THE LIFE
AND TIMES OF
STANLEY SPANK

LYNDON HAYNES

authorHOUSE®

AuthorHouse™ UK Ltd.
1663 Liberty Drive
Bloomington, IN 47403 USA
www.authorhouse.co.uk
Phone: 0800.197.4150

© 2014 Lyndon Haynes. All rights reserved.

No part of this book may be reproduced, stored in a retrieval system, or transmitted by any means without the written permission of the author.

Published by AuthorHouse 09/16/2014

ISBN: 978-1-4969-9044-0 (sc)
ISBN: 978-1-4969-9045-7 (e)

Any people depicted in stock imagery provided by Thinkstock are models, and such images are being used for illustrative purposes only. Certain stock imagery © Thinkstock.

This book is printed on acid-free paper.

Because of the dynamic nature of the Internet, any web addresses or links contained in this book may have changed since publication and may no longer be valid. The views expressed in this work are solely those of the author and do not necessarily reflect the views of the publisher, and the publisher hereby disclaims any responsibility for them.

They both laughed hard intoxicated by the strong cider and their big Bob Marley joints as they called them. Sat on the banks of the river Ty the evening sun still provided enough rays to warm the face of a clearly stoned Stanley and Jerry. Stanley rested back on the grassy verge still chuckling at the silly jokes made by his best mate, his top gun Tom Cruise Ray ban pilot glasses covering partially his rose coloured flushed cheeks. This was another normal day for the so called Tyford two, both jobless and champion layabouts it allowed them to spend days on end chilling out living off of their parents getting drunk and high having crazy conversations about anything from building and owning a space shuttle to having sex with the latest movie screen siren in this case Mila Kunis.

"Seriously there's got to be more to life than this" slurred Jerry, Stanley laid still with his hands behind his head which was perched on his folded jacket digesting the philosophical words from his friend, "I quite like this" he responded sounding disengaged and contented speaking out of the side of his mouth as the smoldering half smoked joint teetered from his lips.

Stanley Spank son of Greg and Brenda was 23 years old he had lived in his family home all his life and generally cruised his was into early manhood ever since he was a pupil at the William Langley school, Stanley always sauntered through life he had good looks but was never aware of them and half a decent brain as his mum would always tell him but he just did not feel the need to apply himself.

His father Greg was a local bus driver and had worked at the same company for neigh on twenty years he was a hardworking union man and had been married to Stanley's mother Brenda for almost thirty years, she was a nurse and worked at the local care home. They were a close knit family with Stanley being their only son whom they adored hence why he got away with being a champion dosser; he had a boyish charm which always melted his mother's heart "your my own little James Dean" she would always crow although his father Greg would often grumble that he did not push himself to be anything special especially as he himself had worked almost all his life, he secretly frowned almost bitterly upon the fact that Stanley never earned a crust since he left school instead living mainly off of his mothers handouts. Home was a modest two bedroom supplied by the council nothing fancy but it had been home to the Spank family for over twenty years.

It was almost six o clock in the evening and the burnt flushed looking Stanley arrived back home with his faithful mate Jerry Dooley another slightly oversized waster in tow, as they entered the house the aroma of a home cooked beef casserole hit their noses immediately, both being slightly tipsy from their afternoon excursion they were famished by the time they had eventually arrived, "is that you Stanley?" a high pitched shriek came from the kitchen area, "yes mum only me" Stanley answered back trying his best to sound as coherent as possible, while Jerry chipped in "me too Mrs. Spank" he chuckled immaturely as the two headed into the lounge.

Both sat in the comfort on the brown corduroy settee slumped back they gazed at the TV giggling at the game show hosts over exuberant patter. Brenda who looked nothing like her forty five year old age stepped into the room, she wore an apron which had an image of a portly opera singer in a tuxedo, conflicting against her slim figure, "hiya Stan, Jerry, you boys hungry? Tea will be ready in ten", both nodded in unison looking like cheeky school boys attempting to suppress their intoxication not that it got past Brenda who shook her head disapprovingly before walking out and back into the kitchen.

Jerry with his tubby friar tuck features nudged Stanley as they sat relaxed awaiting their meals, his rosy red cheeks still burnt from the afternoon sun, "Stan mate" he started hesitantly "I got to find a job mate my dad's on my back" he sounded fed up almost disheartened at the prospect of having to actually work, "well you better find a job then" Stanley mumbled back still with about as much enthusiasm as someone not remotely interested as he continued to gaze into the direction of the large TV screen, "what's up with you mate?" Jerry said attempting to perk up his lethargic friend, "I thought we could get a job together, would be a laugh" he chuckled.

Stanley still remained unmoved blowing out his cheeks as if he was bored of the whole subject now shuffling uncomfortably "why not?" His response was flippant almost throwing his arms up in the air as if to signal his distain at Jerry's persistence. "Seriously?" Jerry questioned excitedly perking up onto the edge of the sofa the obvious glee in his face apparent, "yes but I'm not sure what I'm letting myself in for working with you" Stanley retorted throwing an old newspaper in Jerry's face, "mum I'm starving" he then shouted his hunger contributing to his frustrated cry.

It was now late into the night the house was quiet with only the sound of the television on downstairs as Stanley sat in his room alone smoking another joint and playing FiFA football on his X box game console, he did this most nights until whatever time of the morning he finally would crash to sleep.

The sound of footsteps creaking up the wooden staircase interrupted his thought process he stubbed the smouldering remains of his joint out and quickly opened his window in an attempt to air out his room.

The was a light knock on the door before it was opened slightly, his dad Greg poked his head into his room waving his hand under his nose "Stanley how many times have I told you about smoking that stuff in the house!" his dad stood in the doorway still dressed in his green and red driver uniform he removed his silver rimmed spectacles and rubbed his eyes reacting to the smelly haze which swept into him as he entered the room.

Stanley sat with his back against the headboard with his knees clutched against his chest, he looked stoned and sleepy as his dad sat on the edge of the bed, "what are you going to do with your life Stanley?" he questioned with a tired grizzly look on his face, Stanley sighed heavily he knew what was coming he had heard this speech a million times, he really was not in the mood to receive another late night lecture from his dad but it was inevitable.

Greg was now talking for over fifteen minutes his words meandering from the ethics of hard work to money being tight, Stanley sat passively every now and again nodding in acknowledgment, "don't you want to start a family or travel the world son?" he continued to mutter, "you're a good looking lad I'm sure someone is out there for you", Stanley as always seemed far away somewhere else, whether it was the effects of his joint or the sheer boredom from another speech from his dad he just sat staring into space, "they are looking for packers in the super market" his dad continued getting up and throwing a crumpled rolled up newspaper onto the bed intimating Stanley to take it up and look, "alright dad I'll have a look" the lack of enthusiasm in his voice prompted his dad to put his glasses back on and raise his eyebrow, as he left he mumbled a parting shot "and stop smoking that funny stuff it's no good for you", he exited slamming the door shut. Stanley pondered for a second picking up the bedraggled newspaper and glancing through the pages casually before throwing it onto the floor before he continued to play his computer game.

The next morning the sun once again filtered brightly into Stanley's room through the slashes of his blinds causing a bleary eyed Stanley to stir belatedly, his television was still on from his previous night's gaming, his room had a musty aroma as the smell of smoke mixed in with his natural bodily odours.

Stanley tossed and turned pulling the duvet cover over his head to block the piercing rays, he groaned in his attempts to prolong his sleep only to be interrupted by the loud chiming sound of the doorbell, Stanley did not budge instead curled up into the fetal position to gain more comfort before the chime rang loudly again, this time he let out an even louder groan knowing he was going to have to get up from his slumber, "mum get the door!" he shouted his frustrated moody tone bellowed out, again the chimes sounded this time causing Stanley to literally fall out of his pit and make for the stairs.

Dressed in only his tight red boxer shorts a grumpy Stanley stamped his way down to the front door as the bell continually chimed, "alright I'm coming bloody hell" he moaned sniffing and spluttering before opening the door squinting into the sunshine to see a cheerful smartly dressed Jerry standing on the doorstep looking full of himself, "what the hell?..." Stanley stated shocked to see his best mate done up to the nines wearing a blue suit and black shoes, his hair was gelled back slickly, a pair of shades sat tightly on his face which contrasted his rosy red cheeks, "morning Mr Spank" he said cheerfully barging his way past his lethargic bleary eyed friend "I brought you a bacon sarnie" he quipped as he strode into the kitchen leaving Stanley stood in the doorway his hair flopped over his face causing his normal boyish good looks to give way to a ruffled and creased furrow, "come in" he said gesturing with him arm sarcastically closing the door shaking his head in disbelief.

They both sat at the kitchen table a contrast of two postures, while Stanley could barely keep his head upright enough to face his mate, Jerry however was sat stiff and poised chewing carefully on his bacon buttie breakfast, "the kettle's boiled" Jerry mumbled stuffing the last piece of bread into his already overcrowded mouth spitting out pieces of crumbs as he directed Stanley who groaned loudly dragging himself up towards the counter where he proceeded to slowly make tea.

"So what's the occasion big man?" Stanley quizzed still stood in his boxers his athletic body still unwilling to accept he was awake, "there's an open day at the town hall for a holiday company, time to get me a job Stan" Jerry stated optimistically, wiping his mouth with a white tissue he looked like Oliver Hardy minus the moustache, suddenly Stanley burst out laughing, "open day…job!" he continued to laugh it was probably the most energy he expended in the last few minutes as he continued to cackle whist pouring the steaming hot water into a large grey mug.

Jerry sat looking defiant unaffected by his friends comments, "why don't you get dressed and come with me?" he asked hoping Stanley would take something serious for the first time in his life, "come with you?" he questioned almost offended at the suggestion stirring the mugs of tea, "your are joking? I'm going back to bed when you're gone mate", he continued, he sat back at the table planting down the mugs and launching into his bacon sandwich "thanks for brekkie though" his arrogance abound as he chowed down heartily almost choking as he continued to chuckle to himself.

Jerry still was unrepentant determined to follow through regardless of Stanley's immature remarks, he stood up and fixed his glasses back onto his face "I'm off to land me a job mate" he declared fixing his shirt and tie before striding towards the front door, he turned momentarily looking back hopefully at Stanley who was still giggling albeit a forced show of petulance, "good luck mate" he casually threw his wishes towards Jerry who in turn took a deep breath and stepped back out into the sunshine.

Stanley sat silently for a few minutes before it began to dawn on him that his best friend was determined to make something of his life and for a moment he almost got up to follow him, but for all his idleness he was also stubborn and did not like to feel forced to do anything. "Mug" he muttered under his breath before getting up and walking slowly back up to his room yawning scratching his flat taught stomach, on entrance he stepped onto the newspaper his dad had left for him the night before which was nestled amongst all the other strewn clothes, game covers and console wires which decorated his floor.

Stanley laid back onto his pillow lighting up the remainder of his joint from the night before, he flicked through the pages as he puffed away on the small rolled cigarette, suddenly he sat up squinting as the smoke hit his face, he stared intently stubbing out the remainder of his joint in the ashtray, a smile spread across his face then he read out aloud "Male escorts needed, age between twenty three and forty excellent rates…" he began to laugh maybe it was the high from his joint or just the literal fascination but he quickly scampered towards his dressing table looking for his phone, "I'll show Jerry Dooley how to get a job!" he declared hopping around the various obstacles in his room until he finally found his device.

He began tapping away feverishly the number into his phone, he began to compose himself as the connection was made, a few seconds in he actually cut the call, "nah can't be …" he stopped again then hit the redial button this time taking a deep breath he stood up rigidly still in his red boxer shorts with the rays of the sun striking his back as they sliced through the window, again the connection was made and the phone started ringing, he held the paper up to his face peering at the advert, "hello Elite escorts Cassandra speaking can I help?" a soft gentle toned voice spoke, Stanley was stumped at first barely able to mumble his words out, "erm ah yes" he spluttered before adjusting himself, "yes I'm calling about the advert" he continued attempting to put on a broad English gentleman accent although with a hint of hesitation.

The voice on the other end of the line suspected this and answered back "are you talking about the escort position?", Stanley was taken aback and tried to stifle his voice realising that this was not a joke anymore, part of him wanted to hang up again but the thought of getting one over Jerry spurred him on, clearing his throat he spouted again in a regal voice "yes that's right I wish to become an escort" he affirmed holding back his laughter by covering his mouth with his hand.

By now Stanley was getting excited playing this role of an interested gentleman to the unsuspecting Cassandra who continued running through the protocol of questions, "so Mr.?" she stopped awaiting his reply, Stanley could not think quick enough to conjure an alias on the spot so blurted out his own surname "Spank", "Spank?" she repeated back now sounding just a little more curious "ok…Mr Spank I need some details from you" Cassandra continued her speech stagnated, by now Stanley's initial court jester act descended into him sitting down on his bed silent and seriously beginning to like what he was hearing as Cassandra ran through some of the information especially the hourly rate per job, he nearly forgot himself letting his guise slip when she asked for him to send some personal information including a picture by email, "ok I will do" he answered in his normal boyish tone before quickly realising and coughing vigorously again before resuming to his alter ego.

The call lasted for about half an hour and once Stanley hung up the call he actually did not think the whole thing was funny anymore, he picked up the tatty newspaper again and kept staring at the advert which by now had Cassandra's email details scribbled beside it, he giggled and shook his head at the same time trying to comprehend what he just committed to, quickly he jumped up and grabbed his laptop from his dressing table he was intent on following through even if it was just a game of one upmanship on his best friend.

"Done" he declared rubbing his hands after hitting the send button on the email, he laughed out to himself fiendishly before laying back onto his bed satisfied that he had put one over on Jerry, the glee on his face was apparent and he could not wait until Jerry got back to rub it in his face, he closed his eyes but still had the smuggest expression even thinking about his act.

The strong vibration from his phone awoke Stanley from his doze, he scrambled around before grabbing his phone seeing Jerry's name flashing in fluorescent on his handset "what do you want?" his voice croaked in a baritone "you still sleeping you lazy bum" an excited sounding Jerry shouted down the phone "do you know what a glorious day your missing?" Jerry continued in reference to the bright sunshine which continued to shard through his bedroom window, Stanley mumbled adjusting his eyes to the green clock radio digits on his dressing table, 12:08 it read "oh man it's late" he said yawning and stretching, "I'm in the crown having pub lunch in the beer garden, get down here mate", Jerry signed off leaving Stanley spread-eagle on his back lifeless as if the effort was just too much.

An hour later a clean fresher looking Stanley emerged into the sunshine, Jerry was right he was missing a glorious day he pulled his sunglasses from out of his shirt pocket and placed them on his face before strolling causally towards the high street observing the many people who were out enjoying the weather, kids playing football in the local park and the unmistakable melodic tones from a distant ice cream van as he continued his walk. Stanley thought about what he had done, the phone call to the agency played on his mind, really it was all a joke to him he never really considered anything so bizarre but he could not be outdone by his mate, Stanley was a first class layabout and he liked it that way he also liked the fact that his best mate was the same as him and selfishly did not want him changing anytime soon.

Upon entering the crowded beer garden which was full of office workers enjoying an extended lunch break in the sun, Stanley pint in hand pushed and jockeyed his way through until he spotted a red faced lobster looking

Jerry sitting alone at a wooden table, he had clearly been indulging the empty pint glasses which were lined up like skittles across the table next to an empty plate "Stan! Over here mate" he boomed clearly excited to see his friend.

Stanley took a seat opposite a beaming Jerry who was clearly itching to tell him his news, "so what happened on your little open day?" Stanley questioned supping heartily from his glass, "guess what mate I got the job can you believe it!" an ecstatic beaming Jerry exclaimed with a big smile taking off his sunglasses revealing the red tan lines around his cheeks, Stanley took a big gulp from his pint nearly choking in the process "you what?" he spluttered almost spitting out his mouthful in Jerry's direction, "yeah I'm off to Magaluf for three months for the holiday season mate, I'm going to be a holiday rep, cheers!" Jerry raised his glass in celebratory mode belching loudly whilst a gobsmacked and clearly shocked Stanley looked on, eventually he picked up his glass although half-heartedly "yeah well done mate" he forced a smile but deep down his heart sank, "can't believe it, I'm well chuffed", Jerry continued clearly delighted, "don't want to rub it in but birds beach and sun", a clearly contented Jerry sat back basking in his own fantasy world for a moment, Stanley cut a disconsolate figure, "I should have come with you, have they got any more jobs?", he asked hopefully, Jerry snapped back into focus again before answering "doubt it mate there were tonnes of people there, even Tracey Wilkins from school got in", "really? Tracey Wilkins" Stanley repeated in disbelief.

The realisation that his best friend was soon to be embarking on what sounded like a fun filled jolly whilst getting paid for the next few months stuck harshly in Stanley's throat, he moped enviously as he watched Jerry Dooley grinning like a Cheshire cat and continually having to listen to the proposed adventures he was planning on having, his obvious glee about having his first job holding no bounds for his excitement.

After a full afternoon in the beer garden both wearily sat weakened by the draining sun pondering their respective futures, Jerry by now was flagging bent over on the table affected by the numerous empty pint glasses dotted around, Stanley sat smoking slowly staring through his shades into the distance anonymous through his silence he was gutted faced with a whole summer of being alone whilst Jerry embarked on a new life and adventure.

"Jerry mate it's time to go" he said pushing his conked out mate in the back, Jerry stirred slowly regaining his focus, it was only four thirty in the afternoon but he looked like he was finished for the day his nice shirt was now untucked and tie loose and bedraggled as he clung to Stanley. They both tottered off through the bar onto the high street "I'm going to miss you Stan" an emotional Jerry droned barely able to get his words out, "yeah me too you big lump" Stanley responded as the sheer weight of his friend began to converge onto his lean frame.

Stanley walked home after taking the over sunned and drunk Jerry back, his mind was filled with many thoughts as to where he would go from here in his life, he could hear the echoes of his dads voice always telling him to pull his socks up and get in to the working environment he knew what he would say when he heard that Jerry of all people had landed such an enviable position.

As he turned into his street he saw his mum Brenda struggling ahead with some shopping bags, he trotted up towards her making her jump with fright in the process "I'll take them thanks madam" he whispered as he moved up behind her, "oh my god! Oh Stanley it's you" she shrieked stopping in her tracks as Stanley grabbed a couple of bags from her, "where have you been? Or should I ask?" Brenda quizzed knowingly, "I can smell the pub on you" she continued looking up disapprovingly at her son, "I was celebrating with Jerry he got a job as a holiday rep", Brenda stopped dead in her tracks again "Jerry Dooley got a job?" she looked and sounded surprised "well I never" clearly shocked she shook her head and began to walk as they approached the house "so you will be losing your left arm" she quipped jangling her keys prior to unlocking the door, "chin up son these things happen in life" she added a small crumb of consolation.

Stanley sat alone in his room he was trying to brush off his mood the feeling of loss knowing he would soon be a Billy no mates, he accepted Jerry wanted to change his life but never even contemplated it would be abroad but maybe it was time for a change time to grow up after all he could if he really wanted to find a good job, his Dad Greg was always trying to get him some kind of job at his bus station, not that he wanted to follow in his dads footsteps.

The smell of shepherd's pie billowed through the house enticing Stanley downstairs into the kitchen where his mum was putting the final touches together for dinner, "you come down to help?" Brenda's sarcasm abound knowing a moping Stanley was no use to anyone in the kitchen, "no just thought I'd keep you company" he mused standing close peering over her shoulder checking the food.

As a mother Brenda's maternal instinct instantly sensed Stanley's downbeat mood, "come on son sit down I'll serve up" cajoling him towards the table, she knew by his long face he was still feeling down. After wolfing down his dinner Stanley had to sit and listen to his mother going on about life and how change was a good thing, Brenda always shot straight from the hip and was now going on for at least five minutes which was normally the maximum limit in Stanley's attention span "and another bit of advice" she continued picking some food out of her teeth using a fork as a makeshift toothpick, "you should be thinking of getting yourself a nice girlfriend and starting a family" her voice now beginning to go completely in one ear and out of the other as Stanley's mind began to wander leaving his mums voice to fade into the background, "thanks mum" he interjected sharply stopping her in mid flow "dinner was great" he mumbled then got up from the table and walked out leaving his mum to sigh heavily rolling her eyes.

Stanley sat on his bed and flipped open his laptop he clicked onto his music library and began to play some tunes, it had been a draining day although the temperature was still warm from the sun drenched day, his computer bleeped continuously signifying the receipt of an email, with his mind so occupied on Jerry's news he actually had forgotten about his conversation to the escort agency, he was perked up by seeing the name Cassandra Hill as the sender suddenly he showed an injection of energy as he clicked open the mail, not sure what he was going to see his eyes widened when he began reading the text "Stanley we are delighted to offer you an opportunity" were the first words that stood out, he grinned nervously and chuckled to himself more in disbelief than anything, for once the surly Stanley had something to smile about, it was only a game to him but when he kept reading and saw the figures of five hundred pounds per night he actually burst out laughing "sweet!" he exclaimed scrolling down the rest of the email which asked for him to contact Cassandra again to arrange a meeting.

Stanley rested back into the pillow and breathed a satisfying sigh suddenly everything had lifted, his despondence turned to anticipation as his mind began to work overtime, many thoughts came into his head he had not dated a girl since Eliza Copthorne at the end of school disco many years ago and that turned out to be a disaster with Stanley and Jerry getting extremely drunk and embarrassing the poor girl, he laughed as he reflected before sharply focusing again turning his attentions back to the email which was still glaring at him on the LCD screen, "an escort?" he again laughed shaking his head in disbelief.

The next morning an energetic Stanley was surprisingly up showered and standing in front of his mirror deliberating on which style to have his fair mop of hair, it was rare for him to pay so much attention to such things as looks but he was now paying attention to every little detail, he flicked and stroked, preened and brushed it into an assortment of looks but then got frustrated blowing up to his fringe, he continued to stare at himself checking out his reflection striking some embarrassing poses attempting to look cool. He flexed his muscles and puffed out his chest, twisting and turning in an attempt to get an all-round view, unknown to him his dad Greg was peeking through the door trying his hardest to stifle his laughter, "you might need to add some pirouettes to that boy" he finally cracked into a husky laugh, "oh my god dad why don't you ever knock!" a mortified Stanley flew back with shock trying to cover up, "what's all this you got a date or something?" Greg quipped, Stanley still looking sheepish pulling on a plain grey tee shirt answered "nah I got to go somewhere later" he replied, his dad looked on curiously before retreating "your mum and I are off out for a bit" he declared while striking a funny pose mimicking his son, Stanley stuck his fingers up in defiance "get lost then!" he shouted back laughing finally seeing the funny side of his dad's mocking "can I lend some money dad?" he asked quickly just about hearing Greg moan while stomping down the stairs.

This new energy saw Stanley out in the beautiful sunshine he strolled through Tyford town centre, he was on a mission to buy some new threads, he wanted to make an impression at the escort agency even on a very limited budget, this was the first time in a long time that he seemed to have enthusiasm for something other than smoking or drinking, he had a purpose although it was driven by the fact that Jerry had actually proved him wrong and beat him to an exciting job and burgeoning new lifestyle in the sun.

As he strolled his mind wandered through all the scenarios he really did not know what was expected of him, who would he be escorting? Where would he take them? and most importantly how much would he get paid?, he really began to think seriously about his choice whilst staring in the windows browsing at the flash suits and shoes in the shops all which seemed to be well out of his price range.

After an hour of meandering from store to store a frazzled Stanley found himself sat outside on a bench next to a couple of pensioners who seemed to be having a picnic eating sandwiches and drinking from tea from a flask, Stanley looked around him and thought maybe Jerry was right if this all his life had to offer maybe it was time to change surely there was more to life.

He realised that in a couple of weeks his mate would be gone embarking on a new adventure and he would be sat right here in the middle of a dead town on his own doing nothing, maybe it was time to grow up he could hear his dads voice in his head repeatedly telling him to get a job to be a man, he sighed heavily looking at the old couple who were sat still only their mouths moving in unison as they chewed down there homemade sandwiches he shuddered as he got a flash forward of how that could be him in twenty years time not having achieved anything.

Spurred into action he found himself stood in a noisy trendy store where he was approached by a young sales assistant "hello sir do you want some help?", her enthusiastic spunky voice pierced through the already throbbing sounds which reverberated around his ears, Stanley perused through a rack of shirts before turning to the girl "well…" he paused not really sure what to say "I'm just looking for something smart" he said to the girl who had several face piercings and pink coloured hair "something smart?" she questioned back looking as puzzled as him, "ok" she said sizing him up "come with me", she ordered before bounding across the shop floor with a hesitant Stanley following in tow.

Loud music bounded from Stanley's room Dirty Harry by the Gorillaz turned up full blast anyone walking by would think a full party was going on, but this was Stanley getting ready for his appointment getting himself up for something that was completely out of his comfort zone. Freshly showered he strutted around his room spraying vast amounts of deodorant and smelling under his arms to make sure they were adequately covered, he looked to his bed where his newly purchased white shirt and black trousers were laid out neatly waiting to be put onto his lean body.

As the music subsided he could make out a gentle knocking on his bedroom door "come in" he shouted as the din became reduced, Brenda poked her head around the door peering into his room getting hit by a full dose of deodorant spray which still hung in the air the smell pungent attacking her nostrils "blimey boy what's going on in here, you trying to choke us out?" she continued waving away the excess vapour "you got a date or something?" she asked looking around the room seeing the clothes on the bed and her son standing in front of the mirror preening himself, "well I sort of have an interview" Stanley answered back now moving his gaze away from the mirror still fussing with his hair, "what at this time?"

she replied looking at her watch bemused "I'll tell you about when I get back" an over fussed Stanley countered now getting annoyed as his hair would not sit perfectly. "Well I never" Brenda shook her head before turning to exit, "oh mum can I have some money? I spent my last lot on these" he said picking up his shirt "oh Stanley" she sighed before going down the stairs "I take it you don't want your tea then?" her voice waned as the music once again began to reverberate around the room.

For once Stanley had energy and drive he looked cool dressed in his crisp white shirt and smart black trousers the only thing that looked out of place were his shoes which were borrowed from his dad as his old pair were too worn, they looked big and clumpy compared to the rest of his slick look but he was not bothered as he stomped his way into town to get the bus to the offices where he was meeting with Cassandra.

Sat at the back of a crowded bus squeezed up between an old man who smelt of a boozy afternoon in the pub and a spotty teenager who proceeded to blast rock music from her headphones, Stanley tried to keep his cool persona he shuffled uncomfortably trying hard to retain his polished look, thankfully he did not have to sit for too long as his stop was just around the corner.

Armed with the address and Cassandra's phone number he walked down the street looking at all the office blocks ahead for some reason he anticipated as plush twenty first century building something that he may have seen on grand designs or MTV cribs, but when he found the building he was actually a bit let down as it was just a unit in a deserted industrial estate. He stopped to check the details again looking around him before slowly continuing to walk down the darkening path towards a small contained building "hello Cassandra it's Stanley Spank I'm just trying to find your office", he said almost forgetting his distinguished gentleman accent in the process being so consumed in finding the premises, "ok Stanley I am in unit 5 it has a bright red door", Cassandra replied.

Stanley looked around all of the buildings looked the same he tried to get his bearings before looking across and seeing one solitary building where the lights were still on and the red door, "at last" he exclaimed relieved fixing his hair and striding towards the entrance, as he walked his heart began to race, the realisation that he was actually going through with this hit home as he neared the very bright red door, he arrived and saw a gold metal entry door system with the name Elite escorts beside it, "must be it" he muttered pressing hard on the button initiating the harsh buzzing of the bell, "come in Stanley" the muffled voice came back as the door released.

He walked in and straight up a flight of black metal stairs it was cool and airy, he could hear a door being opened, it was all very covert and understated not at all what he expected, he could see at the top of the stairwell a short plump old lady "come up Mr Spank" she motioned, his mind raced with all sort of thoughts he half felt to turn around but he did not he continued until he reached the top "Mr Spank so nice to finally meet you" the short old lady greeted him by holding out her tiny wrinkled hand "hello.. Cassandra?" he questioned hesitantly, he had not expected her to look the way she did, in his mind and going by her phone voice he was expected a super fit young secretary type just like the ones on the movies, so stunned he paused before shaking her hand "nice to meet you" he said shyly as Cassandra looked him up and down giving him the once over before inviting him in.

Sat in the confines of a cosy office Cassandra toddled back behind her desk plonking down a tray of tea and biscuits she was barely five feet tall and looked like any ordinary grandmother, her blue rinse curly hair slightly thinning shone under the lights she wore a grey knitted cardigan which covered her ample frame, "how many sugars Mr Spank?" she offered cordially, Stanley looked at her bashfully before replying "two please and call me Stanley", he fixed his shirt making sure he still looked clean and fresh as Cassandra spooned the sugar into his tea stirring slowly peering over her glasses.

"So Stanley you know the nature of my company?" her voice was gentle and soft in tone, Stanley shifted in his seat "yes you hire escorts right?" he answered trying to sound assured and confident although he was actually quite nervous and felt nausea inside, he looked around scanning the room which was bare with not much to indicate the industry just a small computer on Cassandra's cluttered desk, he expected pictures of sexy women and male strippers types in raunchy poses, yet he was surprised to see there was not much evidence to back his perception.

Cassandra pulled out a huge black diary book from a grey filing cabinet the weight of it causing her shoulders to sag as she strained to put the book on the table,

Stanley immediately leapt up clearing the some space on the table for her to put it down "thank you" she huffed acknowledging Stanley's show of chivalry, "you are a handsome boy Stanley Spank a little bit young, but I think I can really do well with you" she mentioned, her lips quivered as she shakily hovered her cup of tea under her mouth before taking a quick sip.

Stanley sat staring at Cassandra he immediately had a sense of compassion for her she reminded him of his Nan. His nerves were finally gone and he felt more relaxed knowing that this little old lady was in charge. Cassandra opened the book which contained a bundle of documents, "now Stanley" she continued sounding more assured and composed licking her fingers before scrolling down the notes in the folder at close range "have you ever been in trouble with the police?" she asked, Stanley sat up surprised "no never" he answered back truthfully, again shuffling in his seat he almost wanted to get up and leave thinking he was out of his mind to be sitting there, it was just a spur of the moment reaction which was meant to be a joke, but the more he watched Cassandra meticulously combing through her lists he began to warm to her and the possibility of earning a few easy pounds.

After about an hour Stanley was signing consent forms and was officially a new escort for Cassandra and her Elite escorts agency, his heart was beating fast the laid back Stanley Spank had finally committed to something other than downing pints and smoking joints although not knowing the full extent of what he had let himself in for, "well if your free tomorrow evening I have a beautiful widower who loves the theatre Stanley, maybe you can escort her?" the soft comforting tone of Cassandra's voice enticed Stanley who sat back now daunted by the prospect, "yeah why not?" he spoke confidently but inside his stomach did somersaults, "ok I will email the details to you" Cassandra confirmed with a sweet smile, her eyes twinkled as she cast them over him again, "I have high hopes for you Mr Spank", she said winking at him closing her hefty black book.

"Do you own a suit?" she questioned rising from her seat once again struggling to place the book back into the filing cabinet, Stanley shook his head "I don't" he replied feeling a tad embarrassed, "well.. I recommend you invest in one", she gave a stern suggestion, "my clients like class", she continued, leaving Stanley feeling like he was back in school being told off by the headmistress "er well ok I'll see what I can do" he muttered back feeling awkward knowing he would have to ask his mum for more cash as he rose from his seat ready to depart.

His tall lean frame towered above the petite Cassandra, again she cast her eyes admiringly over Stanley who grinned uncomfortably, "good features …nice teeth" she commented continuing to give her latest asset the once over inspecting every inch of him looking more than pleased with her latest recruit.

Sat on the bus on his journey home Stanley pondered on the events of the evening, he couldn't believe how Cassandra was literally just a little old lady on her own running this type of company, part of him felt sorry for her but he wondered how much money she must be making, judging her thick book of clients she must be pretty well off.

As well as feeling surreal about the whole experience Stanley was excited about what the opportunity would bring, it was a chance to get out of the house, meet different people and of course make some money, he could also brag to Jerry. He looked at his reflection in the window "Stanley Spank male escort to the ladies" he whispered under his breath fixing his shirt collars imitating the cool of James Bond, he laughed and shook his head in disbelief he'd never taken anyone anywhere before one thing he needed to do was brush up on his etiquette as he was lacking in the gentlemanly manners department.

He arrived home still wondering what he had got himself into his mind was awash with different ideas and scenarios he even thought to contact Cassandra and tell her he had changed his mind but for some reason he felt strangely connected to her, maybe it was just the fact she was an old lady trying to make people happy sort of like a fairy godmother.

His keys jangled in the lock he stepped in as quiet as he could but upon his entrance he saw his dad still sitting up in the kitchen doing some paper work, "hi dad what you still doing up?" he asked, Greg looked up and did a double take looking Stanley up and down "are those my shoes?" he grunted scratching his head with his pen, "why you all dolled up, had a date?" his dad continued trying hard not to laugh.

Stanley sat down at the table opposite his dad he was coy and put his head down taking a deep breath before raising up to be in his dads eye line, "well I have a job", he blurted, Greg Spank nearly fell off of his chair, "you have a what?" his dad chuckled, taking off his glasses to rub his eyes before repeating his sentence again, "you have a job, I don't believe it", he was aghast resting back in his chair with the expectancy waiting to hear the rest, "well what is it?", he asked eagerly, Stanley began to laugh nervously before mumbling out "a male escort", he coughed attempting to stifle his words, "come again?" his dad now sat up rigid leaning inwardly towards his son, "I'll be taking women to the theatre and stuff" Stanley repeated quckly, his dad let out a wheezed laugh, he tried to contain himself his body jerking vigorously "when?…what?…please explain" he chuckled, Stanley looked embarrassed "cup of tea dad?" was his response before getting up from the table and turning his back, "look whatever you do just be careful and not a word to your mother", Greg Spank nodded towards him continuing to wheeze a suppressed laugh shaking his head before putting his glasses on and getting back to his paperwork.

Stanley sat on his bed, shirt open and untucked and sparked up a well-earned joint by flicking his lighter rapidly igniting a small flame which he hovered on the end of his rolled cigarette, he was somewhat surprised by his dads reaction he had expected a tougher talking to than what he received maybe he was just happy that he was doing something useful with himself.

The bedroom window was wide open, the warm balmy conditions suffocated any breeze in the night air, he kept going over what may happen tomorrow evening in his head, what would he say? How would his client look? What if he gets seen by people he knew? Many questions swam around his relaxed brain he kept getting visions of Cassandra smiling over him as he relaxed on his bed, her words of optimism floated into his ears, he continued to pull hard on the remainder of his joint before crushing the rest of it into his sliver tinned ashtray, he laid back onto his bed prone still with his dads shoes on now in a full sedative state "better get some sleep" his drowsy words barely managed to escape his lips before he was completely conked out.

Stood staring enviously at the expensive suits that adorned the cool looking mannequins in the shop window, Stanley cut a confused figure as the sun reflected his mirage, he was up early surprisingly after making sure he caught his mum before she went to sleep from her night shift. He was armed with one hundred and fifty pounds borrowed with the promised of a payback when he got paid, he told his mum he managed to get some work in a local bar but really he was eager to impress his unsuspecting escorts with a brand new classy suit.

It seemed like many minutes had passed before he finally plucked up the courage to enter the store to browse. Stanley felt awkward as he walked in he was not really dressed as if he could afford the clothes which were neatly folded on the shelves and displays, blue combat shorts, flip flops and a black tee shirt were his ensemble topped off with his ever present Ray Ban sunglasses.

He looked around overwhelmed by the array of garments in this contemporary and stylish store, the sounds of European techno music throbbed in the background "can I help you?" the voice of a female instantly interrupted his static gaze, he spun around to see a very well put together attractive assistant, she looked foreign Swedish at a guess, blonde short hair a la Mia Farrow in Rosemary's baby and stunning ice blue eyes.

Stanley was momentarily taken aback and slow to respond such was her beauty, immediately he thought he would try out his new persona on the unsuspecting assistant who continued to stare at him blankly awaiting an answer, "yes" he replied giving the impression he knew exactly what he was after, he removed his shades hanging them onto the collar of his tee shirt, "good morning Miss?" he somehow obtained his selective queen's English accent sweeping his hair away from his eyes, "how are you this fine morning?" he continued feeling slightly out of his depth but pursuing regardless.

The young assistant looked back at him with a confused expression before breaking into a smile albeit a forced cheesy one, "I'm very well sir" she responded also trying to apply a well-spoken accent although her mother tongue crept in, Stanley pushed further, "Spank" he continued, "I beg your pardon" the shop assistant replied her expression was now one of disgust as she felt he was alluding to some form of sexual innuendo, Stanley became embarrassed as he twigged "no I meant that my name is Spank…Stanley" he back tracked apologetically just about rescuing the situation as the unsuspecting assistant who finally realised what he was saying.

Stanley by now was dying on his feet cringing "I'm so sorry I feel like an idiot" he stated slapping his forehead with his hand, "suits, I'm looking for a suit", he quickly spouted feeling the blood rush to his face as the warm feeling of embarrassment surged up his body resulting in him being red in the face, the shop assistant smiled wryly before leading Stanley to the suit section.

He stepped out from behind the curtain of the changing room the face of the young shop assistant lit up she nodded in approval almost in disbelief as the transformation from casual beach bum to sophisticated stylish playboy "well… suits you sir!" she put her thumbs up at an awkward looking Stanley who shyly modelled his well fitted choice. He looked like a totally different person and as he gazed disbelievingly into the mirror eyeing himself from head to toe even the flip flops could not spoil the look, it was only then that the realisation hit him he saw somebody that he had never seen before he was barely recognisable but was happy to embrace.

The touch of the assistant's hand on his shoulder interrupted his dreamy thoughts as she brushed his shoulder and stood in front of him buttoning the jacket boring her blue eyes into him it was bordering on seduction which Stanley was too naive to appreciate, "thank you" he replied hesitantly his eye line meeting with hers, "how much is it?" Stanley quickly deflected the energy oozing between them still looking directly at the assistant who finally had let go of the jacket and composed herself "this one is one hundred and twenty pounds", she smouldered stepping back to appreciate him in his full glory, "ok I'll take it" Stanley confirmed before quickly turning and heading back in to the safety of the changing room.

Stanley proceeded to the till to pay for his purchase still being snared by the attractive shop assistant he felt slightly awkward especially he was now back in his normal everyday clothes, he bashfully handed over his cash to the now very keen and friendly assistant who cheekily smiled and handed over the bags "Spank!" she said winking, Stanley smiled "thanks" he replied bashfully he didn't dare look back and concentrated on making sure he walked out without tripping up or bumping into anything.

He lit up a cigarette and continued to stroll down the busy parade of shops still shaking his head in amazement, he slung the bag containing the suit over his shoulder moseying slowly browsing in some of the other shop windows, he walked about one hundred yards before he felt a firm gripped on his shoulder "Mr Spank come with me" a gruff voice shouted startling him causing him to turn sharply, "blimey! it's you, what you trying to do scare the living daylights out of me?", his relief was apparent when he turned to see the familiar face of his compatriot Jerry Dooley, the larger than life personality pouncing on him "what you doing down here mate shopping?" Jerry as ever was bubbly still lobster pink in a bright yellow shirt which only enhanced his luminous colouration, Stanley laughed "what do you look like?" he said grabbing Jerry's chubby cheek, with his cigarette hanging off of his lips, "fancy a pint?" he asked, "can't" Jerry replied to Stanley's surprise "I've got to go and pick up some stuff, I'm off at the weekend mate".

Stanley stopped in his tracks shocked at the realisation he would be losing his mate so soon he lifted his sunglasses from his face squinting in the sunlight "this weekend?", he questioned with a disconsolate frown, "I thought you had two weeks yet", he said placing his glasses onto his head looking Jerry straight in the eye, Jerry noticed the disappointment in Stanley's face it then dawned on the both of them that time was nearly up "sorry mate I'll only be gone for three month's" Jerry tried to reassure his crestfallen friend who stood motionless except for pulling the cigarette to and from his lips, "well mate we have to have an end of an era drink and joint don't we?" Stanley perked up encouraging Jerry who frankly did not need much encouragement or persuasion, "oh go on then you've twisted my arm" he responded playfully cupping his chubby hands onto Stanley's face, "anyway what's with the clobber?", Stanley dismissed Jerry turning around and walking away "come on fat boy let's go", placing his shades back onto his face marching off purposely in the sunshine with his bag slung of his shoulder.

After a couple of early pints and some breakfast Stanley began to make his way home, he had left Jerry to complete his tasks knowing that after the weekend he would be practically on his own, feeling a little high and worse for wear he suddenly stopped and remembered that he needed to get shoes, he casually did a u turn and wearily meandered his way back towards the town centre.

As he walked his thoughts turned to Cassandra and the job for tonight he chose not to tell Jerry about his new job out of both fear of ridicule and not wanting to put himself under any pressure, this was his journey and as sure as Jerry was going to have fun abroad he knew that he also needed to do something equally as entertaining, of course he had no thoughts of how this could turn out but he now warmed to the idea and was actually looking forward to his first experience as a male escort.

"Stunning Stanley if I say so myself" he acknowledged indulgently admiring himself in the mirror, he did look good, the suit fitted his tall lean body well defining all the right contours, the trousers fell perfectly onto his new black shiny shoes, he looked like someone straight from the set of a magazine shoot, he tried a different style with his fair mop of hair, gelling it slickly all back in one, even he was amazed by the transformation and the difference a suit could make, he kept staring and then began to practice delivering his line "good evening madam call me Mr Spank" he joked swiveling around and putting his glasses on, attempting to appear uber cool posing ridiculously.

A final squirt of his dads Dunhill aftershave onto his chin and he was ready to go, he did not want to be late as Cassandra had stipulated the importance of timekeeping and he had to catch the bus which was not ideal.

Stanley waited patiently at the bus stop his nerves began to kick in now with the different thoughts racing through his head he lit up a cigarette to calm his nerves while checking himself out again in the reflection of the shop window. He only had time for a few quick puffs before his bus arrived he tossed the half smoked cigarette to the floor before boarding.

He arrived at the office pressing hard on the gold intercom system; it took a couple of minutes before he finally received an answer hearing the muffled sweet voice of Cassandra come through "come up Stanley", she sounded occupied as she buzzed him in, Stanley took a deep breath and quickly ran up the stairs his steps echoing as the heels from his new shoes hit each of the metals steps, he suddenly had a rush of energy mostly adrenalin fuelled but he was now ready to take on his task.

Stanley reached the office door and gently knocked before entering, "hello" he signalled as Cassandra answered back "hi Stanley come in let's see you" her voice heightened in anticipation as he stepped into the office looking like a totally different person, he walked in confidently knowing that he looked good in his new suit and shoes, "oh my well look at you!" she exclaimed taking off her glasses and rubbing her eyes in astonishment "you like?" Stanley struck a pose before bursting out laughing knowing how silly he must have looked, "you've had a makeover!" Cassandra shrieked again clearly delighted clapping her hands at her newly acquired commodity.

With all the pleasantries over it was now down to business, Cassandra gave details to Stanley of where he was to meet his client, her name was simply Ms White, "she's a new divorcee just wants to be shown a nice time" Cassandra said firmly as she shuffled around her desk searching through some paper work, Stanley stood with his hands clasped in front of him, he was nervous inside his heart galloped a pace as he now began to feel daunted by the prospect of his date, "now Stanley I'll give you a sub for the taxi the rest is on Ms White, smile be courteous and be a gent" she continued handing him some money then fussing around making sure his suit was spotless casting her eye over him once again before ushering him out of the door.

Stanley was a bit overwhelmed he felt like a kid again like when his mum used to get him ready for school, "ok well shall I call you later?", he quizzed sheepishly, "no son you just get Ms White home safely after and we'll speak tomorrow" she reassured. Stanley took the paper details from Cassandra inhaling a deep breath and then bounded out of the door with purpose; this was it he was on his way Stanley Spank male escort who would have thought it, Tyford's biggest layabout was actually working.

Sat in the taxi Stanley was silent and in deep thought he was half anticipating and half apprehensive the reality was looming large he nervously chuckled to himself not quite believing what he was getting into but it was too late now he was on his way and just wanted to see his prospective date, he visualized she must be quite an old lady maybe a spinster who lived alone with loads of cats, probably around Cassandra's age.

The car swept into Oakfield lodge this was home to the richest folk of Tyford, large houses exclusivity, long country lanes in the most scenic part of the town, Stanley's eyes marveled at the houses set back in amongst the trees it was quiet peaceful and gave the impression that the people who lived here were high end the types that were never seen down the local pubs and high street shops but still were part of the community.

A fleeting thought passed through his mind he wondered about the amount of money Ms White had even more so how much she was spending on his services?, for now he did not want to weigh up the curious questions which flashed through his mind he was more interested in what his date was going to be like.

Finally the car had slowed down veering off to the left of the path, a large metal fence separated the house from the outside world Stanley stepped out of the car and marched up the stony path to the gate and pressed the buzzer, it just had a bronze plate with a circular button as soon as he pressed it a bright security light beamed out to the path. Stanley stood back shielding his eyes from the light, a voice crackled through the intercom "hello" it bellowed "yes hello it's Stanley…I mean Mr Spank" he quickly came to his senses and adjusted his voice attempting to sound mature and assured, he looked back at the car glancing at the driver flashing a nervous grin, before adjusting his suit making sure he still looked good. By now his anxiousness was at a peak he stuck his hands in his pockets and stood tensely tapping his fingers against the inside of his trousers. In the distance he could see the light from the door as it opened he could just about make out the figure that stepped out she seemed quite short but due to the brightness of the security light he could not make out her features, Stanley began to fuss he licked his hands and slicked his hair making sure his style was still intact he coughed clearing his throat, his jitters became uncontrollable how he longed for a cigarette or a joint now just to calm his nerves.

The short figure crunched her way down the gravel path, he noticed that she walked with elegance very deliberate in her steps taking her time, he could see the outline of her body which was silhouetted almost as if she was walking from a heavenly beam, Stanley's mind raced in all directions he just wanted to see her and get the introduction over with so he could do his job, as she neared he took his hands out of his pockets and straightened up, his eyes widened as he was able to see what she looked like, "bloody hell" he muttered under his breath shocked as she approached the gate, quickly remembering his manners he moved forward to greet her "Good evening Ms White" he offered sounding ridiculously nervous. The gate opened and she stepped through holding her hand out for a shake "Mr Spank I like that" she replied her tone high pitched almost in surprise "wow!.. I mean hi…hello" Stanley spluttered as the combination of nerves and shock concocted to explode through his vocal chords. She was stunning a mid-forties blonde cougar who obviously kept herself in good shape she could have walked straight off of the Desperate housewives set, a very well kept lady someone Jerry Dooley would describe as a yummy mummy, dressed in a black fur coat which covered her petite frame, "my I have done well" she purred looking a clearly impressed Stanley up and down with a glint in her emerald eyes.

Stanley stood admiring before he jerked himself back into escort mode scuttling towards the car to open the door remembering to apply his gentleman's etiquette; Ms White gave a cursory glance towards Stanley before elegantly sliding into the car.

The drive to the theatre was awkward one Stanley sat shuffling uncomfortably beside her as he felt a bit giddy and became more infused by her sweet aroma, the driver obviously recognising the beauty of his passenger kept looking in the rear view mirror smirking every time he caught eye contact with Ms White.

Stanley could not believe his luck to be sat beside such a sexy woman being driven to the theatre in a fancy car was something he and Jerry would struggle to dream up on a crazy intoxicated night; he daren't look at her he was too nervous although inside he wanted to really talk to her instead he tapped his fingers onto his knee jittery staring out of the window, "do you get to theatre much?" asked Ms White as she leaned in towards Stanley's ear her warm breath wafting against the side of his face causing him shudder, "no not much" he answered back meekly trying his hardest not to act intimidated he even stared back looking her directly into her eyes, "don't worry Stanley, you will enjoy this show" she leaned in again placing her hand onto his already shaking leg, sensing his nervousness she asked "are you ok Mr Spank?" squeezing his thigh with her tiny hand.

Stanley tensed up shocked at her boldness he immediately responded "yes I'm ok" he cleared his throat adjusting his position suddenly feeling very hot under the collar, his mind raced wildly he was thinking if only Jerry could see him now all dressed up going to the theatre with a classy chick beside him he'd be spitting out his pint.

The evening progressed quickly with the both of them sitting in a comfortable private box through a performance of Chicago, of which in fact Stanley quite enjoyed probably as much as his date who sat staring at him for long periods during the show, Stanley felt quite comfortable now and began to use his wit to charm Ms White who really did not need too much encouragement anyway judging by how tightly she gripped his arm as they whispered to each other as the songs were belted out by the actors, "shall we do drinks after Stanley?", a very relaxed and flirty Ms White breathlessly whispered into his ear, "of course I would love to" he responded sounding official. Stanley was having fun no longer nervous he was actually now warming to his date his guard was slipping and the facade of his English gentleman act began to soften and the real Stanley started to creep out which was something Cassandra had warned him about it seemed his brief lasted about as long as the show which was now coming to the grand finale.

Stanley leaned over to the smiling middle aged temptress and indicated it was time to go by grabbing her fur coat "are you ready to go now Ms White?" he asked in a hushed tone also offering his hand to help her up "hmm yes my sweet Mr Spank" she purred while gripping his hand tightly and easing herself out of the comfortable burgundy cushioned seat pushing her body against a now relaxed and in control Stanley who continued to play the well-mannered gentleman. He simply draped her coat around her shoulders and ushered towards the exit, Stanley looked back towards the stage and could see the cast about to complete their final bow before being dragged out through the doors by an eager little pocket rocket of a woman whom seemed more than ready to whisk her escort away.

For the first time in his life Stanley felt at ease with someone from the opposite sex there was no more pubescent nerves or immature antics that he would normally display to the sheer dismay of any girls in the town, he now was more the Stanley his mother liked polite well-mannered and respectful, the nerves had disappeared and he actually began to feel cool about his new found job although the actions of a certain seemingly man hungry Ms White certainly opened his eyes as to what existed in the country lanes of Oakfield lodge.

On arrival back to her house after a few cocktails in a nearby bar Stanley got out to open the door for a now fairly tired Ms White, she held her hand out to seeking to be helped up out of the vehicle "ooh thank you kindly Mr Spank" she purred her emerald eyes dreamily gazed as she forced her petite frame vertical, "do you want to come in for a coffee?", she sashayed towards the gate throwing her comment towards Stanley's direction, for a second he stood and contemplated looking back at the driver who turned his head as if he was none the wiser of the seductive invitation, tempting as it was Stanley could see and hear Cassandra like the little fairy godmother in his conscious telling him to maintain his professionalism. "No I'm ok Ms White" he replied internally kicking himself at the chance of supreme bragging rights at Jerry, "well thank you for a beautiful night" she smiled back demurely before stepping through the gate and walking up the long path towards her home.

Stanley stood and watched for a moment keeping his eyes firmly on the silhouetted figure as she disappeared into the distance dwarfed by her sprawling building, "blimey!"

he emphasised pushing his fingers through his hair and stepping backwards towards the car turning around and catching the drivers face who was also staring as hard into the distance as Stanley was trying to get a last view of their passenger.

Stanley sunk back into the leather seated car and rested his head on the headrest "can I smoke in here? I'm dying for a fag", the driver nodded his head slowly before driving away "I would have gone in for the coffee" he remarked in a deadpan tone, Stanley just sucked hard on the cigarette blowing out smoke and shaking his head in disbelief "I wish I could have" he replied slouching back into the seat.

Stanley tossed and turned in his bed as the ferocious buzz and vibration from his IPhone shocked him into consciousness, he groaned frustrated at be woken as he stretch his body and scrambled around with his eyes still closed trying to locate the device. He rubbed his eyes squinting as he tried unsuccessfully to fully open them, instead curling back into the fetal position and pulling his bed covers over his head.

All around him were the remnants of his previous night's exertions the evidence of a night out laid strewn across the floor, shoes which had been kicked off his shirt and trousers left in a heap at the foot of his bed, Stanley was never the tidiest but it seemed like his first night of work had taken its toll, he wriggled himself into a more comfortable position, a knock on his bedroom door further annoyed him as his attempts to catch some serious shut eye were hampered, "who is it?" his gruff deep voice croaked as he now pulled the cover back yawning, "it's only me Stan" his dad Greg poked his head around the door, "thought you might want a cuppa" he continued to let himself in to the obstacle course which Stanley called his bedroom stepping over the minefield of clothes, gaming accessories and CD's carefully, "what time is it?" he finally sat up rubbing his face hard in an attempt to wake up and be alert, "how did it go last night?", Greg questioned quietly shutting the door behind him and sitting on the bed intrigued handing Stanley the piping hot tea.

Stanley took a sip of his hot morning liquid before revealing to his eagerly listening dad, "yeah it was... interesting shall we say", Greg Spank nodded silently digesting the comments pensively scratching his chin "care to expand?" he asked awaiting some more juicy information adjusting his glasses before turning to his son who was now sitting upright his fair hair flopped messily over his face, he took a deep breath as his dad looked on waiting curiously with baited breath "well?" again he reiterated his inquisition.

Stanley placed the cup down onto his bedside table before breaking into a big smile "nothing happened dad, we went to the theatre that's all, nothing to report here" he laughed, Greg took his glasses off to look his son dead in the eye, "dad don't worry it was all harmless fun", his dad rose from his seated position shaking his head "I really don't know" he said as he walked towards the door, "just be careful, and make yourself useful and clean this room", he turned to Stanley before exiting "not a word to your mother" he gestured putting his finger to his mouth and nodding toward the next room indicating his mum was asleep, Stanley gave him the thumbs up before grabbing his tea.

It was the day of Jerry's leaving do time had gone fast and for the two best friends it finally was their day of reckoning, it was something that played on Stanley's mind as he slowly began to get himself together, it was going to be a big night and although he was happy for Jerry he knew from tomorrow onwards he was going to be on his own, it was like breaking up with a girlfriend his gut ached knowing that it was soon to be an end of an era the Tyford two as they would fondly call themselves would soon become one.

Stanley's mind cast back to the night before, his experience with Ms White left him seriously thinking about whether he could continue doing the escort work, I mean he loved her company her smell and most of all her aesthetic, he would never in his wildest dreams have an opportunity to meet such a fine looking and rich woman.

He sat on his bed slowly putting on his socks lost in thought when he was interrupted by his loud musical ring tone which he grabbed quickly, on his screen he saw Cassandra's name flashing, "hello Cassandra" he answered jovially, "hello Stanley are you busy?" a soft and polite Cassandra asked, Stanley quickly pulled up his socks and immediately sat up straight "yes I'm just getting ready to go out" he hurriedly replied, a paused ensued Cassandra could be heard flicking through some papers and shuffling about before she came back "Stanley I received a call from Ms White this morning …she was very complimentary", a now more energetic sounding Cassandra remarked, "really?" Stanley responded happy yet surprised "well that's good right?" he continued slightly puzzled, "well she has requested your company again tonight at a function she's willing to pay double" an impressed Cassandra excitedly stated leaving Stanley to linger on the thought, "tonight? …I can't" Stanley scratched his head awkward and flustered knowing he could not miss Jerry's last night, "oh" a surprised Cassandra replied sounding surprised by his response, "this is a high paying and loyal client Stanley".

Stanley stamped his foot in frustration he became fraught quickly trying to decide, he was torn but knew he could not leave his mate Jerry without going to his party, "I'm so sorry Cassandra but tonight I can't" he grimaced as he spoke knowing this was potentially damaging to his already fledgling career, there was a long pause he could here Cassandra breathing heavily and flicking through the pages of her big book, Stanley was on tender hooks awaiting her reply "ok, I'll let her know" she spoke with restraint but her disappointed tone could not be veiled, "call me tomorrow" she concluded before slamming down the phone, "oops" Stanley threw the phone down onto his bed sheepishly he knew Cassandra was disappointed and also he had spurned another chance to see the beautiful yet frisky Ms White, "she requested me personally" he shook his head as he began to apply the finishing touches to himself before his big night with Jerry.

By the time Stanley had got to the Crown he could see that Jerry was already drunk and in full party mode, flanked by a couple of Tyford local girls who Stanley looked at with distain clearly not matching up to the delicious Ms

White "oi look who it is Stanley Spank!" Jerry shouted at the top of his voice giving Stanley a great yet embarrassing introduction, Jerry was clearly in a good mood he had the biggest smile on his face he wore a bright pink tie around his chubby neck with a white shirt and jeans, the two girls beside him stared at the more handsome and clean cut Stanley as he approached definitely excited that he would be joining them.

"Alright mate" Stanley said grabbing his friends cheeks "you plastered already?" he quipped, Jerry hugged his friend tightly before introducing him to the girls "Stan this is Donna and Kylie" he said throwing his arms around both of the girls who both in unison replied "hi Stanley", they looked very ordinary compared to Ms White both blonde dressed in jeans and tight fitting strappy tops "no class" Stanley thought as he forced a smile towards them "a pint for you mate and for you girls?", "a white wine please" one of them answered, before Stanley forced his way up to the bar.

"I'm so not going to miss this place Stan, I can't wait to have some fun in the sun" a sweaty red faced Jerry slurred into Stanley's ear spitting as he spoke leaving Stanley with a wet ear "yeah lucky you, I'm jealous" Stanley replied supping his pint contemplating his own future as straight in front of him Jerry's two female guests annoyingly giggled and whispered into each other's ear before breaking in to more fits of laughter.

For some reason Stanley was not his normal self he was not fulfilling his usual sidekick role for Jerry who was way too drunk to notice chuckling away pulling faces trying to impress his two female friends, Stanley tried his hardest to gee himself up even laughing out loud to another meaningless joke, his mind was on other things namely the second outing with Ms White plus the cash he could of earned. He stared forlornly gazing at all the usual faces that gathered in the Crown and for a split second in that moment he saw his own life encapsulated by what was in front of him he shuddered to think that he would also be stood in the Crown in twenty years' time probably married to the vacant Kylie or Donna.

His parents were right and so was Jerry Dooley there was more to life he had just been too pig ignorant to acknowledge it, his brief encounter with a certain Ms White got him thinking, he continued to day dream watching all the punters in slow motion laughing and drinking around him, "Stan…oi Stan!" he got jerked back into reality as Jerry's jovial voice interrupted his moment of clarity "what's up with you? You got a face like a wet weekend" Jerry quipped cackling towards the girls who both looked at each other and broke into a fit of giggles in unison, "come on let's go outside I got a joint to puff", Jerry patted him on the shoulder as he attempted to manoeuvre his tubby frame from his seated position winking at Donna and Kylie as he rose.

The two girls also began to get up and follow, "you ladies wait right here" he ordered "men's stuff" his face turned serious pulling the large rolled joint out of his pocket before breaking into a heinous laugh before bounding towards the beer garden, Stanley reverted to type doing his best James Bond impression "excuse me ladies" he shoved past still gripping his pint.

Outside both stood at the back of the garden away from the main sway of the boisterous locals, a red faced Jerry sparked up the big joint and pulled hard on it as if his life depended on it like he was sucking on an asthma inhaler before exhaling a thick plume of smoke which literally stank the surroundings with the lethal herb, Stanley looked around sheepishly catching a few non approving eyes, "I'm so going to miss this Stan" Jerry choked out the words the hoarse husk of his voice made him sound like a hippy, Stanley nodded in approval silently still aware of the beady eyes being cast in their direction.

"So are you actually going to work or just going for a free holiday?" Stanley quizzed whilst taking his turn to suck on the charred joint, Jerry grabbed Stanley's pint and proceeded to gulp it down finishing it and rounding off with a loud crass burp, "I'm going for fun it's a free pass to fun Stan my boy" he replied, Stanley took another healthy pull before passing it back, "just be careful alright?" a concerned Stanley replied, "so what are you going to do without me Mr Spank?" a now far gone stoned and drunk Jerry asked barely able to speak let alone stand swaying back and forth, "well.." Stanley was about to tell him about his own little side job but he stopped short and thought it better not to evoke a response from a clearly drunk and high Jerry. "I'll be alright mate" he said passing back the joint "just have fun and don't do anything stupid", Stanley said slapping his both his cheeks then embracing his friend tightly almost burning himself on the still lit joint, "come on let's go before your dates leave us" Stanley joked referring to Jerry's friends Donna and Kylie, "the Tyford two lives on!" Jerry screamed as they're entered the bar drawing curious stares from some of the publicans.

It was now past closing time and as all the late night revellers emptied onto the streets a clearly hammered Jerry stumbled out he was the worse for wear his pot belly bulging out of his shirt which was now unbuttoned exposing his pink hairy gut, Stanley struggled to hold up his friend whose arm was over Stanley's shoulder, "I fancy a kebab… who wants a kebab?" Jerry shouted to the other stragglers who were all trying their best to avoid a clearly drunk Jerry, "come on mate I think I need to get you home" a surprisingly sober and sensible Stanley suggested. Donna and Kylie stood by waiting and watching as the two stumbled their way back towards home "what about us?" Donna, the larger of the two screamed in all of the mayhem, "see you later girls" Stanley replied bluntly without even turning around to acknowledge them, instead he stopped to adjust his leverage trying to cope with the dead weight of a nearly passed out Jerry, "I love you Stanley Spank you are my best mate in the whole wide…", Jerry slurred before tripping up on the kerb pulling Stanley down with him as they both ended up in a heap on the floor.

They both sat heads bowed on the side of the road Stanley pulled out a now crumpled cigarette box and fiddled around until he managed to extract a bent cigarette, he rifled through his pockets for a lighter while a clearly wasted Jerry sat slumped forward on the kerb, the fresh night air sent a chill through Stanley making him shudder slightly whilst he dragged hard on his cigarette tipping up the collars on his jacket, it was quiet now most of the crowds had dispersed to their warrens of life only the sound of a heavily wheezing Jerry interjected into what was a serene surrounding.

Stanley looked at Jerry he smiled to himself as memories flooded his mind of the many years of dossing and endless days spent larking around getting high, again he tugged hard on the cigarette his fears of loneliness and boredom seemed to evaporate he knew it was time for a new chapter for both of them, sure life could not continue as it was even a lovable oaf like Jerry knew that, so it was time to grow up and as Stanley stubbed the remainder of his cigarette out onto the concrete, Jerry stirred momentarily breathing in and slowly rubbing his face, Stanley placed his hand onto his shoulder rocking him back and forth "come on mate let's get you home" his now tired voice instructed, it was the end of the night and for now the end of the road for the Tyford two.

Stanley sat hunched at the kitchen table mulling over his morning tea his mood was sombre for once his usual buoyancy seemed deflated as he stirred the silver spoon belatedly he did not even have a hangover, instead he was solemn, quiet and lost in his thoughts, until his mother Brenda breezed in full of life "morning Stan" she chirped still in her pink towelled dressing gown and a white towel wrapped around her head like a turban, as she walked past her fresh fruity shampoo smell wafted past stirring Stanley, "what's wrong with you sour chops" again her early bird cheery outlook did nothing to arouse any kind of senses in Stanley, "oh.. Jerry" she suddenly cottoned on to the fact her son was in mourning at the loss of his right hand man and best friend.

Brenda poured herself some hot water from the kettle and sat opposite her desolate son, plonking two lumps of sugar and a tea bag into her cup, "heavy night was it?" she continued to probe in a reassuring motherly tone, Stanley raised his head to find his mother's eye line "no not that heavy" he grumbled slurping his hot tea, Brenda sat adjusting her head towel looking on surprised at the fact her son was so down and it was not alcohol induced "come on Stan you have to pick yourself up son, your life starts now" she continued whilst dunking her tea bag casually as she spoke.

Stanley looked up from his bowed position his eyes were reddened as he sniffed in deeply "I'll be alright" he whimpered getting up from his chair the wooden legs scraping against the lino floor screeching as he pushed the chair backwards, Brenda knew better than to badger him further, she sipped her tea without reply knowing that she had to give her son the time to mope.

Stanley sat on his bed his room was darkened he had not even opened the curtains; the familiar aroma of weed circulated in his confined space, the small TV screen projected a colourful melee which was attributed to his computer game, he was in no mood for company or lectures from anyone, he dragged hard on his joint dressed in a baggy tracksuit with a hood which covered most of his face, he remained sullen there was nothing that would lift his mood, he glanced at his phone looking at the digital clock display knowing that by now Jerry would be half way to his destination he rested back onto his pillow and closed his eyes drifting into a slumber as the intoxicating fumes began to hit his brain cells.

His eyelids became heavy as Stanley struggled to stay awake, he was taking it pretty badly it was as if he had lost his right arm. For the next half an hour already stoned Stanley continued to roll another joint clearly in no mood to do anything except smoke himself into a coma, he meticulously sprinkled his weed into the thin rolling sheet of paper trying not to lose any, his slanting eyes struggling to focus in the limited light made even more difficult by his fair fringe flopping over his face.

Stanley continued regardless and he expertly rolled a perfect cone shaped joint, he scrambled around on his bed for his lighter before being interrupted by the fierce vibration and ring of his phone, he sighed and tutted loudly disgruntled by the interruption before picking it up to see Cassandra's name flashing, he was in no mood to speak with anyone and stared hard before bothering to answer "hello Cassandra" he attempted to sound upbeat but instead sounded a little bit crazy as his voice cracked into high pitch, "Stanley is that you?" a bewildered Cassandra asked, "yes it is" he responded again sounding high, Cassandra hesitated before answering "I need you to work tonight, you seem to be very popular with Ms White she wants you again" she sounded enthused.

Stanley suddenly sat up the mere mention of her name seem to rouse him into some sort of life he stretched out and tried to shake some energy back into himself, "ok I'll do it" he said with a healthy dose of enthusiasm about as much as he had mustered all morning the fact Cassandra had called somehow managed to remind him that he actually had a life still here in Tyford.

The day passed and was fairly uneventful for Stanley he spent the rest of the day playing computer games he had stopped smoking in an attempt to clear his head and fantasised about meeting the cute and delectable Ms White, he tossed the idea through his mind that if she was to ask him back to her place again he would take her up on her offer but then again he had to remember that it was not a date he was simply providing a service.

He could not help but get excited at the thought and in his little fantasy world he pictured himself as the suave cool James Bond type sweeping her off her feet in a black tuxedo whisking her up the path to a secret location lined with palm trees a remote island surrounded by turquoise oceans and pale white sandy beaches, he sat staring hard at the small screen frantically pressing the buttons on his game control as he became more entranced by his vivid imagination.

He finally began to redeem some self-worth and focus and by the time his mother poked her head in through the door to announce she was off to work he had reverted back to his normal self, no longer the brooding sulk that she faced over breakfast, "Ok Stan I'll see you tomorrow, your tea's in the fridge" she stood in the doorway her blue and white nurses uniform clean and immaculate, "alright see you later" Stanley replied waving her away, "and Stanley…open the bloody window will you!" Brenda shouted back intimating the whiff of his stale weed smoke was still pungent in the air, "yes mum" he replied again sheepishly.

Brenda slammed the door the sound of her stomping down the stairs signalling her disgust. Left to his own devices now Stanley began to look through his wardrobe selecting his attire for his evening he did not have much to choose from as he only had the same suit he wore before and the shoes but at least he could wear a different shirt and tie, he looked at his digital clock the big green digits displayed the time 5:45 "ok time to get ready" he muttered, he turned to his cd collection looking through "need music" he spoke under his breath "ah ha" he exclaimed before selecting his choice, N.E.R.D the title read, he flicked open the case and cranked up the volume blasting out the Hip hop rock tunes.

Once again Stanley Spank was reinvented into Mr cool, he stared into the mirror admiring himself and the makeover like transformation this time he chose to add a quiff to his hair and donned a pair of spectacles which made him look a bit geeky but somehow added to the overall sophisticated look, he had seen this look in one of his mums female magazines and thought at least it may divert Ms White's attention from the fact he had worn the same suit twice.

He left the house after much preening and pampering smelling like a perfumery and looking like a model from the pages of GQ, he shoved his hands into his trouser pockets and began his march towards the town he had to make a quick stop to Cassandra's office first to get his brief and pick up his money from the last time he worked, which was something else he was looking forward to, maybe life after Jerry would not be so bad after all he thought striding purposefully towards the bus station feeling more optimistic about life and the future.

As he approached the stop from the corner of his eye he saw the bus careering around the corner which made him have to jog the final few steps, luckily there was a few people boarding which gave him enough time to make it, he fixed his jacket which became slightly disjointed as the rest of the passengers jostled for position.

Still perplexed and adjusting his jacket Stanley heard a distinctive sounding voice beside him "hello sir nice suit" it said, Stanley was just about to step on board when he turned around and noticed a beautiful blonde girl looking up at him at first he just smiled back at her too occupied with getting onto the bus it took him a few seconds to register before the penny dropped "you're the girl from the ..." he paused before they both said in unison "the shop!" both laughing at the coincidence of it all, Stanley turned and paid the driver his fare before looking around for a seat waiting for her to board.

They both sat together she looked stunning her ice blue eyes jolting Stanley's memory back to the day he bought his suit "ah yes I remember now" he said as he stared back at her piercingly through his spectacles, "Stanley" he was about to introduce himself before she finished of his sentence "Spank! Yes I know" she giggled "I didn't know you wore glasses" she continued, nodding her head impressed by his new look, Stanley adjusted his eyewear "and your name?" he asked unable to distract himself away from her pretty face, "oh I'm Ami", she held out her hand offering a shake to which Stanley obliged.

Her sweet fresh aroma captivated Stanley into silence, his heart actually pounded hard he felt a little chemistry in her company, Ami sat shyly waiting for the next part of the conversation from Stanley who seemed to have frozen in the moment, "so where are you off to?" he asked suddenly plucking up the courage, he was taken in by her beauty and could not remember paying her too much attention when he purchased his suit from her shop at that time his mind was too preoccupied with grabbing some threads but on this occasion he realised how stunning she was. She had little dainty diamond earrings dangling from her rose pink earlobes, she coyly looked back at the suave looking Stanley "I'm on my way home, I share a flat with a friend in Underbridge, and you?" she countered her accent abound a slightly Scandinavian dialect which Stanley found endearing, "Oh er I'm on my way to a dinner party" he stuttered remembering the nature of his mission, "nice" Ami responded, "well you look very dapper Mr Spank" she continued brushing the collar of his suit her sweet tone enticing Stanley.

He felt as if he wanted to stay and chat to Ami some more comfortable with the organic nature of their conversation but his stop was fast approaching, "mines the next stop" he mumbled resigned to ending this one off chance encounter, they both exchanged glances and smiles as the bus sped rapidly towards the next stop "maybe I can meet you for lunch one day?" Stanley blurted out a rushed statement before standing up to depart.

Ami smiled amiably her eyes looking up towards the tall lean geek chic gent, "ok that sounds nice" she responded again fluttering her eyelids and smiling sweetly. The bus veered into the stop squelching to a halt allowing Stanley to step off, he was chuffed but at the same time baffled by what had just happened.

He stood statuesque watching the bus trundle away and found himself smiling as Ami went past waving with a smile in the window. "Wow" Stanley exclaimed to himself completely shocked but happily surprised, his mind now wandered he was consumed with thoughts about Ami, he never would have imagined being able to take someone as nice as her out never in a million years, he was so bewildered he had even forgot to ask for her number his mind fleetingly passed on Jerry and the days they spent fantasising about girls like that, "wow" he shook his head again and started to walk towards the industrial estate where Cassandra's office was located, for that time he had almost forgot he was escorting the lovely Ms White she had just been eclipsed by Ami.

Stanley approached the bright red door he looked at the time on his phone 7:05 it read, he was just on time and pressed the gold buzzer entry phone, "Stanley is that you?", once again he heard Cassandra's feeble voice crackle through the intercom, "yes Cassandra it's me" he answered before the buzz sounded signalling the releasing of the lock.

Cassandra stood by the door to welcome him in "hello Stanley, look at you" she squealed in her excited high pitched tone she ushered in a pleased Stanley, Cassandra who was dressed in a black dress with a red cardigan shuffled back towards her desk she was clearly happy to see Stanley, "we've not much time, do you want a tea?"

she asked looking up at him, "no I'm ok thanks" Stanley replied watching as Cassandra began flicking through documents which lay strewn across her desk, "right" she declared clearly attempting to regain her focus in amongst the melee of paperwork "this is for you" she handed Stanley an envelope before licking her fingers and flicking through another folder.

Stanley looked at the envelope with a bemused look on his face before peeling back slowly the fold to open it, he pulled out a cheque and was quite startled when he saw the amount written on it "£1500 pounds" he tried to suppress a smile "are you sure this is all mine?" he questioned naively, Cassandra stopped her fussing and paper shuffling and looked directly at Stanley her small wrinkly face yielded to a warm smile she almost laughed when replying "Stanley this is just the beginning, you can earn double that the more clients you escort", again she smiled knowingly "I think you can do very well indeed" her sweet voice was coated in enthusiasm as she looked back at Stanley who was still transfixed by the piece of paper in his hands, "anyway you have Ms White to meet tonight so let me give you the brief", she was quickly back to business her serious tone jolted Stanley back to reality especially on hearing Ms White's name he regained his focus remembering he actually had a date to attend, his mind was a bit of a whirl what with Ami still fresh in his thoughts too.

It was back to familiar territory as Stanley stood outside the gates that guarded the house of his special client, he stood with his hands in his pocket slightly apprehensive as to what the night had in store. The soft purr of the waiting cars engine was the only sound to interrupt the beautiful silence of the countryside, in the distance he could see the feline petite figure and blonde hair silhouette of Ms White.

She walked with a sexiness which had Stanley homing in on this mysterious alien like creature emerging through the shadows, he gulped in anticipation and braced himself for the inevitable temptation and frolics which awaited him. He stared ahead fixing his stance attempting to appear relaxed and cool but inside his stomach churned with nervous excitement, as the forty something vivacious minx prowled towards him.

The closer she got a shiver went through Stanley as her almost Bardot like image became clearer, "Mr Spank how lovely to see you again" she stated enthusiastically as the gate slowly opened in front of her, "Ms White" Stanley replied his eyes fixated onto her gloriously dressed body. Once again she had surpassed all of his expectations by shimmering her way into his sight, "wow you look amazing" Stanley exclaimed almost losing his cool persona and sounding like and excited teenager watching Baywatch for the first time.

She oozed a powerful and sexy style which admittedly Stanley found hard to resist especially when she came forward and planted a succulent kiss onto his left cheek, "loving the spectacle look today Stanley" she whispered in her undeniable soft mischievous tone, her hot breath dancing around his ear.

Stanley smiled before inviting her to link arms, again she was dressed immaculately in a beautiful sea blue full length dress complete with sparkly silver strappy shoes, and a dark blue fur scarf to cover her bare shoulders, Stanley was totally mesmerised nearly losing his footing as he stepped towards the waiting car.

Her smell again was fresh like a bouquet of flowers, she glanced up at her tall young escort and flashed a knowing smile "are you ready for dinner?" she questioned seductively her green eyes twinkled like diamonds caught in the light, Stanley grinned trying to contain himself as he opened the door of the car, his nerves had dispersed he was now feeling as if he knew Ms White and was really looking forward to another night in her company.

Any thoughts of Ami disappeared he was focused and ready to have some fun, as he squeezed up close next to her in the car, her pretty face remained flawless as she encouraged Stanley to sit close by pulling his arm inviting him to budge up next to her "don't be scared" she chuckled sensing Stanley's hesitation, he duly obliged he was looking forward to the evening and relishing the chance to spend time with a certain Ms White.

The dinner party was taking place at a hotel about forty minutes away from Tyford which gave Stanley plenty of opportunity to get cosy on the Journey with Ms White, he felt more confident and was at ease with her enough to engage in conversation, she told him that she was divorced and that her former husband was a wealthy steel magnate who died of a heart attack leaving her a substantial amount of money she seemed unmoved and unemotional when telling him her past, "I'm now all about companionship Mr Spank" she winked at him rubbing his leg with her jewel encrusted hand, Stanley as excited as he was chose to smile back in a genteel manner placing a comforting hand onto hers.

As they pulled in to the venue which looked more like a stately home than a hotel, it was evident that they were going to be in the company of some very rich people going by the assorted hi performance luxury cars which pulled into the grounds. Stanley peered out of the window "blimey" he muttered under his breath, a healthy selection of Lamborghini's, Ferraris and Rolls Royce's queued to find their space, Stanley turned to Ms White who was busy powdering her nose staring into a tiny silver pocket mirror, "do I look beautiful Stanley" she mused whilst clipping the mirror and placing it back into her bag "of course darling" Stanley replied in his English gentleman voice which he practised so well just about taking his eyes away from the fleet of cars which fascinated him.

They pulled in to the drive Stanley could not help noticing that most of the guests were a lot older than him, he began to feel an little out of his depth "are you sure it's ok for me to be here?" he said sounding a little lost and fearful, Ms White looked at him her eyes sparkled transfixing a nervous Stanley, she reached over and cupped her hand onto his face, Stanley felt a shiver run through his body, "you are with me it'll be fine" she reassured rubbing his cheek, Ms White took charge fixing his tie and brushing off any fluff from his jacket, "now deep breath Mr Spank it's time to make our entrance", She pointed to the door which made Stanley jump into action once he realised he was supposed to be the escort, "Oh ok I'm ready" he stuttered turning to get the door.

They both strolled arm in arm up to the main entrance Ms White walked with a swanky sexy style clearly happy to have a young good looking man beside her, "now I'll introduce you as Stanley, it makes us seem more shall we say Intimate", she began to purr again like a lust induced sexpot, poor Stanley gulped and took a sharp intake of breath nodding in agreement, in his head he was just thinking its only for a couple of hours easy money.

As the guest streamed in he noticed how lavishly dressed everybody was he was glad he wore a suit, he could not help being slightly overawed by the occasion, he had nothing in common with all of these rich affluent people it was a world apart from the life he and his parent's lived in fact his dad Greg would frown upon such a flagrant show of materialism and pomp.

The foyer bustled with guests as the champagne reception kicked in, Stanley gazed in amazement at the opulent splendour it really was something straight out of a Bond movie set, there were smartly dressed cocktail waitresses walking around with giant trays of drinks, well dressed couples in black dinner suits and an array of slinky dresses in vibrant colours.

The constant mumble of conversation droned around the room, Ms White grabbed a glass of champagne swiftly from the passing waitress leaving Stanley feeling as if he needed to be coached in dinner party etiquette showing his boyish naivety looking around trying to catch the eye of the next pretty waitress that waltzed by.

Ms White was already in mingle mode and began to drift off when she saw a friend "Charles Carter!" she screamed catching sight of one of her acquaintances "Marilyn White how in the devil are you?" a booming yet camp voice responded, Stanley swiftly managed to grab a glass of champagne from the giant tray which flew past him like a flying saucer just in time to turn round and see a tall broad chubby faced man grabbing a kiss on the cheek from Ms White, "Marilyn?" Stanley muttered taking a large sip of the fizzy golden liquid and watching his client embracing this larger than life character, who was dressed in a blue pin stripe suit with a cream paisley cravat.

Stanley looked him up and down he thought to himself it was quite funny for such a big strapping fella to be so camp, Stanley continued to stand watching as the big guy continued to flap about obviously excited to see Ms White, "come on I'll introduce you" she said grabbing his hand and pulling him towards Stanley's direction. "Charles Carter this is Stanley Spank my young hot escort for the night" she purred in that familiar lusty tone which she often used when talking to Stanley, "oooh Spank!" Charles Carter replied "you can spank me anytime" he said suggestively whilst gripping Stanley's hand and giving him a firm handshake, Stanley smiled bashfully he could feel his cheeks filling with a rush of blood as he blushed at the introduction.

Ms White stood smiling her eyes shimmering with happiness as her friend gave Stanley the once over, "you lucky bitch" Charles cattily spouted turning to Ms White "What a fine catch", he continued, "welcome to my dinner party Mr Spank" he continued giggling at the mention of Stanley's surname, "have drinks and then join me in the Windsor room we chow down at eight", he swivelled like a ballerina towards Ms White clasping her hands before prancing away "toodles til later" he bounced away and into the room full of guests.

"Oh my god what?... I mean who was that...Marilyn?" Stanley laughed focusing his attention back to Ms White, she linked her arm into Stanley's and looked forward with a proud look on her face "come on sexy, let's take a look around".

After walking around and drinking more champagne and wine the already tipsy couple made their way to the main dining area located in the sumptuous Windsor room, Stanley who by now had loosened up considerably and warmed into the evening mainly due the flow of alcohol whispered and giggled with his client, he was literally blown away by the amazing layout and spread he adjusted himself and took off his spectacles rubbing his eyes when he saw the beautifully decorated chandelier lit room, it was the most splendour he had ever seen in his young life.

As they entered they drew stares from the older guests not that it bothered Ms White who sauntered in clearly comfortable being the centre of attention. Stanley could see the names of the guests written on small gold leafed cards on the table, and searched for their place which was right next to the party host himself one Charles Carter.

There were thirty guests all older rich folk dressed as if they were going to the ballet, Stanley sat opposite a couple called the Marshes, a gentleman of about sixty with his wife who seemed a lot younger but not as pretty as Ms White, Stanley looked down at the table counting the different types of shiny silver cutlery which lay next to the clean white china plates, he was uncomfortable and did not really know what to do or say he felt awkward and began to get agitated not knowing where to place his hands.

He began to think he was out of his depth especially as the conversations around him ranged from land owner rights to scuba diving in Sharm el Sheikh things and places he knew nothing about, he sat fidgeting with his cutlery tapping the fork onto his hand nervously until he felt the foot of Ms White rub against his leg "relax Spank" she purred quietly "just enjoy the evening", she continued while also rubbing her hand ever closer to his thigh, Stanley twitched and sat up rigidly the effects of the alcohol now beginning to subside, he laughed nervously while shooting Ms White a furrowed glance to which she responded by rubbing her left hand close to his crotch which again made Stanley shoot up sharply, grabbing his glass of wine and rapidly taking a big gulp.

The host Charles Carter stood up, his colossal frame seemed even bigger as he towered over the table but as soon as he open his mouth he turned into a big lovable teddy bear red cheeked and sweating profusely, he clinked his spoon onto his glass "attention purlease!" he squealed excitedly as he commanded a hush in the Windsor room, all murmurs descended and everyone sat silently, he had his audience even the waiters stood steadfastly awaiting him to speak "it's an honour and pleasure to have you all here" he started buoyantly, he then giggled hiccupping before declaring "tuck in darlings!" in a flamboyant high pitched tone, drawing roars of laughter from his guests.

Stanley sat slightly bemused and laughed along with everyone else he did not even know why but he joined in regardless to the delight of Ms White who used the distraction to once again grope young Stanley grabbing a quick squeeze of his inner thigh.

Ms White winked at him seductively clearly in a playful mood, Stanley felt a hot flush slowly travelling up to his face he went red with embarrassment, part of him loved the fact she was so hands on and tactile but the other part he was frustrated as he knew he was working and could not reciprocate any kind of feelings, so he was literally her plaything for the evening.

The smartly dressed waiting staff came in serving tray after tray of lavish foods, lobster, shrimp, beef, sauté potatoes, oysters and vegetables' all nicely arranged richly coloured which smelt delicious and vibrantly leapt off of the silver trays, he had never witnessed a feast like it, bottles of champagne and wine were being poured into their glasses relentlessly as the energy around the large table intensified the more food and drink were consumed.

Stanley tucked into the sumptuous array but he felt a little bit guilty he knew his father would frown upon such acts of snobbery and wanton self-indulgence, he was playing a role and quite frankly enjoying it he thought of his old mate Jerry and what he would do in the same situation, you bet he would be milking it for all it was worth, free food and booze a no brainer.

After what seemed like hours of eating and drinking the worse for wear couple said their goodbyes Stanley had a little too much to drink he wobbled his way through the lobby as the patrons filed out to their cars, Ms. White who was clearly drunk clung on tightly to his arm, "I just need to powder my nose Stanley" she spoke with a slur as she stood steadfastly trying to hold some kind of poise, her emerald green eyes now looked a little misty as she swiveled and tottered off in the direction of the ladies restroom, "I'll wait here shall I?" Stanley offered sarcastically, he was dying for a cigarette so he staggered outside patting his pockets in search of his box of fags;

He got outside and lent against a concrete pillar the cool evening air hit him stiffening him up he shuddered as the late fresh breeze bit into his body, finally he was able to quickly light up and inhale his cigarette blowing out the smoke with vigour, "got a light?" a recognisable voice could be heard although Stanley was so engrossed in his smoke he did not pay any attention and on auto pilot replied without looking "yep", as he casually took out the lighter, he could feel the presence of somebody next to him but did not even offer a passing glance until he flicked the flint of his lighter, the flame lit up the face of the person requesting "oh it's you" Stanley said as he finally saw it was none other than the host Charles Carter himself "nice party Charlie", he replied as he held the flame up towards the brown wooden pipe which hung from Charles reddened lips.

Charles grabbed Stanley's hand holding it tightly as he sucked hard lighting the tobacco, by now he had lost his smart suit blazer and his cravat was loosely hanging around his neck, "so…" he spoke while blowing the pipe smoke from the side of his mouth still holding on to Stanley's hand, he looked him up and down like a designer staring at the allure of his creations on a mannequin his eyes big and beady "how do I get one of you then?" his question profound and to the point, which at first Stanley did not completely pay attention to, "one of me?" he replied innocently whilst taking another pull of his fag, "yes well Marilyn, excuse me I mean Ms White suggested…" he continued playfully, the penny had dropped as Stanley caught the innuendo taking his hand away from the clammy grasp, "oh …well" he coughed "I mean I don't.. well you know" again he coughed trying to be polite in his reply, "listen Mr Spank I am very wealthy and have a trip abroad planned, I'll pay triple for you to accompany me", Charles Carter was straight to the point. Stanley looked back shocked at what he was hearing again he shuddered as the evening chill swept through his body "erm I don't…" before he could finish his sentence, Charles Carter pulled out a small business card and thrust it into his top breast pocket of his blazer "call me" he asked calmly patting Stanley's chest hard and winking before turning away leaving a trail of tobacco smoke of which the raw whiff attacked his nostrils, within seconds Ms White sauntered outside looking a little fresher "oh there you are!" she walked towards him.

Stanley stood with a confused expression still attempting to digest what had just happened, "let's go" she demanded sounding tired and ready for bed, she grabbed his arm tightly almost owning him as the car pulled in towards them, Stanley was still stunned by Charles Carters proposal he had sobered up considerably, flicking back into escort mode as he opened the door for Ms White to climb into the car.

On the way back to Oakfield lodge Stanley relaxed calmly on the leather seat he was quite glad the night was over and although he had a good time his mind was still disturbed by the thought s of the hosts request, he was not angry but was beginning to think of this job in a different way, almost feeling like he was just an object to be used as a bit of eye candy by rich folk, he frowned as the thought passed through his mind, Ms White snuggled in close to him she was not quite asleep as he could hear her making soft purring and groaning sounds as she made sure she continued where she left of at the dinner table by rubbing her hands along his legs and inside his blazer onto his chest, for some reason Stanley did not seem to mind he gazed out of the window watching the passing lights blur into the distance attempting to remain calm as his racy client continued to spread herself all over him.

"Stanley Spank" she called his name playfully intensify her assault on his lean body, Stanley was trying to remain relaxed and calm but it was obvious he was now not going to get any respite from a clearly horny tipsy siren of a woman, she began to writhe her body up against him surrendering herself, again she said his name this time bringing her face close to his grabbing his chin and turning his head towards her arcing for a kiss her breath was hot and the alcohol remnants were still abound on her pallet, Stanley was becoming aroused he had never been in a situation like this before and was not sure if he could resist the overtures of such a fine foxy lady who was clearly in the mood for some frisky fun.

The drive back to the house seemed to take longer than usual and by the way Ms White was grabbing at Stanley's shirt trying to undo the buttons he hoped the journey would end soon, he was squirming uncomfortably on the back seat trying his hardest to stay evasive, "come on stop now" he told a moaning Ms White who just ignored his plea and ploughed on relentlessy in her lusty pursuit. Again she moved her face up towards Stanley's, "hmm just one kiss please Mr Spank" she begged in a low growl her breath reeked of alcohol while her fragrance wafted up into Stanley's face, she stared provocatively her glazed eyes looking longingly up towards her handsome young date "I'll pay you extra to stay with me tonight" she continued her voice hoarse, Stanley looked shocked his own blue eyes widened at the request but for some reason could not bring himself to take advantage of the situation this was a good position to be in maybe something he would have never imagined sitting on the banks of the river Ty with Jerry, but he strangely had pity for her, sure he found her very attractive in fact extremely attractive but he kept getting images of Cassandra popping into his head like a little fairy godmother repeating her company's etiquette and rules, "please stop" he sounded quite pathetic really but Stanley was one for good old fashioned morals and he knew he would be crossing the company line by doing anything more than what he was paid to do.

"Look I can't" he struggled free pushing her away unceremoniously "look I'm sorry I've had a good night but we should leave it there" he stated commandingly looking flustered and a bit disheveled fixing his shirt and buttoning it back, Ms White sat up looking hurt and slightly embarrassed at the harsh rejection she fixed her hair and her ruffled dress as the car pulled into her drive, looking at her reaction Stanley sensed he was a bit too harsh on the vexed vixen "look I've had a lovely time let's just call it a night" he pleaded sincerely hoping that she would accept his reasoning. Ms White turned and forced a paltry smile "yes you're right", her smile did not mask the disappointment her tone dry and hoarse she sounded tired.

Stanley opened the door and leapt out offering his hand to help Ms White out, she held his hand her small jewelled fingers clutched his hand tightly as she stepped out into the night air. The night time chill stiffened her posture upright she swept her blue fur scarf around her shoulders and neck, she stared longingly into Stanley's eyes "thank you for a lovely evening Stanley" she said proudly moving in stretching upwards to plant a kiss onto his cheek. Stanley gave her a hug as the two shared an extended embrace, her petite frame felt warm as they pressed against each other Stanley held her firmly making sure he completely consumed her into his chest, inside his mind his thoughts battled between lust and sincerity, in the end his sincerity won.

He eased himself away and cupped her face, she hummed with satisfaction, "Ms Marilyn White" Stanley smiled broadly as he said out her name "you are one in a million", he reverted back to his Bond like persona, she looked up adoringly and touched his face "you too Mr Spank, you too" she replied shivering the chill reminded her it was time to go, she activated the iron gates which opened smoothly, she turned and began to walk into her drive the percussion clicks of her heels resonated as her deliberate steps lead her towards her house.

Stanley stood and watched he almost felt cruel for allowing such a beautiful woman walk away from him but he knew there would be further adventures to come just that gut feeling that he would be seeing her again.

Greg Spank sat at the kitchen table nursing a large mug of tea whilst flicking through the morning papers; it was silent except for the sound of the pages turning he looked studious concentrating as he carefully read, his calm was soon interrupted by the sound of heavy footsteps a fully dressed and vibrant Stanley bounded into his quiet haven, "alright dad?" he offered cheerily as he clinked the cups grabbing his mug and flicking on the kettle, much to his dad's annoyance who replied clearly grumpy "Stanley" he said without raising his head from its position buried in the pages.

Stanley continued to whistle cheerily and make as much noise as he possibly could while making a cup of tea, "is there a reason for all of this?" his dad now very ruffled due to the sudden interruption taking off his glasses and putting his newspaper down "well, good night was it?", Greg Spank said folding his arms and sitting back in his chair as Stanley walked around and sat opposite his dad holding his steaming mug of tea.

Stanley was dressed in a plain white tee shirt and jeans, his fair mop of hair was messy not combed which was a stark contrast to his slicked back look of the night before he had a sly grin on his face as he sat down and took a quick sip, he looked excited and fresh he was tapping his foot on the floor as if he had a disposition, "I met someone last night" he whispered enthusiastically bowing his head shyly still tapping his foot, his dad raised his eyebrows in surprise "well I know you go out and meet people" Greg replied mocking his son slightly by emphasising the meet part of his sentence, "who was she? Some old lonely bingo biddy" he continued sarcastically affording himself a small chuckle.

Stanley looked back at his dad with furrowed eyebrows not amused by his attempts of humour, "no actually I met a nice young girl called Ami, she works in the town", Greg leaned back in his chair surprised "oh really? tell me more" he continued now leaning forward eagerly, "and that's it" Stanley smiled broadly taking another sip of his tea before getting up from the table, he definitely had a pep in his step and seemed very vibrant, "where are you off to now?" a bemused Greg quizzed, Stanley bounded out towards the door "I'm off into town to see Ami" with a smile on his face grabbing his jacket from the coat hook in the hallway and was out of the door leaving his dad sitting at the table scratching his head.

Stanley walked briskly with purpose his hands were shoved into his pockets he felt fresh and vibrant a total turnaround from the normal lazy lethargic person he'd been for the past few years, as he walked he wondered how his friend Jerry was doing he had not heard from him since his departure, lighting a cigarette he smiled knowing that his best friend was probably larging it up on a beach somewhere hammered out of his mind, it was all about him now and he was actually enjoying his new lease of life, he had money a job and now a possible date things were looking up.

Finally he reached the town which was quieter than normal maybe because he was early the shops had just opened and there was only a few people milling about, a large dustcart slowly edged its way through the centre with the road sweepers and garbage men in their luminous hi vi vests shouting banter as they swept up and tossed large blacks bags into the back of the truck. Stanley walked straight towards the cashing office he had his cheque that he wished to get his first wages again this was a new experience for him as he never really had his own money before usually his relied on his mum for hand-outs.

After collecting his cash Stanley stood outside staring at the clothes store where Ami worked, he pondered for a moment trying to muster up the courage to step over the road and go into the store, this was a different Stanley it was actually himself not the dressed up smooth looking James Bond gentleman, he took a deep breath and stepped in the direction of the shop he had nothing to lose and deep down he really wanted to see her.

Upon entrance the heavy bass of the electronic techno music thumped hard, the shop floor was pretty empty not many early shoppers about, Stanley began to browse at the various coloured outfits which were all neatly positioned and hanging off the rails, he nodded his head in rhythm to the beats as he perused through the clothing, affording himself a quick glance around to see if he could spot Ami. He continued to look around at the various displays scanning carefully each section grabbing a couple of tee shirts as he moved from rack to rack, "do you come here often?" a soft voice politely asked, Stanley spun around quickly and to his delight a fresh faced Ami dressed in a tight white top with bleached jeans and white plimsolls standing right behind him "hey good morning" he said surprised but at the same time trying to hold his excitement of seeing her, he stepped forward and stretched out his hand for a handshake, Ami seemed just as delighted as she giggled "you really are very English Stanley Spank" she said as she jokingly did a curtsy as if she were greeting a member of the royal family, Stanley let out a nervous laugh, he could not help himself and gave her the once over look from head to toe before plucking up the courage to speak, "so ..." he said nervously "I came here to see you and I wanted to ask if you were free for lunch maybe ...?".

He tailed of finally letting go of her soft hand, he had this knack of switching between shy Stanley to the cordial gentleman and to Ami she found it endearing it made her blush she fidgeted ruffling her hair "ok yeah I'm free let's say about twelve?" she responded with a cute smile. Stanley's heart thumped harder than the music that continued boom throughout the shop "how do you work in this every day?" he laughed as he pointed to the speakers breaking the uncomfortable moment, Ami laughed shaking her head and shrugging her shoulders, "I better get back, are you buying those?" she pointed to the tee shirts in his hands.

Stanley was still in awe staring into her blue eyes "erm oh these yeah thanks" he stuttered, "it's ok I'll take them to the till", she stepped forward and took them from him again both their body language spoke volumes as they hesitated their movements Stanley grinned nervously as Ami took his purchase to the till "I'll see you at twelve" she mouthed before walking off towards her colleague.

After a couple of hours hanging around the town centre spending some of his well-earned cash on a few computer games Stanley slowly made his way back to the shop to wait for Ami, he was happy that he had got over his initial fears of speaking to girls and had suddenly acquired a new found confidence probably which was down to the wonderful Ms White.

Right on time Ami emerged to see a bag laden Stanley stood in front of her, she was enthusiastic and approached him with verve grabbing his arm as she greeted him certainly not shy, Stanley smiled when he saw her she looked fresh and happy to see him her lips shimmered from a fresh coating of pink glittered lip gloss, "so where are you taking me Mr Spank?" she said cheerily her accent still evident when she pronounced certain words.

Stanley looked back at her you could see from his face he was delighted to be going on a date with Ami, in fact he felt very lucky and surprised that she would give him the time of day, Stanley looked at her admiringly before declaring "I thought we'd have a pub lunch", linking her arm and striding off towards the venue not very inventive but he knew the Crown served a good lunch.

They sat in a quiet corner of the half empty pub both reading the menu's, Stanley could not help but peek at her at every opportunity hoping that she was not looking but she caught his eye "I know what I want" she put down her menu looking directly at Stanley, "oh good a girl who is decisive" he laid on the charm switching back to his smooth English gentleman voice "what you having then?" he asked, Ami stretched her hand out and touched Stanley's, he tingled with trepidation grinning nervously, he had a churning feeling in his stomach, she was very forward but he liked it, it was in a nice way not like the ravenous Ms White, "I'll share whatever you want", she purred before bursting into a giggle herself which left Stanley flummoxed at her overtures before he broke out into a laugh himself, "ok" he drew breath trying to regain control of his composure before declaring "we'll get a mixed grill platter then".

The two sat and joked, she was a real bundle of energy talking nonstop about her homeland in Sweden and her favourite bands which oddly enough were exactly the same taste as Stanley's Arctic monkeys and Gorillaz, she was a breath of fresh air she was pretty, vibrant and funny he sat back almost mesmerised as he listened to her voice, in his mind thinking she was perfect he could not ask for more she was definitely girlfriend material.

He was in dream land as they continued their fits of laughter while sharing chunky chips and chicken dips, they were having so much fun that the hour went quickly to both of their disappointment, "I have to get back" Ami injected a tone of seriousness "ok I'll pay and walk with you", Stanley responded wiping his mouth with the serviette then touching it around Ami's mouth playfully, again they both burst into laughter like a couple of school kids, it was just what he needed someone who was on his level and liked his stupid sense of humour a bit like Jerry but a whole lot prettier.

After walking Ami back to the shop he was lucky enough to get a kiss and her phone number, Stanley's walk back home was like he was walking on air, he had a spring in his step a new found swagger about him, confidence was now coursing through his veins like never before all he could think of was Ami's sweet smile he could still smell her sweet perfume, he replayed in his mind every single moment he was with her he sang the words to his favourite Arctic monkeys song as he happily made his way home.

Stanley sat in the kitchen with his mother Brenda she watched him carefully as he fiddled with his phone dragging his finger across the touch screen prodding it as he checked out various pictures and internet videos, he was lost in his own world not even acknowledging his mother's presence, she continued to sit diligently staring at him with a knowing look call it mothers intuition but she knew when Stanley's mood was good, "so you going to share?" she said with a voice of intrigue, this made Stanley look up with a smile he could hardly contain his happiness "come on I know something is going on" she pushed again her eyes twinkled which happened whenever she got excited.

Stanley began to grin he got shy and ran his fingers through his hair "alright mum gosh you don't give up", he said all embarrassed, "I think I have a girlfriend" he spoke shyly and softly, his mum shrieked "you? ... a girlfriend?" she questioned rhetorically chuckling uncontrollably her face went bright red at the self-amusement, "who is she some trollop from the pub?" she continued to crack up to herself at Stanley's expense. Stanley squirmed clearly uncomfortable at his mums reaction before blurting out in response "no actually she is a gorgeous Swedish girl who works in retail", he sounded defensive which cut Brenda's cackling dead, "oh" she said in a high pitched voice eyebrows raised clearly surprised at her son's impassioned response.

Just as the atmosphere became taut Stanley's phone began to vibrate and kick into his musical ringtone, he looked at the screen and could see Cassandra's name flashing "got to go mum I need to take this call" he winked at her switching his tone to a business like seriousness, "hi Cassandra" he answered loud enough to make sure his mum heard, she meanwhile sat mouthing the words "well I never..." shaking her head in total disbelief.

It was late into the evening now and Stanley was sitting playing his games console very relaxed smoking a joint, rain lashed against his window as the elements signalled the end of the summer, as much as he tried to relax his mind ran on Ami, he was not sure whether to call her for some reason he was nervous about making contact he had never been in this position before suddenly the dark cloud which loomed over him from Jerry's departure had evaporated, he was now popular, the escort job was beginning to take off he had another booking for tomorrow night so that meant more money and definitely more fun and games which whoever his next client would be, and then there was Ami.

Stanley kept looking at his phone his mind dabbled with the thought of calling, he took another long drag of his joint and blew out the smoke with gusto, picking up the mobile device and playing with the touch screen gadget he scrolled through the contacts until he found Ami, "ok let's do it" he willed himself slightly hazed in a sudden act of bravado he pressed the dial icon on the screen his heart fluctuated beating hap hazard as he awaited the inevitable.

The phone rang twice before a tired sounding Ami picked up "hey Mr Spank" her cute sleepy tone came back through the handset Stanley sat up as if he were struck by a bolt of lightning "hey …I mean hi" he stuttered breathlessly "did I wake you?" he questioned politely attempting to mask his high state, "no its ok I was just resting" she replied still sounding rather sleepy. He loved her accent the slight foreign twist that she had to her words he could sit there and listen to her all day, there was a silence between them he could hear Ami shuffling "what you thinking about Stanley?" she asked knowing that he was momentarily lost for words, Stanley naive in the art of conversation with the female species swallowed before taking a deep breath he was still in awe that he was actually talking to someone as hot as Ami, he gathered himself before replying "was just thinking it was nice today…with you" the words came out in an almost fragmented fashion as if he was unsure whether he was saying the right things or whether it made sense at all.

The rain continued to pelt onto the windows the smokey room created a bluesy ambiance Stanley relaxed into his pillow closing his eyes as he became mesmerised by her voice, "ahh Stanley you are a cute English man" she responded almost as dreamily as him earlier, they talked for about twenty minutes laughing at the silliest things it was the most comfortable he had ever felt with a girl maybe the dates with Ms White were actually paying off.

"I have to go to London tomorrow night" Stanley declared yawning as the sedation from his joint kicked in, "London? What is it you do?" Stanley laughed nervously before switching sarcastically to his bond styled accent, "I'm an international playboy" he sniggered indulging in his own sense of humour for a little too long, "you are playing right?" a worried sounding Ami quizzed, Stanley paused figuring out whether he should continue playing or should he come clean, again he giggled immaturely before revealing it was a big joke but so wrapped up in his own bubble of fun he failed to think of a proper answer. "So what do you do? why you have to travel to London?" again Ami fielded the question to Stanley who suddenly realised her serious tone, "well let's just say I'm in the hospitality industry" Stanley stuttered slightly he gave her a shaky answer, he wanted to tell her and be honest but he felt it was too soon to be coming clean about his extracurricular activities.

Stanley had only been to London once when he was a young boy that was when he traveled with his Nan to visit the sights, he could only remember vaguely the big red buses and big Ben, so he was excited about his journey later this evening.

He danced around his room with a cigarette hanging out of his mouth strutting around like Mick Jagger he was only in a grey vest and boxer shorts he swayed and jerked out of sync with the heavy bass influenced songs which pumped out of his stereo, he looked like the quirky rock star without his trousers on, swiveling around creating clouds of smoke at every move.

He picked up his suit and noticed a white card which fell from the pocket of his blazer he stopped and bent down to pick it up the name Charles Carter stood boldly out, dragging the cigarette away from his mouth Stanley rose up blowing out the smoke staring hard at the professional looking business card, he got quick flashbacks of the extroverted camp dinner host and shuddered at the thought of him smiling frequently and giving him cheeky glances at the dinner table.

He was about to tear up the card and throw it away but something stopped him, he thought to himself for a second as the music on the stereo died leaving the sound of Stanley breathing heavily from his exertions, "hang on a minute this could come in handy" he spoke to himself as if there was another person in the room, pausing for thought flicking the long ash which had hung from his cigarette into a burnt yellow stained ashtray positioned on his window sill.

He continued to look somewhat deep in thought until he was interrupted by his mobile phone ringing which snapped him back into the present, he grabbed his phone and saw a strange looking number flashing on the screen reluctantly he answered, "hello" sounding somewhat hesitant, distorted noise came back through the handset, it sounded as if someone was either caught up in a merger between a sandstorm and disco, a cacophony of noise and interference bled his ears, he could faintly hear a voice calling out his name before the phone went completely dead.

Stanley stood shaking his head still holding his blazer and Charles Carter's business card in his hand. Stanley placed the card back into his jacket pocket and was about to begin dressing when the phone began to ring again, a frustrated Stanley grunted irritably and turned to grab it again seeing the same number flashing, "hello!" Stanley shouted angrily frowning "who's this?" he asked with attitude with his hands outstretched almost pleading to the other person, "Oi Spank its Jerry mate how you doing?" in an instant Stanley went from perplexed to completely euphoric "mate!" he screamed "Dooley!" again he shouted his best mates name chanting as if they were at a football match before they both broke into uncontrollable laughter.

"How's it in Spain then?" Stanley reclaimed his calm to ask directly, the noisy background indicated that Jerry was somewhere which was busy and loud, he could hear people shouting and screaming car horns tooting and just general mayhem in the background. Jerry sounded hyped up clearly excited, "Stan..." he shouted above the din, "I'm having the time of my life it's crazy here!" his high pitched octave voice screamed "I'm loving it, how's good old Tyford?" he mocked knowing that Stanley could not possibly compare their quiet little town to the party lifestyle in Spain, "yeah things are good" Stanley shouted back down the phone "I've got a job… oh and a girlfriend…" he tried to convey his news but as he did the line went dead, "Jerry?" he called out with disappointment knowing he had lost the line "arggghh" he shouted in frustration again as they lost connection.

He threw his phone onto his bed before breaking out into laughter, "Jerry what are you like?" he said to himself knowing that his lovable friend was having fun at least he was alive and healthy he thought before continuing with getting himself ready for his trip to London.

It was now late afternoon and Stanley was well and truly on his way to London sitting on the train playing games on his phone with his white headphones attached, he was dressed casually in jeans white trainers and a grey hooded top beside him he had a small sports bag and his suit in a cover hung up on the window handle.

The carriage was half empty just a few other passengers a business woman who was engrossed in her laptop also a young couple with their children who were making the majority of the noise. Stanley had been given his brief by Cassandra, he was to make his way to the Premier Inn hotel in Kings Cross which was luckily the station where the train was heading in to, his clients name was a very flamboyant Sunshine Devroux he only knew that she was a rich American lady and that he was to accompany her to a media function.

It was funny because as he took his eyes away from the bold colourful screen on his phone to assess the green country fields which blanketed the view out of the window as the train sped past he was not even nervous he was actually looking forward to it.

He was in a good place right now he was earning had a beautiful girlfriend in Ami, and knew his friend Jerry was as always in good spirits, he knew to himself that it was about time he took charge in his own life for once the former lazy layabout actually now had some drive, he knew he could potentially earn good enough money to at least do good things for Ami, his thoughts were now to look towards the future in a funny shift of change he now thought in an inadvertent way Jerry making that move was actually the reason for all these changes that were happening in his life.

He looked back at the young couple sitting with their young family and for the first time ever he thought maybe he could be that one day, but first he was looking forward to having as much fun and making as much money doing the escort thing, he knew there were far more interesting adventures awaiting him with his first port of call being London, he was excited and intrigued to meet this Sunshine person.

The metropolis which was a busy mainline London station at first bamboozled Stanley, he had to get his bearings amongst the hustle and bustle which greeted him, it was frenetic there were all sorts of people rushing around, it was a hub of activity which left Stanley's head spinning like a carousel.

The smell of coffee wafted through the concourse from the Starbucks cafe which was right in front of him, the crowd were merciless pushing past him and bumping into him without any words of apology, it was quite an eye opener for the boy from a small town like Tyford.

Eventually Stanley gathered himself and began to step forward, his sense of direction was void but he felt he had to at least start walking otherwise he was standing out like an accidental tourist, he looked around at the barrage of people the sound of the multiple announcements echoed through the station P.A system, more and more people seem to swarm around him dragging suitcases, chattering away into their phones, the constant hum of conversations buzzed around him accompanied by music from the in house station buskers.

He strolled causally trying to remember the instructions given to him by Cassandra, he was still going over these thoughts in his mind when he was approached by a scruffy looking man who wore a dirty green jacket and had long curly matted hair he was holding a little scrawny black dog which was clearly underfed and looked just as spooky, "you got a spare fag mate?" he asked Stanley in a thick broad cockney accent, he was shivering and sniffing loudly and stared at Stanley with reddened hollow eyes.

Stanley stopped in his tracks and was about to search his pockets for a cigarette for the man but then thought better of it and began moving away "no sorry I don't" he replied sternly before making his way towards the main entrance and onto the street, he looked behind him as he walked out into even more mayhem outside. It seemed to never stop people en mass shuffled and dodged throughout the crowded streets, a homeless man sat outside the station groaning loudly and asking for change, everyone seemed to be in a world of their own hurrying to get somewhere, it was in stark contrast to where he was from and used to.

After the initial shock of the fervent activity set in Stanley composed himself enough to ask a passer-by for directions, which was not easy as everyone seemed to have an urgency about them, shyly Stanley made his way to a newspaper stand which was manned by an old bearded stocky gentleman, he looked battle hardened and weary with a pipe hanging from his mouth and the smell of smouldering tobacco oozing from it.

The man seemed busy but was the only stationary person who Stanley felt he could stop and ask amongst the melee of movement from the crowds around him, he approached stood with his travel bag and suit holder hooked over his shoulder "excuse me please" he spoke quietly but politely which had no effect or impact as the man behind the stand continued to shout to his potential punters, again Stanley tried to get his attention "excuse me please do you know where the Premier Inn hotel is?", this time a more firm and vocal request. The man turned and glared at Stanley with the pipe still dangling from his lips, he looked over towards Stanley whilst continuing to fold and sell his papers, "walk straight and take the first left at the lights you will see it" he responded in a craggy tone.

Stanley stood still to get his bearings and compute the information, "cheers" he responded the man gave him a cursory glance before continuing his trade. This was a culture shock for Stanley he was not used to the hardened approach, "London's crazy" he whispered to himself as he turned and began to make his way.

A short five minute walk and eventually the hotel was in sight much to the relief of a now tiring Stanley, he stopped just short of the entrance to light up a cigarette before checking in. From the outside the hotel looked smart with several business types coming in and out through the rotating glass doors all in deep conversations either on their phones or to their colleagues, Stanley observed that everyone seemed to be very self-centred and always on the move there did not seem to be the laid back approach as the folk had in Tyford.

He took slow drags from his cigarette he felt it was an opportune time to phone Ami, at least to let her know he had arrived, just as he a pulled out his phone two stunning women power dressed in business attire emerged from the hotel, for a moment Stanley along with other passing men clearly distracted by the couple just gazed as the two well-heeled females walked past, it was almost a slow motion scene as they both held the gazes of drivers and pedestrians alike, "wow!", Stanley shook his head before continuing his call.

"Hi Ami it's me" his voice quickly changed to a soft tone as soon as he heard her distinctive dialect, they spoke only for a few minutes but it was enough to satisfy Stanley who was still getting used to the whole concept of having girlfriend, "ok I'll be back tomorrow see you then" he reassured before disconnecting the call.

At the check in desk Stanley was given an envelope "this was left for you Mr Spank" the young freckle faced receptionist chirpily said, Stanley looked bemused as he was given his room card key. The hotel was busy with many sharp suited men and women milling around the lobby, there was a business conference happening which would explain all the corporate looking people, Stanley felt pretty under dressed as he swerved his way through the flocks of chatty office types, he was amazed at the amount of young people that were probably around his age it made him start to believe more that there was definitely life outside of Tyford.

Room 119 was on the fifth floor, the doors of the clean shiny mirrored lift breezed open to reveal a quiet clean corridor, he walked slowly looking at each door number counting upwards until he reached his room, "home sweet home" he mocked as he pushed the card into the slot which unlocked and opened the door revealing the nice spotless double room with king-size bed and flat screen television, "yes!" he exclaimed excitedly "this is what I'm talking about" he continued surveying the pristine room and furniture.

This was really his first time that he had ever been in this situation and was now feeling more like his James Bond alter ego, he threw his bag and suit onto the perfectly made bed and took a look outside through the window, he could see all of the hustle and traffic of London below, people and cars moving around like ants "this is nuts" he again spoke to himself as if he was the second person in the room, he laughed out loud fiendishly rubbing his hands turning back around and spotting the mini bar fridge which was positioned under a wooden desk "what have we here?" he quizzed loudly opening the small door revealing the neatly stacked miniature bottles of assorted alcohol beverages "sweet!" he commented again with glee he was really out of his comfort zone but strangely loving his new found surroundings.

He continued to explore opening the door to the bathroom, "oh my god" he commented taken aback by the neat presentation of the glistening en suite, he laughed again as he stood in front of the grand mirror which gleamed in the light, the layout of soaps and other bathroom necessities were set out very deliberately.

Stanley stared at himself his understated looks vividly apparent before he got too carried away he remembered the envelope which he had stuffed into the back pocket of his jeans, he took it out and ripped it open it was a note from Cassandra, he smiled knowingly it was unsurprising she was so organised he knew she would planned everything down to the last detail. The hand written note just explained all he had to do, "be ready and in the reception at 19:00 prompt ask for Ms Devroux at the desk", it read with an underlying tone which Stanley knew she was serious he could see her little face in his head wagging her finger at him.

The bathroom door swung open letting out a gust of steam, Stanley emerged through the white clouds of the sauna "wow" he commented emerging with a fluffy white towel wrapped around his taut body, he sat on the bed picking up his phone quickly to check the time 6:05 it read. He laid back blowing out his cheeks his faced reddened from the heat, trinkets of sweat drizzled down the side of his face, he closed his eyes, he was in heaven this was luxury beyond his wildest dreams a new experience for the one half of the lazy Tyford two, those days now a distant memory this was a new high end Stanley Spank the male escort to the rich and lonely.

He opened his eyes and sat up sweeping back his wet hair daubing his forehead with the towel, "time for operation Sunshine" he said in his now familiar upper crust accent perking himself up in preparation, again he turned to his phone and this time touched some buttons on the screen which invoked the loud audio music of Mark Ronson "that's better" he said as he rose to finish getting himself ready.

The time now was six forty five, and Stanley's transformation was nearly complete his room now resembled his own bedroom at home with various items of clothing strewn on the bed and floor the air was humid from the hot bathroom and his activity, he stood running a comb repeatedly through his hair ensuring that there was not one hair out of place.

He was almost ready and just had to apply a tie to his crisp white shirt, he knew tonight would be different even though he was still in the dark as to what to expect, all he knew was that he was beginning to like his little adventures and all of its perks he was no longer the nervous young man who first embarked on his date with Ms. White he was now becoming the confident charming prince who was getting used to all of the fuss and opulence these mysterious women and adventures were bringing.

The mechanical hum which accompanied the smooth seamless journey in the small yet comfortable elevator was the only thing that could be heard above Stanley's breathing, he stood facing the mirrored wall checking himself out from every angle, he looked very dapper this time it was a charcoal grey fitted suit with a white buttoned down collared shirt and a black skinny tie, he checked his face which was smooth and clear barely a blemish or any facial hair such was his boyish features.

He had obviously stepped up his efforts tonight wishing to make the best impression possible, the recorded voice indicated they had reached the reception as the shiny silver doors slid effortlessly apart to reveal a very busy lobby, people were everywhere coming and going, well dressed couples along with groups of families milled around.

Stanley cleared his throat and strode forward his shiny polished shoes clicked rhythmically as he walked towards the reception desk, his sandalwood fragrance left a trail of his scent, he felt cool and he looked cool drawing sly glances and stares from some of the other females who happened to catch him strutting his way to the main desk, Stanley himself did not know where to look except for straight ahead, he was in his zone and just wanted to follow his brief.

After standing calmly in the queue he finally reached the front desk, the young attractive receptionist looked up "hi…I'm mean hello can I help?" she said cheerily with her tone changing from serious to borderline flirty, she did a double take when she saw the fine tall figure standing in front of her, her eyes bulged with delight and her smile was even warmer.

Stanley modest as ever did not even pick up on the flutter of her eyelids he was far too concentrated now on meeting his client and finding out exactly what was in store for him.

"Mr. Spank reporting as per this" Stanley was back to his cool persona the debonair bond character was fully in place, the receptionist barely able to withdraw her gaze took the folded piece of paper from his hand, "ahh yes one moment please" she picked up the phone and began to dial. Stanley fixed his shirt cuffs making sure his appearance remained immaculate, "ok Mr. Spank, Ms. Devroux is waiting for you in the white car outside" she said handing back the note with a definite glint in her eye to which Stanley finally picked up on, he smiled back at her "thank you Tina" he responded confidently taking note of the young receptionists name badge winking before turning away leaving her smiling and swooning in his wake.

Stanley stepped outside, the area was now even more vibrant than earlier in the day people were coming and going rapidly most of them dressed up for an evening on the town gaggles of party girls all dressed in hen night fancy dress attire as well as couples and families, he surveyed the area looking for a white car until he clapped his eyes on a gleaming Rolls Royce with a smartly dressed chauffeur stood outside it, surely not Stanley thought his eyes stared transfixed on the beautifully crafted vehicle, he slowly began to walk towards it his heart pumping hard now with a small measure of nervousness, other drivers and pedestrians also lent admiring glances towards the car.

As he approached the stiff upright chauffeur dressed in a black uniform mouthed his name "Mr. Spank?", Stanley smiled the realisation that it was in fact to be the car he was going to be in hit him, "yes sir" he cooed enthusiastically as the chauffeur opened the door, "Ms. Devroux awaits" he managed to crack a small smile at Stanley before remaining straight faced ushering him in.

This was just like a movie Stanley felt surreal as he stooped down to enter into the back of the car he felt like a superstar, this was the first time anything like this had ever happened to him, "come on in!" a big voice boomed out as Stanley entered the smooth clean leather interior, as soon as he entered he saw the larger than life beaming smile of Ms. Sunshine Devroux. "Wowee!" her unmistakable Texan drawl screeched loudly as Stanley finally slid in onto the comfortable seat, "you are a very fine young man" she said holding her hand out to Stanley, she had a large smile which lit up the car she was voluptuous and very sparkly sitting there in a tight fitted shimmering gold dress with accessories to match and a face full of make up, bright red lipstick which covered her big juicy lips.

Sunshine was of mixed race descent and her sweet perfume smell was overpowering as she clasped Stanley's hand almost dragging him towards her buxom body, "and what might your name be?" she asked her eyes beaming with delight, Stanley sat and tried to maintain his composure still taking in the whole Rolls Royce experience "I'm

Stanley Spank" he shyly responded, "Spank!" Sunshine shouted her reaction led to a big hearty laugh which reverberated around the cushioned comfort of the plush interior, she snuffled attempting to stop her booming laugh, "well Mr. Spank we are going to have some fun tonight" she slapped his leg hard as she continued to chuckle.

Stanley shifted uncomfortably the sting of the slap lingered on through his thigh, as the drive continued Sunshine Devroux chatted nonstop on her mobile phone she sounded intimidating barking orders to her personal assistant she seemed like a woman who was very much in charge and demanding certainly her personality did not match her wholesome and spunky image, if there was one thing that passed through Stanley thoughts it was that he knew he was going to have a crazy experience tonight.

He sat back resting his head as Sunshine continued to chat away down the phone she was obviously a successful woman he gleaned from the content of her conversations which ranged from ordering cases of champagne for a charity ball to booking a hotel suite to meet with television executives, she in fact spoke nonstop for most of the journey only pausing to instruct Stanley to open the wood grained minibar which was built into a compartment behind the passenger seat, she jabbed her finger towards the fridge, Stanley took a while before he realised what she was alluding to before he twigged.

He lent forward and pulled it open revealing the large quantity of stocked miniature champagne bottles and spirits, he was actually happy at the array of free booze staring him in the face he needed a drink to steady his nerves from the overbearing nature of his client, "what would you like?" the well-mannered Stanley spoke politely looking towards Sunshine who continued to ramble for all she was worth, again Stanley posed the question still calmly and polite "what can I get for you?", he waited for a response before the animated Ms. Devroux snapped back "just pour me a glass of champagne child!", her voice escalated to the point where it made Stanley flinch her smoky southern drawl became abrasive and cutting forcing an offended Stanley to quickly grab the bottle and glass fumbling the bottle which fell and rolled around before he quickly snatched it up.

Sunshine clipped down her phone and tossed it onto the seat before assuming her soft country girl character again relaxing provocatively in the spacious seat, "oh I'm sorry Mr. Spank" she giggled again as she said his name sweeping her brown hair back causing her earrings and wrist trinkets to jangle.

Stanley looked up at her his face was an expression of worry he was not used to this kind of treatment, she scared him she seemed to have a split personality, his hand shook as he tried in vain to pop the cork of the small bottle of Moet Chandon, he grinned uncomfortably still trying his best to play the role of the clean cut gentleman, but something about his date irked him, "do you need some help with that young man?" Sunshine purred placing her jeweled hand over Stanley's squeezing tightly, her soft hands and fingers deliberately intertwining with his.

Stanley's face went red he became a little flustered and hot under the collar as the cork popped finally causing some of the bubbly liquid to fizz over onto the carpeted floor, "ooh" Sunshine squealed laughing heartedly while Stanley squirmed embarrassingly only managing to feebly exert a chuckle, he reached over to grab a glass but Sunshine intervened and just took the bottle forcefully from his hand, "child just give the bottle I'm mighty thirsty" her tone became serious as she guzzled down the champagne putting her red lipstick stained lips over the top and sucked it down.

Stanley actually laughed he thought her actions were hilarious such crassness was hard to fathom he stared in amazement as she continued to consume the full contents after which she let out a frog like croak of a burp before declaring "that's what I'm talking about", she handed an awestruck Stanley back the empty bottle, "driver how long until we are there?" she shouted at the driver who was obedient in his response "be there in a minute Ms Devroux" the driver replied he did not even turnaround he kept his head straight and continued to drive.

"You are something else" Stanley managed to speak through the laughter, he knew this night was going to be a crazy one, Sunshine Devroux was one of a kind she was in essence a real diva well that's what he thought anyway, as the car slowed to a standstill.

From what Stanley could see out of the window it seemed they had arrived at another hotel only this one was on a grander scale and unique in its impressive architecture, "wow there's a lot of people outside" Stanley commented quite alarmed at the flashing lights from the bulbs of the cameras, "don't you worry, just look good on my arm that's what you're here for" she laughed out loudly quickly powdering her nose and fixing her hair looking into the reflection of the tinted glass windows ending the sequence by squirting a vast amount of sweet scent onto her neck and chest.

Stanley coughed exaggeratedly as the spray filled the back of the car "blimey" he said covering his mouth just as the driver opened the door. Stepping out was just like something he'd seen on one of his lazy days watching TV, the first thing what was obvious was the bright red carpet which starkly lay in front of them, followed by a hoopla of sounds, screams from a gathered crowd in anticipation of whoever was exiting the car then the whirring of clicks and sporadic flashes of cameras.

Stanley froze momentarily uneasy at entering the fray before he was shoved in the back by an over keen Sunshine, "come on boy let's not make my people wait!" she shrieked excitedly clearly the effects of the champagne going to her head as Stanley stumbled out in an ungainly fashion onto the carpet initiating a flurry of flashbulbs he was literally blinded and pulled some funny faces before he was able to regain some kind of composure until he was dragged to one side as the larger than life Sunshine exploded out of the car.

She was a real professional smiling broadly and blowing kisses to all of the waiting crowd and media who were gathered. Stanley stood steadfastly posing as best he could but his mind was a dizzy carousel he was thinking he still did not know who she actually was?

Sunshine stood lapping up the adulation and shouts from the frenzied camera men of where to turn and how to pose, Stanley felt way out of his depth he was thinking what if his mum were to see his picture in a gossip magazine how would explain that? Sunshine was in her element her cheesy smile showed no hint of reducing, "can we go in now?" Stanley begged shielding his face pulling her away from the mayhem increasingly self-conscious of all the photographers snapping away he suddenly felt a little vulnerable and began to walk hastily into the hotel literally dragging a reluctant Sunshine with him.

Once inside Stanley recomposed himself "that was scary" he commented glancing back at Sunshine who was still blowing kisses, "who are you?" Stanley broke escort etiquette by asking a direct personal question towards his client, "child I am Sunshine Devroux TV personality and talk show host!" she sounded insulted that he did not know who she was fixing her ample bust into place ensuring she did not suffer any type of fashion faux pais whilst making her grand entrance.

Stanley was clearly baffled as he looked at her trying hard to recall if he had seen her before but he did not have time in amongst all the melee which was around him, "sir" a polite voice from behind calmly called out, he spun around to see a waiter dressed immaculately in a black waistcoat and white shirt thrusting a tray full of tall champagne flutes "sir" again the waiter spoke politely offering up the golden sparkling liquid, Stanley was about to gleefully accept when Sunshine reached over a grabbed a glass rudely stretching across him, Stanley raised his eyebrows at the waiter embarrassed giving him a knowing look before he took a glass himself "thank you" he winked back at him before walking away behind his abrasive yet intriguing client who had already walked away without a word and was air kissing a couple of well-dressed gentleman.

The foyer was awash with pretty celebrity types all glittering in long evening gowns there were several camera crews filming and reporters interviewing various people, Stanley sipped his champagne and just took a minute to take it all in the sheer glitz and decadence of the whole occasion, it was slightly overwhelming he had never seen anything like it he could not help noticing how many good looking women were gliding around all looking very stunning most of them shimmering more that the giant chandeliers which hung from the cavernous ceiling.

His client was in her element moving around the room laying on her thick southern charm, schmoozing her way through each guest, Stanley stood in the background watching as she was being interviewed, the bright light attached to the camera shone illuminating Sunshine's already glowing face, "she must be famous" he mused racking his brain trying to work out if he had seen her on television before. By now the early light headiness from the champagne began to hit, he found himself smiling at a couple of the women who shot admiring glances as they floated around moving from person to person.

Stanley though chose to played it safe and kept his distance just in case, he was conscious of Sunshine's somewhat volatile temperament so he just kept his cool and observed all of the action stood next to a giant screen which flashed numerous commercials.

After all of the craziness of the reception all of the guests had made their way into the main room which was set out like an auditorium, red velvet covered cushioned seats were aligned next to each other leading up to a silver glittering podium which stood in front of long red drapes tied back with gold coloured rope tassels.

A giant screen which was centered behind spoiled the vintage look and feel of the room which buzzed with the quiet hum of conversations, Stanley who had by now felt a little tipsy still clinging onto a half filled champagne flute escorted an excited Sunshine, her head seemed to be in the clouds she was just smiling and making approving noises whenever she spotted or acknowledge a friend.

Their seats were reserved one row back from the front, Stanley smiled to himself as he was sat next to a gorgeous blonde who could not help but to wink at him seductively before turning to converse with her partner, Sunshine sensed this and yanked Stanley's arm as if to reinforce her authority, Stanley patted her hand in a show of reassurance but inside he had just about enough of his bossy superficial date he decided to sit back and watch the show unfold silently seething.

"A television award show never been to one of these before" Stanley whispered into her ear as the announcer excitedly rambled on doing his best to rouse the crowd, "is there any famous people here except for you" he said with a slight chuckle, "no just me" she smiled back at him insincerely diverting her eyes back to the shiny podium. Stanley shifted uncomfortably in his chair and folded his arms, this was clearly not his bag and although surrounded by beautiful people and the smell of money everywhere he frankly would rather be at home in Tyford drinking a pint with Ami.

He pulled his mobile phone from his pocket and checked to see if he had any messages, there were none, he yawned placing his phone back into his pocket fidgeting and looking around the room, he caught sight of a beautiful hostess who was walking through the aisle with a tray of drinks, they exchange glances before Stanley caught Sunshine's beady eye boring into him, she again clasped his hand tightly and nudged up her chair in an attempt to get closer to him before facing the front again but not without a look which made Stanley shudder and sit up straight fixing his suit, he felt as if he was out with his mum and he had done something wrong.

After about half an hour of awards and speeches Sunshine suddenly became excited and animated "this is my category" she mentioned jabbing her elbow into Stanley's arm she became poised and expectant fixing her hair and making sure her dress was draped correctly even Stanley became quite intrigued as the host began to read out the nominees.

The room darkened as footage of each of the nominees were shown to the audience, "Miss Sunshine Devroux for Days of Sunshine!" the host stated as footage of the very glamorous looking Sunshine appeared on the screen to a round of applause, Sunshine gripped Stanley's hand tightly she was clearly tense as they showed her in her element as a daytime chat show host, "wow" Stanley said in amazement he finally realised he was sitting with a star of American TV, she was similar to Oprah Winfrey sitting on a couch in a comfy studio talking to movie star Cameron Diaz, "that's really you?" Stanley asked gobsmacked Sunshine's grip got stronger as the intensity heightened.

"And the winner is…" the host said the famous words a hush went around the room, images of the four hopeful nominees were flashed up onto the giant screen Stanley saw himself sat alongside his famous client his heart began to race and he blushed looking at himself on the screen, an elongated silence ensued Sunshine was visibly shaking mumbling to herself "please god" she muttered, it felt like forever the suspense really held until "Sunshine Devroux!", the host screamed excitedly, "yes yes!" she squealed clapping her hands before turning to Stanley and grabbing him for a big kiss.

Stanley could not help himself and jumped up too punching the air "yeah" he shouted before helping up a now emotional and weeping Miss Devroux who looked every inch the star as she stood for a second milking the applause, her gold dress shimmered as the spotlight shone directly onto her, she waved to the audience before beginning her walk to the main podium.

Stanley's adrenalin was flowing he let out another yelp before suddenly coming to his senses and subduing his excitement attempting to reclaim his composure. Sunshine stood clasping the abstract gold gong to her chest she held the audience captive as the voluptuous bodied American snivelled her way through her speech "thank the lord!" she yelled out thrusting the award towards the sky to rapturous applause, "blimey" again Stanley shook his head unable to fathom or take in what was happening.

He was part excited and part nervous he knew that now all of the spotlight would be on his client, which meant he would surely be captured in all of the publicity, he stood and clapped as she received a rousing ovation which of course she milked every last minute waving and blowing air kisses lapping up the applause strolling slowly back to her seat where a bashful looking Stanley stood waiting, it was awkward as the spotlight shone on her all the way until she arrived at Stanley who kept his head bowed in his attempt to keep a low profile.

"Congratulations" he smiled when she arrived, "thank you Stanley" she gushed emotionally her eyes reddened from the flowing tears of joy, "let's have a look then, I've never seen a real award before" Stanley said enthusiastically reaching for the shiny ornament, Sunshine gave it to him as she dabbed her tears away with a tissue and continued to apply some make up and lip gloss staring into a tiny circular pocket mirror. "Gosh this is fantastic" Stanley marveled "you really are a star then?", he asked rhetorically handing back the award, "oh Stanley" she drawled "I love your British charm, maybe you can show me more back at your hotel", she rubbed his hand and leaned in towards him resting her head onto his chest.

Stanley became uneasy and flustered he laughed out nervously as Sunshine's strong floral scent tingled his nostrils, her big mane of thick curly hair nestled between his neck and chin he could feel the rush of blood flush through his cheeks as the embarrassing clinch surprised him, he sat frozen as she continued to hum to herself before standing up and looking him dead in the eye before declaring "let's skip the after party and go back to your hotel I fancy a drink and a joint" she spoke seriously with an emotional husk in her voice.

Stanley was taken aback and looked around him checking if anybody heard her random request the blonde girl next to him again looked and winked smiling getting in a quick ogle before turning back to her man, before he replied in a hushed suppressed whisper "are you serious?", he looked Sunshine dead in the eye, she looked back with a naughty twinkle in her sparkling jade coloured eyes, "hmmm" again she hummed to herself fixing Stanley's tie seductively licking her full lips.

Stanley became hot and politely grabbed her hands pulling them down, "ok shall we go Miss Devroux?" he quickly quelled the intimate up close and personal moment, to the frustration of Sunshine who smiled wryly before digging her mobile phone out of her golden clutch bag and called her driver, "we're ready to leave" she said assertively grabbing Stanley's hand.

Stanley could not believe the way this evening was panning out, chauffeur driven Rolls Royce, awards ceremony, celebrity TV host he had to pinch himself to believe exactly what was going on as he was led by a striding Sunshine through the crowded auditorium she smiled and waved to certain acquaintances who shouted her name and blew air kisses as they walked past.

Stanley felt surreal almost as if he were in a dream and for that moment he was actually enjoying it, he could feel the adulation as they approached the exit. As they left the hotel the crisp night air hit them instantly sobering their faculties the driver and gleaming Rolls Royce stood waiting the two of them with arms linked walked briskly through the remains of the eager paparazzi who belatedly snapped the couple as they made their way to their vehicle.

Stanley sat back in the comfortable back seat he finally was able to loosen his tie and unbutton his shirt "well that was an experience" he said exhaling a breath of air relaxing with his head back, Sunshine sprawled herself across the back seat putting her legs onto Stanley's lap her shiny gold shoes dangled as she half kicked them off "I could do with a nice foot rub now" she mentioned dropping a heavy hint to her hired partner. Stanley who was just getting ready to close his eyes felt duly obliged to provide a full service albeit reluctantly, he eased her shoes off revealing her petit pink painted toenails, she moaned when Stanley clasped his hands onto her soft skinned feet, he felt awkward pushing up his face and was unsure of what he needed to do as this was the first time he had actually touched or let alone massaged a woman's feet.

For about two minutes he rubbed slowly the caramel coloured feet of an award winning American TV host in the back of a Rolls Royce he felt as if he was having an out of body experience "Stanley" she called his name in a low husky voice obviously very relaxed and enjoying her moment of indulgence, "crack a bottle of champagne we are celebrating after all", his reaction was confused he felt more like her servant, but he just kept thinking about Cassandra always banging on about the reputation of her business and did not want to let her down, so he stopped rubbing her feet and lent forward to the inbuilt drinks cabinet which had been restocked with an array of different coloured liquors and pulled out a bottle of champagne. He began to peel away the golden foil and unscrewed the wire to release the cork, Sunshine sat up still holding her award and leaning over to plant a lingering kiss on to Stanley's cheek, "that's for being a gorgeous escort Mr Spank" she spoke softly now in a very relaxed tone just as Stanley popped the cork "woooo!" Sunshine let out a scream followed by a hearty laugh "forget the glasses we'll drink from the bottle" she exclaimed, Stanley laughed before putting the bottle to her mouth she sucked down the drink which spilled down the side of her mouth onto her dress, she shook her head her cheeks became bloated as the champagne filled her mouth, Stanley thought it was funny and began to splash some of the champagne onto her face, before taking a long swig from the bottle himself.

After a crazy thirty minute drive the chauffeur swung open the door they had finally arrived at Stanley's hotel, both spilled out laughing clearly drunk and having fun, it was quieter although there were still a few people milling about outside the entrance, the driver kept a straight laced expression upon seeing the drunken couple stumble their way out of the car.

Sunshine now looked a little worse for wear her makeup had disintegrated and her dress was now stained with blotches of drink she was also barefoot, Stanley clutched her shoes in his hand, "thank you sir" he said saluting the driver as he tried to walk past him knocking into him holding up Sunshine, "I'll call you" Sunshine slurred waving at the driver who remained expressionless watching the pair stagger into the hotel.

Giggling like a schoolgirl in love Sunshine had to be helped across the clean tiled floor lobby which was empty except for the sole receptionist who watched as the pair made their way to the lift. Sunshine seemed to be more affected by the alcohol than Stanley who felt a little more clear headed, enough to be able to fish out his hotel room key card, he also had time to check his phone while an excited babbling Sunshine seem to be amusing herself.

He had now three missed calls from Ami which left him cursing under his breath. The bell chimed and the lift door gracefully slid open "come on my Sunshine" he joked as they both entered the clean warm mirrored space, Sunshine searched in her bag furiously as if he had lost something before producing a clear plastic bag full of marijuana, "hope you can roll sir" she stated before bursting out into another fit of laughter, "sssh…where did you get that from?" a shocked Stanley responded grabbing the bag and opening it to examine it at close quarters, he poked his nose into it and sniffed "hmm smells good" he acknowledged as a dreamy eyed Sunshine rested her head wearily onto his chest.

They finally reached their floor and exited into the quiet corridor quite what was going through Stanley's mind as he approached his room with Sunshine hanging on to him only he would know but once he unlocked and entered his room, the only thing on his mind was enjoying some of her weed and having a night cap.

Sunshine flopped onto the bed sprawling her whole body out across the duvet, "come on Spank let's get high baby" Sunshine tried to muster some energy, Stanley took off his suit jacket and tie, "ok just give me a second" he replied before disappearing into the bathroom.

Stanley emerged after five minutes he was now relaxed and seemed awake and energetic, his shirt was now hanging outside of his trousers and he had taken off his shoes and socks and picked up some of his clothes that were strewn all over the room tossing them onto the chair. "Care for a night cap?" his voice stopped suddenly as soon as he noticed that Sunshine had slipped out of her dress and was laying on the bed dressed in only her black lacy bra and knickers, "what the..?" he froze "what are you doing?" he gulped shocked he tried to train his eyes away from the rather large boobs and thighs of his American date, "aww come on Stanley don't tell me you haven't seen a woman's body before?" she teased pulling back her hair clearly comfortable with having her ample charms on show.

Stanley spluttered distracted knocking himself on the dressing table as he tried his hardest to not to focus on her, "I'll fix us a drink then" he said proceeding to bend down opening the small fridge and pulling out a can of lager and a small bottle of wine, too embarrassed and visibly shaking he could not bring himself to tell her to put her dress back on, "hurry Mr Spank let's get rolling with that joint too" she demanded seemingly regaining her energy and bossy nature.

Feeling pressurised but could not bring himself to stop staring at her reflection in the large mirror, he had never seen a real life half naked woman before, only on the internet, he did not know what to do with himself and continued to pour the drinks into the two tumblers provided.

He walked over to her his hand shaking "here you go" he gave her the glass of white wine and could not help noticing how good her caramel skin looked on her legs also her cleavage which seemed very restrained in the lacy black bra, "right" he said going back to the table, he knelt to rummage through his bag searching for his cigarettes and rolling paper, "got it" he exclaimed before sitting on the edge on the bed with his back to her, "I'll just skin up then" he said beginning to extract the rolling papers. He seemed calmer now relaxed as he concentrated on rolling a joint he felt like he needed one after the eventful night he just had.

After a few minutes he could feel Sunshine's feet rubbing against his back for a moment it felt good but Stanley quickly stiffened up when he realised where this could lead "I'm all done let's open the window" he quickly twisted around looking at the half naked chubby body of Sunshine who had propped her award up onto the pillow next to her she lay seductively tilting the wine slowly towards her lips, Stanley actually began to laugh the surreal nature of this situation was getting weirder by the minute.

He pushed open the window the sound of passing traffic could be heard below as the cool air filtered in, he lit the joint a took a long draw and blew the thick pungent smoke out into the night air flapping his hand to make sure none of the smoke escaped into the room, "are you coming?" he quizzed turning around to Sunshine who was up and standing closely behind him "I'm here now pass me that joint" she shoved her way past and in front of Stanley squeezing herself in front of him.

She was shorter than he thought without her heels on and her large derriere pushed into Stanley's midriff, she snatched the smouldering joint from his hand and took a large puff, "this is what I needed" she now sounded relaxed looking out to the city views her hair blowing gently onto Stanley from the night breeze, she continued to take large pulls the waft of smoke flailed back into Stanley's face, "this is good stuff" she said her voice hoarse choking as if to emphasise before turning round to face Stanley.

Her voluptuous breasts pressed against Stanley she looked up into his face with a glazed dreamy look, Stanley's heart began to beat faster as he felt her warm body tightly up against him, "smoke Mr Spank?" she put the joint to his lips he followed her instructions without a word and pulled on the burning rolled stick, she broke out into a fit of giggles watching him slowly blow out the smoke above her head, "hmm this is nice" she said grabbing him around the waist and leaning her head against his chest, "I just want to take you home with me" she continued to ramble squeezing him tighter.

Stanley now stood unfazed he took another draw of the white rolled joint which dangled from his lips, the smoke billowed above their heads and Stanley once again waved his hands attempting to keep the smoke outside the room.

"I need to lie down", a slowly spoken Sunshine conceded, "are you joining me Mr Spank?" she tugged onto his shirt attempting to coerce him away, "ok give me a minute" he answered back sticking his head out of the window trying to clear his it before coming back inside where he turned to see a high Sunshine laying seductively on the bed, her hair like a mane spread above her head onto the white pillow and the rest of her body contorted into a shape which made him twist his head to make sense of.

For a moment he completely was lost he sat on the side of the bed with his back to her, he downed the remains of his lager and ruffled his hair, he was unsure of what was to come next as this was the first time he had ever been in a position like this alone with a willing participant not even with Ami had he been this isolated and intimate, "Stanley hurry what are you doing?" a desperate sounding Sunshine pleaded stretching out her hand to rub his back.

Stanley began unbuttoning his shirt slowly thinking this would buy him some time all the while he was thinking what he was expected to do now? Was this a part of his job? He knew he was inexperienced when it came to sex and thought that maybe he wanted Ami to be his first proper intimate encounter, "your taking too long" Sunshine again wailed her voice now trailing off as the effects of the weed began to sedate her.

It was at least ten minutes by the time Stanley had manage to unbutton his shirt, he was clearly dithering and in two minds whether to go through with what some would call a perk of the job, inside his head he was fighting with loyalty to Ami and the sheer intrigue of sleeping with an award winning TV host he dithered some more before eventually turning round to address Sunshine, "listen it's not that I don't find you attractive but…" he stopped in mid flow he saw Sunshine lying on her back sprawled out with her mouth open sleeping taking shallow breaths, high himself he ruffled his hair and let out an exasperated sigh not quite believing what he was witnessing he laughed to himself it was not quite a hearty one more so a chuckle of relief, being the gentleman that he was he went over to the chair and grabbed his suit jacket and covered up Miss Deveroux's ample assets.

He continued smiling to himself before sitting down on the edge of the bed, he was tired but still high with thoughts of his night, he was in a different world now who would of thought his path would take him to this moment, he picked up the gleaming abstract award and held it studying the gold template with Sunshine's name engraved "wow" he muttered quietly transfixed by the gleaming gong, he placed it on the table next to the bed before lying down next to her his eyelids were heavy and eventually closed, lights out for Stanley as the sound of a snoring Sunshine faded he gave in to sleep.

Sat on the 12:35 train to Tyford and now very casual but tired Stanley leaned back in his chair reflecting on his outing and night out, he was dressed in a grey hoody and jeans with the hood covering most of his head with just a tuft of his fair hair showing, he was in a world of his own lost in thought, he had woken up that morning to find his hotel room empty apart from himself still lying in the same position, Sunshine had disappeared only the smell of her strong scented odour lingered sending a reminder of what had ensued the night before.

He had woken up with a hangover almost believing he had dreamt of the whole night, a note written on white paper was stuck to the mirror above the dressing table eye catching because of the bright red lipstick kiss mark which vividly drew Stanley's attention, he looked around and there was no sign of his flamboyant client, he rubbed his eyes they were stinging from the lack of sleep and consumption of alcohol.

He sat up and looked around for his phone to check the time,, the bright screen illuminated "oh my god" 10:55 it read Stanley had an hour get check out and get himself together, but as soon as he tried to get up the woozy feeling from a champagne night out slowed him in his tracks.

He was intrigued as to how Sunshine had got up and vanished without making a noise or waking him up to say goodbye, he ripped the paper from the mirror and stood whilst he carefully read the note *"what a man Mr Spank you are truly one of a kind!, I hope our paths cross again you can come and be a guest on my show!"* Stanley managed to exert a laugh he could see and hear Sunshine as he read the note, *"keep in touch you charming English gentleman SD xx"* she had left her email address and telephone number on the note also, Stanley took a deep breath then let out a big sigh "blimey" he scratched his head before stepping into the bathroom.

As he continued his journey back on the train he stared out of the window the green landscaped was lost of a young man whose mind was somewhere else, Stanley smiled to himself remembering certain points from his eventful night, he had a small taste of another part of a life that a few months ago merely existed to him through the TV or in music, but he was actually now living it and if he was honest he was enjoying it.

He nestled back in his seat trying to relax as much as he could before getting home when he was interrupted by the vibration and ring of his phone, Ami's name flashed on the screen, Stanley's heart skipped a beat he was excited to talk to her now, he sat up and composed himself clearing his groggy throat before answering " hi Ami you ok?" he attempted to sound refreshed, "where are you Stanley?" the high pitched voice was just barely audible as music played in the background "I'm on my way back should be there in an hour" he responded, "ok well come and meet me from work I've missed you" she sounded urgent.

Stanley was happy on hearing her voice and the fact she had missed him a feeling of warmth tinged with a nervous excitement rushed through his body "I miss you too" he stuttered not quite comfortable with expressing his feelings yet but he knew it felt right with Ami, "see you soon hurry!" she sounded even more excited.

Stanley was energised he kicked his feet up onto the vacant seat opposite him and continued to look out at the vast lush green and yellow meadows which whizzed past and the train hurtled its way towards Tyford.

It seemed quite a contrast from the busy buzz of energy of London to return to the sedate rather slow motion atmosphere which was the town of Tyford, compared to where he had just come from this was coma induced but it was home and Stanley albeit tired was very happy to be back in familiar surroundings.

He walked slowly towards his home lugging his travel bag and suit bag on his shoulder still with his hood covering his head, as he walked most of his thoughts were consumed with coming up with a plausible story to tell Ami of his nights so called hospitality work, he did not want to risk anything by telling her the real truth of his shenanigans.

His thoughts could not help being distracted by sharp flashbacks from the previous night, the red carpet entrance which should have made him feel like a celebrity but really caused him embarrassment as it was something he was really not ready for, sitting amongst an elite swathe of high end media and industry people that he really had nothing in common with but strangely slotted in without question, he smiled to himself remembering the first time he laid eyes on Sunshine Devroux the sparkle she gave off which matched her energetic personality she was fun he thought but a bit crazy.

He had finally made it back to his home and was about to push his key in the door when it was opened by his mum, "oh so look what the cats dragged in" she said with a non-impressed expression on her face, "I didn't know the supermarket did twenty four hour shifts" she added stepping to one side to let a sheepish Stanley in, "hi mum" was his only response as he dumped his bag to the floor, "I'll put the kettle on shall I?".

Brenda strode past into the kitchen where Greg Spank was sitting at the table cleverly burying his head into his union newspaper, "alright son" he grumbled from beyond the pages making sure he had no eye contact with either Brenda nor Stanley who sensed his mum was not in the best of moods, "I'm going to shower then I'm meeting Ami at work" he said doing a u turn and swiftly running up the stairs.

Brenda Spank was no one's fool and shouted after him, "need to talk Stanley!" as his heavy footsteps could be heard stamping around his room, "and you don't think you can keep quiet either" she said giving a sharp look towards her husband. She was in a bullish mood and made sure it was felt by crashing the dishes in the sink as she cleaned up, Greg winced the sound cut through spoiling his tranquil moment with his newspaper he dare not respond he full well knew this was not the time to test Brenda's patience.

Stanley bounded down the steps looking refreshed now changed, his attire was smart he wore a navy blue v necked jumper with a yellow polo shirt underneath and dark denim jeans with white trainers, he grabbed his jacket which hung on the banister and made his way towards the front door, "Mum dad I'll see you later I'm off to see Ami" he shouted barely giving any of them time to answer back before the door slammed shut, both Greg and Brenda looked towards the door before making eye contact with raised eyebrows surprised bewildered by the new energy and disposition of their son.

This was a new Stanley a confident purposeful person he had plenty to look forward to and was actually enjoying his liaisons not least because of the money but just because it was a chance to get up off of the sofa. He was now beginning to see there was a whole new world out there which he had not explored before, so many of his days spent wasted only because him and Jerry had a blinkered vision of the world, certainly the last few months had added weight to the contrary, there was a zest in his steps and he was full of energy as he made his way towards to town centre.

Just as he was approaching his phone began to ring he could see Cassandra's name flashing boldly on the screen, "hello Cassandra" he answered politely, "Stanley Spank you little star!" her excited voice resonated back into his ear, "once again you have had a glowing report from our client", Stanley became embarrassed and bashful "thanks that's good right?" He queried stopping briefly, "well I have two more lined up for you this week, can you come in tomorrow and we will go through the details?" Cassandra asked clearly happy with her new investment.

Stanley paused for thought sweeping his hair back over away from his forehead, "ok yes tomorrow sounds great" his upbeat tone reflected his new attitude, "oh and I have your cheque ready too", she said quite happily "see you then Stanley", again she sounded very happy.

Stanley ended the call and continued his journey definitely with a more of a spring in his step he felt cool and contented and was looking forward to seeing the one person who would restore some normality to his now interesting and relenting life. He walked thinking to himself in all of the years he'd been lazing around with Jerry this was a feeling he had not experienced before he was happy and now seemed to look forward to every juncture and turn ahead of him in his new life. He approached the shop he saw Ami waiting with one of her colleagues he began to smile a big one from ear to ear upon seeing his girlfriend and as usual she looked stunning even in a casual pink ruffled tight blouse, faded tight jeans and white wedges, "how lucky am I?" he whispered to himself.

Ami smiled towards him her warm endearing face lit up when she saw him coming towards her, she looked at her friend who mouthed to her "he's gorgeous", she gushed clearly checking him out looking him up and down nodding in approval, "hello you" Stanley's eyes were fixated on Ami not even acknowledging her companion they embraced holding each other tightly before shyly giggling and letting go "good to see you" a nervy Stanley flicked his hair back still staring deeply into Ami's eyes which were blue and sparkling with excitement as she stared back, "blimey you two get a room!", Ami's colleague who was a buxom blonde with a face full of bright make up tutted before cracking into a fit of laughter, "sorry, Stanley this is Mikala", Stanley laughed and held out his hand to shake, "nice to meet you" ever the polite well-mannered gentleman.

Ami clutched Stanley's arm as they walked towards the bus stop "come to my house Stanley I will make you some dinner" an enthusiastic Ami asked almost begging she seemed so happy to be with him they seem to be inseparable clinging onto each other like a couple of lovesick teenagers, she swept Stanley's hair away from his face and kissed him passionately on the lips then cutely smiled hugging him "I missed you" she squeezed him tightly "anyway how was London?", she stepped back to look into his eyes, "it was ok" Stanley replied attempting to play down his adventurous evening with Sunshine, "I missed you too" he reciprocated touching her face tenderly before the bus pulled into the stop brusquely.

The one thing that did not sit well with Stanley was the fact that he had to lie to Ami, he was too scared to be totally honest with her he thought who would want their man socialising with rich lonely women night after night, he felt that he had to build her trust first but it was killing him inside. Every time he looked at Ami's face he felt a wave of guilt especially when he sat discussing his boring "hospitality" job, but he knew this was one secret that he had to bury until the time was right, anyway why spoil things when they were going so well.

After a thirty minute journey they reached Underbridge a nice quiet leafy area just outside the main town of Tyford, it was lined with large houses with drives filled with expensive cars it seemed quite desolate there were really no signs of people "it's really quiet" Stanley whispered as they strolled down the Cul de sac, "yes and that's how I like it" Ami answered in a quiet tone before turning into a gated residence, "this is nice" Stanley spoke sounding surprised but impressed as he laid his eyes on the purpose built premises, "the girl I share with is away for a while so it's just me and you" Ami smiled seductively unlocking the door and entering her home.

The flat was warm, clean and had a fresh rose scent, it had a very contemporary feel the main room was spacious with a large black leather sofa small table and a TV, "come in and get comfortable" Ami instructed she threw her keys onto the wooden table which was in the centre of the room, "check you out" Stanley commented as he looked around suitably impressed "nice pad" again he commented. He continued to have a nose around and spotted a couple of framed pictures on the window sill "is that you?" he quizzed picking up the photo which had a younger looking long haired Ami alongside another woman.

Ami strode towards him "ahh yes that's me and my mum" she commented throwing her arms around his waist and resting her head against his chest, "that was a few years ago before I came here", she looked up towards Stanley who was still studying her picture, "Stanley" she said softly, "kiss me please", she continued staring adoringly into his eyes.

Stanley's heart literally skipped a beat as he looked down at her yearning expression, he melted, the twinkle in her eyes rendered him putty in her hands, her sweet scent lingered as they stood close, Stanley hesitated before slowly and tentatively leaning forward to plant a tender kiss onto Ami's lips, he could feel a number of unknown sensations running through his body he was nervous, excited and felt a rush of blood jolt from head to toe all at the same time especially when he felt the softness of her lips, he knew at that moment this was the girl he had been waiting for dreaming of even, a pure fantasy which was now very real.

Ami moaned as they continued to kiss, "Stanley your shaking" she giggled as they held each other closely, "I know stupid aren't I" he nervously grinned, "don't be scared" again her tone was sultry and soft she held his face and planted another tender kiss, Stanley held her closer feeling her warm body against his, his mind was exploding he could only wonder if she was feeling the same too.

After about ten minutes of kissing and canoodling Ami pushed him away, "I have to make dinner" she laughed looking at a forlorn Stanley who was clearly still taken by this experience, "put the TV on and relax, is chicken and chips ok?" Ami asked as she detached herself from Stanley who still attempted to hold her hand, "err yes that's fine", he finally snapped back into the now.

As he sat watching the TV his mind wandered he thought about his nights out with Ms White and Sunshine, he hated deceiving Ami but he knew he had to keep his extracurricular shenanigans to himself, he thought the best way to balance it was by separating it as work although he also enjoyed his little escapades, but he knew there was something different and special about Ami. He watched her while she was busy in the open planned kitchen, she was perfect he thought, just his type if ever he were to have a type, he wondered what it would be like if Jerry was still around whether any of this would be happening, he was glad it was, it was time to grow up and be normal he thought as Ami caught his gaze and winked at him, he reclined into the sofa with a smug smile on his face, this was his life now his time and he was certainly enjoying it.

The following morning Stanley opened his eyes, he stared up to the ceiling then vigorously rubbed his eyes the room was certainly unfamiliar and not his own, he turned and could feel a sleeping Ami snuggled up next to him, he almost jumped up and out of the bed then he remembered that this was a continuation of a special night, he was slightly uncomfortable at first feeling her sexy warm naked body next to his but then he realised just at that moment how good it felt to finally pop his cherry, he held her tighter looking at her while she lay peacefully her warm milky skin and perfect pert breasts nestling against his chest gave him an instant rush causing him to stretch out his lean figure he knew at thaat moment this was where he was supposed to be, tucked up with the beautiful Ami.

He affectionately planted a gentle kiss on the top of her head causing Ami to stir then Stanley in an act remotely unrecognisable of the old him thought he would surprise his girlfriend and promptly slid out of the bed leaving her while he went to the kitchen to make her a cup of tea, he always remembered what his mum would tell him about treating a lady in the right way and thought this could be a small gesture to show her how much he appreciated her.

Stanley bumbled his way around Ami's kitchen looking for the cups, cutlery and tea bags trying not to make too much noise he was not the most nimble when it came to domestic dexterity hence a yawning Ami entered the kitchen dressed in a baggy t shirt her hair ruffled "hey what are you doing?" she quizzed still half asleep she managed a tiny giggle at seeing Stanley stood in his boxer shorts fishing around for everything, "I just wanted to make you a nice cup of tea" he said stood with his hands on hips looking lost and slightly embarrassed, "I'll give you a hand shall I?" she yawned cupping her hands onto his face and giving him a gentle kiss on his lips.

Stanley responded by putting his arms around her and giving her a big hug, he felt so comfortable this was the best he felt in his life the warm embrace of Ami he had the feeling that he had now turned a new leaf he could look forward to the future with hope his mind now activated to what the real world could offer.

Stanley had returned home after an exciting and pleasant stay over at Ami's he literally could not stop himself replaying the events of his last night, he felt like the boy who had become a man, nothing was going to spoil his day he even stopped to at Cassandra's to collect his cheque from his previous night's work. Feeling generous he had purchased a large bouquet of flowers for his mum and a six pack of bitter for his dad something he had not been able or bothered to do this in the past, but along with his new verve for life he felt this would just be a small getsture of his gratitiude and he was happy to do this.

His phone vibrated as he strolled back to his home, it was Ami although he had just left her "hi you", he said gushing as he answered "you ok?" he continued to speak with the phone attached between his neck and ear as he carried the bag of drinks and flowers in his hands, he spoke like a carefree love bird nonchalantly meandering without a care in the world, "ok babe I'll catch you later" a very confident sounding Stanley continued before wrapping up the call just as he turned into his road, he shook his head in disbelief before digging in his pocket to find his keys.

Squeezing himself through the door Stanley yelled out announcing himself boldly upon his entrance, "Mum, Dad" he called out only to be met with silence, he opened the front room door poking his head in before walking to the kitchen, they were both out. He dumped the beer on the kitchen table and placed the flowers next to them, not one for classy decoration he then proceeded to plonk himself on the sofa in front of the TV, he sighed heavily before grabbing the remote control and laying back to watch whatever was on the large screen in front of him.

It was strange for Stanley as for once he was unable to focus or concentrate on anything else but Ami his mind swam with thoughts reflections of his night and the time they spent curled up in bed he felt like the cat that got the cream his world was coming together and he wanted to share it with Ami all except he could not let her know exactly what his job was he hated keeping secrets from both the special women in his life his mum being one, but he knew at some point he would have to spill the beans before things became too obvious he knew he could not hide behind his lies and to be frank he felt really uncomfortable doing so.

Stanley continued to lay prone gazing at the screen he heard the lock in the door followed by the shuffling of feet and voices, it was his parents by the sound of it returning from a shopping trip "Stanley!" he could hear his dads voice bellowing out but as usual he did not move a muscle instead opting to shout back the effort to move his body any further than his fingers pressing the remote control was too much.

"I'm in here dad", his muted tired response croaked out through the doorway, "come and give us a bloody hand then" Brenda's voice interjected forcing a belated Stanley to sit up and finally make moves towards the hallway opening the door to see both of them laden with bright orange shopping bags. "Need a hand then?" he cheekily replied only to receive a scalding look back from his mum his dad shook his head and strode past towards the kitchen forcing Stanley to step forward and relieve his mum's bag carrying duties.

"Flowers! well that's a first" Brenda exclaimed as she entered the kitchen noticing the colourful bouquet which laid on the table unceremoniously next to the bag of beers, "what's all this is aid of?" his dad countered inspecting the six pack then turning to look at Stanley, "just a thank you" he shrugged continuing to unload the bags to his parents amazement " oh and mum here's the money I lent from you plus a little extra" he handed his mum some scrunched up notes much to her suprise, she looked at Greg in disbelief before looking back at her son, "I don't know what to say, flowers and money?" she questioned giving Stanley a confused stare "hmm can I have my son back please we seem to have an imposter" she joked causing Greg to muster a chuckle.

Greg Spank sat with a can from the six pack sipping slowly as to show he was really enjoying the free beverage, all three sat in silence in their own thoughts Brenda clipped the stems of the flowers taking her time pruning each one looking at the bright colours of each flower, "so Stanley tell me some more about this job in the supermarket" she asked still with her eyes transfixed on the bouquet, Greg coughed as if he was choking on his beer then shot a hard look at Stanley, before Stanley could answer again Brenda continued "because Mable Thirlwell told me that she has never seen you and she works there too".

Stanley shifted uncomfortably in his seat and looked at his dad who in turn stared wide eyed tense holding his tin in front of his face, "no point looking at him" Brenda continued raising her eyebrows at Greg who again stifled a cough in between supping, "well ok mum you got me" Stanley tried to laugh and inject some humour into the questioning "I'm actually doing some hospitality work" he announced much to Greg's relief at his sons sudden talent for thinking on his feet emerged "hotel seminars and that" he quipped brushing his hair aside comfortable with his response while Greg continued to squirm excruciatingly.

Brenda sat looking unconvinced switching her gaze between the two of them, "I tell you the pair of you are as bad as each other" she scoffed before she continued tending to her floral ensemble aggressively clipping the stems.

Up in his room Stanley sat back on his bed for once he was not smoking a joint or drinking a bottle of lager he was lost in his own little world of thought, he could not stop thinking about Ami but he also smiled when he remembered the crazy night he had with Sunshine, he was loving the unexpected nature of the escort business and of course the money he was earning, he got up and went over to his desk the card from Charles Carter was propped against his computer, he stared at it before picking it up for some reason he felt a compelling urge to contact the over blown camp and flamboyant dinner host.

In his mind all he was thinking about was the opportunity of earning more money and he knew privately Charles Carter would pay over the odds despite the trouble it would cause with Cassandra if she found out about him moonlighting but in his mind he just wanted to earn as much money as he could for him and Ami, his mind was now thinking on another level which was another first for the former layabout. He was beginning to make plans which is something previously he had not been able to afford he had his mind set on a nice holiday for him and Ami somewhere hot and exotic, he was loving the taste of wealth although it was only at an early stage he knew the financial potential could be huge, a dream that was now easily in reach of becoming a reality, it was still better than having nothing.

Still for a few minutes he contemplated before finally picking up the phone and slowly began to dial the number on the card, his heart thumped he did not want Charles Carter to get the wrong idea "it's only business" he kept repeating in his head trying to convince himself as the number connected and then rang.

Stanley stood up and walked over to his window leaning his head out feeling the fresh evening air, the phone continued to ring he was just about to hang up until a weary sounding voice answered "hello Charles Carter" he sounded as if he had been woken up his normal falsetto pitched voice was now more baritone and grumpy. Stanley paused before hesitantly answering "hello Mr Carter this is Stanley", he could hear Charles Carter shuffling the phone being moved about, "Stanley who?" he answered back slightly annoyed at obviously being disturbed, "Stanley Spank I met you at the dinner with Marilyn White remember?", Stanley spoke in a hushed voice, a pause ensued before a suddenly energised Charles Carter answered back "oh yes Spank, I remember you the young dashing lad OMG!, to what do I owe this pleasure?" he suddenly had an injection of energy and the normal excitable flamboyant persona seemed revitalised.

"Well…" Stanley paused again he was lost he did not quite know how to get his words out he really was not even sure why he was calling, "I just wanted to know" again he stopped himself short clutching the phone to his chest "what am I doing?" he whispered to himself shaking his head he cleared is throat then continued, "I just wanted to know if you needed me for any work" he spat it out quickly looking up to the heavens as he spoke quite unbelieving what he was doing, down the other end of the phone Charles Carter shrieked with laughter all of a sudden he was very excitable, "well there must be a god" he responded still having a hearty chuckle.

Stanley rolled his eyes he half felt to just hang up he knew this was a crazy thing to do which could compromise him before Charles Carter came back "well my little petal I am about to go away on business and could use some company" he spoke enthused the camp nature of his voice sent a shiver down Stanley he turned around to make sure none of his parents were approaching his room, "ok give me the details", he spoke with authority as if he were in business mode.

"Do you have a passport Stanley?" Charles Carter asked, "I think my mum sorted something" Stanley countered, "well I suggest you check, I have a business trip to Monaco planned it would be nice if you could join me", Stanley was stunned Monaco? he had only just left Tyford to London let alone get on a plane and fly to another country, "er well I'll check" he answered back meekly still reeling at hearing this news, he could hear the loud cackle of laughter down the phone "Mr Spank it will be worth your while, I'll make sure your taken care of" he spoke suggestively "I'll be leaving in three weeks give me a call and let me know".

Stanley was now in a dilemma he knew he could potentially earn some good money and also get a free holiday, "ok I'll call you" he muttered, "ok toodles" Charles Carter hung up the phone, leaving Stanley holding his device in his hand still digesting the information.

He paced up and down in his room running his hands through his hair thinking, he had a mixture of emotions he was excited at the thought of going abroad but then he also the thought about being alone with Charles Carter and the implications. He also felt a little bit disloyal to Cassandra after all if it was not for her he would never even be in this position and what about Ami? could he leave her and go away? He scrambled for a cigarette as the pressure began to tell, he lit up and aggressively inhaled walking back to his window to blow out the smoke, staring out into the distance his mind was awash with thoughts "it's only business Stan" he spoke to himself again reassuring that he would be doing the right thing although his gut instinct told him otherwise.

The next day and what was now becoming a normal routine Stanley was up early he had just put himself through a rigorous workout which was also something he had introduced into his new lifestyle, he sat up on the floor after completing a set of squats coughing violently and wheezing as he spluttered out loudly. The days of smoking and drinking were catching up with him but he was determined to get healthy he knew Ami was worth all of the pain "I'm going to give up the fags and the weed" he mentioned as he huffed and puffed sweating crouched over.

After his shower Stanley made his way downstairs where as usual Greg Spank was sitting at the table peering over his half cut glasses into a pile of paper work, he gave a double glance shocked at seeing his son up showered and half dressed, "it's a bit early for you isn't it?" He questioned looking at his watch then giving his son a curious look. Stanley pretended to ignore him instead he began whistling happily looking through the fridge "I'm starving Dad is there nothing for brekkie?" his dad looked at him sternly and asked in a dead pan tone "what did your last slave die of?", before returning his eyes back to the strewn pages on the table. Stanley groaned with discontent scratching his bare chest ape like before stomping out and back up the stairs to his room, Greg did not bat an eyelid instead just continued to study the sheets of paper in front of him.

The sound of the front door slamming indicated Stanley's exit he marched down the road with a scowl on his face headphones plugged into his ears he strode purposely with a cocky swagger it was almost as if his attitude was now changing his new found confidence was bordering slightly arrogant he flicked up the collars on his denim jacket and shoved in hands in both of his pockets cutting a disgruntled figure.

He had made his way to a cafe just near the town centre it was near empty just the waitress and a short tubby cook who was consumed with frying up some bacon and eggs. Stanley sat nursing a large mug of tea his music still blasted out into his ears he seemed very distracted in deep thought hardly noticing the large plate of hot steaming food being marched his way, the waitress plonked the plate in front of him a full English breakfast with all the trimmings, "hmm thanks" Stanley gleefully appreciated the feast in front of him bare acknowledging the waitress as he prepared to tuck in.

Gulping down the last of his tea Stanley pushed aside the empty plate, he belched loudly to the disgust of the waitress who was within earshot "excuse me, that was lovely" he exclaimed a bit emabarrassed with his own laddish behaviour, taking out a wad of cash and tossing down a ten pound note "keep the change" he shouted before putting his headphones back in and getting up to leave, the waitress looked over at Stanley and offered a fake smile before moving in to clean the table. Now he had filled his stomach a much happier Stanley made his way towards the town with one person on his mind. He walked in tune to the beat he was listening to, it was kind of a strut full of confidence someone who was now more in control and beginning to see his growth into a new person, the power of attraction and acceptance had now fuelled Stanley's appetite for life for someone who had never earned a crust in his young life to have money and Ami was a great achievement and also the cause of his mini power trip.

Outside the clothing store where Ami worked Stanley stood gazing in through the shop window he was trying to see if he could spot her without her seeing him as he wanted to surprise her, he peered through and caught a sight of her fixing some clothes which were on display, his heart literally skipped a beat as he watched her working, she looked cute as usual even in just jeans and a red fitted tee shirt, he must of looked odd from the outside standing on his tip toes peeking through the mannequins positioned in the window, he began tapping lightly on the glass not that his attempts of distraction could be heard amongst the din of the music blasting inside of the shop.

He carried on tapping and waving thinking that he could divert her attention away, he was laughing to himself getting some form of enjoyment from larking around until he felt a hand pat him on his shoulder, he quickly spun around and saw the big blonde figure of Mikala, Ami's work colleague chewing gum ferociously with a cigarette dangling between her fingers, "and what do you think you're doing?" she said sternly her face full of bright coloured war paint, Stanley looked startled and pulled out the ear plug from his headphones "blimey! You trying to give me a heart attack?" he shouted much to Mikala's amusement who laughed out loud before taking one last draw on her cigarette and stomping it out with her high pink platform shoes, "why don't you just come in and say hello to her?" she nudged past him and strode into the shop.

A red faced Stanley quickly attempted to fix himself up by stroking back his hair and adjusting his jacket collar before a baffled looking Ami emerged from the shop "what are you doing here? silly boy" she asked moving in for a kiss and hug, Stanley smiled whilst drawing in the hug he loved her sweet smell and warmness as he clinched her tightly, "I just wanted to say hello" he gushed, his mood now visibly lifted from his grumpy exit earlier. "Shall I come round later?" he asked while sweeping his hand on her cheek tenderly, Ami looked up at him her stunning eyes sparkled as she connected with his, "you are very handsome Mr Spank" she mused whilst peering lovingly up at his face, "ok I'll see you later" she responded quickly before kissing him again and running back into the shop.

Stanley stood temporarily frozen still mesmerised he felt all warm and fuzzy inside before popping his headphones back on and walking away nodding his head to the urban beats which brashly pumped into his ears.

Once he had got home he went straight up to his room and began to sort out his clothes for his evening with Ami, still with his music on he danced around his room visibly happier now that he knew he would be getting his dose of his Ami time, he posed and postured in front of the mirror throwing various items of clothing onto his bed, so involved he did not notice his dads unimpressed figure standing just inside of the door shaking his head.

Stanley froze immediately the minute he saw the hunched shoulders and folded arms of his dad standing there, "oh dad!" he stopped sharply pulling out his headphones and laughing nervously "you alright?" he asked still frozen in an awkward pose, "what's up?" again he asked as his dad stood silently his face still stony, "you're out of order Stan" he said sternly his voice sounded tired and gruff, Stanley's demeanor suddenly reverted back to his normal relaxed shape, "what do you mean?" he questioned.

Greg Spank shook his head he looked disappointed, "we didn't bring you up to be disrespectful", he wagged his finger in Stanley's direction getting increasingly animated "you are changing boy and not for the better!" he continued to rant his voice now raised something that was seldom seen in the Spank household. Stanley could tell his dad was seriously not amused suddenly he felt like a child again being brought down a peg or two, "I'm sorry dad but what exactly have I done?", he questioned unable to comprehend the reasons for his dad's rage, "all I'm saying is while you're here you need to show some respect" again the tone of his voice was merged with emotion, Greg Spank then turned away slamming the door behind him and stomped back down the stairs. Stanley was shocked into silence his momentum halted he sat down on his bed amongst the pile of clothes his shoulders sagged as if he had just had the energy sucked out of him, he had been brought down to earth his short lived moment of euphoria stopped in its tracks, maybe his dad was right just because everything was happening for him now he should not forget who he was or where he came from, he actually felt really gutted he knew his dad was right in principle he had been acting a bit cocky lately maybe he just needed to reign in a little and focus on making money and spending time with Ami.

The good thing about doing the job he did was definitely the money and spending time with interesting clients the bad thing was still lying to Ami and keeping up the pretence that he was working in hotel hospitality but while she suspected nothing Stanley saw no reason not to continue going undercover as an escort, in a way it was now a form of adventure for him although he had to be careful not to indulge too much in the offerings of the clients especially when he felt so drawn to Ami and also knew how much she was drawn to him.

He made his way to Cassandra's office sat on the bus he stared out of the window still thinking about his dads remarks, it seemed that his life was becoming more complex he thought about the people in his life now that he had to please, for some reason he could only think about Ami he knew for once in his life he had an aim, and that was to make as much money and spend the rest of his time with her. On approach to Cassandras distinctive red door he received a phone call, he pulled his phone from his pocket the screen flashed "unknown" a puzzled looking Stanley placed down his sports bag and took the call, "hello who is this?" he said awaiting a response, he could hear a crackled signal there was a delay until he could hear the faint voice of Jerry, "allo mate it's me", a barely audible almost hoarse voice replied, "Jerry Dooley how are you mate?" Stanley responded excited yet surprised to receive such a random call from his old sparring partner, "I'm good mate really good" Jerry spoke back, "just wanted to tell you I'm staying out here for a bit longer now, found a nice lass" his voice continued to crackle down the phone "Dooley! …yeah me too!" an even more excited Stanley shouted back "that's class mate, anyway I'll call you soon" Jerry shouted out before the line went dead, Stanley took a moment to digest the news before picking up his bag and pressing the buzzer to see Cassandra. As he reached the door at the top of the stairs he saw the tiny figure of Cassandra waiting to greet him she seemed energetic and bouncy, "hello Stanley come up" she ushered, she wore a grey cardigan a long black skirt and flat leather shoes, they made their way into her small office Cassandra was talking continually sort of in a mumble but excited mutterings.

They sat down and Cassandra began to shuffle around some papers, her desk was unusually untidy, she seemed too excited and was trying to do too many things at the same time as well as chattering away, "well Stanley I have had so much good feedback" she continued licking her index finger and thumb before turning over some pages. Stanley sat back in his chair relaxed and still mooching over Jerry's news, "you are my most popular request at the moment" she continued to witter on her excitement causing her voice to peak at a high pitch tone.

Stanley was in a world of his own only catching a few words, "can you do a double date for me tomorrow?", Cassandra paused for breath and looked up over her tiny glasses directly at Stanley "you'll get paid as if it were two jobs" she said hopefully, Stanley pricked up "yeah why not?" he confidently replied, "wonderful Stanley" Cassandra seemed chuffed with his reply, "you know you have been a godsend" she continued tapping slowly on her computer keyboard.

"Ok thank you Cassandra" Stanley politely said as he exited quickly, he ran down the stairs and out of the building, he wanted to get to Ami's as quickly as possible, he was happy he had another cheque in his pocket and a double date booked for the following evening, he ran out of the dark trading estate towards the bus stop bag in hand his heart pumping fast as he ran as quickly as he could to catch the bus.

The bus sped round the corner as soon as he got back to the main road Stanley began to sprint knowing missing it would mean at least another half an hour delay in getting to Ami's place. He made it just wheezing for breathe as he stepped onto the deck, "really should give up fags" he joked with the driver as he boarded. He sat down barely able to catch his breath the bus continued on with the driver obviously in a race to get home such was the speed they were hurtling, Stanley took out his phone and sent a text to Ami, *"on my way"* it read, he rested back in the seat exhausted, "I really must give up the fags" he whispered to himself, leaning his head onto the window.

It was late now but Stanley had finally arrived at Ami's place in Underbridge he was tired now but still had a spark of excitement which was reserved for his beautiful girlfriend, Stanley pressed onto the intercom and leaned against the wall until he heard Ami's voice which made him barely prick up, "hello" she sounded robot like through the remote system, "hi Ami its Stanley" he responded playfully before the door opened, he strolled up to her flat he was surprised that Ami had come out to meet him "hey you" she said looking a bit shifty, as usual her look was effortless even this late she had a long flowing white and yellow floral dress on.

Stanley was happy to see her he dropped his bag and walked forward to share an embrace "what are you up to?" he quizzed a bit concerned, the two hugged her subtle sweet scent tickled his nostrils, Ami looked up at her tall man her eyes raced all over his face before she kissed him repeatedly, Stanley chuckled and touched her hair, "oi what's up are you ok?" he continued slightly taken by her enthusiastic greeting, "ok I have a surprise for you" Ami stepped back grabbing his hand, "really?" a now intrigued

Stanley questioned, he picked up his bag and walked towards the flat with an unsually trepid Ami, "what's going on?" Stanley asked again very wary, "just come" Ami responded playfully.

They entered the flat together Stanley sensed that they were not alone he could smell food and heard someone else moving around, "hold up Ami, who's in there?" he stopped pulling her back, "just come in" she reiterated with a cute smile, they both walked in and Stanley could see two people sitting in the front room. "Ok mum, dad this is Stanley", Stanley's jaw dropped and his face went red with shock when he heard the words from Ami's mouth "huh mum…dad" his voice tailed off then he quickly fixed up smartish wiping his hand on his trousers anticipating a handshake and looking at Ami confused, she in turn shrugged her shoulders as if to say I did not know they were coming either.

A short squat figure bounded towards Stanley "hello Stanley I'm Lars, Ami's father and this is Kirsten" he turned and saw a very hot young looking woman with long flowing blonde hair she looked mature but was very well preserved. "Hello Stanley" Ami's mother Kirsten smiled warmly they both came forward, he shook Lar's hand a stern handshake, he looked military very sturdy he was dressed like a tourist in khaki combat shorts and sandals with a white short sleeved shirt, the first thing Stanley noticed was the amount of blonde hairs he had on his arms "pleasure Stanley" he had a slight accent also, Stanley was too shocked to really take it all in then Ami's mother Kirsten came forward and embraced him she seem very calm and poised, she looked healthy and tanned he could see where Ami got her looks and eyes from as she had the deep ocean blue eyes, a very shocked Stanley responded to them both, he suddenly reverted to being shy "hi very nice to meet you" he was bashful but remembered his manners, Ami stood back watching as an awkward silence ensued "well surprise!" she cut into the atmosphere causing them all to start laughing "come in sit down" Lars offered him in grabbing his bag.

Stanley stepped in he certainly was not prepared for this he glanced at Ami who could only smile awkwardly, "are you hungry Stanley?" Kirsten fired a question at him which again caught him while he was attempting to take it all in, "yeah starving" he answered back without thinking, "I mean yes I am thank you" he responded causing Ami and her parents to laugh.

He sat down with Ami clinging onto him for dear life squeezing his hand "don't worry we are only here for a few days" Lars joked as they all sat down to eat spaghetti Bolognese "yes we wanted to meet the man that Ami always talks about" her mum Kirsten interjected with a warm reassuring smile she rubbed her hand onto Ami's, Stanley looked at Ami and smiled "I hope it's all good" he said playfully "oh it's all good" Kirsten responded back "yes yes all good" Lars then repeated he then boomed out a big laugh which vibrated through Stanley before he began choking causing his face to go beetroot red "water dad?" Ami intervened pouring some water out from a jug, "I'm ok" he spluttered, "I wanted to say she has spoken very highly of you" he managed to finish his sentence before downing the rest of his glass, "that's nice" Stanley replied impressed looking lovingly at Ami, "I love her she's a great girl" he gushed before getting all embarrassed and looking down at his food smelling the rich aroma of the sauce, "we like to pray first" Kirsten spoke calmly towards Stanley sensing he was about to directly tuck in to his meal, "oh I'm sorry" he replied taking his hands away from the table and giving a strange look to Ami who just closed her eyes.

After the meal Ami's parents disappeared into her bedroom to get ready to sleep, Ami came back with blankets and pillows dumping them onto the sofa, "well this is us for the night Stanley" she looked towards him "and no hanky panky!" she threw a cushion his way, Stanley laughed, "come here gorgeous you set me up" he whispered, Ami walked round and literally fell on top of him using the pillows to cushion her fall. The two embraced and shared a passionate kiss, "I love you Stanley Spank", she said lovingly staring her beautiful eyes right at him and ruffling his hair, "I love you too" he whispered back his eyes glaring wide, he never thought he would be in such an unenviable position to utter those words but he felt good and knew he was not going to let Ami out of his sight, it was hard for him to look into her eyes knowing that he had a double date the next evening but to him it was the only way he could save enough money to take them on a nice holiday that was his main aim as deep down he knew that Ami would love that.

Stanley lay wide awake while a clearly tired Ami snuggled up tightly into him he stared up into space his mind mulling over everything, he loved the feel of Ami her warm body touching his it felt just right, he could not believe that one half of the infamous Tyford two would be lying with his body intertwined with a beautiful Swedish girl with a cheque for close to a grand tucked away in his jeans pocket, he felt sweet and well chuffed with himself he turned and kissed Ami on her forehead tenderly before resting back and closing his eyes, the toll of the day began to hit him, he could barely hear Ami as she slept her shallow breaths warmly tickled his neck, he smirked before drifting off into a deep sleep.

It seemed like merely a few minutes had passed before Stanley could hear a voice whispering in his ear he rolled his gangly body away from Ami's grasp groaning as he turned, he could still hear a persistent and playful Ami "Stanley wake up" she continued, nibbling his ear and tickling his side at the same time, Stanley felt irritated he grumbled louder signalling his discontent, "hey sleepy head" Ami continued to whisper into his ear clambering onto him with her thighs rubbing his tight stomach seductively.

Stanley stirred again this time grabbing her leg and squeezing it gently he rolled over and pulled her in towards him cuddling her tightly "you are up early naughty" he spoke in a gruff deep morning voice kissing her gently on her forehead they embraced tightly and writhed underneath the cover Ami giggled as they continued to fool around only to be interrupted by a noise "ish… ish… ish" could be heard along with deep loud breathes, "what the..?", Stanley stopped instantly popping his head up from the sofa "oh my god!" he rubbed his eyes in disbelief he saw the sight of Lars in a tiny pair of tight black shorts performing a series of intense sit ups, "ish… ish… ish" he continued his stocky body glistened in sweat, he looked like a mini hulk and no wonder the way he was energetically putting himself through the paces, "Jesus your dad is a beast!" Stanley whispered laying back down as Ami graoned frustratingly "he will do this for at least an hour" she sounded upset that her snuggling session was stopped short "I guess we better get up" she moaned flipping the covers off of them both.

Everyone was now up and changed Ami was in the kitchen with her Kristen making breakfast while Stanley sat on the sofa with Lars who was nowshowered changed and more relaxed than his earlier exertions, his blonde hair was swept over to one side he was quiet flicking through a brochure, "you must come to Sweden Stanley sample the great outdoors" Lars mused looking up whilst licking his fingers and turning the pages.

Stanley seemed to be in another world only nodding and grunting a reply, he was preoccupied gazing into space now dressed in a plain white tee shirt and jeans with flip flops, "what else do you plan to do while your here?" Stanley asked politely refocusing his attentions towards Lars, "oh we will just relax until we travel to Scotland for a few days", Lars answered, Stanley nodded in approval before Lars placed the brochure down and leaned into Stanley, he glared sternly into his eyes he was all butch and brawn with chiseled square jawed features, "Ami speaks well of you, she seems to love you" he began speaking quietly grabbing Stanley's immediate attention, he looked towards the women in the kitchen slyly before focusing back onto Stanley, "she is my little princess make sure you never break her heart" his voice sounded a little bit menacing he then stuck out his hand for a handshake.

Stanley drew breath he knew this was a warning shot he hesitated before clearing his throat "of course I mean I love her too", Lars gripped his hand and squeezed tightly he was like a bear, Stanley could only smile through gritted teeth trying to hide the fact he was intense pain "yes I will look after her I promise" he replied almost in surrender his voice tone went squeaky as the grip took over his whole body before Lars broke out into a big laugh "I like you Stanley" he patted his leg with his big heavy paw like hands. "Ok guys breakfast is served" Kirsten announced just in time as the glare from Lars signaled his earnest feelings, Stanley coughed nervously before smiling and getting up to get his food "thank god …I'm starving" Stanley mentioned his voice still a high pitch squeal a timely interjection to break away from the awkward heavy father speech from Lars.

They all sat around the table mixed aromas of bacon eggs mushrooms and hash browns swirled upwards, Ami looked fiercely towards Stanley who was already tucking into his full plate ravenously, Lars and Kirsten sat quietly watching as an embarrassed Ami cleared her throat loudly attempting to get Stanley's attention, "Stanley!" she shouted squirming uncomfortably, Stanley stopped and looked up "what?" his mouth full chomping feeling the icy stares, "oops sorry" he said putting down his knife and fork realising his bad manners.

Kirsten who seemed always calm then took charge "we'd just like to say a quick prayer" she winked at Stanley and smiled before closing her eyes, Stanley looked at Ami who gave him a frosty glare before joining her parents and closed her eyes.

Stanley felt embarrassed and awkward kicking Ami under the table as if to let her know she should have stopped him from dying a thousand deaths he felt so stupid he wanted the ground to open up and swallow him the way he swallowed that mouthful of food. Kirsten continued to softly recite a prayer before opening her eyes on the words Amen, she looked straight at Stanley and smiled warmly, whilst Lars had a face like thunder before he cut aggressively into his bacon snorting loudly before snapping away at his fork.

After breakfast Stanley ambled up to Ami and asked if she needed help washing up the dishes he could tell she was not best pleased and he was not the most assertive when it came to doing chores but he sensed she was upset at his earlier faux pais "do you want me to dry?" he asked, Ami continued to ignore him clinking down the plates deliberately with measured force, her eyes stayed fixed at the sink, "babe …" again Stanley misled up to her and attempted to put his arms around her, "no Stanley!" she was adamant and by the tone in her voice he could tell she was seriously cross, splashing the cutlery around in the sink then through gritted whisper and in no uncertain terms she said "sometimes Stanley you frustrate me" the tone was heartfelt yet venomous and shook Stanley he had never really seen Ami like this.

"I'm sorry" he spluttered, "I'm just not used to doing stuff like that", Ami shrugged then turned to Stanley, "well you better get used to it especially when my parents are around", Stanley's shoulders sunk he cut a forlorn figure he could feel himself getting heated the rush of blood from rejection flooded through his body "Ok I'm sorry" he said backing off looking lost and bewildered before sauntering off mumbling something about getting his things.

Within a few minutes Stanley was back holding his bag he stopped and stood skulking behind Ami he hesitated sensing she was still fuming "babe I have to go I've said goodbye to your parents can I get a hug?" he bravely requested, Ami walked towards him she still had a face like thunder and she gave him a flimsy hug and token peck on the lips before pirouetting and walking back towards the kitchen leaving a confused and dejected Stanley at a loss he knew in this mood it was not worth trying to retrieve situation, "ok I guess I'll speak to you later then" he moodily replied before walking out.

The journey to his next assignment was a lonely one he had to hit the bright lights of London again this time to an exclusive club in the heart of the city, he stared at his phone almost willing it to receive a call from Ami, he dithered with his fingers on the icons on the phone hovering over Ami's number but he could not bring himself to press the buttons.

His thoughts turned to business staring out of the windows of the train at the greying evening skies for the first time he felt guilty for doing this job his thoughts and feelings were with Ami and he was struggling to get his mind on the job. Digging into his pocket he pulled out a scrunched up spliff, it was bent and crumpled Stanley looked around before carefully straightening it out, it had been a while since he actually smoked and this was mainly down to Ami, but for tonight he thought what the hell.

He placed the now smooth cone shaped spliff behind his ear and lent back in the seat, once again he scrolled through his phone he then tapped away a message *"I'm sorry love u lots xx"* before switching his device off.

A couple of girls boarded the same carriage giggling and squealing with laughter they seemed in full party mode heading into London they were taking it in turns to swig from a large cider bottle this instantly went against the shiny stiletto heels and posh frocks they were wearing. Upon noticing a distant Stanley one of them called out "oi oi what have we here then? David Beckham" breaking out into a loud cackle of laughter, Stanley stared back at them and shook his head "pitiful" he mumbled which for him was quite self-righteous as it was not so long ago himself and Jerry were the exact replicas of the two girls.

He went back to gazing out of the window lost in his thoughts too distracted to entertain the two goodtime girls. The train pulled into the city station Stanley got up and grabbed his bag his mind was still occupied but he knew he had to switch to the charming Mr. Spank for the evening, he was about to get off the train when one of the drunken girls sidled up to him and brushed past "sorry sexy" she broke into laughter looking back and winking at him, Stanley rolled his eyes to the heavens before shaking his head and stepping off the carriage to be absorbed into the city.

A short taxi cab ride into the heart of London brought Stanley to his hotel, he paid the driver and stepped out, as usual the area was busy with people all milling around or rushing to get to wherever they were going, cars roared up and down the roads and the big red buses rushed past incessantly.

Stanley stood outside the hotel he surveyed the area around him and spotted a little side street just to the left of the hotel entrance, he walked down it was quieter and away from the main street, he dumped his bag on the floor then took the ready rolled spliff from behind his ear, he took a big sigh before placing it to his mouth it was as if the pressure was getting to him somewhat.

Stanley dug into his pockets rooting around for his lighter he impatiently searched his pockets until finally pulling out a silver metal lighter, he flicked back the top and sparked the flame instantly burning the tip of the coned shaped spliff, he dragged hard and took down the smoke sucking in aggressively the smoke caught the back of his throat causing him to draw for breath choking, he leaned against the wall now relaxed letting the potency hit home.

The smell of the weed engulfed his immediate circumference, Stanley pulled his phone out of his pocket and slid the button to switch it back on, he continued to draw on his joint with it hanging from his mouth whilst his hands tended to his phone, he was hoping for a message to pop up from Ami but his heart sank when no messages came up he shoved the phone aggressively into his back pocket and huffed loudly, he sucked again frantically taking pull after pull until a fog of smoke literally surrounded him "right time to have fun" he said discarding the burnt remains of the joint and picked up his bag before stomping off towards the hotel entrance.

It was becoming a normal scenario now for Stanley as he checked into room 88 of the Thistle hotel for a night back in London again and a nice big room to chill out in all paid for by the client. Stanley was light headed and high from the rush of the marijuana he looked around his room and nodded in appreciation before chucking his bag onto the floor, the room was vintage in style and deluxe, a nice large queen-size bed with iron cast frames, an antique dressing table with a large oval shaped mirror it even had a small unused fire place "very nice" Stanley commented before poking his head around the door to the bathroom which had both a stand-alone bath and a shower with neatly folded white fluffy towels piled onto an oak wood stand.

Stanley looked at the time it was a quarter to seven he had an hour to get ready before being picked up, he still was not sure who he was meeting or where he was going, in his mind he was thinking maybe it was Sunshine Devroux again? He sat on the bed bouncing up and down testing out the mattress for comfort purposes, he paused taking it all in rubbing his face aggressively in an attempt to shake off the lethargy he was feeling from the joint he smoked "maybe I shouldn't of had that" he murmured rubbing his eyes yawning now feeling way too relaxed to get himself together. Again he pulled his phone out of his pocket and stared at the screen he contemplated calling Ami for a split second but then just threw the phone onto the bed before lying back and closing his eyes.

The loud shrill of the hotel telephone startled Stanley out of his temporary slumber "oh shit!" he leapt up quickly realising he had dozed off, the continuous and annoying ringing made Stanley literally leap across the bed to grab the handset, "hello" he shouted his brain totally scrambled, "Hello Mr Spank this is reception informing you a car is waiting for you downstairs", the official yet foreign voice explained "ok yep five minutes", replied a gravel voiced groggy Stanley before slamming down the phone.

He had not even showered or got dressed but suddenly leapt into action knowing he was going to have to get a wriggle on "damn" he said scrambling around tripping over his bag in the process and knocking into the dressing table, he hastily got his shirt and trousers out of the bag and threw them onto the bed then followed by his shoes, he then spun around and headed into the bathroom thrusting his hand into the shower turning the shiny chrome handle until the powerful water spray spurted out.

Five minutes later a dripping wet frazzled Stanley stepped back into the room digging into his bag to get his toiletries he was breathing heavy he knew Cassandra was a stickler for timekeeping with her clients, he sat down on the bed and dabbed himself dry rubbing the towel on his head vigorously only stopping once the room telephone again sprang into life ringing aggressively, "ok ok" a frustrated Stanley again got up "hello!" this time he shouted "I'm coming tell him ten minutes" he continued before slamming down the phone again petulantly.

The room door slammed shut and heavy footsteps could be heard running down the corridor before becoming a faint dull noise, the random ringtone of James Blunts song Beautiful began to play as Stanley's phone buzzed nestled in amongst his clothes and the soft quilt, Ami's picture flashed as it continued to ring until the music cut *"Missed call Ami"* faded from the screen before the phone blacked out.

Stanley was still fixing his hair in the mirror of the lift on his way down to the main lobby of the hotel, he was flustered and felt awful and groggy, he ran his fingers several times through his hair trying his hardest to perfect the slick style he craved, he wore a plain white shirt open necked with a black blazer, fitted jeans and his black shoes, he pulled faces attempting to exercise his facial muscles and relax "arrgh" he groaned "that'll do" he talked to himself as the loud bell indicated the lift had reached the ground floor.

The doors opened to a flurry of Chinese female tourists who were waiting excitedly outside chattering away they seem to be ready to converge into the lift before seeing Stanley and then all stopped before shrieking in awe watching the cool James Dean lookalike step out, almost in unison they all drew a collective breath as he strolled out, his tall lean frame striding confidently forward as he headed straight to the reception desk, "err can you tell me where the car for Mr Spank is please?" he politely asked, "just outside the driver is waiting" the snooty middle aged receptionist replied not even batting an eyelid at Stanley, "thanks" he quickly turned and made for his exit.

A black limousine style Mercedes gleamed parked stationary outside the main entrance of the hotel, a tall sexy Indian female dressed smartly almost military in shiny knee length black boots and short black admiral style coat with gold buttons stood almost to attention her long dark hair covered by a chauffeurs cap gave her a very official look, Stanley stopped in his tracks before smiling finally he summoned a spurt of energy knowing the night was about to begin. He approached switching into his English gentleman persona "I believe you are looking for me" he spoke suavely walking towards the beautiful yet stern looking driver, "you are late sir" her pretty petite face remained stern, no smile was offered although she clearly gave a seductive once over look at her subject the cool suave Stanley. Her deep red lipstick stood out vividly from her brown sheened skin, "I apologise" Stanley offered a sincere token of acknowledgement, "please this way" the driver motioned to Stanley ushering him towards the door at the back of the long stretch vehicle.

She bent slightly to lever open the door, Stanley could smell her sweet rose petal fragrance as she moved past him, "thank you" he replied before bending to get into the car, once the door completely opened Stanley firstly was hit by a concoction of sweet and spicy aromas then secondly he noticed two identical looking gorgeous Asian women sitting in the spacious and luxurious car, "I hate lateness" one of them snapped, watching Stanley climb in, "don't you know its poor etiquette to keep a lady waiting" she continued her posh cum cockney accent sounding unimpressed, "but I'll wait for him", the other interrupted seductively her eyes lighting up as Stanley finally slid his body into the comfortable crème leather seats, "big apologies… ladies" his voice tailed off, Stanley was taken aback and did a double take as he laid eyes on the two rich socialites both were stunning plus a lot younger which was quite a shock as he had been used to escorting older women.

He settled into the car sat directly opposite them he noticed they were twins which at first baffled him their faces looked exactly the same except one had a lip piercing and was dressed in a hot red leather cat suit whereas the other wore a simple black dress with a thick gold chain draped around her neck, "so sorry" Stanley said smiling relieved at the sight of these two beauties "My name is Spank", he said confidently offering his hand for a handshake.

The twins looked at each other and both repeated in unison "Spank!" they burst into fits of high pitched giggles "no way…really is that your name?" the cat suited twin replied holding her chest her fingers covered in sparkling diamond rings as she tried to contain herself, "well Stanley Spank yeah" Stanley replied feeling slightly embarrassed at the usual reaction to his name. He still felt slightly groggy from his cat nap and was not fully tuned in yet, "well Mr Spank" she continued attempting to hold in her laughter "my name is Melissa Le Chad and this is my sister Carissa", Stanley lent forward still in a bit of awe and shook both of their hands "Melissa and Carissa got it" he confirmed pointing to both resting back fixing his blazer.

The driver took them through the busy and heavy traffic of the London streets, he sat nervously as the twins stared directly at him, it seemed weird he was not expecting two beautiful identical twins, they definitely played the roles of their look Melissa seemingly the more forward and aggressive one whereas Carissa was quieter softer and more polite. "Crack open a bottle then Stan let's get this party started good lad" Melissa ordered causing Stanley to jolt into action almost forgetting his manners, "sorry" he murmured before leaning towards the polished wood grain drinks cabinet, he opened it revealing a fridge full of gold bottled Cristal champagne which literally glowed back in his face like gold bullion, "ok we are in business" he joked pulling out one of the bottles from the fridge and began to peel back the gold foil from the cork.

After about a minute of twisting the metal wire the cork popped causing both girls to let out a hysterical shriek, Stanley felt good at not spilling any of the fizzy liquid in the pristine vehicle, "cor I could die of thirst here Stan" Melissa spouted again thrusting her empty glass forward, this only made Stanley more nervous as he tried to steady his hand whilst pouring the drink out, "and for you" he said looking at Carissa who seemed distracted and bored and was not really paying too much attention.

As he poured into her glass he looked at her she seemed a touch more refined than her brash sister, this made Stanley more affable towards her, "say when Carissa" he spoke calmly, "when" she replied with a smile and a wink, her voice was seductive yet sincere as she placed the glass to her mouth and sipped the cool champagne, "pour yourself one", she continued leaning back and peering out of the window, "and yeah I'll have another one" Melissa thrust her glass into his face again causing Stanley to once again jump to attention "I'm thirsty and yeah I'm bossy too" she cracked fake cheesy smile as Stanley did his best impression of a silver service waiter, "sure say when" he quipped keeping up the 007 persona and charm tilting the bottle and nodding towards the feisty Melissa.

"Do you like partying Stan?" a motor mouthed Melissa continued, her speech becoming more rapid and excitable the more champagne she drank, Stanley shrugged "I'm here for you so let's party!" he replied in his attempt to inject some enthusiasm into proceedings even though he was not really the party type, he sat back and sipped his glass of champagne feeling full of himself knowing whatever happened tonight was going to be very interesting.

The car slowed to a stop both girls began to check themselves and touch up their make-up fussing and pulling their outfits into place, "how do I look?" Melissa asked an open question, "yeah you look fine?" both Stanley and Carissa replied in unison before bursting out into laughter which judging by Melissa's expression did not go down well at all, "ok let's do this" she said sternly as the driver opened the door, "are you ready for this Stanley?" the softer more genuine toned Carissa asked, "ready for what?" Stanley replied as he was being ushered out of the car, again both girls giggled mischievously before an almighty clamour and the flashing of cameras began.

"Oh my god!" a startled Stanley covered his eyes and face as the hordes of hungry paparazzi all circled, the clicking of camera's whirred away the bright flashes temporarily blinded him, "take my hand" Carissa ordered stepping elegantly out of the car, "and mine" Melissa ordered too, a disorientated Stanley tried his best to compose himself and reach back for his double dates, "now take a deep breath and pose Stanley" Carissa pulled him into line "Jesus who are you girls?" a baffled and flustered Stanley commented as the cameras continued to click.

He stood frozen trying to at least not look dazzled he was taken aback by it all before a burly security guard came through the midst of the pack and told them sternly to make their way into the club, the girls seem to lap up the adulation and madness and took to it as if it were nothing special, striking various poses holding onto their man for the night while Stanley got flashbacks of the Sunshine Devroux experience, he was amazed at the amount of attention the twins were receiving before being bundled hastily into the club.

On entrance Stanley tried to adjust his eyesight from the strobe like flashes from the camera's to the booming music and strong vibrating bass line which thudded and reverberated around the red velvet line walls, a tall female emerged dressed in a tight black cat suit with a big gold chain which read "Cyber Babe", her jet black hair was pulled back into a tight ponytail she seemed very stern and robotic "hi girls I'll show you to your table" she mentioned before turning and leading them into the heaving club.

Stanley became excited he never really had done any sort of clubbing before so to him this was like an adventure he nearly got lost with the fact he was at work as such, he stared wide eyed at all of the people dancing and acting crazy there was a boundless energy he could feel the adrenalin as girls gyrated on tables in the tiniest shorts and bra tops he craned his neck as they walked past before he felt the hand of Carissa pull him towards her direction, "Stanley your ours tonight no looking" she shouted back at him.

All three made their way through the crowds they were led to an area near the back of the club it was cordoned off with a red velvet rope and guarded by a burly muscle bound security man who looked like an American professional wrestler, he stepped to the side as the hostess unhooked the rope and let them into a coolly purple neon lit booth, on the table were three silver buckets of champagne and glasses which were turned upside down on a tray, "ok ladies and gent, anything you need I'm your hostess Stacey", she said before stepping out and hooking the rope back.

"Well this is nice" said Stanley he looked around nodding his head in appreciation, from their position they had a vantage point where they could look down towards the dance floor, "time to dance baby" Melissa screamed out stepping forward to get her space to dance "pour some drinks then Mr Spank" she turned towards an impressed and gawping Stanley, "right away" he responded jumping to attention like a butler anytime Melissa barked an order.

Carissa sat calmly looking vacant while Stanley did the honours, it was strange how the twins were so different Stanley sensed that this was not really Carissa's type of thing but she was keeping up appearances for the wilder and more outgoing sister, "champagne?" Stanley popped the cork and began to pour a glass and reached over to give to Carissa, "cheer up" he said as Carissa looked beyond him towards her sister giving him a plastic smile after his comment.

Stanley poured another glass and turned towards Melissa who was grinding up and down to the booming dance music, he felt a bit uncomfortable approaching her hesitant as he walked up behind her, this made Carissa chuckle to herself watching him tip toeing around her crazy sister who continued with her hi energy Zumba style dance moves "err Melissa champagne" he shouted above the din.

Melissa spun around and draped her arms around Stanley knocking the glass and spilling the drink onto the sleeve of his jacket she stared demonically at Stanley and continued to grind up against him, Stanley became hot and flustered he was not much of a dancer never had been he just felt clumsy which did not help his smooth persona he sort of half smiled not really sure what to do, "boring!" Melissa screamed grabbing her drink and stepping off back towards the edge of their area. Stanley walked back taking off his jacket and wiping off the champagne spillage, "wow is she always like that?" he quizzed Carissa as he walked back towards her and sat down, "I need a glass after that" he said sounding relieved leaning back into the comfort of the black cushioned seat, "let me pour you a drink" a compassionate Carissa grabbed the bottle and poured a glass for Stanley who laid his blazer to the side on the seat, "thank you kindly" Stanley said holding up his glass which fizzed over to toast with Carissa.

"So who are you girls?" a more relaxed less tetchy Stanley asked, "our dad is Vincent Le Chad he owns a multimillion cosmetic brand, we are his only offspring", Carissa said casually her soft voice barely heard as Stanley lent in to listen to her, he turned and stared into her eyes she smiled back before sipping her champagne, Stanley's eyes were wide open "wow I can't believe it, so I'm sitting with a millionairess" he mused leaning back to digest the information.

Suddenly in a rare moment of clarity Stanley realised he was living his dream the one him and Jerry would always fantasise about on the banks of the river Ty, beautiful women albeit not Mila Kunis but rich successful women fancy cars plush hotels and champagne, he took another sip and sat back watching a clearly energetic Melissa going through an array of lung busting dance moves, he surveyed the bouncing club with all of the lights and multi-colour lasers flashing across the dance floor, he stroked his hair back, before turning back to Carissa "cheers!" he said raising his glass again surprising Carissa who responded by clinking her glass against his.

"Come on let's dance" Stanley suddenly plucked up enough courage and enthusiasm grabbing her hand, "are you crazy?" she responded laughing and feeding off Stanley's new energy, she laughed cutely actually getting up and finally began to dance very seductively with Stanley who himself did not actually have any moves of note but he was high on life and just did a happy jig followed by a poorly executed robot move which definitely amused Carissa, "hey are you trying to leave me out?" Melissa bounded over sweating profusely from her exertions grabbing the champagne bottle and swigging it before bouncing up and down as the three of them threw some shapes, Stanley's world at this moment was a good one he was finally having fun even smiling with the caustic Melissa.

A few hours later the three of them stumbled out of the club Stanley in his white shirt which was now untucked and holding his blazer, he had his arms over the shoulders of the twins who were both clearly drunk and merry, a few more flashes from the gaggle of paparazzi who remained outside and continued to shout orders towards them, the three were oblivious too drunk to really give a monkeys as they walked towards the waiting car. The beautiful tall model like driver opened the door with a pert smile as she greeted them all, for the first time Stanley's English gent mask had slipped he was just being plain Stanley Spank enjoying himself his clients were not complaining as all three bundled their way into the back of the car.

"Ok what's next?" the still very hyped up Mellissa asked, only to be met by fits of laughter by Stanley and Carissa, "well I'm yours for as long as you want me" a clearly giddy Stanley responded attempting to sit up straight adopting a now more congenial stance, which lasted for about two seconds before the rampant Melissa kicked her legs onto his lap and rubbed them up and down "well is that right now?" she said putting her finger into her mouth and sucking it slowly and provocatively while purring like a cat, Carissa pushed her twin sisters legs away "leave him, he's better than that" she sprang to Stanley's defence passionately staring at Melissa who scowled and kissed her teeth before petulantly whipping her feet away, "thank you" an impressed Stanley countered, "please ladies no fighting" he continued trying to hold a serious face before they all cracked up laughing as the car sped through the city.

They approached a grand looking building it was magnificent with orange spot lights shining against the brown medieval brick work, a door man dressed immaculately in a black overcoat with red stitching on the cuffs stepped towards the car and opened the door.

Stanley still in awe at the beautifully crafted architecture was slow to move arcing his head through the window, "come on Stanley we're home" said Carissa she tugged his sleeve pulling him towards an exit, "home? wow" a now more sober Stanley continued stepping out into the fresh air still straining his neck ogling the tall building. "Fancy a night cap Spank?" a still feisty and energetic Melissa asked alluringly before flouncing up the steps and through the swish glass doors, leaving Carissa to link arms with Stanley and walk with him towards the building "don't worry Stanley our driver will take you back when you're ready", a caring and tired sounding Carissa Le Chad mentioned she clung on tightly as Stanley stiffened up feeling the night breeze cut through his shirt.

Once up and into the apartment Stanley's breath was taken away by a cool contemporary penthouse sparsely furnished with a large red sofa and a long glass coffee table Stanley stood in the middle of the circular lounge room with a panoramic view that was to behold, all of the city lights were radiant in the distance an orange glow amongst the varied buildings that formed the concrete backdrop.

Stanley's gaze was interrupted as Melissa came and placed her arms around his waist leaning her head onto his back "oh Stanley come away from the window" she said spinning him around to face her, Stanley looked directly into her eyes his mind was awash with thoughts driven by alcohol and a boyish giddiness induced by being surrounded by such beauty and splendour, "what a great view" Stanley declared his voice only quietened when he saw the light brown cat like eyes of Melissa delving deep into his.

He stood back to admire her she really did have a measured beauty her brown skin smooth and flawless, "are you talking about me?" she questioned before breaking out into a fit of giggles which slowly subsided into an awkward silence, she pulled Stanley towards her by his shirt collars and kissed him hard on his mouth, at first he hesitated and tried to pull back but Melissa reasserted her grip and pulled him towards her lips again locking on to him forcefully. Stanley's heart pounded as she continued to devour him sticking her tongue into his mouth to both his surprise and weirdly delight, Melissa groaned then pulled away leaving Stanley in a suspense like state, "not bad Mr Spank not bad at all" Melissa licked her lips before sauntering away, "fix yourself a drink Stanley", again she ordered walking slowly towards her room.

Stanley was still swooning from their clinch barely able to fathom what was occurring before Carissa returned dressed in a fluffy white bathrobe with a towel wrapped around her head she walked barefooted towards him, her face was clear no make-up her features were softer than her twin which was the only trait to distinguish the two "that feels better" she said removing the towel from her head allowing for her wet hair to drop down onto her shoulders "did my sister offer you a drink?", she seemed now more relaxed and confident clearly at home.

Stanley still stood shellshocked he was lost in the sheer beauty of the twins but more captured by their ying and yang difference, Carissa walked over to him and grabbed his hand "come and sit down" she spoke so softly pulling him towards the large red sofa, they both collapsed onto the cushioning "why are you two single?" a puzzled Stanley asked throwing up his hands "look at what you have, money, beauty a great place to live" he continued to babble on, Carissa just smiled sweetly, "you don't get it do you Stanley?" she spoke and placed her hand onto Stanley's face turning it towards her, again her beauty shone back at him her big full pink lips and distinctive light brown eyes even her nose was small and cute with a smattering of freckles, Stanley could only shake his head and whisper the word "no", Carissa smiled "ahh babe all we get is jerks and gold diggers, that's why we chose this route", Stanley finally got it a light bulb came on in his head, "ahh yeah ok I get it" he nodded before relaxing back into the comfort of the large seat.

"Let me get you a drink" he said suddenly remembering his manners and getting up to grab a bottle of champagne and flutes which were on a side table, "here we go" he said handing Carissa the flutes before twisting the cap off and forcing the cork which flew into the air accompanied by a loud pop, Carissa let out a shriek as the bubbles spilled over onto the carpet. Stanley poured some into Carissa's tall frosted flute, she giggled as he filled her glass up to the brim the bubbles fizzed "thank you" she replied courteously, he finally took a seat holding both the bottle and his flute.

"Wow what a great night" he commented looking directly at Carissa who seemed to blush and giggle like a school girl every time she locked eyes with Stanley, "why are you an escort Stanley?", Carissa asked again her voice was soft she dreamily stared at Stanley who himself laughed nervously stroking back his hair "well I.." before he could answer the other twin Melissa marched out of the bedroom "hey where's my drink?" her impromptu entrance as the bold drama queen interrupting the moment, she clambered onto the sofa on the other side of Stanley brusquely grabbing the bottle from him and taking a large swig gulping it down before croaking out a large burp accompanied by a crass laugh she then dipped her fingers into her bra pulling out a small folded piece of paper.

She too had now changed and wore a revealing black lace two piece underwear which showed off her ample assets her long jet black hair was also now tussled down to her shoulders, Stanley stared at her nipples which protruded though her underwear, Carissa rolled her eyes "no class" she uttered under her breath before sipping daintily from her glass.

Stanley sat back he was once again in the middle enjoying the dynamic of the twins fighting over his attention, Mellissa lent forward and poured the contents of the paper onto the table, a small mound of white powder she laughed heinously and her eyes lit up she looked back at the both of them with a cheeky grin again followed by a nervous giggle "and here's one I made earlier" she declared pulling a rolled fifty pound note from her other bra cup, "who's on it?" she continued leaning forward carefully flattening and separating the powder into lines.

Carissa rolled her eyes and shook her head covering her face with her hand while Stanley looked on in a trance like state this job did not feel like work for him it was more of a hot date with two stunners one who was completely crazy and the other who was completely to die for his thoughts were a long way from Ami as he lay back embracing the attention "come on girls can't we all get along" he laughed putting his arms around them both "come on group hug" he continued pulling them both into him. Carissa was happy to snuggle up to his chest while Melissa who was still helping herself to the cocaine sniffing loudly and aggressively until she turned with the remnants of the white powder smattered around her nose "ahh yeah that's better" she grabbed him tightly pushing her sister to the side in the process.

He seemed confident probably due to the alcohol consumption Dutch courage maybe but he found the twins receptive they both broke into laughter and squeezed up to Stanley who clumsily caused a spillage from his glass onto Melissa's chest "oops sorry" he sat up quickly knocking his elbow onto Carissa's head "ow!" she screamed rubbing her hand on her still damp hair, "oh god sorry" a flustered Stanley turned to Carissa who started laughing looking up at him.

"Stanley" a seductive call from Melissa who was now laying back stretching out on the sofa with the champagne bottle raised above her torso, "I quite liked that, want to do it again?" she began to slowly pour the contents of the bottle over her chest splashing the liquid everywhere with a naughty laugh both Carissa and Stanley sat watching her, "Mel! What's wrong with you?" she screamed at her sister, who continued to dowse herself clearly enjoying her antics.

Melissa continued to hysterically laugh as the bubbles frothed up on her brown skin she gyrated slowly clearly enjoying the feel of the champagne on her body, "come and help yourself Stanley and don't stop until you've licked it all up" again Melissa looked up seductively sticking out her tongue to emphasise her point, Stanley did not know what to do or where to put his face but he was grinning like a crazy man he had never seen anything like this and found it quite funny.

Carissa was not impressed and got up stomping away "I'm going, you two can carry on with your debaunch stupidity!" she moaned frustrated by her sister's antics, "Carissa wait!" Stanley suddenly found enough reason to get distracted away from Melissa he swiftly got up and chased after Carissa "wait" he said again catching her before she disappeared into her room, he grabbed her and unbeknown to him why he planted a firm hard long kiss onto her lips to which a shocked Carissa succumbed and responded by kissing him back hard.

The kiss lasted for about a twenty seconds before Stanley felt hands grab his waist from behind he spun to see

Mellissa standing dripping wet in next to nothing "what about my kiss Mr Spank?" she asked before taking control and grabbing his face pulling him towards her, she kissed him hard almost sucking his tongue from his head, it felt totally different from the soft lips of Carissa much more aggressive with the taste of alcohol and bitter cocaine swishing around in his mouth, "hey that's enough now" Carissa moaned trying her best to part them both, which she was nearly successful with until Melissa began to rip Stanley's shirt off by roughly popping off each button.

Stanley laughed nervously he was being twisted back around by Carissa who seemed to be in direct competition with her sister she rubbed his bum before again kissing him softly, "No more" she stopped abruptly putting her finger against his lips leaving Stanley breathless and moving his lips like a fish out of water, but before he was able to compute what was happening Melissa again grabbed his head and twisted his face around to kiss him again ravishing her hands on his chest wildly.

Stanley was perplexed he did not know what was going on, he glanced over and saw Carissa standing watching she looked genuinely upset biting onto her thumb nail, for some reason at that moment Stanley felt wrong he prised himself away from the hungry Melissa and held onto her stopping her from trying to devour him "ok let's just cool down for a sec, I'm supposed to be working" he declared, still staring in the line of Carissa, "no Stanley you're working for us", Melissa countered grabbing at him, "no we should stop" he said stepping away, "I need to be going now" he said looking around for his blazer hastily clearly in a bit of a tizz.

Carissa turned and disappeared into her room slamming the door as she went in, "well Spank that just leaves me and you", again she prowled following Stanley around the room in hot pursuit, he backed off grabbing his jacket and retreated tripping over his own feet in the process, suddenly his mind sobered he began to babble to an insistent Melissa "look I think we should call it a night, it's been great but..." Stanley continued to back away almost pleading with Melissa who seemed hell bent on getting her man or at least some of him. "Stanley don't run you want this" she teased striding forward putting her finger in her mouth and sucking it seductively twirling her tongue around it, her eyes were trained directly onto her prey, Stanley backed away some more until he was cornered between the wall and the front door, he started putting his jacket on "look it's been lovely but..", Stanley did not get time to talk again before the lips of Melissa connected to his locking them together she ate away on his lips hard and forced her tongue into his mouth again this surprised Stanley who got his arms caught up in a tangle trying to quickly put his jacket on.

Melissa forced him back into the corner and pressed her wet body up against him, she became more frantic her approach was lustful and animated, Stanley pushed back finally managing to release his lips, he gasped a sharp intake of breath "look" he said sternly, "we can't do this", as he spoke Carissa reappeared from her room peering from a distance, "let him go Mel", she ordered her voice carrying in the pause of action.

Melissa huffed and turned round to give her sister a fierce stare before focusing back onto Stanley she let out a hysterical laugh then rolled her eyes and groaned "ok you can go home Stanley" she spoke in a husky deadpan tone dismissing him defeated twirling away playfully before strolling back to the sofa, her peachy bum cheeks tantalisingly protruding from her black lace knickers.

Stanley finally relaxed and untangled himself from his twisted jacket sleeves, he took his time and pulled on his jacket tugging the sleeves into place, he swept back his hair and stood upright composing himself, "the driver is waiting downstairs", Carissa spoke the calm voice of reason. Stanley stared a last gaze at Carissa who looked sexy her dressing gown open showing off her fine figure in a pink two piece, Melissa stretched out on the sofa, waving to Stanley as she laid down, Stanley turned sharply and left closing the door behind him.

He took a big breathe a sigh of relief, before walking towards the lift, "that was mental", he said to himself pressing the button attempting to gather his thoughts he was still feeling the rush of adrenalin which had taken over from the liquor which fuzzed his mind.

The elevator arrived with the sound of a loud bell signifying its ascent, the door slid open and Stanley was about to step in when he heard the front door of the Le Chad twins apartment open, he turned to see Carissa poke her head out he was somewhat shocked when he saw her, "Stanley wait" she mouthed in a hush tone, as she walked fleet footed towards him she still wore her dressing gown open revealing her sexy underwear.

Stanley was mesmerised if not a little surprised, as she approached she began to giggle shyly she closed up her gown folding her arms across her body, "look I'm sorry about all that, Melissa is a bit crazy but she means well", she began to speak still in a barely raised voice, Stanley kept quiet and listened he was too tired now to really figure out where this was all going, "let me put my number in your phone Mr Spank I would love to see you again, you are a true gent" Carissa looked up coyly slightly blushing her eyelids fluttered.

Stanley was shocked but smiled back at her warmly "ok thank you" he replied nodding his head in approval, he began to put his hands into his pocket searching for his phone, he became concerned when he did not feel the device and began to pat down his pockets "I don't believe this" he sighed his eyes rolling towards the heavens, "I've lost my phone" he spoke sounding frustrated. Carissa looked up at him "don't worry I've brought one of these" she said cheekily pulling a card from inside of her pink satin bra, "call me Stanley please" she sounded sincere while reaching up planting a longing kiss onto his cheek and shoving the card into his trouser pocket squeezing the top of groin before walking away.

Stanley sat alone in the back of the car, the world seemed normal and sober now he was tired and rested back into the seat staring blankly out of the window, for the first time his mind was full of thoughts for Ami, he was feeling guilty as much as he had enjoyed his night he could not help but feel as if he had cheated, this was supposed to be work not as much fun as the night turned out to be, it was a crazy but Stanley was beginning to think whether he could continue leading this double life, he glanced up and could see the beautiful driver peering back at him through the rear-view mirror, she was stunning but her beauty did nothing to waver his thoughts at this time, he just wanted to get back and sleep.

After arriving back at the hotel the stunning driver opened the door, "sir" she motioned to a weary Stanley he pulled himself up and out of the car, looking the tall glamorous driver straight in the face, they held a stare for a few seconds before Stanley smiled and held his hand out to shake her hand, they touched then Stanley pulled her hand up and kissed it "thank you", he said politely, before stepping towards the hotel entrance shaking his head in disbelief, he did not look back he just heard the car drive away.

Finally he was back in his room the early signs of dawn began to creep in as the skies became a lighter shade of blue, Stanley looked around the room, it was just as he had left it with his clothes strewn all over the place similar to his own bedroom, he tossed his jacket onto the back of the chair kicked off his shoes then flopped onto his large bed, "oww" he grimaced feeling a dull pain in his back, he flipped around and felt the object underneath him, "bloody hell" he said he saw his phone and picked it up quickly looking at the screen, there were over ten missed calls from Ami, "ahh man" he blurted out the realisation hit him he was already in the doghouse and now she would be even more angry and suspicious, Stanley half thought to call her but at five in the morning it was probably not a great idea, he laid back clutching the phone to his chest and closed his eyes he was totally drained.

A strong buzz vibrated ferociously almost shocking Stanley into life like a defibrillator his bleary eyes opened as he clutched the phone which was still balanced on his chest, he groaned annoyed at the fact he was being woken until he looked at the screen and saw Ami's name flashing up before him, "ahh crap" his mouth was dry and his head still fuzzy but he knew he could not ignore her call, he fumbled with the screen before answering his voice gruff and low "morning" he said sounding half asleep.

"Stanley where have you been? I've called you all night", her voice was strained and she sounded emotional "where are you?" she continued now noticeably getting more upset as she spoke, Stanley sat up jerked in to a upright position the guilt from his eventful night began to creep in as he paused searching for an answer but his brain was still not engaged enough he stuttered and coughed before he answered "it was a late one babe", those few words trickled from his mouth in a slightly insincere tone, "is that all you can say Stanley?", Ami's sharp answer stabbed him right back he was shocked at the seriousness and anger in her tone.

He raked his fingers through his hair his mind still vacant and fuzzy "I worked a double shift Ami" he said firmly feeling agitated now but he did not want to argue "look babe I'll be back in a few hours we'll catch up when I get home", he laid back down breathing out a big sigh, an awkward pause ensued he could hear Ami whimpering clearly upset, his mind seized up he strangely could not find any words of comfort "look" he said before being interrupted by Ami, "It's ok Stanley I'll see you later" she just about got her words out she was clearly on the brink of tears, again another moment of silence, "bye" she snivelled then cut off the call.

Stanley's stomach churned he felt physically sick "damn man" he let out a cry of angst suddenly he was wide awake stunned he could not believe that he would ever upset Ami, that sickly feeling returned to the pit of his stomach, it was galling he was now so consumed by guilt his thoughts turned to the moral essence of his job, to him it was all about the money but last night showed him that he was loving the life maybe more than the pay, he did not want to hurt Ami in his head he was doing this for her now, but he knew it was going to get harder to mask the true nature of how he earned his bread.

He stood up and began to change from the clothes he slept in he was still lost in his thoughts emptying his pockets when he felt the card left by Carissa, he took it out and looked at it "*Carissa Le Chad Pemberton Mansions 07854669885*", it read, he stared at it and recalled all of the action from the last few hours it did not feel like escort work more like a crazy night out, he knew Ami meant more to him than his bank balance but also he knew that he loved the unpredictability of each job, "what she don't know won't hurt her" he mumbled to himself defiantly shoving the card into his jacket pocket he sounded ruthless and moody now grumpy even before he stepped into the shower.

Stanley was now home relaxed in his bedroom he was totally absorbed by his computer game sitting on the floor in a grey tracksuit with the hood over his head, it was dark and only the manic glare from his TV flickered a beam throughout the room. He was in a sombre mood pensive even obviously still stewing from his exchange with Ami, he sat rapidly pressing the buttons on the remote control a piece of his fair mop of hair protruding from the top of his hood, his phone began to flash and although on silent mode the heavy vibration alerted him to it, "hello" he answered in a deep grumpy husk.

The voice that came back certainly perked him up just by the sheer energy which translated "hello Mr Spank how's you sir?", it was the unmistakable voice of Charles Carter a flamboyant ball of energy he always seemed to put Stanley on edge just due to his natural effervescence, "I'm fine" Stanley responded with a little more enthusiasm just to be courteous, "are you on board with my proposal?", Charles Carter cut straight to the chase, Stanley mulled for about thirty seconds, Charles could hear his brain cogs churning "look you get a free holiday, get paid handsomely and get to spend time with me" Charles laughed playfully.

Stanley still stalled he could only think of the drama this would cause with Ami but then something in his mind snapped, "yeah why not I'm up for it" he said defiantly' "ohh wonderful" Charles Carter squealed very excited "ok darling I will text you the details we disembark in one week bye!", a clearly exuberant Charles Carter disconnected the phone, Stanley was quite nonchalant and tossed the phone onto his bed before getting back to his game.

As the night wore on Stanley knew in his heart that at some point he would have to call Ami and face the music he had deliberately avoided contacting her as he had the feeling she would still be annoyed he thought best to leave it a while at least enough so he could figure out how he would handle the situation, womens emotions were not really a strong point in Stanley's make up only the recent escapades with the clients could serve as any reference.

"Stanley Spank get down here now!" Brenda shouted her voice strained as she continued to call up the stairs, "what mum?" Stanley replied frustrated by her untimely interruption he got up and moved towards his bedroom door he could hear his mum stomping up the stairs by her heavy footsteps he knew she was not happy at something. He opened the door to see his mum who had climbed the stairs with some effort by the look of her face which was red and flushed, "now young man I don't know what you get up to at night but you need to start talking fast!" she was at the top of the stairs and pushed a copy of the national newspaper into his chest, the force of which made Stanley step back one foot into his room, "what are you going on about?" he fired back himself now quite confused and shocked, "is that how I raised you?" again Brenda forcefully pushed the daily rag into him.

Stanley took the hood off his head and stared down at the paper, "oh no…" he sounded defeated looking down and seeing a picture of him and the Le Chad twins stumbling out from the club the night before with headline "*Twin action*", the actual photograph made Stanley look like quite a playboy with his arms draped over both of the twins who themselves looked worse for wear not that it helped in any way, "well I'm waiting" Brenda continued her annoyance hardly subsiding, Stanley stood open mouthed staring the picture "well I went out with some friends" he feebly offered which irked his mum more "I should give you a bloody clip round the ear" she said biting her lip, before turning away and marching back down the stairs "your father will be home soon" again her vexed tone left Stanley scratching his head, "mum I need my passport" he shot a paltry request which was ignored by a clearly steaming Brenda.

Before he could even digest everything again his phone was buzzing away in his pocket he was still absorbed in the headline making piece, he pulled the phone out of his pocket and saw Ami's name flashing his heart beat harder he knew he would have to face many questions from the last episode at her home, "hi Ami" his voice sounded hesitant, he could hear her but instead of speaking he could only hear what sounded like somebody whimpering, "Ami?" he called out concerned but again all he could hear was her snivelling "why Stanley?" her voice cracked with emotion she was clearly upset "who are those girls? Why are you in the papers? who are you?" her voice heightened the tension and angst seeped through. Stanley's heart sank it felt like of all the blood had just literally drained from his body he was overcome with guilt and lost for words he moved into his room and slumped onto his bed, "babe it's not what you think I promise" he managed to solemnly reply which fuelled Ami's emotion, she began to bawl uncontrollably unable to hold back her tears.

Stanley felt awful his stomach churned like a tumble dryer he went numb there was no way he would ever intentionally hurt or upset Ami not in this way he could not even muster two words of comfort he could only listen the snuffle and snivel of his girlfriend, "you break my heart Stanley" her broken dialect abound as she released her words "please do not call" before she disconnected the call clearly distraught. Stanley felt sick he held the phone and stared at it his first reaction was to redial Ami his heart was pumping even his emotions were now charged, Ami's phone rang while Stanley held his breath just waiting again to hear her voice but to no avail as the ringing was cut short and diverted to her voicemail. Stanley chucked his phone onto the floor in frustration as he stared back at the ruffled newspaper with the picture the more he looked at it he realised what an idiot he'd been and just how this must of looked to Ami he felt more gutted with the fact he did not come clean at the beginning and his judgment was so off it dawned on him that he may have just lost the best thing that had happened to him.

As he sat staring pensively ahead he could hear more footsteps coming up the stairs followed by a polite knock on his bedroom door, he was not in the mood for another earful from his mum but braced himself regardless, "Stan can I come in?" this time the quiet voice of his dad came as a sense of relief although he knew Greg would have something to add to his mothers fury, "yeah come in dad" he said his tone barely raised his downbeat mood reflected his feeling.

Greg sat down beside him on the bed at first he did or said nothing but just stared ahead at the crazy coloured screen which had the computer game still running, "it's not what it looks like dad" Stanley broke the silence "I was just working and having fun", he offered disconsolate in his expression, Greg scratched his stubble chin grating his fingers coarsely he searched for something to say, "look son your mothers upset because you lied to her", he offered diplomatically picking up the paper and studied the photograph, "they aren't bad either" he chuckled to himself attempting to inject a slice of humour, to which Stanley responded by cracking a small smile "it's not just mum I upset it's Ami too", again Stanley's furrowed expression came to the fore as soon as he mentioned Ami's name, again Greg scratched his chin, he mused for a few seconds before offering his son some pearls of wisdom, "you see son..." he began candidly "women like to feel special unique even", he continued turning to Stanley and placing his arm around him "all I'm saying is if she is special then fight to make her happy", he shrugged and patted Stanley on his shoulder offering a tiny crumb of sympathy, "oh and your mum told me to give you this" he stood up and dug his passport out from his back pocket then handed it to Stanley, "I won't ask", he continued holding out his hands before walking towards the door, "thanks dad" Stanley replied gratefully looking up at Greg who winked back at him before closing the door behind him.

Another call to Ami's phone and another voicemail, she had clearly switched her phone off to avoid his overtures, this time Stanley left a message "Ami please call me we need to talk", he sounded desperate and dejected, lost even, he thought of her father Lars and the warning he gave him before that night, he knew he would be spitting feathers and out for his blood he wanted to get to Ami before she relayed any news to her parents, he jumped up from his bed and began getting himself ready to go out, with his dads words still fresh in his mind he decided to take action.

It was getting later into the night but Stanley was determined to see Ami's regardless, he bounded down the stairs and went straight out without notice, he walked quickly knowing that he could catch the last bus to Underbridge if he hurried up even breaking out into a casual jog sporadically, his breathing became heavy as he rushed towards the town the years of smoking clearly doing him no favours as he wheezed his way through the streets in the night air.

Finally Stanley boarded the last bus to Underbridge he checked his phone and saw it was 11.35 he knew time was against him but he had to try he had a new zest about him after the lull of guilt had consumed him, for the first time he was showing a bit of passion for something, he did not even know what he was going to say once he arrived but he knew he had to try and retrieve something from their fledgling relationship.

The bus was empty only an elderly couple sat at the front the woman with her head lent against her partners shoulder, it dawned on him whether he and Ami would ever get the opportunity to grow old and graceful together or would his misdemeanor cost him, it was a fleeting thought which shook him as the bus swept into Underbridge.

Stanley nodded to the driver as he stepped off and walked the short distance towards Ami's building, it was dark and quiet as he made his way towards her flat, there were no lights on which indicated that she was most probably sleeping but he had come this far and was not about to turn around now.

On his approach he stopped and gathered himself just pausing briefly and taking a breath, "ok here goes" he mumbled before pressing on the intercom buzzer which seemed twice as loud in the night silence. At first there was nothing but Stanley waited patiently before pressing it again, the sound again droned before a sleepy voice responded "yes who's is it?" Ami asked her voice clearly surprised by the late visitor, "it's me Stanley" Stanley put his mouth close to the intercom, before hearing the door release.

Stanley reached the front door which was left slightly ajar he could hear the shuffle of Ami's feet as her slippers slapped against the floor, he pushed his way in gently tip toeing into her place, he was met by an unimpressed half asleep and fed up looking Ami who stood with her arms folded defiantly half dressed in a baggy tee shirt which ironically belonged to him, her face looked tired and pale with her short hair for once messy and ruffled.

Stanley closed the door and took careful pigeon steps towards her "hi" he whispered tentatively his head slightly bowed clearly embarrassed "what do you want?" Ami asked her voice creaking with emotion mixed with tiredness, her eyes were red she had clearly been crying, Stanley moved forward he just wanted to give her a hug but Ami's response was to walk away with her back to him, "please babe I came to talk", he pleaded "just give me a few minutes" he opened his hands almost begging for an opportunity to state his case.

Ami moved further away from him and sat down on her sofa, "talk then let me hear what you have to say then you can go", again her response was cold and cutting each repel landed like a blow to Stanley's heart, "ok well" he stuttered clearing his throat before announcing "it's my job I'm a male escort" a spluttered confession which caused Ami to shake her head she even managed a slight chortle to herself, "is that the best you can come up with?" she asked whilst continuing to laugh out of utter disbelief "male escort really Stanley?" again she repeated his claim which followed by a disparaging laugh, "it's true I'm doing it for us" Stanley blurted out his comments fuelled with emotion rather than tact.

Ami grabbed her ears with both hands she no longer wanted to listen to his excuses she continued to shake her head before letting out a loud scream, which made Stanley jump out of his skin, "I can't take you seriously" Ami shouted at him amazed at his gall, "ok please just let me explain" again Stanley pleaded he could see she was now getting upset, "I just wanted to make enough money for us it's not what you think" his words were impassioned he moved closer to Ami with his arms outstretched yearning for a hug or some sort of reconciliation but his overtures were rejected by a clearly hurt Ami who began to freak out shaking her head and waving her hands "no just go now please just leave me alone" her voice shook with emotion she did not even look up towards him.

Stanley felt awful seeing her that way was not something he was prepared for he backtracked towards the door feeling the tension "alright I'm going" holding his hands up in surrender his tone now low and sullen "I love you", he mouthed before turning and walking through the door closing it quietly.

Stanley wandered slowly back down the path outside Ami's flat he was gutted and felt a truly hollow feeling, his head was absent he did not even know where he was going or how he was getting home this was the worst he had felt ever, the thought of being without his girlfriend filled him with dread, he stopped and sat on the floor his energy sapped, he looked up towards the window of Ami's flat he could still see the light on and gazed upwardly for a few seconds before putting his hands into his head shaking it continuously, he could not believe what was happening the last twenty four hours had been a merry go round and one that he was not equipped to handle.

Stanley pulled his phone from his pocket and began to type on the screen a spontaneous text hoping to at least touch Ami's heart, *"I'm sorry hope we can work it out"*, he paused before defiantly pressing the button which sent the message, he blew out heavily before rising to his feet and walking down the dark path towards the town centre.

It had been a few days now since Stanley last heard from Ami, he mooched in his room on most of those days not doing much at all just hanging out playing his game and listening to music, he was moody and thoughtful very quiet and distant, he reflected on the last few months and how much his life had changed he chewed ferociously on gum rocking his head as loud music pumped from his cd player, the many questions that entered his mind all led back to the moral dilemma of doing the job and having a girlfriend for many hours he had tossed around everything his head similar to clothes in a washing machine different thoughts churned jumbling his mind, the problem was he actually liked the money and adventure of working for Cassandra it gave him an escape but it did not give him something he wanted which was Ami.

"Oi Stan…Stan!" Greg's strained voice could just about be heard above the din causing Stanley to spring up quickly reaching for the volume button, the music subsided enough before a relieved Greg stepped into the room, "son what are you doing?" Greg looked at a dejected figure as Stanley flopped back onto his bed slumping back into the pillows, "nothing" he grumbled staring up towards the ceiling, "listen son give her time she'll calm down soon then you can talk", his wise words falling on a distracted Stanley who frowned before responding, "I'm going away at the weekend dad got business abroad" his low tone lacked enthusiasm, "oh yeah business is it?" Greg responded rolling his eyes and shaking his head before walking out mumbling to himself.

The day had finally arrived for Stanley's trip with a certain Charles Carter a long weekend in Monaco had become very appealing now especially with everything that had been going on at home and with Ami, Stanley squeezed down his suitcase and pulled the zip tightly around the robust black luggage, he had tried to call Ami several times in the last few days all to no avail, she was still not answering any of his calls or replying to the number of texts he sent her but still determined in his mind Stanley was of the thinking that when he got back he would still win her round.

The instructions had been sent from Charles Carter a car would be picking him up from his house and then he would meet Charles Carter at the airport, although this was a new and exciting venture for Stanley he was still in a reflective mood and very casual, in his mind he was just thinking a few days away somewhere foreign and a hefty financial reward at the end of it, all he had to do was look pretty for his client. The house was empty as both of his parents had gone to work he was still not on the best of terms with his mum who was still quietly seething at the newspaper picture, it seemed to sum up his whole world at the moment very empty on one hand but with something to hang onto in terms of his work.

Stanley humped his case down the stairs as the call came through from the driver to notify him of his arrival, he looked good in a plain white polo tee shirt with shades which dangled from the collar and fitted jeans with a new pair of black suede loafers, he knew in this business it was mainly about first impressions and although this was a private job he knew that if he was working for Cassandra he would have to present himself in the best light.

As he stepped out onto his doorstep he was amazed to see a gleaming black Rolls Royce complete with a well heeled chauffeur stood upright and steadfast awaiting his passenger, "morning sir" he greeted Stanley stepping forward to grab his case and then retreated to open the door. Stanley quickly did one last check to make sure he had all of his bits, keys passport and phone, before stepping into the vehicle, he looked out he could see one of the neighbours curtains twitching obviously having a nose at the outside activities, Stanley smiled curtly before leaning back into his seat, he knew Charles Carter was a very eccentric man and obviously never did anything by half, he just told himself to enjoy the adventure as he knew it definitely would be one and at least for the time being he was able to escape all of his domestic woes.

The drive took him through lush country fields and lanes it was quiet and smooth with the driver not even breaking into conversation, Stanley felt like a celebrity being driven to a secret location, he was able to stretch out his lean frame in the spacious luxury car, which looked and smelt brand new, it gave him a sense of power as if he were someone important. He was able to ponder how his life had changed as he sped through the vast green scenery the fact of the matter was he loved all of the pomp and ceremony which surrounded each job it was as addictive as the money and he knew it, it almost gave him an arrogance probably that was what his mum was trying to tell him in her reaction to the Le Chad twins picture, but as far as Stanley was concerned he just wanted to make more money his dream of whisking Ami to a surprise holiday still remained a force in his motives regardless of their current situation.

After an long drive they arrived at a private airfield Stanley sat up and looked around he could see in the distance another Rolls Royce this time a shiny white one which shone brightly against the back drop of the green airfield it was parked beside a gleaming private jet which definitely made Stanley perk up from his low slung disposition.

It was a scene which resembled that of a movie or one of those MTV rap music videos he and Jerry used to watch, it was a definite adrenalin rush. The car slowed to a halt pulling up adjacent to the identical Rolls Royce "one moment sir" the drivers monotone voice sounded as he stepped out and walked around to the back of the car to remove the luggage, a sense of anticipation came over Stanley nerves even as the extent of what loomed ahead began to hit home. He was eager and felt ready to get out of the car and jump onto the plane he was so excited this was the first time he had ever been near a plane let alone a plush gleaming private jet.

His gaze was interrupted when out of the corner of his eye he caught sight of his client Charles Carter for the first time it was then when the butterflies really hit his stomach, the large figure clambered from the white Rolls Royce looking resplendent dressed in a lime green shirt, white shorts and same coloured flip flops his shirt buttons just about holding together with the strain as his large belly bulged, he was chattering away on his phone and peering into the window at Stanley.

"Spank!" he shouted before gesturing to the driver to open the door, Stanley smiled awkwardly "oh god here we go" he muttered under his breath before the door was eventually swung open, a moments hesitation followed before Charles Carter's energetic squeal ejected Stanley from his seated position, "hi Mr. Carter" he spluttered shyly bumbling his way out of the car and extending his hand, "well hello gorgeous and call me Charles" Charles Carter was a gregarious man he exuded happiness as he grabbed Stanley's hand tightly almost pulling him in towards his vast frame, "one sec" he whispered indicating he was still on the phone call.

Stanley stretched and then swept his hair back surveying his surroundings while Charles Carter continued to chatter a million miles per hour into his phone, "well Beatrice I have to go we'll catch up in Singapore mwah" he finished the call with an over exaggerated air kiss and then turned to divert his attention towards Stanley. The drivers from both cars dragged the luggage towards the jet, "well look at you sir as handsome as ever" Charles Carter seductively gave Stanley the once over looking him up and down his eyes sparkling with excitement, Stanley shifted uncomfortabley shoving his hands into his pockets and twisting awkwardly, Charles Carter let out a big hearty laugh, "don't be worried I don't bite" he continued to chuckle rearing his teeth smiling broadly.

"Let's go" he swiveled dramatically before bounding off in the direction of the waiting jet, it was quite a sight and one that actually made Stanley have a quiet snigger to himself watching Charles Carter strut like an over excited diva with his flip flops squelching against the tarmac, his chunky legs waddling in the tiny white shorts, it was quite amusing, Stanley took a deep breath and placed his shades onto his face and strode forward.

Stanley entered the plane his eyes instantly lit up through his smoked lenses firstly they were greeted by a smartly dressed pilot complete with a fresh white shirt decked with gold and black pilot stripes on his shoulders and aviator shades on his face also a stewardess who was also very smartly dressed a gorgeous blonde decked out in a clean white blouse and crème pencil skirt, "welcome aboard" they both said in unison the stewardess's eyes coveting Stanley bearing a pearly white teeth smile.

Charles Carter swanned on screaming like a child on a merry go round "hi" he squealed high pitched before flouncing down the aisle before turning around and beckoning an open mouthed Stanley to join him "come on Mr. Spank let's get ready for take off", the demanding tone shook Stanley into action he managed to tear himself away from his gaze into the stewardess's eyes enough to look into the rest of the jet he was so overcome by the luxurious interior of a private jet his first thought were that it was even nicer than his own front room at home.

The soft beige leather seating separated by marble tables which were covered with buckets of champagne and bowls of brightly coloured fruit even the soft crème carpet under his feet was immaculate and it smelt fresh like that just off of the showroom smell. Stanley stood for a moment to take it all in before composing himself enough to find a seat opposite the relaxed Charles Carter who in turn flipped out his IPad and began tapping onto screen without paying any mind to his guest or surroundings "let's go people I have a business meeting in five hours, sit Stanley sit" he demanded waving Stanley to take a seat and buckle up.

Stanley rested back in his comfortable soft leather chair he was cool although inside his stomach was doing somersaults, his first flight ever on a beautifully crafted jet with luxurious interior he kept marveling at the whole specter of the event even though he was sat with a fat camp gay man but the whole sense of adventure melted away any concerns or taboos for the time being, he was just nervous and excited.

The plane began to slowly roll into position turning three hundred and sixty degrees before facing the runway a sense of anticipation overwhelmed Stanley he clicked the seatbelt into position across his waist breathing in deeply as the nerves and apprehension slowly begun to take over. Charles Carter peered over at him "first flight?" he quizzed smiling taking a moment away from his device, Stanley nodded slowly in reply "don't worry it will be over before you know it" he reassured before casting his eyes back to his IPad.

The planes engines began to rev up only interrupted by the pilots announcement that they were ready to take off, Charles Carter finally put away his IPad and pulled the seatbelt tightly around his portly frame which was wrapped in his loud shirt, he let out a boorish yawn before looking at Stanley "well Mr. Spank we are going to have some fun chill out" he snorted as the fit sturdy stewardess ambled her way down the aisle "gentlemen we are ready for take off, once we are in the air I shall bring you some refreshments" her sweet voice was high pitched and nasal her inflictions managed to pierce the taught atmosphere, Stanley looked up and smiled she winked back and walked back towards the cockpit.

Charles Carter smiled at Stanley before closing his eyes, it was the weirdest situation Stanley had ever been in sitting on a luxury private jet about to go to a place labeled the millionaires playground sat opposite a large gay businessman he could not even write it if he had too, leaning back into his seat he stared at his client and host who was now clearly relaxed and dozing into a deep sleep, he reminded Stanley of Jerry a little maybe just the large belly and bubbly personality.

He looked to the side and moved the curtain slightly away from the oval shaped window, the acceleration and speed began to kick in the plane raced along the concrete runway, Stanley's stomach churned again he drew breath when the jet began to rise and take off, the speed at which it elevated into the air surprised Stanley he could see the green fields and sparsely spaced buildings dotted below get smaller and smaller rapidly it was quite exciting and an new experience which again he enjoyed, for once he felt free and looked forward to the next chapter and his first trip abroad.

It was about forty minutes into the flight Charles Carter was now snoring loudly with his mouth open his face had a sheen of perspiration which glistened under the spotlight above he was spread-eagled in his seat now bedraggled his body twisted, Stanley smiled and pulled his phone from his pocket to take a picture of his host, "excuse me sir would you like a drink?" the unmistakable bubbly high pitched voice of the stewardess distracted him from his mischief, "oh er yeah why not?" he replied shoving his phone back into his pocket quickly.

He looked up as she stared at him smiling curiously Stanley smiled back admiring her beauty almost forgetting to answer her question "so sir what would you like?", again she asked still smiling her white teeth dazzling Stanley's thoughts somewhat "do you have lager?" he asked coming to his senses enough to remember to answer, "of course sir we have everything on board" she chirped before turning away, "excuse me Miss" Stanley called out stopping her in her tracks, "my name is Stanley no need to call me sir" he said politely coolly winking back at her, she giggled and trotted off to get his drink. "Cheeky boy" the sound of Charles Carter's croaky voice interrupted Stanley's gaze causing him to swivel back round in his chair, he saw Charles Carter wiping his face with his hands and yawning like a lion before coughing violently spluttering before catching his breath, "ohh I need cocktail, hello! Mojito purleease" he squealed his face now beetroot as he attempted to gain his composure fanning himself to cool down, Stanley sat and calmly watched Charles Carter look like he was about to spontaneously combust.

Drinks were served and followed by plates of smoked salmon and avocado strips drizzled with French vinigarette and slices of fresh bread, this was not Stanley's staple diet but he tucked in regardless feeling hungry now, he felt like a star he was thinking this was the lifestyle of the rich and famous his nerves had subsided and he was slowly beginning to get to grips with the idea of spending a long weekend with the most eccentric and flamboyant man he had ever met.

Shoveling his fork into his mouth and chomping down Stanley with mouth full asked Charles Carter if he had seen or heard from Ms. White, in a mumbled effort he barely was able to spit out the words audible enough for Charles Carter to understand, "manners young Stanley manners" he replied implying him to finish his mouthful first before attempting to speak "and for your information Marilyn, excuse me Ms. White is in good health", he replied flippantly swallowing a large glass of water then daintily patting his mouth with a white napkin.

"So what do you actually do?" Stanley asked pertinently whilst swallowing his last mouthful, "well I dabble, it's all about a little dabble Mr. Spank" Charles Carter playfully replied not giving too much away, "so this business trip…" Stanley hardly finished his sentence before Charles Carter intercepted, "ask me no questions I'll tell you no lies" he clicked his fingers moving his head from side to side, it reminded Stanley of Sunshine Devroux she did the same move but then again she was quite a diva.

"Ok so why me?" Stanley asked limply awaiting some sort of indecent reply, Charles Carter let out a hearty laugh patting his belly clearly humoured he shuffled in his seat, "because your hot boy!" he continued to laugh raucously with his eyes twinkling back in Stanley's direction, "strictly business though Stanley you are just my eye candy hmmm" he licked his thin pink lips slowly leaving them with a slither of saliva gloss before cackling hard to himself again.

Stanley found him hard to work out he was like a cuddly teddy bear one minute but the next he could switch to this hardnosed sharp cutting character not the sort of man you would want to upset, he certainly did not dice his words.

The pilots announcement came over the radio again "afternoon folks I'm happy to report we are approximately twenty minutes from the Cote d' Azur, the weather is fine and sunny, clear skies as we begin our descent", Stanley leaned his head towards the oval shaped window and peered outside, "wow that's nice" he viewed catching sight of the vast turquoise coloured water and the coast lined by what looked like small boats around the edges of the coastline he had never seen anything like it apart from on the TV when his mum would watch programs such as A place in the Sun.

Charles Carter sat back smiling like a proud father taking his son on his first adventure, "you've not travelled much have you?" he shot his question to Stanley with a distinct tone of cynicism really knowing Stanley was a novice when it came to jet setting, Stanley just shook his head not even turning to respond he was too absorbed with the view, inside he began to get butterflies in anticipation of what escapades awaited them down on the ground in amongst all of the tiny boats and houses.

The stewardess once again walked over to clear the tables and prepare for landing again she looked at Stanley and smiled, Stanley smiled back politely much to the scorn of Charles Carter who just scoffed as she breezed back through the plane waltzing down the aisle, he began to fix himself up wiping his face and tucking in his shirt, Stanley played it cool just relaxing back in the comfortable seat adjusting his seatbelt in preparation to land.

It had been a weird first flight and actually having to spend this time with Charles Carter a stranger in essence but a rich one at that, the plane began its descent he rested closing his eyes just thinking all he had to do was make it through the weekend then he would be home with a lot of money in the bank and hopefully back with Ami.

Finally landed an eager Charles Carter hastily unbuckled his seatbelt he picked up his IPad clutching it to his body and was ready to leave "come along Stanley time waits for no one" he sounded hurried as he scuttled down the aisle towards the exit, "toodles" he screamed passing the still fresh faced stewardess and pilot who had barely just left the cockpit.

Stanley was more languid taking his time and readying himself for the inevitable unknown adventure, he strolled casually towards the exit door giving a broad smile towards the stewardess taking her perfectly manicured hand as he approached and kissed the back of it bowing down to her "thank you" he said calmly "I guess I'll see you on the rebound?" again the James Bond alter ego reared, "no… thank you" she replied back gratefully still clinging onto Stanley's hand her eyelids fluttering with delight at his cheeky comment, he took his shades from their dangled position on his neck and placed them on before shaking the pilots hand and departing down the stairs.

As soon as he stepped out he felt the heat hit him like the opening of an oven door, the temperature was soaring as he hit the tarmac "blimey this is nice" he took a moment to let the heat seep in before stepping quickly to catch Charles Carter who was already walking at speed ahead of him.

They arrived through customs and Stanley requested for his passport to be stamped something he was very proud of he gazed at the ink emblem drying onto the page but his moment of pride did not last long he was interrupted once again by the squeal from his pushy client, "come on Spank we have another flight to catch", he yelled, "another flight?" Stanley replied confused he quickly jogged to keep up with his energetic client, "yes from the heliport" an out of breath huffing Charles Carter slowed down enabling Stanley to catch him.

They exited and were met by a tall driver who instantly recognised Charles Carter, "Mr. Carter" he announced sticking out his hand to shake cordially "the car is over here and your bags are being brought round now, sir" both Stanley and Charles Carter paused for breath in the sweltering heat. Stanley had just about caught his breath enough to take in the beauty of his surroundings it was something to behold he removed his shades, his eyes lighting up seeing the tall palm trees swaying in the light breeze it was a lot to take in he almost forgot about his host in the moment. He wiped the sweat from his brow still appreciating the exotic paradise, "come on Stanley" again the demanding voice of Charles Carter shook him into action him turning his focus squarely back to the need to move.

"Oh wow" Stanley was yet again dazzled this time by a gleaming silver Bentley which seamlessly glided smoothly towards them his jaw dropped "how cool" he managed to utter some words while a clearly flustered and agitated Charles Carter waddled his way towards the car, "let's go dream boy", he instructed snapping his fingers.

Stanley was actually getting a little fed up with his clients unrelenting badgering he just wanted to relax and enjoy the environment but he knew he was on business he was warming to the idea of a long weekend in a new country especially if all the trappings were similar to the ones he had just encountered.

Speeding through the palm tree lined Riviera sat in a classy cool air conditioned Bentley with the sun beaming into the windows Stanley sat back feeling like the real James Bond his shades reflecting the bright light he was in a fantasy world his eyes could not take it all in quick enough. Charles Carter was again in full business mode this time yapping into his phone his voice was even louder and animated than previously he seemed excited as he chattered away his face already reddened as the heat took it's toll. "We are nearly at the heliport darling see you in a few", he turned to Stanley who was still sat back coolly absorbed with his new surroundings until felt felt a slap on his thigh "Mr. Spank we are going to have a wonderful time", he enthused crossing his legs and dangling his flip flop from his foot.

Stanley remained unmoved just continued to look out of the window, he was spellbound the fact he was abroad was something he could never have believed also that his life would take such twists and turns, a fleeting thought towards Ami passed through his mind it still wrenched his stomach when he thought of how they left each other but he knew she was also the driving force behind this whole trip and he could see as they approached the heliport that his client the enigmatic Charles Carter was rolling in cash.

The Bentley smoothly breezed into the international heliport where in the foreground a shiny black helicopter stood majestically in the distance this made Stanley instantly sit up "whoa are we getting into that?" he asked excitedly sounding like a child at the fairground, "this Mr. Spank is the only way to go, you really must get out more" came the catty reply from Charles Carter who grabbed his various devices and pushed open the car door literally just as it came to a halt, "let's go Spank" again he commanded Stanley into an impromptu reaction even though he was still allured by the black sun glinted metal bird so much so even the beautiful Bentley he had just been chauffeured in became secondary.

Stanley waited as the slightly irked driver opened the door, he stepped out nodding in acknowledgement, Charles Carter was already marching towards the helicopter it was clear he literally took all of this in his stride but for Stanley this was sheer adventure he took his phone out and began snapping away taking pictures of both the car and helicopter quickly before the shrill of Charles Carters voice once again alerted him to make haste, he turned to the driver and gave him a thumbs up and the driver in turn saluted towards him with a smile before Stanley loped his lean frame towards the next waiting transportation.

It was a surreal feeling being sat in a helicopter in close proximity to Charles Carter who's tubby body just about squeezed into the tight seats, they were both buckled in and fitted with microphone headsets and ready for take off. It was such a buzz as the vibrations of the propellers whirred into action and the helicopter rose from the ground hovering before picking speed and thrusting them airborne leaving the palm tree lined streets below.

The pilots voice crackled through the radio his French accent apparent as he gave a running commentary mentioning they would be landing in the short time of seven minutes. Charles Carter sat silently his garish green shirt now soaked with sweat patches under his armpits, Stanley in contrast still appeared cool and fresh his white polo tee shirt unwrinkled and his mirrored shades sat firmly on his face as he peered out at the coastline below. He was thoughtful he wished his mate Jerry Dooley could see him or even be part of this crazy experience although he knew if he found out Stanley was escorting a rich fat gay client abroad he would most probably wet himself laughing in sheer disbelief. A broad smile appeared on his face as the thought passed through his mind, "what's so funny?" Charles Carter quizzed, "oh nothing just enjoying the view" Stanley replied causually as the helicopter veered to one side and swooped into Monaco.

After an exhilarating short flight they touched down Charles Carter seemed relieved and hastily unbuckled his seatbelt "that was fun, well it's Monte Carlo or bust!" he laughed pulling a silk paisley handkerchief from his shorts pocket and dabbing his forehead, "time for a stiff drink now I think" he gasped clearly affected by the heat and travel exertions. It was now becoming a familiar pattern with Charles Carter leaping from the helicopter and striding towards the exit leaving Stanley trailing alone to follow behind him as a couple of eager charges scuttled over to unload the luggage.

It had been a long day Stanley was feeling tired and grubby all he wanted was to freshen up in the hotel after the action and excitement of private jets, expensive cars and helicopters across golden coastlines. He still had no clue as to what he was letting himself in for or where they would be staying he was solely in the hands of his colourful client who was not renown for his communication in fact he was a bit wary of him as he had seen his mood swing from totally happy to a sharp and cutting dictator with the drop of a hat.

He recalled his dad Greg always telling him in one of his infamous working class dinner speeches at home that's how the rich got rich by being cut throat and ruthless and looking down on the normal people maybe that's how Charles Carter acquired his wealth he thought how many other people had been subject to his non relenting remarks.

"Do you like the sea water Stanley?" a more mellow and relaxed Charles Carter asked stretching out in the back of yet another luxury car this time a Rolls Royce, he was now clearly more affable and in holiday mode than at any point of the trip so far, Stanley remained quiet and thoughtful musing over the question before answering "I'm not Michael Phelps or anything but yeah why not?" he carried on while still focusing on the beautiful scenery as they drove along the harbour. "Well the reason I asked is because over there is our hotel", Charles Carter chuckled leaning his heavy sweaty frame across Stanley and pointing out of the window towards a large white yacht in the distance, aside from the uncomfortable nature of Charles Carters hand firmly pressed onto his thigh the stale smell of sweat mixed with aftershave and his belly in close proximity to his chest annoyed Stanley who felt invaded almost.

Stanley removed his shades to feast his eyes on the spectacular floating vessel "really? we are staying on that?" again he answered in amazement it was enough to make him grin from ear to ear it was almost too much he felt like he was on a movie set and he was the lead, this standard of high life was pure dreamland compared to Tyford, "yes it's owned by my good friend Baron Von Arnold" Charles Carter continued fanning himself frenetically with his handkerchief as the car turned into the harbour and slowed to a halt.

"We are here!" Charles Carter exclaimed once again prematurely jumping from the car and trotting off in his flip flops as he always did leaving Stanley in tow, Stanley took a deep breath to settle himself then marched forward towards the yacht. "Hello sailor!" a gruff English voice projected from high on board, Stanley looked up and could see three people standing on the deck it was daunting but he tried to be as cool as possible walking casually behind the now very jovial and bouncy Charles Carter.

They reached the end of the wooden pier and were greeted by a man dressed immaculately in all white holding a tray with two large and exotic looking cocktails complete with colourful umbrellas, "welcome on board Mr. Carter" he bowed then thrust the tray forward, Charles Carter grabbed one glass aggressively "hmm thank you Fredrick I'm dying for one of these" he revealed before guzzling it down all in one then wiping his mouth with his handkerchief "lovely" his satisfaction confirmed before he sauntered on board. "Sir" the man nodded in Stanley's direction "thank you" Stanley politely responded taking his drink and also thirstily drinking it all in one his face contorting when the lethalness of the cocktail hit home, he coughed sharply before composing himself and walking on board to catch up with his client.

Once on board Stanley stood back to take everything in it was quite overwhelming the supersized yacht surrounded the blue sun kissed water and of course watching Charles Carter happily hugging his friend Baron Von Arnold a sturdy looking gentleman with a thick grey Sherlock Holmes type moustache with a matching long head of grey hair which was straggled out and blowing in the breeze, he was still in mid clinch with his seemingly old cohort before they broke off and remembered Stanley was there.

The other thing that really caught Stanley's eye were the two other people stood on deck, two women one who was a stunning young lady with long black hair wearing a gold shiny two piece bikini and big Victoria Beckham style sunglasses the other was almost a carbon copy slightly shorter but just as beautiful but mature, she wore a large black wide brimmed sun hat and a black off the shoulder flowing dress.

"Stanley come" a very bubbly Charles Carter motioned for him to step forward, it was then at that very moment Stanley's nerves took hold, the butterflies in his stomach went into overdrive he tried to remain cool walking forward his legs jelly like taking his shades off as he neared Charles

Carter who launched and grabbed his arm pulling him forcefully, "and this everyone is my weekend eye candy Stanley Spank", his big announcement sank Stanley, he felt so uncomfortable especially when the gorgeous girl in the gold bikini began to laugh only to be nudged by the Baron, "welcome Mr. …Spank?" he even tried to disguise a sneaky chuckle on hearing Stanley's name brushing his bristled moustache and covering his mouth.

Stanley got a hot flush of embarrassment which charged through his body he grinned nervously with his head bowed he became squeamish and felt awkward, "this is my wife Heidi and my daughter Anais" the Baron continued, Stanley sheepishly waved still keeping his head down.

It was a strange set up but one thing he could not help was how his eyes were constantly drawn to how beautiful Anais was she looked like a model tall and leggy especially in that incredible swimsuit, she actually did sparkle in the sunshine against the blue sea, her hair was luscious and long swept back and unfurled down her back her skin was bronzed obviously she had spent a lot of time in the sun, he also noticed her face lookin a bit miserable and disinterested which did not suit her stylish magazine cover girl look.

Heidi Von Arnold herself was an older version of Anais, clearly she had years on her stunning daughter but she still looked strikingly gorgeous her black hair blowing in the breeze from just under the large black sun hat.

Straight away she walked over to Stanley "oh my" she said removing her big round black sunglasses from her face "he is gorgeous Charles", her tone was soft calm and sultry she reached out and touched Stanley's face with her hand which showed her age slightly wrinkled her long fingers tipped with bright red nail polish stroked the side of his face from his cheek to his chin.

Stanley shuddered and nervously grinned, "he is isn't he" Charles Carter uttered with a playful giggle, "can I get back to my sunbathing now?" Anais interrupted she sounded how she looked at that moment sour and distracted clearly feeling as if her guests had taken up too much of her tanning time before she twirled away, she walked across the large wooden decking to the point of the yacht where a couple of blue and white sun loungers sat empty. "Lets all go downstairs shall we?" a slightly embarrassed Baron declared his big brusque voice boomed out he was like an army drill sergeant corralling his troops, "come on Stanley" Heidi took his hand gripping tightly before leading him away and down a spiraled stairs to the lower deck.

The yacht was amazing even better on the inside as the four descended into what was called the lounge "come in young man make yourself at home" Heidi continued to lead Stanley winking at Charles Carter, Stanley was instantly struck by the size and beauty of the place "this is crazy" he could not help himself from reacting vocally to the spacious high spec living quarters.

It was decked out nicely and had all the mod cons, contemporary in design and furniture, large plump green and blue cushions neatly arranged on a white soft leather sofa, the room had curved contours in shape with the vessel, a built in giant flat screen TV with various maritime and sailing paraphernalia which were dotted neatly around on built in shelves.

He could not take it all in but was certainly impressed "this is class" again he spoke forgetting he was here on assignment, "well take a seat, let me get some drinks then show you around", Heidi again was happy to play hostess while Baron Von Arnold and Charles Carter stood smiling in Stanley's direction he was like a small child fascinated, "there are four bedrooms and a sauna and steam room", the Baron informed Stanley, "he's green" Charles Carter added again the slight remark aimed was unnecessary but Stanley paid no attention sitting down sinking into the plush sofa.

Heidi waltzed back in holding a tray of drinks now wearing a floral patterned sarong which covered the bottom half of her body, she was a bright and energetic person and Stanley felt quite taken to her already. Charles Carter sat next to Stanley his big frame sinking the cushions lower as he settled, "here we are" a bright and breezy Heidi put the tray onto the oval glass centerpiece table "Pimms o clock!" she exclaimed happily causing the Baron and Charles Carter to break out into a roar of laughter.

Charles Carter looked flaked out now that he was sat down he had finally stopped sweating but still smelt of stale body odour which hit Stanley's nostrils like a harsh whiff of smelling salts it reminded him of being knocked out on the rugby field at school, "well it's so good to be here" Charles Carter's high pitched voice roused everyone raising his glass triumphantly, Stanley followed suit then sipped on his beverage. "Anais!" the gruff shout came from the Baron as he attempted to call his stunning daughter down to join the welcome committee, "these kids" he shook his head "she's so stubborn sometimes" an embarrassed Heidi chipped in smiling.

Stanley was too distracted by the size and comfort of the yacht it was much better than any hotel he had stayed in he was still paying attention to all of the details such as the dotted spotlights in the floor which reflected onto the ceiling, "your first time here Stanley?" Heidi politely asked, causing Stanley to refocus "er yes it is" he answered politely, for the first time remembering to apply his English gentleman persona. This really did not feel like work and for his first trip abroad Stanley could sit back and relax knowing that he did not do too badly he felt like this was the life he should be living in earnest even though he knew there was a lot more ahead especially being here with the label of Charles Carter's escort.

After five minutes Anais stepped elegantly down the stairs and sauntered into the room, she looked healthy and super tanned, the gold swimsuit shimmering against the white walls as she casually strolled in still wearing her sunglasses, "darling won't you come and join us", Heidi insisted getting up to usher her to a seat and grabbing a drink from the tray on the table.

Stanley sat calmly he was trying to be cool sipping on his drink when really his eyes kept diverting from the yachts splendour to the beauty of another, Charles

Carter picked up on this and instantly stretched his arm around Stanley's back, "wow Anais you look gorgeous you have definitely grown up since the last time I saw you", he commented making sure Anais stared over in his direction Stanley cringed knowing her focus would now be on them she probably thought they were a couple. Anais removed her shades slowly and stared intently, "thank you" she spoke smiling politely sipping her drink seductively and averting her eyes towards Stanley, who in turn shifted awkwardly and slid slyly a couple of inches away from Charles Carters lair and also his odour.

"Would you like to see the rest of the yacht?" a sultry Anais shot a direct question at Stanley to his surprise, he sprang forward needing no further invitation, "of course I'd be delighted" he responded giving a cursory glance towards Charles Carter who stared at him wickedly thern declared to the others "I told you he was green" followed by a exaggerated cackle, it was as if he were jealous or needed to show him up in front of everybody just for his own satisfatcion.

Stanley rose shrugging it off with forced laughter himself more interested in getting some time with his gorgeous host, he nodded towards the Baron and Heidi before turning to Charles Carter, "don't keep him too long" Charles Carter commented as he yawned sprawling his body out into the space vacated by his young client.

Stanley followed gleefully behind the comfortable and sexy Anais as she walked in front of him she had a shimmering aura that was similar to her outfit although her personality was coy until this point. They walked through the beautifully crafted vessel the floors and parts of the walls decked with clean beech wooded panels, to Stanley this did not feel like a yacht it felt like a glamorous brand new apartment it was even hard to tell it was floating moored on the Mediterranean.

"So this is the kitchen and dining room" Anais said casually stepping out into a spacious modern area which had a long glass dining table with iron cast chairs every piece of cutlery and crockery was immaculately placed it looked like a brand new show home yet decadent with the personal touches. Stanley nodded in approval clearly impressed he watched Anais glide round the oval shaped room before turning and staring directly back at him finally revealing her beautiful dark mystical eyes. It made him smile nervously not knowing where to look each time he tried to move his eyes around the room they seemed to get easily drawn back to her eyes, "yeah nice really er nice" he rubbed his chin attempting to look intelligent enough to qualify a learned opinion.

Anais smiled playfully for the first time she gave a glimpse of another side to her intriguing personality "come on I'll show you the rest", she spoke the way she looked her smokey tone was almost hoarse but had a guise of sweet inflictions on certain words, either Stanley was feeling tired or just simply enchanted but he stood motionless for a few seconds collecting his thoughts before again walking behind the bronzed perky buttocks and gorgeously slanted back of Anais who was beginning to lighten up little by little.

"Ok this is my room" Anais swung open the large white door revealing a large neatly compartmentalized room the first thing he noticed was the many built in shelves full of tiny coloured slim shoe boxes all packed tightly side by side along one side of the room, he then saw a circular bed adorned with cute teddy's and red heart shaped cushions "wow now this is nice" again Stanley's vocabulary eluded him he was just struck by how each room was decked out perfectly.

A white and gold vintage dressing table also stood in the corner with a melee of coloured perfume bottles, jewelry and trinkets "come in sit down I'm going to change you can chill in here, you don't mind do you?" again it was like every time she spoke Stanley was stuck for words the trance like effect she had on him was a force one that he had never exoerienced not even when he first met Ami.

Her sultry tone caressed his ears and senses he was literally mesmerised by everything he had seen today but nothing was more eye catching than she that stood in front of him, "I have an en suite bathroom through her, sit down I'll be back soon" she was so relaxed as if everything was normal but to Stanley he certainly knew he was a long way from Tyford and this was far from normality for him.

He sat quietly on the bed and waited patiently the sun now dipping lower but was still strong enough to impart an orange glow into the room through the horizontal shaped bay windows, he stretched over and could glimpse the deep blue sea which shimmered with the tints from the now reducing sun, it was the only thing that reminded him that he was actually on a boat of some kind.

He rested back just taking it all in still unsure of how he had got here, he could still hear the voices of the Baron, Heidi and Charles Carter conversing in the lounge, he felt much more comfortable in the presence of Anais even though he had just met her maybe the age similarity was the main factor or maybe just because he absolutely fancied her rotten and reveled being her centre of attention.

Anais remerged now wearing a silk patterned robe which did not leave much to be desired she looked refreshed her long dark hair was wet and left to dangle ruffled down to her shoulders, she sat at her dressing table and lit a slim white cigarette "smoke?" she looked in the mirror back at Stanley who nodded and stepped up to take up her offer, "do you mind lighting mine?" she casually requested whilst she began to comb through her hair with the cigarette teetering from her lips.

Anais looked and acted like a princess her relaxed ways had Stanley in a state of submission, "so tell me about that name then Spank isn't it?" she asked with a glint in her eye looking towards him her hoarse sultry tone massaged Stanley's ears she had a twist of French with her English accent. Stanley's hand shook as he held his lighter up to her cigarette it was weird how he could not control himself he was so nervous maybe because she was the first seriously rich person he had met that seemed to not care about her wealth or surroundings she just took everything naturally in her stride.

Stanley lit both of their cigarettes and retreated back to the bed, blowing out his first plume of smoke he answered candidly "that's my real name Stanley Spank" he said attempting to be relaxed, Anais stood up and turned towards him the slight gap in her robe allowed for just a peek of her black lace under wear which fitted her body snugly.

Stanley tried to train his eyes away from her perfectly toned figure and stared directly up at her as she stood above him in close proximity, she puffed slowly and deliberately everything she did was done with a hint of class even the way she blew the smoke out of the side her mouth looked sophisticated the way she pursed her lips after each exhale was also a cute anomaly "well I think that's such a cool name" she confirmed, before grabbing a white porcelain ashtray from her table and sitting besides Stanley.

She seemed so in control and cool herself almost to a point of moodiness, "shame your gay otherwise…" Stanley nearly choked on his cigarette coughing violently before composing himself enough to speak "gay? I am not gay!" he exclaimed in a surprised rebuff before Anais quickly covered his mouth with her hand, "sssh" she said accompanied with a giggle, "he might hear you" she spoke again her eyes indicating towards the room where her father and mother sat with Charles Carter, "I didn't think you was" she let go of his mouth and placed her finger to his lips hushing him "I can just tell" she again looked alluring at him her almond coloured brown eyes squinting slowly as the smoke flitered towards her face.

Stanley stared back at her and smiled he was relieved but found it funny at the same time, "well I'm glad you can see that" he responded moving her hand away as he spoke, "look I'm just working, him I mean Charles Carter is my client", he continued in a hushed whispered tone stubbing his half smoked cigarette out in the ashtray, "I just do it to earn a bit of money. I'm an escort" he continued almost pleading to justify his existence alongside his flamboyant client, "that's good then you'd be wasted", again her response was cool ice even before she got up "let me show you the rest of the place", she turned back and winked at him and walked slowly towards the door.

After his interesting whirlwind tour of the amazing vessel Stanley made his way back to the main lounge to re-join Charles Carter and his hosts, his mind was wandering everywhere he could not get Anais out of his head he certainly did not expect to meet her on this trip but he was glad she was thrown into the equation she seemed to also be glad that he was there as it came across that she was somewhat isolated herself even though her lifestyle must have afforded her plenty distraction, he had to try and focus on the job in hand he remembered he was there to be with Charles Carter who was now firmly secondary in his mind.

"Ah ha the wanderer returns" Charles Carter boomed when Stanley re entered the room they were all sat still relaxing and drinking their Pimms Stanley smiled politely and sat down back in his original seat next to Charles Carter who gave him a bit of a frosty stare before continuing his conversation with the Baron, Stanley looked at Heidi she gave him a sincere warm smile as the two men talked about what seemed like important business.

"This evening we are going to the hotel Grande for dinner then on to the casino" Charles Carter announced to Stanley who although excited just nodded in approval, "yes I have some friends at the Grande Stanley it will be a great night" the Baron chipped in smiling broadly his bright white veneered teeth protruding from his bristling bushy moustache, "I look forward to it" Stanley chimed in now in working mode trying his best to sound intelligent and well spoken as if this surreal scene was normality for him, far from it but while he was here on his secret mission he may as well submerge himself into the lifestyle even though he found Charles Carter's personality a tad trying to say the least.

He knew that for the next few days he had to be the quintessential gentleman just as long as Charles Carter kept his hands to himself he would play the game, the money aside he had to show some form of gratitude to the man who had given him one of his greatest life experiences to date so far.

"Darling let me show Stanley to his room, you must want to shower before dinner no?" Heidi ever the nice affable person rose from her seat her svelte frame defying her years, she came over holding her hand out towards Stanley "come on Charles knows his way around this place", she said as Charles Carter continued to talk shop with Baron Von Arnold, "ok thank you" Stanley replied politely then looked at Charles Carter for approval, "its ok I'll join you in a while" he replied dismissively continuing to rabble on with the Baron.

Heidi's hand was as warm as her personality she was refreshingly genuine she seemed to have a big heart and was a typical mother hen character very accommodating which helped him feel at ease. They walked through the spacious yacht passing Anais who was sitting alone in the kitchen looking at her phone, Stanley looked over and smiled still being led by the hand of Heidi, Anais smiled back and pulled a silly face which made Stanley have to suppress a laugh.

"Darling we are going to the Grande this evening", Heidi informed as they breezed past she made it sound as if they were just popping out to the local shops or to the pub or something which again was hard for Stanley to fathom but by now he was just beginning to get accustom to all of the glamour only to be knocked for six again.

Heidi led him to a fabulous room "here we are, this is where you and Charles Carter will bed down" she gave him a comforting stare and squeezed his hand before opening the large wooden door and walking in, "there are two double beds and two en suite bathrooms" she emphasised the fact there were two of everything winking at him, "go ahead get yourself freshened up", she ushered him in before closing the door behind him.

Stanley stood in awe just looking around at the large circular room, it was pristine with the theme of white and wood consistent with the rest of the yacht, all smooth curved contours and clean furnishings with bright burnt orange and green cushions on each bed where his suitcase was stood next to.

He ventured into one of the en suite bathrooms poking his head round the door "oh my god!" he exclaimed before covering his mouth to quell his excited reaction, the bathroom displayed such decadence tiled with white marble and gold fittings it was clean and breath taking a large gold shower head stood above in an area with what looked like a matching marble bench. The smell was fresh and fragrant "unbelievable" he was enamoured by the detail "this is the nuts" he confirmed enthusiastically taking out his phone again taking pictures randomly, he lined up shot after shot making sure he covered every angle he could even taking some of selfies, "such a tourist" he heard the unmistakable sultry voice of Anais behind him she laughed and pushed him in the back causing him to stagger forward before spinning around to catch sight of the cheeky beauty who was clearly tickled by her unexpected guest.

Stanley himself was stuck in a trance like state he stared at his perpetrator he could only stand there with a grin on his face he could not feel any better at this moment his movements were staccato his thoughts seem to be disconnected from his body. He stood frozen eyeing the young socialite who playfully still giggled placing her finger into her mouth, "go on shower you stink!" she laughed again before turning and walking out of the room leaving Stanley literally motionless, she was a beautiful creature a temptress and someone who he was keen to get to know some more.

Stanley emerged from a wholly refreshing shower he felt clean and rejuvenated, he was looking forward to the evening and could not wait to get dressed up and hit the town, he whistled his way back into the room and was confronted by Charles Carter laying on the other bed half stripped his hairy barrel chest and bloated belly on show, he had his eyes closed and his hands behind his head his bright green shirt was tossed to the side he did not move except for his torso which indicated he was breathing as you could see his belly rising up and down.

Stanley dripping wet tip toed towards his bed attempting not to wake him from his slumber until he heard him speak in a dead pan croak, "it's a black tie dinner make sure you dress to impress" he snuffled out scratching his nose wriggling shifting himself into a more comfortable position "and Spank don't forget you are mine for the weekend" he shot a cold order which made Stanley frown looking down on the lobster faced eccentric who laid flat on his back still with his flip flops dangling from his feet and white shorts crumpled tightly into his crotch with the top button undone.

Stanley sat on the edge of the bed and began tentatively opening his suitcase trying not to make too much noise he felt awkward and did not want to show his half naked body to his client, he made sure the towel was tightly wrapped around his waist as he slipped on his underwear then continued to dab himself dry with one eye on the resting Charles Carter.

Standing in front of his large en suite bathroom mirror now near fully dressed Stanley combed his hair over and over ensuring that his signature slicked back style was perfect, he afforded himself a wry smile appreciating his suave transformation excited about venturing out to the

Monaco nightlife. He wore a new black dinner suit and fresh crisp white shirt, the only thing he lacked was a bow tie as he had never thought about attending a black tie dinner, still he was happy with the way he looked as finally he stared at his reflection with satisfaction, "cool I'm done" he mentioned confidently as he licked his fingers and smoothed his eyebrows.

He stepped back into the room and was greeted by a much refreshed and energetic Charles Carter who was buttoning a white pleated shirt over his paunch without his trousers but in bright yellow paisley patterned boxers shorts his thick pale hairy legs partially covered by short black socks held up by elastic garters.

Stanley acknowledged him but shyly looked away going to sit on the bed to put his shoes on, "ohh very smart Mr. Spank you do scrub up well" he commented as he strode around still fiddling with his buttons, "thank you" Stanley responded cordially spraying on some aftershave then slapping his cheeks vigourously as the vapours hit his facial pores with a vengeance.

Charles Carter sat opposite him and began putting on his trousers he stared intently at Stanley drawing on his strides, "tonight will be fun Stanley it's a formal dinner but just relax and enjoy", he mentioned with a smile, he seemed more jolly now probably because they were going to eat, "I only have a skinny tie is that ok?" Stanley hesitantly asked, "I have a spare bow tie in black you can wear that" Charles Carter replied digging into his case and pulling out the bow tie tossing it across the room towards him, "cheers" Stanley replied catching the tie, he then looked at it with a confused face trying to figure out how to put it on "come here I'll do it" Charles Carter sighed heavily before getting up and standing behind Stanley taking back the bow tie from him and began to fasten it around his neck.

Stanley flinched he felt the hot breath of Charles Carter literally warm the back of his neck as he stood in close proximity fixing it tightly into place, "there now turn around let me see you" he demanded again in a tone of authority.

Stanley turned slowly and faced his client who was no more than a inch away from his face there was a pause a painfully awkward moment before Charles Carter broke into a broad grin his bright enamel teeth gleamed like the white keys on a piano. Stanley was so close he could see the sweat beads begin to form on Charles Carter's top lip, he himself smiled back awkwardly before they were interrupted by the Baron who's deep voice broke the tense yet intimate face off, "are you guys ready? it's time to leave" he put his head around the door his grey hair was pulled back into a ponytail "ahh splendid your both ready", he reacted seeing both Stanley and Charles Carter dressed.

They all walked out into the living room area where both Heidi and Anais were waiting "oh how dashing" Heidi remarked impressed when she saw the transformation of Stanley, Anais stood shocked also processing the newly transformed Stanley her brown eyes twinkled into life, she was dressed elegantly equally looking splendid in a long black fitted dress her hair was slicked tightl back into one with a long straight ponytail and she wore a diamond choker with small tear drop shaped earrings which glistened. She stopped Stanley in his tracks a broad grin appeared when he saw her unable to help himself she responded also by delving her smokey brown eyes into his, then scanned him up and down practically undressing him with her eyes, for a moment he felt like it was only the two of them in the room such was the intensity of the stare.

"Right are we ready the car is waiting" Heidi as usual the mother and chief organiser rounding everyone up she came towards Stanley and linked her arm into his "come on handsome" she smiled her crows feet wrinkles by her eyes were covered in a layer of bronzing foundation which masked her obvious age however she still carried herself off well she again winked before leading the way towards the spiral stairs to the upper deck.

It was a short but interesting drive to the hotel Grande with all five comfortably sitting in a stretch limousine the concoction of perfume and aftershave created an ambient sweet infusion everyone was done up to the nines looking perfect and preened none more than Stanley and Anais.

As usual the conversation was mostly between Charles Carter and Baron Von Arnold they continually bantered back and forth gesticulating and nodding in agreement as they chatted away fervently, in Stanley's mind they may as well had been talking in Chinese as he could not understand all of the business speak which waffled from their mouths.

He was sat next to Heidi who looked a little tired yet still managed to pull off a poised posture staring straight ahead and fairly distant from the verbal actions of her husband, on the other side was Anais who sat calmly and pensive she stared directly at Stanley with a mischievous glint in her eyes, there was something rebellious about her a streak which maybe came from having it all and being spoilt but it attracted Stanley she was pure fantasy someone who himself and Jerry would happily spend hours drooling over. She had a sense mystery about her sitting there looking like plenty more than a million dollars, her lips glowed with red shimmering lipstick she had applied her face was immaculate flawless even the golden brown tone suited her, it was hard for him to avert his eyes away from her he began to fidget with his bow tie as they continued to exchange stares, only Heidi who was as ever very tuned in really caught the exchanges between them both as the Baron and Charles Carter were too engrossed in conversation to notice the simmering undercurrent building between them.

Heidi shuffled fixing her dress deliberately breaking the invisible chemistry which was developing between her daughter and Stanley, she cleared her throat looking at Anais who just smiled sweetly back at her mother like butter wouldn't melt.

Stanley was enjoying the ride checking out the vibrant Riviera catching different sports cars whizzing by and the shimmer of the early evening moon against the vast dark sea which reflected onto other boats and yachts along the harbour, it provided a fitting backdrop to his own elevation.

He glanced at Charles Carter who looked back at him fleetingly before continuing his chat with a very engrossed and animated Baron, again he afforded himself a sly grin looking back at Anais who in return winked back cheekily smirking herself, his stomach filled with butterflies she had a magnetism which definitely was pulling at Stanley, he was a long way from Tyford and anyone there including Ami, who he had not had the time to give a second thought to.

The car swept into the bended drive of the hotel Grande abruptly coming to a halt before the doors were opened by a smartly dressed valet wearing a black tailed jacket dotted with shiny gold buttons "Madame Von Arnold" he lent towards the car holding out a helping hand for Heidi who accepted his assistance and stepped out first, "time to eat I'm starving" the Baron finally broke off from his business talks his gruff voice rose in ascension as he moved forward. Anais also took the hand of the valet and stepped out managing to keep her poise in the tight dress, Stanley looked on gazing out towards Anais before he was grabbed aggressively by the firm hand of Charles Carter "Mr. Spank shall we?" he spoke firmly ensuring Stanley knew his place.

The entrance was exactly like the name of the hotel, grand and it was very upper class wide marble steps coated with sumptuous red carpet its tall pillars made it look very regal, Baron Von Arnold led the way it was easy to tell he was very well known to everyone as all of the hotel staff nodded and greeted him as he strolled confidently through into the vast and spacious lobby.

Charles Carter clung onto Stanley keenly as they all walked through he felt uncomfortable and was embarrassed as all eyes were on there group from the other guests who stopped and watched as the Von Arnold procession were shown through to the dining room.

It was a bitter sweet moment for Stanley he tried to admire and take in the beautiful ambience and architecture of the old hotel, the red draped curtains and high painted ceilings, he stared ahead at Anais who walked confidently her high heels clinking against the washed marble stone floor, Charles Carter seemed bent on making sure everybody knew they were together puffing out his chest like a proud peacock strutting after all he was his escort.

They were led into an intimate private room where the table was set with gleaming silver cutlery and white china plates, three servants all in pristine black and white uniform stepped forward and began pulling out the chairs for their guests.

Heidi and Anais sat first opposite Charles Carter and Stanley while the Baron chose to sit at the head of the table, Stanley was relieved to finally be released from Charles Carters grip who himself seemed to become quite moody shunting his chair forward with vigour and giving Stanley the evils.

It was becoming a bit of a battle for Stanley he was not impressed by Charles Carters mood swings and was beginning to regret agreeing to accompany him he was controlling and bossy and acted quite childish towards him especially if he did not get his way, he came across like a moody boss he was beginning to see why he had no partner in his life, but the silver lining for Stanley was looking across the table and seeing Anais light up the room with her beauty and radiance if anything that was worth more than the money and hassle he had to endure.

A menu was given to each of them by the ever courteous waiters, Stanley perused the fine gold leafed scroll's italic writing he honestly could not pronounce half of the meals on there they were all fancy French described meals, confused he kept his nose stuck in it staring at the well written definitions of food, he was more of a meat and two veg man like his dad Greg and was not used to all of these Michelin star dishes.

"I'll have the skewed veal with sauté potatoes and raspberry jus" Charles Carter announced slamming down his menu clearly satisfied with his choice, Stanley looked towards Anais and then Charles Carter who was still watching him like a hawk, "would you like me to order for you Stanley?" he asked sarcastically backed with a healthy guffaw. Stanley was stumped he could not think and before he could answer Anais chimed in "you should order what I'm getting Stanley the poached salmon it's nice" she sounded assured and confident looking over at Charles Carter with a frown as if to say stop being an arse, "ok I'll have that too" Stanley quickly replied he was relieved yet a little embarrassed but tried to hold it together despite being ridiculed by Charles Carter.

He looked back up at Anais who was coolly pouring out some water from one of the large crystal cut decanters which were placed down with several baskets of bread, she exuded confidence nothing seemed to faze her everything was taken in her stride very cool and this was a growing attraction to Stanley he admired her strength as well as her beauty.

Baron Von Arnold clinked his glass with a spoon and cleared his throat getting the attention of the others at the table, standing up with a large glass of red wine in his hand he resembled a mafia don stood tall in his black suit, his red bow tie and cumber band matched, his grey hair swept back into a pony tail made him look cavalier he had this habit of always brushing down his moustache with his hand whilst he was talking, he like Anais and Heidi was the owner of a glowing tanned skin except his was more weathered leathery even.

All eyes were diverted towards him as he began to speak, his deep commanding voice like a Naval grenadier certainly carried around the room as he delivered a welcome speech to Stanley and his old friend Charles Carter, he certainly knew how to hold court in the room even the waiters stood to attention to the side while he continued to ramble on about the wonderful Monaco lifestyle and loving his beautiful wife.

"So let's enjoy this meal and welcome to the family Stanley" he finished off by holding out his glass "salute" he said gleefully before gulping down a fair quantity of his wine, the others followed the toast and shouted back raising their glasses towards the Baron, Stanley smiled back looking towards Heidi he felt comfortable with her she reminded him of his mum he could tell she was a very down to earth genuine person despite her obvious wealth.

The eager waiters came forward in an orderly procession bringing dish after dish of sexy sophisticated looking food, Stanley was starving and just the seasoned aroma of the culinary delights which floated past his nostrils caused his stomach to rumble hard in anticipation.

It was all upper class silver service as the waiters presented the food and even wiped the side of the plates before stepping back with one arm placed behind their backs almost bowing as they retreated.

The opulent array of food covered the well laid table Stanley's eyes bulged as he looked at the marinated pink salmon and rich coloured vegetables, he was not really accustom to this level of fine dining but the minute he placed the first mouthful onto his tongue the succulent butter and garlic flavours danced in his mouth teasing and tantilising his tastebuds, "hmm" he could not help himself as the taste exploded, he nodded in approval as the others including Charles Carter laughed in unison, "that is so nice" he enthused with his mouth full chomping hard much to Anais amusement.

The rest of the meal became very relaxed the fact that everyone had now filled their stomachs allowed for a better atmosphere even Charles Carter was witty and vociferous sharing jokes and stories. Both food and beverage were flowing constantly back and forth from the table in sync and well timed, wine was poured regularly although it was mainly the Baron and Charles Carter who were responsible for the copious consumption.

Stanley was happily talking to Heidi listening to her stories of a young Anais and her hidden talents as a young champion equestrian, Anais herself remained quiet she seemed to be lost in her own thoughts picking at her fruit dessert, she was hard to read at times her body language seem to go from perfect poise to practically bored in minutes.

Stanley managed to catch her eye with Heidi still in mid flow he gave her an intrusive stare to which she responded by winking at him licking her spoon provocatively, Stanley smiled back but was then distracted himself when he felt her leg rubbing up against his under the table he suddenly sat up rigidly and adjusted himself coughing attempting to refocus on Heidi who was still taking great delight in talking about her daughters exploits.

Anais was ice she continued to stretch her leg against Stanley reaching as far as his inner thigh he could feel her ankle and the heel of her shoe which rubbed dangerously close to his private parts, she stared at him continuing to play with her dessert until her mother included her in part of the conversation, "what was that teachers name again darling?" Heidi nudged Anais sensing some kind of horseplay, "the rotund one with the funny eye?", Heidi asked nudging her again for good measure, Anais broke off from her under the table antics and turned to her mother they shared a wide eyed stare before Anais softly answered "Miss Theobild, mother", Stanley picked up his glass and guzzled the remainder of his wine, "that was lovely" he mentioned looking ahead towards Anais, "the meal and dessert thank you", he stuttered feeling hot under the collar and again fidgeting with his bow tie.

"I say we take it to the casino I feel rather lucky" Charles Carter's exuberant voice rose as did his excitement he was much more in party mode now with a few glasses of vino and a filled belly his face once again reddened. "Allez!" he shouted clapping his hands laughing hysterically rising up unsteadily from the table almost knocking the drinks over as he bashed into it "whoops!" he cried out holding onto the strong arm of the Baron as they both broke out into fits of raucous laughter holding each other like a couple of drunken sailors.

Heidi quickly signaled her intention to leave "darling I'm going to go back too tired for a casino night" she yawned heartily emphasising the point, "Ok darling I will arrange the car and follow you downstairs", he patted Charles Carter on his back and gestured to Anais and Stanley to follow him, "goodnight guys have fun" Heidi blew a kiss towards Stanley and hugged Anais before her and the Baron exited.

The three of them walked through the glamourous corridors of the hotel, Charles Carter led the way he was merry and wittering to himself about loving roulette, he stepped briskly ahead of both Stanley and Anais who trailed casually in comparison, his heavy footsteps echoing through the cavernous corridor.

Anais heels clinked loudly against the polished floor, she looked at Stanley then lent over to whisper into his ear "you look so hot Mr. Spank", a breathy compliment which Stanley received with a nervous laugh "really?" he answered looking towards her, she held her hand out towards his, Stanley hesitated knowing Charles Carter was only a few steps ahead of them although he was blissfully in his own world.

Stanley slowed down and in turn held his hand out to her, they were about to touch when Charles Carter spun around causing them to both pull away quickly, "come along you two chop chop!" he shouted still buoyant in his mood. Stanley put his hands behind his back and smiled back at Charles Carter, "yep we're coming", he looked back at Anais who could not suppress a cheeky giggle before cantering ahead seductively.

Stanley stopped and took a moment to just admire her walk watching as she took deliberate steps swinging her hips, "wow" he shook his head and took a deep breath in before continuing on behind them.

The actual casino was in a private suite and much to Stanley's amazement very calm and orderly, there were around twenty people sitting at different tables playing cards and roulette, the smell of cigarette and cigar smoke instantly hit him and he could see through the mist some very attractive cocktail waitresses tending to the guests, the room was dressed like a palace large burgundy sash drapes partially covered the large arched windows vintage wooden tables and red velvet covered cushioned chairs.

"I'm dying for a cigarette" Stanley whispered to Anais away from Charles Carter's earshot, "me too" she replied her tone filled with mischief "follow me" she grabbed Stanley's hand and waltzed through the smoky room towards one of the young cocktail waitresses, "excuse me I'm Anais Von Arnold, two Singapore slings to be brought to the balcony please", she spoke with an air of assertiveness reserved for important people, the young waitress immediately acknowledged and replied "yes Miss Von Arnold" before scampering away towards the bar.

"Ok that was impressive" Stanley nodded in appreciation, clearly taken aback, "Charles we are just going for a smoke" she again took authority "don't mind me" he replied too busily engaged in getting a seat at the roulette table, Stanley stared at him he was waiting for permission from his boss, Charles Carter gave him a cold steely stare pulling out his famed pipe and stuffing it with tobacco before breaking into a laugh "well toodles then Spank" he waved his hands dismissing him away before turning his attentions to the game.

The fresh air brought some welcome relief to what had been a tense evening it was still warm and the smell of the sea hung in the balmy breeze, Anais pulled out one of her all white slim cigarettes from a gold pocket holder, she placed one in her mouth then offered one to Stanley "are these the Von Arnold brand?" he said affording himself to begin turning on the cool English gentleman charm, she looked back at him her red lipstick shaped into a coy smile as she sparked the flame from her lighter and put it to Stanley's cigarette, "well your about to suck on a Von Arnold" she returned her cool witty reply her husky voice sent a genuine shiver through the lean frame of Stanley who choked with laughter as he took a strong drag on the newly lit nicotine stick.

Anais held the bright orange flame and followed suit her face still vividly flawless as the flame flickered in the cool light breeze, she pulled hard and walked over to the concrete balcony "come and see the view" she requested just as the young waitress returned with their drinks "Miss Von Arnold" she politely spoke standing with a circular tray which held the colourful beverages, "I'll take those" Stanley stepped forward winking at the waitress his cigarette hanging from his mouth he grabbed the glasses and stepped towards Anais, "Miss Von Arnold" he spoke eloquently presenting her with the drink and stood next to her, they both took a moment to puff on their cigarettes and take in the view which was a wondrous one.

Palm trees and slick apartment buildings some lit in the distance, the sea could been seen in the background, "cheers for an interesting evening" Stanley turned to Anais raising his glass containing the deep red mix of alcohol, she coolly blew out her smoke before turning to Stanley and touching her glass to his "well down the hatch" he said mockingly in a very posh snooty English accent before they both took a hearty sip.

"Stanley I'm glad you are here" Anais for the first time showed a slight hint of vulnerability she for once took on the shy honest mantle averting her eyes away from his, "well I'm glad I'm here it's better than Tyford" he replied cheerily looking out into the distance, "no I mean its cool to have someone in my age group, you being charming and handsome is a bonus" she faced him speaking candidly.

Stanley's heart skipped a beat he felt a rush through his body Anais definitely oozed sex appeal and class he did not know how to respond instead just opted for a polite "thank you", the moment was picture perfect and the intensity of their undeniable chemistry held them both in suspense and for that moment Stanley felt something he had never felt before, in control.

He looked deeply into Anais eyes he knew there and then that he had arrived as a man his confidence was high "come on you we better get back my boss will be wondering" he managed to break away and led a doe eyed Anais back into the Casino.

Sat next to Charles Carter who was clearly absorbed and having fun playing roulette, Stanley for once went back to being the cool professional escort he began to have fun seeing Charles Carter so excited he felt duty bound to join in and play the role, he already knew that him and Anais was a story about to unfold so he allowed himself to get reacquainted.

Charles Carter was clearly in his element his brown pipe leaned from the side of his mouth, he had been joined by the Baron the night became literally fun and games, Stanley himself had only seen roulette on tv but started indulging himself "Charles Carter place it on thirty six red!" he shouted as if he really knew what he was doing, the excitement of Charles Carter when the little white ball popped up and landed on the right number and colour was both funny and amazing to see, they were all screaming and shouting much to the interest of the other patrons who were drawn to the table.

Charles Carter was in full fun mode squealing with delight and high fiving Stanley each time their bet came in. Across the table the Baron stood steadfast hugging

Anais his booming voice would shout whenever Charles Carter won, it was fun and a great night.

"Last game wish me luck Spank" the exuberated Charles Carter in the full throes of joy screamed out by now looking a little bedraggled and hot he had loosened his bow tie and unbuttoned his shirt collar his face flush red the more animated he became, "put it on red twenty" Stanley shouted "I got a good feeling" he became embroiled with the wave of adrenalin, the roulette wheel spun rapidly as the little ball popped about until it landed bang on red twenty "yes!" Stanley shouted as the croupier even applauded.

Charles Carter gave Stanley a big bear hug squeezing the life out of him, "well done my lucky mascot" he squealed with delight before scraping up all of his winning chips, "wow that was good", Stanley said fixing his hair back into position, "I say we call it a night" Baron Von Arnold declared, everyone was now tired and a little worse for wear.

They all made their way outside of the hotel and waited for the car Charles Carter was happy counting his bounty of cash, "this is for you Stanley Spank" he placed a fold of notes into Stanley's breast pocket, a surprised Stanley responded "oh thank you" as Charles Carter patted the money on his chest, he looked over at Anais she looked tired leaning onto her father as the car breezed to a halt in front of them.

After a short drive they had arrived back at the luxury yacht it was late into the night the mood was more subdued,

Anais had taken of her shoes and walked barefooted up the wooden decking Stanley followed behind her while the Baron and Charles Carter took up the rear still deep in conversation they always seemed to have so much to discuss which was fine by Stanley as it took the attention away from him.

He kept his hands deep in his pockets as he strolled on board, "hey" he called out to Anais he rushed down the spiral stairs, Anais stopped in her tracks turning around she still looked stunning even at this late hour "hey yourself" she replied with a smile, Stanley quickly trotted up to her "I just wanted to say goodnight and thanks" he said in a hushed voice again his polite tone made Anais crack a smile "I'll see you in the morning good luck" she said winking then looking beyond him towards Charles Carter who was just bounding down the stairs, she twirled and continued to walk through the yacht to her room swinging her hips, Stanley could only look on longingly he knew he had never met or seen anyone as sexy and sassy she was truly box office.

"Fancy a night cap Spank" a hoarse and yawning Charles Carter asked, the Baron chuckled as he walked into the spacious lounge "well if you two are then have some of my finest single malt whiskey" he growled his deep tone now sounded even deeper due to tiredness, "I'll see you in the morning for our meeting" he handed a wooden box containing an old black and gold labelled bottle to Charles Carter "go easy I need you refreshed for tomorrow" he choked out a wheezy cough before patting Stanley on his back with a heavy paw like hand and trudging off towards his room taking his hair out of the pony tail, he grunted loudly before slamming the large wooden door at the end of the open plan room. "Let's go to the upper deck, grab some glasses" Charles Carter ordered, Stanley nodded reluctantly resigned to spending more time with his client.

He arrived upstairs onto the upper deck where the large frame of Charles Carter minus his jacket and tie which were strewn across the floor, he laid back on one of the two sun loungers still with the wooden box containing the bottle in his hand "come and sit Stanley let's taste this" he managed to sit up and took the bottle from the box.

Stanley was tired yet apprehensive as he took a seat in the empty lounger beside Charles Carter, he placed the two thick glass tumblers onto the deck then took his suit jacket off folding it neatly before placing it on the floor.

The night was mild just the bright moon and a cluster of stars twinkling brightly in the dark sky, the reflection rippled onto the sea as the cool breeze gently massaged the water, "ahh yes Stanley Spank this is the life eh?", Charles Carter's voice was now a calm deep gravel tone he looked tired his face still a lobster pink colour from the afternoon heat and the whites of his eyes had reddened.

Stanley lent forward as Charles Carter poured out two neat shots and put the bottle back into the wooden case, "here's to your first night abroad" he raised his glass towards Stanley's, they touched glasses before downing straight the potent vintage fluid, "arrgh woo!" Stanley reacted the whiskey literally tore strips from his throat and fermented down to his chest, "wow that is strong" he beat his chest with his closed fist.

Charles Carter did not make a sound instead he just relaxed back into the lounger dropping the tumbler from his hand, his breaths became heavier, "Spank I brought you here" his now wheezy low husk got deeper and more slurred, Stanley laid back also tired his body still trying to digest the burning sensation of the whiskey, "yes and I really appreciate it" he spoke quietly looking out to the dark wide ocean which surrounded them, "I think somebody likes you more than me", Charles Carter's voice went up a couple of pitches he suddenly sounded playful and tipsy, "but I own you Spank at least until tomorrow night" he giggled pathetically it was more of a warble that turned into a evil chuckle, Stanley pricked up "own me?" he quizzed surprised at Charles Carter's choice of words, again Charles Carter chuckled then turned to him lazily "Anais is not for you Spank" he shot a warning the fumes from the alcohol on his breath wafted across he looked a shocked Stanley dead in the eyes.

He reached over and gripped Stanley's arm tightly continuing his stern stare, Stanley looked back at him he felt creeped uncomfortable and violated his skin crawled, Charles Carters eyes began to waver his lids becoming heavier before he patted Stanley's arm tenderly "hmm you are gorgeous Mr. Spank so cute" he trailed off before closing his eyes and reeling back into the lounger.

Stanley slowly removed Charles Carters heavy hand from his arm, he lent over looking closely at him he had fallen asleep the sound of snoring ascended as he drew for every breath, Stanley rose wearily and leaned over him just about holding his own balance as the yacht slowly rocked in the sea, he gently shook Charles Carter pushing his shoulder which only caused him to snort louder before going back into a rhythmic snore.

Stanley shook his head "ahh leave him" he said to himself placing Charles Carters suit jacket over his slumped body before making his way down to his room, his head now pounding the last shot of whiskey taking its toll.

"Wake up Stanley wake up!" a vexed Charles Carter shook a shocked Stanley from his comfortable slumber, he jumped up out of his sleep to see a red faced Charles Carter looming over him he was angry and clenched his teeth as he spoke to Stanley who was still half asleep and feeling the effects of a long night, "you should have woke me instead of leaving me up there" Charles Carter said in a forceful whisper attempting not to wake the others "I tried to" a frustrated bleary eyed Stanley replied pulling the warm blanket over him "I have an important meeting this morning I could have done with sleeping in a bed!" Charles Carter continued to fume before turning away in a huff and stomping off to the shower room still dressed in his crinkled shirt and suit trousers.

A shell shocked Stanley lay still his eyes barely open and his head feeling groggy he checked his phone and could see it was barely six o clock in the morning he groaned again before closing his eyes and placing his hand over his head.

The sound of a text message came through forcing Stanley to open his eyes again he squinted looking at the bright screen his eyes widened seeing the name Ami illuminated, hastily he opened the message *"hi Stanley I've not heard anything from you I miss you Ami x*", Stanley stared at the message reading it a couple of times before putting his phone on the pillow beside him, even with a heavy head his mind began racing thoughts of his life back in Tyford especially his bust up with Ami.

Charles Carter re entered the room wrapped waist high in a fluffy white towel and his white flip flops his short friar tuck style hair wet his face was red in comparison to the rest of his pale hairy torso, Stanley peeked momentarily at him then closed his eyes pretending to be asleep wary of encountering another wrath from his unpredictable client.

Charles Carter breathed out heavily lying back on his bed he rubbed his belly slowly whilst grunting, snorting and clearing his throat, his noises were annoying almost as if he was deliberately trying to annoy Stanley, "I won't be needing you for today's meeting, but we will be back for lunch", Charles Carter informed between his farm yard impressions still rubbing his belly and scratching his balls with the other hand, "ok I'll wait here then" Stanley replied dutifully fully aware that he needed to show some sort of gratitude to his client although he secretly loathed him and his bitchy streak.

The rising sun began to peek through the slim windows for the time of morning it shone strong and brightly across the room, Stanley was awake now his tongue dry he felt dehydrated like he needed to drink a pint of water he sat up and rubbed his forehead, "I'm going to get something to drink do you want one?" he asked Charles Carter to no avail he looked across and could see that he had dozed off again lying still with his hands left in the same positions.

Stanley threw on a t shirt and a pair of shorts grabbed his phone and left the room making his way barefooted quietly towards the large lavish open planned kitchen dining area. He went to the large fridge opened it and took a bottle of water out, he twisted off the cap and guzzled down half the contents the cold water quenching his thirst, "ahh needed that" he whispered to himself, he then casually strolled through the now sedate yacht, he looked closely at a couple of pictures which were neatly positioned on a shelf in the lounge he smiled seeing a young Anais sweetly smiling with her parents, his head still felt heavy and his body lethargic he took himself towards and up the spiral stairs to the upper deck, it was warm even for that time of the morning and the sun was now high in the sky.

Stanley walked over to the end of the vessel and leaned over the side checking out the calm water, it felt so nice to be out in the fresh warm air he surveyed his surroundings it was breathtaking the clear blue skies the other yachts which were lined up moored next to each other he gulped down some more water then walked back to sit on one of the sun loungers.

Stanley relaxed stretched out lying back into the comfortable cushioned chair it finally hit him what Jerry Dooley always banged on about there being more to life than Tyford in that moment he could see what his best mate was trying to tell him all along. This was a great life albeit a fabricated one but he now realised that there was definitely another world out there totally different to anything he had been used to and he liked it but he was still rankled by the message from Ami and toyed with the thought of sending her a message back.

His heart was still with Ami but the strong growing attraction to Anais confused him to the point of being afraid to message Ami, he sighed heavily and lent back closing his eyes from the sun which was now heating up rapidly.

Stanley had dozed off for a few minutes and only woke when he heard somebody calling his name, "hey sleepy head Stanley" it was the distinct smoky voice owned by Anais she called his name playfully, he opened his eyes squinting from the sun and saw the fresh clear face and long dark tresses that was unmistakably Anais, "well you beat me to it why didn't you wake me?" she asked whilst poking him in the arm playfully, she still smouldered with beauty even first thing in the morning after a heavy night.

Stanley shielded his eyes from the bright sun as he looked back at her, "I woke up early I was thirsty..." Stanley just about got his words out before being consumed by a long deep luscious kiss that literally took his breath away it was definitely unsuspecting but felt amazing, "good morning Spank" Anais pulled back breathlessly and giggled before relaxing back on the adjacent sun lounger. She wore an oversized white shirt with tiny black shorts and not much else she was so in control and nonchalant as if everything she did was just normal, Stanley was still in shock "what was that?" he said surprised yet feeling exilherated, "it's called a kiss" she fired back assured ruffling her long hair then closing her eyes and laying back.

Stanley stared at her still confused yet still tingling with excitement he swept back his hair and inhaled taking it all in she was a spanner in his works he was developing a strong attraction towards Anais yet he knew Ami was still there at home waiting for him, it was a conundrum but one that would have to wait for now he was happy to be sat on a beautiful yacht in the bright warm sunshine next to the gorgeous Anais, he lent over and planted a soft kiss onto Anais lips his bold action down to his new found confidence abound as he felt desired.

Anais groaned approvingly and smiled opening her eyes looking up towards him "hmm what was that?" she spoke slowly smiling at him, "erm a kiss?" Stanley answered then laid back on the lounger contented he felt good in this moment and knew that Tyford could wait for now he was more than happy to lay back and enjoy his spot in the good life he sneaked a peek towards Anais she looked like a gorgeous goddess basking in the light of the bright sun he drank some more water before relaxing back himself very happy with himself.

"Wakey wakey breakfast time" the strong deep voice of the Baron startled both Anais and Stanley awake from their slumber, "you'll both burn to a crisp out here go get showered and change for breakfast" he was stood looming over the two of them dressed in a white shirt and blue shorts with mirrored sunglasses his teak frame blocking out most of the sun casting a shadow over the two prone bodies curled up on the sun loungers.

Stanley rubbed his eyes looking up at the Baron who seemed like a giant broad shoulders his hair flailing, he sat up and looked over at Anais who coolly fixed her hair before getting up and strolling past her father, "see you at in a minute" she looked back at Stanley who sheepishly sidled along the lounger away from the Baron "good morning" he stood up still disorientated and in a sweat from the heat then quickly made his way down the stairs leaving Baron Von Arnold shaking his head but with a wry smile on his face.

Stanley and Charles Carter emerged together and walked towards the dining table for breakfast they were greeted by two hired helps who handed them a tall glass of orange juice each, Heidi and the Baron were already sat at the table which was covered with a white table cloth and a variety of continental delights such as fruits, croissants and muesli.

Both breezed in now a much more jolly mood after having an extended sleep and even Stanley who was looking as red in the face as Charles Carter who also had a bounce in his step he felt a little more settled and comfortable in his lavish surroundings. He wore a pair of jean shorts and a blue short sleeve shirt opened revealing a white vest underneath, "Anais!" the Baron boomed out as they awaited the presence of their laid back daughter, Heidi greeted Stanley with a wink and a cuddle, she always seemed to give him her attention, she too looked refreshed sipping on a glass of orange juice, her eyes had a sparkle and every time she looked at Stanley it was a warm admiring stare.

Anais made her entrance casually strolling along her hair still wet dangling down her back she still looked gorgeous in a more demure white dress and barefooted, "come on Anais we are waiting" Heidi waved her daughter forward impatiently "ok I'm here" Anais responded taking her seat next to her father and opposite Stanley.

The whole table seemed to watch her and Stanley as she took her seat. Stanley kept his head down shyly picking at the croissant in front of him, "well lets all eat" Heidi announced finally motioning the two helps to bring forward more food and hot drinks. Stanley attempted to keep his head focused on his food he could feel the stares from Charles Carter keeping him in line he always felt that awkwardness with his client but kept his thoughts to himself he knew he only had to get through this last day before it would all be over.

Anais however made sure she kept him as her centre of attention smiling and giggling to herself whilst eating a strawberry seductively much to the annoyance of Charles Carter who stabbed harshly at his food in response to the shameless and blatant flirting from Anais.

Stanley kept calm and continued to eat even though Anais again began to rub her toes against Stanley's shin sending a shiver through him causing him to wriggle in his seat, Heidi once again sensed something untoward and started quickly chattering away to divert any further attention, "so how have you enjoyed yourself so far Stanley?" she said quickly whilst buttering a piece of toast scraping the bread hard to break up the tense atmosphere. Stanley moved his leg away from the reach of Anais's feet, clearing his throat he responded to Heidi who again sneaked her signature wink towards him, "I love it, it's been a lot of fun" he spoke quietly before Baron Von Arnold boomed "you are welcome any time Stanley", he brushed his bushy grey bristling moustache downwards as was his habit.

Charles Carter kept quiet chewing vigorously on a piece of sausage seething silently even he now began to notice the games at the table, a call came through onto Charles Carter's phone which startled everyone such was the volume of the ringtone, "oops excuse me" Charles Carter leapt up quickly to take the call "hi Beatrice…" he answered darting away with urgency.

"So what will you do today while we are doing business?" the Baron shot an open question to both Stanley and Anais, "well I thought I would take Stanley around to see more of Monaco" Anais answered casually, biting into another strawberry.

This was news to Stanley but he was definitely excited about spending some time with Anais, the Baron grabbed Heidi's hand and looked at her lovingly they both then looked towards their daughter "that's a good idea darling make sure you treat her well Stanley" an almost fatherly piece of advice from the Baron causing Stanley to sit up and focus seriously, "I have a feeling it's him who will need looking after" Heidi joked invoking a deep rumbled laugh from the Baron which clearly for once embarrassed the normally cool and casual Anais who put her head down shaking it in disbelief. Stanley shared a laugh with the Baron he felt this could be a potential window into the future, the Von Arnolds were a rare breed wealthy but also very down to earth and welcoming in only twenty four hours he felt comfortable and not out of his depth.

Breakfast was over and a full Stanley was sat in his room relaxing he had his headphones on listening to music thinking about how happy he was even with Charles Carter watching his every move like a hawk, he thought so far he had enjoyed the experience, he toyed with his phone clicking onto his messages and reading over the message from Ami, he felt guilty for not responding but for now he did not want any sense of realism to interrupt this fantasy world, it did cross his mind just to let her know he was ok he knew she would be worried, he began to type a response but stopped at the word "hi".

It was a strange feeling as only a few days ago he would have killed to be able to talk to her after all he was the one who had messed up not being honest in the first place but every time he tried to formulate a response he could not find the urgency, Anais had enticed him there was something special about her and it was not her money.

As he rocked to the sounds of The Script an energetic Charles Carter rushed in frantic and in a flap about something, causing Stanley to jump out of his skin as he bounded into the room looking all flustered, "where's my IPad? I've left it" he mouthed forcing Stanley to take one of his headphones out, "what?" he responded staring back watching Charles Carter rummage through his case, "what have you lost?" again Stanley asked, "my bloody IPad!" Charles Carter replied still in a tizz clearly frustrated sweat patches already forming on his white shirt, "It's over there on the table" a calm Stanley got up and retrieved the device from the small glass table in the room it was still in its grey case.

Charles Carter turned and blew out a big sigh of relief, "oh thank you Spank" he marched over and grabbed it from Stanley who was left standing with one earpiece dangling from his ear, "toodles" he quickly bounded out of the door again his heavy footsteps echoing through the yacht as he rushed up the stairs.

Stanley followed walking up the steps onto the top deck, he watched as Charles Carter quickly rushed to the Barons waiting car which sped off as soon as he slammed the door shut. The weather was gorgeous and now very hot the temperature rising with every hour, phone in hand Stanley took some pictures of the beautiful harbour walking across the vast decking to catch it from all angles.

He stood looking overboard the calm sea gently splashing against the side of the yacht it was such a contrast to Tyford he could stay here forever feeling the hot rays of unbroken sunshine on his skin.

After a few minutes of indulgence Stanley turned to go back downstairs and was startled to see Anais standing directly behind him "oh hello!" he looked surprised to see her standing there "trying to sneak up on me?" he again pulled out his head phones, "as I said before such a tourist" she said in her posh laid back drawl "well let me show you around Mr. Spank" she smiled, again she looked radiant sporting gold rimmed sunglasses with a yellow vest and tiny jean shorts which accentuated her long brown legs down to her roman sandals.

Stanley could see himself in the reflection of her sunglasses his expression was always one of awe whenever he clapped eyes on her "ok let me get my shades and we're out of here" he moved close to her to get past and could not help but lean in for a cheeky kiss which he planted firmly onto her glossed lips, Anais responded with a smile, "don't forget to say bye to my mum she is in her room" she patted his bum as he walked away "oi cheeky" he looked back at her, she made him feel confident and happy he could not wait to spend some quality time with her especially now they had a few free hours away from the gaze of Charles Carter and the Baron.

They walked along the French Riviera a busy stretch along the sea front and harbour full of hotels cafe's and bars which were bustling with people, Stanley was looking around at everything taking it all in, he looked every part his cool Bond like persona in his white vest jean shorts and white espadrilles strolling along besides the beautiful Anais. They were both quiet until Anais spoke to a man who approached trying to get them to drink in a hotel bar, she responded in fluent French which impressed Stanley further "hmm so intelligence as well as beauty" he joked causing Anais to pinch him playfully on the arm, "I'm going to take you somewhere special and nice" she looked up at him grabbing his hand as they continued to stroll, "special yeah?" he responded "what could be more special than this" he stretched his palm out gesturing to all that surrounded them, "you'll see" Anais responded pulling him closer as they made their way through the streets.

The mid morning heat was now searing they had both purchased some ice cold bottles of water which Stanley held to his forehead as they continued their walk he was burning up not having experienced this level of heat before "how much further?" he asked slightly exasperated, Anais continued to stroll smiling at him "not far and it will be worth it" she commented holding his hand firmly and pulling the languid Stanley beside her.

They had arrived at a beach it was serene and beautiful and a quiet spot with not so many tourists around at that time, Stanley stood next to Anais they took in the sun drenched view, "wow this is amazing" Stanley spoke with candour looking out to the sea sipping his water, he put his arm around Anais's bronzed shoulder it felt natural and helped him to appreciate his surroundings "do you like it? it's called Larvotto beach" Anais asked a genuinely speechless Stanley "yeah it's wicked" he continued putting his shades onto his forehead to really take in and appreciate the scenic view, "well good but this is not where I'm taking you ha ha" a cheeky Anais responded laughing "come on there's somewhere else I want to show you". Again she pulled him urgently in another direction "this is where I'm taking you" she pointed to a sign which read Japanese gardens "come on" she instructed grabbing Stanley's hand and putting his arm back around her shoulder as they both walked towards the entrance.

Anais became quiet and more reflective as they strolled through the exotic yet tranquil gardens Stanley sensed her mood had become less sparky and more calm as they walked together, he hugged her tighter "you alright?" he asked sincerely she nodded back in response putting her arm tighter around him as well.

The gardens were beautiful full of vibrant colours and plants it had a quaint red bridge over a mossy green pond which was filled with exotic Koi fish, they stopped and lent over to view and took a moment together, the fish surfaced blowing tiny bubbles just under the surface of water causing small ripples it was quite a romantic moment.

Stanley took the opportunity to lean his head against hers, she groaned before turning directly to face him, he stared back at her but could not see her eyes due to the big framed sunglasses which covered most of her face, "can I say something?" she asked, her sexy smoky voice now was soft and hushed, Stanley was intoxicated by her beauty he watched her lips move and frankly she could of said anything at that point it would not have mattered such was his feeling "well I just wanted to thank you for coming..." she said pausing which allowed Stanley to jump in enthusiastically "no I'm glad I came it's been brilliant yeah" he continued to babble forcing Anais to put her finger on his lips to stop him from committing verbal suicide, "no I meant to say thank you for coming into my life you fool!" she finished her sentence letting out a big breath and a nervous laugh at the same time.

Stanley laughed embarrassed at his eager response "it's a pleasure" he replied regaining his composure, his stomach felt a million butterflies the chemistry between them was intense and at that moment he could not in his wildest imagination believe that someone like Anais would take to him like this, it was a massive boost for his confidence and totally apt in the serene secluded surroundings, he was falling for her big time in the space of twenty four hours and could see that her ice persona was also melting and by the body language the feeling was mutual, "your so lucky your not gay" she laughed and put her hand into his back pocket squeezing his bum as they walked away.

Stanley laughed and shook his head "I'm definitely not gay" he pulled her tighter and kissed her on the cheek they were totally consumed with one another and walked slowly to enjoy the rest of the gardens.

Stanley's mind was consumed with happiness he felt free and totally ignored the fact he had Ami waiting back in Tyford and made sure he did not disclose this information to Anais he simply wanted to enjoy this moment and go with the flow. Everything about Anais attracted him he became quiet so many thoughts rushed through his mind "are you ok Mr. Spank?" she asked casually now seeming very soft and timid herself, "yes I am actually" he replied with a broad grin on his face.

He could smell the fruity shampoo odour from her hair as she lent her head on his shoulder they strolled back along the harbour towards her fathers super yacht, "do you have to go home?" again she sounded wanting looking up at Stanley with her deep sultry brown eyes, "I love it here but remember I'm only here on business" he mentioned again using his English gent accent but this time in a humourous tone, "well hopefully this is just the beginning" she gushed totally immersed in the moment.

They returned both now very drained, hot and sweaty they boarded the yacht separately Anais stepping onto the vessel first, "hello mother" she shouted to greet Heidi who was relaxing on one of the loungers reading a book with a tall cold drink in her hand.

She looked fabulous in a bright yellow swimsuit her dark hair swept to one side and her signature big round sunglasses covering half her face, "oh darling your back" she sat up staring over towards her, "still waiting for your father to return" she shouted across the decking as Anais approached then squeezed herself on the same lounger "I love you mum" she gave Heidi a big hug and a sloppy kiss on the cheek "mwah!" she made sure the noise from the kiss was exaggerated, Heidi laughed and pushed her off playfully "what's all this then?" she asked taking her shades off her skin and face glistening from the glean of perspiration sun induced.

Stanley emerged a few feet behind her "hello Mrs. Von Arnold" he stepped onto the deck and waved from a distance, "hello Stanley" she replied joyfully then looked at Anais raising her eyebrows "ahh I see that's why you are so happy, good day then?" she looked into her daughters eyes knowingly before placing her shades back on "be careful ok?" she commented her motherly tone heightened, she placed her hand onto Anais face, "gosh I have not seen you ever look like this ..." she laughed "puppy dog eyes too" she continued mocking her daughter, forcing a non amused Anais to get up and walk away. "Ok mother enough" she said sarcastically but with a little smile on her face, "I'm going to take a shower" she sauntered back towards an awkward looking Stanley he looked a bit embarrassed and hot as she approached "everything alright?" he asked, Anais lowered her sunglasses just enough for reveal her eyes and winked at him "come on we need to get ready for lunch", she spoke softly clearly still feeling lifted about their day.

The unmistakable voices of the Baron and Charles Carter could be heard raucously through the walls of the lounge a lot of boisterous laughing and excited raised voices it instantly made a refreshed Stanley to prick up and find out what all the fuss was about, he opened the door to his room and could see an animated Charles Carter enacting whatever transpired hours earlier, the sound of the Barons big voice and Charles Carters squeal created quite an atmosphere.

Stanley walked towards the lounge closely followed by Anais who was equally as curious to the shenanigans causing all of the excitement, "ahh Spank come in, Anais join us" a clearly vibrant Charles Carter waved his hand cajoling them in whilst holding a large bottle of champagne in the other hand.

"What's going on?" Stanley asked seeing Heidi also standing in her bikini and sun glasses next to a brimming Baron Von Arnold, "we have just sealed the biggest global franchise deal in the world!" Charles Carter literally screamed popping the cork on the champagne bottle causing the bubbles to fizz over onto the floor his red face was happier than ever and his broad grin could not be hidden. "That's brilliant congratulations" Stanley said clapping getting caught up in the wave of emotion "as I said dabble Spank dabble" Charles Carter continued looking at Stanley pouring out the champagne into a glass and handing it over to him "thanks" he responded looking over at Anais smiling.

"Come on everybody get a glass so we can toast", Heidi and the Baron stood hugging as Charles Carter rambled on with an impassioned victory speech "and I would like to thank the Baron my mum and dad" he gushed jokingly holding his glass to his chest as if it were an award, "and this means I have to leave after lunch and get back to London to tie up some loose ends", he looked over at Stanley who nearly choked on his champagne on hearing that news, "so Spank we'll have to pack our bags our car will be here in a few", he reiterated then guzzled down his glass looking directly at Stanley and Anais who in turn looked at each other. In that very moment Stanley's heart sank he felt like Charles Carter was deliberately pulling the rug from under his feet although he needed no reminding he was there as a client and nothing else but this did nothing to take the feeling of shock away from him.

Sitting at the lunch table outside on the deck was a surreal experience, whilst it was a beautiful setting in the sunshine Stanley's mood was somber, all he could think about was how much he was enjoying his time with the Von Arnolds the life the extravagance and of course Anais.

He picked at his food and tried his hardest to smile but he was gutted to be leaving so soon, Charles Carter by contrast chomped away at his food attacking it with gusto "hmm this smoked salmon is delicious" he spoke with a mouthful nodding his head in appreciation wolfing it down, he was sweating profusely clearly still buoyant from his successful business dealings. Heidi as usual sensed her daughter and Stanley's mood chipped in "it's been a pleasure having you Stanley I'm sure I speak for us all", again her tone was warm and comforting "anyway I'm sure we'll be seeing you again" she continued giving both Stanley and Anais her signature wink whilst reaching over and clutching Anais hand.

Baron Von Arnold nodded in agreement unable to comment due to a mouthful of food, Anais got up from the table and quickly ran across the deck and down the stairs clearly upset "Anais!" her mother called out in vain, "leave her" the Baron chipped in trying to hold back Heidi who just looked at him then got up to go after her daughter "excuse me" she said before sighing and walking after Anais.

"Women eh Stanley hormonal" the Baron chuckled lighting a fat cigar whilst still chewing and blowing up a plume of smoke across the table towards a quiet yet composed Stanley who looked up at the Baron who continued to wheeze a chuckle brushing down his off colour grey moustache.

Charles Carter continued to chew hard on his food not batting an eyelid in Stanley's direction he still seemed visibly excited about his days work sitting back wiping his forehead with a white napkin then washing down the remains of his food with a large glass of water, "that was lovely" he said dabbing the napkin around his mouth "right time for a shower then get my things together and you should do the same young man" he looked at Stanley before leaving the table and hastily walking away towards the lower deck his flip flops squelching against the wooden floor.

Stanley was now left alone with the Baron who looked every inch the nautical aristocrat wearing a white shirt with gold buttons which the bright sun reflected off, he looked out to the sea his eyes surveying his kingdom, "you see Stanley" he began to speak slowly and candid, "Anais is a very lonely girl, but she is special to me" he continued to talk between puffs not looking in Stanley's direction as he spoke, Stanley nodded "I know she is" he concurred sitting back and running his fingers through his hair he was not sure where the Barons speech was going but he knew that he was all ears, "she's happy that you are here I can tell" he mused making a loud sucking sound as he relit his cigar with a large bright flame causing the smoke to billow from around him, "I'd say take care of her and if nothing else be a friend" he diverted his gaze towards Stanley his eyes burned true which caused Stanley to take a sharp intake of breath he nodded his head back slowly at the Baron.

The time had now come bags packed and car waiting both Charles Carter and Stanley made their way to the lounge where the whole Von Arnold family were waiting to see them off. Anais stood close to her mother she wore her shades covering her eyes her head was bowed slightly her body language was that of someone upset her arms folded, Heidi rubbed her back clearly comforting her whilst forcing a smile towards Charles Carter and Stanley, "well time to fly as they say" Charles Carter began his exit speech stepping forward to embrace Heidi and Anais, he kissed Heidi on both cheeks then turned to Anais who coldly just held out her hand limply for a handshake, "ok well you take care now" he said sounding and looking a bit rejected.

Stanley stepped forward he smiled at Heidi warmly "thank you for everything" he spoke calmly as Heidi pulled him in for a big hug "come here young man" she pulled him in towards her he could smell the sweet scent of her lotion as she gripped him tightly into her bosom "hope you enjoyed your stay" she whispered, "I'll be in the car" an impatient Charles Carter swanned off clutching his IPad and small Gucci bag under his arm, he was dressed smartly for his departure wearing a blue short sleeved shirt with jeans and brown leather loafers. He stepped in haste aware that his exit would give Stanley a moment to say goodbye to the Baron and Anais, Baron Von Arnold gave Stanley a firm strong handshake so much to the point he almost squeezed the blood from his hand, Stanley cringed slightly as the Baron continued to shake his hand strongly, "pleasure having you young man" he spoke like a commander not much sensitivity in his voice but with sincerity, Stanley looked at his hardened face and could see he was a straight talker "thank you" Stanley nodded.

The Baron cleared his throat signaling to Heidi they both walked towards the stairs and marched up to the top deck leaving both Stanley and a still moody Anais to say their goodbyes "hey I guess its time to say goodbye then?" Stanley spoke to Anais who for once looked down in the mouth "bye then" she responded showing no form of emotion, he could smell her sharp fresh fragrance infusing his nostrils, he boldly removed her glasses from her face revealing her red puffy eyes a sure sign she had been crying. "Anais look at me" he spoke softly lifting her face by putting his hand under her chin, "I'm ok Spank I'll be fine" she said wiping away a rogue tear which ran down the side of her face, "look I have to go but I wanted to give you this" Stanley smiled and gave her a folded piece of paper, "it's got all my details so I can't hide from you" he started to laugh trying to inject a bit humour into a sad poignant moment. Anais snatched the piece of paper from him, "ok go now your client is waiting" she spoke with emotion her voice cracked she grabbed her shades back from Stanley and placed them on her face to cover her eyes which were welled up with tears, Stanley felt helpless and hurried he quickly pecked her full on the lips he could taste the salty flavour of her teardrops which seeped into his mouth he turned and made his way to the waiting car, "goodbye gorgeous" he turned on his English gentleman voice and saluted in an attempt to make her laugh before he ran up the stairs.

Once he arrived to the car he turned and waved at the Von Arnolds he felt hot and rushed but knew that he may be facing an earful from an irate Charles Carter but when he opened the door he found a chilled out Charles Carter patiently waiting fully engrossed into his Ipad reading some documents "ahh Spank you're here" he spoke cheerfully "are we ready?" he asked, Stanley slipped into the smooth leather seat the car was cool and air conditioned, "sorry yep I'm ready" he answered apologetically. "Ok driver lets go" Charles Carter ordered, they began to drive away from the yacht Stanley looked from the window he could see that Anais had joined her parents he was gutted to be leaving this beautiful fantasy world he felt as if he was getting into the swing of things but business was business, he continued to stare watching as the figures of the Von Arnolds became smaller in the distance, "I told you she is not for you Spank" the cold cutting tone from his client brought him firmly back to reality.

It was strange but the journey back to England was not as exciting as the journey out to Monaco even the comfort and reunion with Charles Carters private jet and the lovely stewardess did not hold Stanley as it did before, the mood between the both of them was much more business like and calm, hardly any words were spoken. For Stanley it was job done and now back home to face the realism of what Tyford had waiting for him, the only real conversation he and Charles Carter had was to give him his banking details so he could transfer the sum of three thousand pounds into his account, "I feel like you barely earned this Spank but a deal is a deal" Charles Carter spoke directly with no emotion almost begrudging Stanley his fee. Stanley did not even turned to acknowledge him instead kept his face turned towards the window where he watched as the plane descended under the grey clouds, it was a bitter sweet moment for him in one way mission accomplished and he had money in the bank but in another he could not help but feel his enjoyment was deliberately cut short hence his sullen mood.

As they disembarked off the jet Stanley winked at the blonde stewardess who was still bright and bubbly as she was before "ok you take care now bye" she spoke enthusiastically still smiling showing her pristine white veneers her blue eyes twinkling at Stanley.

Charles Carter as usual breezed by without even so much of a look "toodles" was his only remark as he flounced down the steps towards the waiting cars, Stanley was more belated taking deliberate steps down and onto the tarmac, "listen Spank it's been fun but I have to go I'll be in touch" Charles Carter was all business stretching out his hand for a shake he still was visibly burnt his face glowing against the cloudy grey backdrop, he squeezed Stanley's hand tightly before turning and walking to his waiting white Rolls Royce "call me we'll do lunch" a last throwaway remark randomly tossed in the air leaving Stanley stood alone to watch the gleaming car slowly drive away.

The chill of the English weather caused Stanley to shiver as he watched his most flamboyant of clients drive away into the distance it was weird he felt a bit short changed but relieved his crazy ordeal was now over and it was time to get back and sort out the mess he left with his mum and Ami. "Sir" the short well heeled driver dressed in a black suit complete with a chauffeurs cap interrupted Stanley's gaze, he held the door awaiting Stanley to climb into the luxury vehicle "ok I'm coming" Stanley responded before getting in and slouching back into the spacious comfortable seats. He took his phone out taking a deep breath then pressed for Ami's number, inside he felt a bit queasy as the phone began to ring at the other end, instantly the unique recognisable voice answered "Stanley… are you ok? where are you?" he could hear the concern and strain in Ami's voice, "I'm on my way home" he responded sinking back further into the leather seat he was tired and still very much had his mind in Monaco still thinking of Anais, "can I see you later?" he asked unsure of what he would say or the response he would get hoping Ami had thawed from her mood when he last saw her "ok I'll see you later then" she answered speaking softly before hanging up.

Stanley sat back and closed his eyes his mind trying to compute all that had just happened he shook his head then looked at his phone scrolling through his pictures until he stopped at the one of the Japanese gardens a snap of him and Anais he gazed at it hard it invoked at cluster of emotions ranging from happiness to confusion his life was now becoming a rollercoaster and he was finding it a challenge to keep a grip.

Back in Tyford the backdrop of his hometown seemed dull in comparison to the palm tree lined Riviera of Monte Carlo nevertheless it was home and back down to earth as the car snaked it's way through the narrow streets. It was a weird feeling be back but at the same time Stanley could not wait to see his dad and tell him all about his escapades.

The car pulled into Stanley's street and slowly crept towards his house the smooth hum of the engine was all that could be heard as Stanley readied himself for his return. It was grey and the temperature was much cooler and bearable, the car slowed smoothly eventually stopping outside the home of the Spanks, "thank you driver" Stanley not forgetting his manners nodded towards the well heeled obedient chauffeur before he slowly eased his way towards the door, taking a deep breath before he exited, his phone began to ring and vibrate just as he stepped one foot outside of the car, he quickly grabbed the phone from his pocket and stared at the number which was not familiar he was a bit flustered as he had the driver pulling his case towards him and could see the curtains twitching from the next door neighbour.

"Hello" he sounded a bit agitated trying to multi task, "Ola senor Spank where the hell are you?" the voice was instantly met with an excited scream from Stanley "Dooley!" he shouted, "I'm back in Tyford mate what are you doing?" an equally excited Jerry Dooley responded. A big smile emerged across Stanley's face "I just got back" he continued shaking the smiling chauffeurs hand hastily before getting back to his conversation "are you back for good?" Stanley asked hopefully cocking his head to the side to hold the phone while he struggled to put the key in the lock of the front door, "well let's meet down the town later for a few and catch up", Jerry responded, "ok cool I will call you when I'm ready" Stanley responded now with a renewed pep in his step "the Tyford two are back!" an excited Jerry shouted before hanging up, Stanley smiled and shook his head before finally pushing his way through the front door.

Stanley stood in the hallway he was finally home he dropped his things at the door and walked through to the kitchen "mum, dad" he shouted but got no response the house was empty which at least gave Stanley time to sort himself out before having to face his mum.

He was happy to be home but still memories of Monaco and the Von Arnolds were still fresh in his mind especially Anais, he scratched his head then went upstairs lugging his case behind him. It was strange to be sat in his room after the grandeur of the yacht he looked around everything was much as he left it with his clothes strewn on the bed, he sighed heavily that feeling of coming back to reality he had a lot to sort out a lot of groveling to do to the two most important women in his life, he open his suitcase and began to pull out all of his clothes some which he did not even get a chance to wear due to the sudden curtailing of his break.

Now showered and changed Stanley felt refreshed and was looking forward to seeing his best mate Jerry, but before that he knew he had to face Ami, he dressed smartly In a fitted pale blue shirt and dark denim skinny jeans he stared in the mirror and took time whilst styling his hair like he always did combing it back into his slicked back look making sure there was not one hair out of place, he looked well even had a slight tinged of a reddish tan to his pale skin his mind was awash with thoughts ranging from Charles Carter to Anais he even wondered about Carissa Le Chad and the crazy night they shared with her crazy sister such adventures. He was finally ready and about to throw on his jacket when he heard the front door slam shut, he rushed towards his bedroom door excited that someone was home he opened the door and looked down the stairs "dad!" he shouted bounding down the stairs over excited at seeing his father, "oh alright son when did you get back?" a surprised looking Greg Spank stood in the hallway holding a bundle of folders and paperwork, he smiled seeing his tall lean son excitedly loping towards him, "good to see you dad I've got so much to tell you, you never guess where I went and stayed" he chattered with speed towards his dad who was overwhelmed by his normally lazy sons enthusiasm. "Ok slow down can I at least get to the kitchen and put the kettle on?" Greg replied almost fending Stanley off by thrusting his bundle of paperwork into Stanley's midriff "well you better have a brew with me then Mr.

International playboy" he chuckled walking off into the direction of the kitchen.

Greg sat staring wide eyed at Stanley as he continued to yap away about private jets luxury cars the helicopter ride and the yacht, it was as if he did not recognise this side of his son, "so who exactly did you escort to this fantasy land?", a pertinent question which stopped Stanley in his tracks, "well that's not important" Stanley coughed brushing aside his dads inquistion catching his breath while Greg quietly supped on his large mug of tea. "And you'd never guess what dad" he continued "I met the most beautiful girl" Stanley enthused, Greg sat back his eyes widened behind his spectacles "oh yeah I thought you were with that Ami girl" Greg tailed off, Stanley paused for thought his face became more serious he leaned forward towards his dad "yeah that's the thing I need to sort out", he hunched over the table deflated at the thought. Greg nodded his head knowingly "you see son all this crazy stuff it's changing you" he began to deliver another one of his wise working mans sermons much to Stanley's displeasure, "money yachts glamourous women blimey its like a film" his tone went up in disbelief "I don't know son, you will have to work it all out" he shrugged resigned to having to let his son figure it all out.

The reality jerked Stanley back to earth he sat back rubbing his forehead, "that's what I'm about to do" he spoke softly now all of the early exuberance waned, "and Stanley I think you need to speak to your mother, make it up to her will you" Greg spoke sincerely albeit wearily removing his glasses and pinching between his eyes he continued to shake his head digesting all of the information "Stanley

Spank I would never of thought it" he wheezed out a laugh before removing himself from the table "I've got work to do big meeting tomorrow" he said grabbing the stack of papers and patted Stanley on his back "glad you enjoyed yourself" he mentioned before wandering off into the front room.

Stanley sat stuck at the kitchen table he was in a reflective mood his dad's words still ringing in his ears he knew his life was becoming a bit entangled and out of his control especially as peoples feeling were involved only he could reign everything in, he frowned confused thinking of how to tackle each issue he was not used to having to sort out complicated stuff like this Stanley had never faced anything before but life had changed and he was the centre of a lot of peoples lives now especially Ami, he decided that would be his first port of call before his reunion with Jerry.

"Dad I'll be back in a while" he said poking his head into the front room, Greg Spank growled in acknowledgment his head buried into a mound of paperwork, Stanley put on his denim jean jacket and flipped up the collars before stepping out. He placed his headphones in and pressed the play button on his phone inducing the strong bass influenced sounds that instantly throbbed into his ears, he stepped with a purpose determined to see Ami and clean up the mess he left. He arrived in the town which was quiet only a few elderly couples dotted around, he kept thinking that Monte Carlo made Tyford seem like the blandest place in the world but it was his home but now he had tasted a slice of paradise he knew that this place was only a mere dot in the world.

He stood outside the clothes shop where Ami worked his heart was now pumping although he was really trying to remain cool "I could kill for a fag right now" he muttered under his breath strumming up some confidence before he stepped in to the store taking his headphones out only to be confronted by an equally loud throb of the booming sound system. Walking through the maze of well positioned racks of clothes he became nervous as his eyes wandered around the shop floor until he finally clapped eyes on Ami, he knew the second he saw her all his feelings would come flooding back. She looked beautiful in a long red fitted dress with white wedge heeled pumps, her hair looked freshly cut into her short pixie style, it was weird because he did not expect this level of feelings to resurge, he casually strolled towards her as she fixed some garments into place unaware of his presence amongst the din of the music. "Hello there" he said calmly tapping her on the shoulder lightly, "oh my god!" the shrill of her scream shocked Stanley as she turned and flung her arms around him, "hi" he responded quite taken aback by her overwhelming greeting, "you shocked me" she began to shake with emotion as she held him, "you shocked me!" Stanley responded holding her tightly both forgetting they were on the shop floor.

Ami looked up at Stanley her eyes were glassed over with tears "you look amazing" she said touching his face "you have sun burn?" she asked looking at him confused her beautiful eyes sparkled like a jewel as she stared with admiration, "give me a second I'll be right back" she touched his face softly before walking over to a colleague. Stanley watched her walk he knew in his heart that he had a lot of feelings for her he did actually really miss her and it was nice to be reunited, but it was only a few hours ago he was kissing the sultry Anais it certainly was a strange few days.

Ami clung on to Stanley tightly as they walked towards the local café to sit down for a bite to eat and have the inevitable talk, on entry they were hit with the smell off fried eggs and bacon, "hmm now that smells good" Stanley salivated from the familiar food aroma. They sat next to the large steamed up window opposite each other Ami could not help by stretching out her hand to touch his face she was very clingy and her body language was very much towards reconciliation Stanley by contrast sat with his head slightly bowed feeling a little bit embarrassed by her show of affection.

"Are you ok?" she rubbed his hand gently, "yeah I'm ok" he replied quietly, the waitress breezed in all perky and bright to interrupt the delicate reunion, "ready to order?" she chirped in "yes two teas and two bacon sarnies" he responded fleetingly looking up towards her, "ok thank you" she swivelled and went back to the counter leaving the couple to continue. "So I wanted to say sorry properly" Stanley began his speech he spoke very deliberately and breathed in deeply "I know you were hurt but I wanted to explain" he continued his voice was calm as he tried to tackle his lie, "I told you I work as a male escort it's good money and I was saving to take you on holiday" he blurted out his rushed confession finally looking Ami straight in the eyes, she squeezed his hand tighter as he continued "I didn't know that picture" he paused briefly he could see Ami was getting upset, "I did not mean for it to hurt you", Stanley continued. Ami began to cry she shook trying to supress the tears now sitting back and folding her arms, "I love you Stanley Spank but you hurt me, what do you do with those women?" she strained to speak as the waitress waltzed back over with the mugs of tea, "here you are" her happy high pitched voice cut into the taut moment neither even acknowledged her they both continued to stare into space Ami turned her head towards the window wiping away her tears.

Stanley was overcome with guilt he could see how much this meant to her it really hit home "Ami I'm sorry" he repeated "come on let's just eat" he continued as their food was brought over distracted by the strong smoky smell of a cooked bacon sandwich, "everything is ok for you right?" Ami shot a direct and straight comment just as Stanley was about to bite into his sandwich pushing her plate away rejecting the food "it's ok just eat Stanley" she again spat out a sarcastic comment causing Stanley to sigh deeply having to contend with seeing a tempting opportunity to chow down on his favourite delicacy taken away from him. "Look I'm sorry I was scared to tell you what I did" his plea was exasperated it was like he was banging his head against a brick wall and Ami rightly so was not making it easy for him.

At this point his phone began to ring just as he was about to pick up his sandwich again and take a bite out of frustration, he plucked it from his pocket and saw Cassandra's name flash up on the large colourful screen Stanley rolled his eyes knowing it was not an ideal time to take the call, he put the phone back into his pocket shifting uncomfortably.

"Who was that?" Ami spat unfolding her arms and leaning forward, "just Jerry" he answered back hesitantly "he's back now" he continued trying to sound as convincing as possible sticking to his guns even though he was probably the worst liar ever. Ami just huffed then sat back wiping another tear from her face, "you have to stop now" again she shot an angry direct statement filled with anger which alarmed an already confused Stanley, he looked up at Ami who sat defiantly he could see she was serious her eyes reflected the hurt she was feeling, he could tell that this was not going to be an easy negotiation.

He felt horrible his head was all over the place he still had Anais fresh in his mind plus he knew the lure of the money and luxury adventures was something that he find it hard to completely detach himself from, his heart told him to be with Ami but his head was telling him he was loving this new life, "look Ami" he began sweeping his hair back as he always did when nervous and fidgeting fixing his collar then ringing his hands fraught and uncomfortable "I love you too but just let me make some more money for us", he limply tried to justify, Ami's jaw dropped in shock, she was clearly disappointed she put her hands over her face "oh Stanley why have you changed?" her voice shook with emotion.

Stanley got up suddenly pushing the wooden chair back scraping the floor loudly causing the other customers to look over he ignored the stares and walked around the table to hug Ami, at first she flinched and resisted he came close and placed his arms around her shaking body, "its ok" he whispered into her ear bending his tall lean frame over drawing her into him, Stanley stroked her face then crouched down to reach her eye level, "come on babe we're going to be ok" he tried to reassure her which only made Ami shake more vigorously as she became overcome with emotion.

Stanley swept her hands away from her face and looked her directly into her eyes he could not believe how upset she was and that the depth of her feelings would be so affected, he felt awful and could only try his best to console her "it's ok Ami, I'll do it for you" he spluttered out not really knowing if he meant what he said but at the time anything to stop her from getting more upset it was his only option.

"I have to get back to work now" a snivelling Ami mentioned whilst blowing her nose timidly into a tissue, Stanley stood up and took a deep breath looking around at the mini audience he had in the café, "can I take these to go?" he asked as the other patrons and waitress pretended to get back to normality turning their heads and talking under their breath pretending not to have seen the altercation.

Ami stood up she grabbed Stanley tightly by the hand "look I'm meeting Jerry tonight I would love you to meet him", he dabbed dry the tears from around her eyes looking down at her hopefully, "I don't think so" she sniffed still clearly upset, "maybe another time" her whimpering voice still cracked with emotion, "here you go" the bright waitress interrupted handing Stanley the brown paper bags containing his coveted bacon sandwich "thanks" he took the bags and took out a crisp ten pound note handing it to the waitress "keep the change" he said arrogantly then walked with Ami towards the exit away from the whispers and prying eyes of the small cluster of customers.

After his fraught reunion with Ami, a lonely thoughtful and hungry Stanley sat on one of the benches in the town centre he was feeling emotionally exhausted and still unsure as to where the latest episode left him and her, the one thing he was sure of was that he was hungry and bit into his bacon sandwich ferociously he breathed heavily chewing down hard on the food his mind still awash with a million thoughts, he took his phone out and saw the missed call from Cassandra.

He pondered for a second just taking a time out to digest the intense welcome committee he had just experienced, his world was a topsy turvy one at the moment, Stanley had to try to figure out exactly what he wanted, again he looked at his phone then pressed the button to return the call to Cassandra his first thoughts were that maybe she had some work for him which would take things off of his mind and get him some extra cash.

The phone rang for a few seconds before he heard a low voice answer "hello Stanley", Cassandra's voice sounded weak and frail he was a little surprised to hear her sound like that "hello Cassandra are you ok?" he asked slightly concerned, "I'm in the hospital I've had a fall" she spoke tenderly her voice barely audible. Stanley stopped chewing and swallowed with a gulp "which hospital? I'll come and see you" straight away he threw away the rest of his sandwich and began to walk to the taxi rank while he was still on the phone with Cassandra, "do you need anything?" he asked his voice riddled with concern his pace quickening on his approach towards the line of stationery vehicles, "Victoria ward, ok I'll be there soon", he finished up the call as he reached the cars.

It took no more than twenty minutes to reach Tyford general hospital, Stanley paid the taxi driver then jumped out quickly he was urgent and looked at the various signposts searching for her ward "Victoria ward" he muttered to himself slightly baffled by the myriad of directions he scratched his head confused and headed off towards a fruit and flower stall which was positioned out side the main entrance gates. He walked up to the old man who was perched on a small stool besides the quaint old style cart, "excuse me, do you know where the Victoria ward is?" Stanley asked politely his brow furrowed, the old man looked up at Stanley and pointed in the direction "just through the main doors and left" he spoke with a low cockney husk with a small rolled up cigarette wedged into the corner of his mouth. Stanley was in such a hurry he began to walk off towards the direction where the old man was pointing before he doubled back "can I have a bunch of flowers and a bunch of grapes please?" he suddenly remembered his manners and not to go in empty handed.

Stanley pushed through the plastic doors which separated the ward from the main entrance area Tyford general was an old style hospital with an old style hospital smell which irked Stanley who was hit by the chemical and somewhat warm musky odour he bowled through the large wide corridors, dodging the slow walking wandering patients, family's and one wheelchair bound stricken pensioner, he hated hospitals but tried to keep his focus looking around him searching for the ward clutching the newly purchased gifts. He was approached by a young nurse she could obviously see he was lost, "are you ok sir?" her bright pale cheery freckled face was in contrast with the plain deep blue uniform that adorned her small frame "yes I'm looking for Cassandra an elderly lady on the …", "Victoria ward?" she finished his sentence for him "I know who she is" she continued, kindly walking Stanley towards the ward.

They arrived at the open ward there were four beds in each corner it was a very bland room with pale blue walls large arched windows flanked by tawdry brown curtains, Stanley looked over and could see one of the beds in the corner with a small lump protruding from the green knitted blanket which covered the prone person "she's over there" the helpful nurse pointed in the direction where Stanley was looking, "thank you" he replied now distracted training his eyes towards the bed.

He stepped in tentatively looking at the other stricken patients nodding respectfully towards an old lady who stared with sorry eyes her face half covered by an oxygen mask, it made Stanley's stomach churn he breathed in deeply before approaching Cassandra's bed, he tip toed around trying his best not to make any noises, he could see she was still, "Cassandra" he called out quietly, she turned around slowly "oh Stanley" her voice barely able to speak, she looked totally different from when he last saw her, she looked tired, ashen faced and her arm in a sling "flowers that's nice" she managed to manoeuvre herself into an upright position with Stanleys help.

Stanley placed the flowers and grapes onto the small beside table then moved forward to help Cassandra into a comfortable position, "you are a good boy Stanley", she smiled before grimacing from the pain, "what happened?" he asked pulling up a chair and sitting beside her, he could see the wrinkles in her tiny face and some bruising on her neck, "fetch my spectacles there on the table", she asked, Stanley passed them over then helped her to place them onto her face before he sat back into the chair. "I stupidly fell over at home and broke my collar bone" she winced turning slowly to face Stanley, "I'll be ok I'm tougher than I look" she cracked a craggy smile. "So tell me what have you been up to?" she asked, Stanley sat up and fidgeted "not much" he replied careful not to get caught up and mention Monaco, "you've been one of my best Stanley Spank" Cassandra rubbed is hand with her frail fingers she felt an affinity towards him and he felt the same for her she was really just a little old lady that had given him a new lease of life, "lovely flowers" she mused looking over at them, "don't worry about work as well Stanley I'll be back soon", she continued speaking optimistically, "yeah you will be fine" he replied touching her hand.

After sitting with Cassandra for an hour Stanley emerged from the hospital, he was feeling a sense of relief seeing that she was at least comfortable, it had been a crazy day full of emotion he was feeling a bit drained, he pulled his phone out and dialled the number for Jerry, "hey Dooley you fancy that pint now?" he asked "I thought you'd never ask!" an excited sounding Jerry responded, "meet me in the Crown in half an hour" Stanley confirmed before jumping into a waiting taxi.

He looked out of the window on his journey back his mind full up of different thoughts how did life get so complicated he thought as the greenery whizzed past outside, it was difficult for him to put everything into context it just seemed like since he returned from Monaco life had been more accelerated and everything centred around him, he felt guilty about seeing Ami so upset and knowing that Anais was still firmly in his mind he was not equipped to handle the mental and emotional issues that were now playing a big part of his life, but as usual with Stanley these thoughts were just fleeting the next thing he was thinking about was catching up with his partner in crime as the car sped into town.

Stanley paid the driver and strutted into the pub he wanted to put all of his troubles to the side for the next few hours and enjoy his reunion, he walked in and saw the unmistakeable large figure of Jerry, "Spank!", "Dooley!" they both shouted in unison walking towards each other "oh my god what happened to you?" Jerry asked loudly looking at the more refined Stanley high fiving him, "and you!" Stanley replied looking back at Jerry who now had a very reddish glow to his skin he was still a portly figure but his hair was now shorn into a crew cut he wore a bright pink t shirt which almost blended in with his skin tone and white combat shorts with flip flops. "Where's the beach?" Stanley quipped looking his mate up and down laughing, "good to see you too!" Jerry replied, he was in his usual jovial mood which also lifted Stanley, "come on I've got a pint for you", he motioned walking back towards the bar as others watched their euphoric shenanigans.

It was strange for the Tyford two to be back together after a long time Stanley could not help laughing at his old friend and his new look, "so talk to me how's the life in Spain been?" he asked taking a long measured sip of his well deserved cold pint he was eager to hear all about Jerry's adventures. It seemed like they had never been apart as he sat listening intently to Jerry wax lyrical about foam parties beach games and meeting women from all over the globe "Stan I tell ya mate I needed a wing man out there" Jerry continued to chat enthusiastically in an animated fashion standing up to emphasise certain parts of his tales, "and then I met Leanne" he continued sitting back reflectively, "I can't believe it Stan I think I'm in love!" he exclaimed taking his phone out and showing Stanley a picture of his new found girlfriend.

Stanley took the phone and looked at the picture, he was surprised to see a nice looking petite blonde in a bikini hugging a bare chested pot bellied Jerry who's face exuded happiness, "wow she's really nice" Stanley sounded surprised handing back the phone, "my life has changed Stan the best thing I did was go to that open day" Jerry continued to chatter clearly consumed, Stanley sat back impressed by his friends transformation, it made him happy to see Jerry so content he was like a different man still the same boorish lad but he seemed a lot more confident even mature.

As Jerry continued to reel off stories of nights of crazy partying Stanley's mind drifted his thoughts quickly turned to Ami, Anais and even Carissa Le Chad for whom he had fond memories, "so how it been in lively Tyford?" Jerry broke Stanley's trance with a question, "if only you knew mate" Stanley replied before getting up "another one?" he asked Jerry picking up his empty pint glass, "of course top me up mate I'm just going to call Leanne" he said excitedly.

Stanley returned with the drinks to find Jerry relaxing in his seat speaking quietly and giggling "Jesus get a room will you" Stanley commented laughing seeing his one time lay about partner in crime all loved up, "ok bye darling love you" Jerry tried to stifle his comments from Stanley who just rolled his eyes and shook his head.

The pub was empty now and only the Tyford two still sat at a table whilst the bar girl began to collect glasses and clean tables around them Jerry was still in hyper mode recalling names of places he had been to "yeah then we went quad biking in the sand dunes and Leanne was screaming", he stopped in mid flow noticing Stanley's short attention span, "sorry mate I'm going off on one, so tell me what have I missed?" Jerry patted Stanley on his leg acknowledging that he had been talking about himself for the last hour. "Well I don't know if your gonna believe this" Stanley put down his pint he tried to look serious but just about was able to supress a smirk "I've been living the high life as a male escort" his delivery was dead pan he looked directly at Jerry who kept an equally straight face before bursting into the biggest roar of laughter for the evening wheezing for a prolonged period before he could catch his breath again, "you a…" before he broke into another bout of sustained laughter, attracting strange glances from the bargirl, Stanley could not help but begin to laugh himself watching Jerry's reaction his face now bright red and sweaty with tears streaming freely down his face, "hold up wait" Jerry attempted to compose himself "a male escort oh Stan that's quality" he continued rubbing his eyes.

Stanley remained cool and composed although the sheer animated reaction from his best friend invoked Stanley to begin reeling off his adventures "I've been earning good money staying in plush hotels even private jets and super yachts" Stanley mentioned quite casually in between sipping his jar of golden frothy liquid, "you are being serious as well?" Jerry quizzed sensing his friend was being totally sincere, "and I have a beautiful girlfriend called Ami" Stanley took his turn to pull out his phone and show off by flashing Jerry a picture of Ami, "wow she's well fit!" a more than impressed Jerry stated nodding his head in approval.

"Stan talk to me how did this all happen?", Jerry sat back in amazement "Ami eh? I can't believe it" he shook his head a baffled expression emerged on his face, "yep that's how I've been doing in boring Tyford", Stanley gave Jerry a cheeky wink, he felt quite pleased with himself watching Jerry's face turn from laughter to fascination, "so was Ami one of your…", "no!" Stanley abruptly interjected "no I met her separately, that's why I carried on, well I thought I… oh never mind" he continued now totally serious and lost in his own thoughts, "anyway I have a dilemma" he spoke candidly "I've met another stunning girl in Monaco and no matter how much I love Ami I can't get Anais out of my head", Stanley's face contorted confusion clearly etched onto his face. Jerry broke into another roar of laughter "are you serious Stan?, we used to dream of this type of scenario and now your confused" he kept chuckling to himself shaking his head his face was getting flush pink like his t shirt, "one thing you were right about Dooley there is a whole world out there" Stanley raised his glass up and clinked it onto Jerry's "welcome home Jerry Dooley" he smiled wearily it had been a long day but Stanley was happy to share some male bonding time with his old mate it was a good distraction from all of the stuff with Cassandra, Ami and Anais although he still had to face his mum.

"Anyway Stan my advice to you is to play the field mate live life to the full!" Jerry spoke with his usual boisterous energy before downing the rest of his pint, "I have a big Bob Marley for old time sake" Jerry laughed mischievously getting up from the table "come on this place is dead anyway" he surveyed around him at the empty bar, "yeah lets get out of here" Stanley concurred doing the same as Jerry and guzzling the rest of his pint and getting up to exit.

"I'm telling you Stan I'm gonna marry that girl" Jerry pulled hard on the large joint his voice cracked as he spoke passing it back to Stanley who sucked on it just as hard blowing the smoke out above his head laying back on the grassy banks of the river Ty, "am I your best man then" he continued to puff hard building up a healthy thick cloud taking multiple sucks of the joint, "of course mate who else have I got?" Jerry turned towards Stanley his eyes were sleepy filled with red lines speckled on the whites of his eyeballs.

"We are gonna have an epic medieval banquet where Leanne can dress as my buxom wench" he continued his tone dreamy his imagination running wild until Stanley burst out laughing choking violently before he was joined by an equally exaggerated vociferous bout of laughter from Jerry. They both rolled around in the dark on the cold dewy grass "buxom wench?" Stanley cracked up again just about managing to breathe in between cries "oh dear Dooley you really know how to make a girl feel special", he continued wiping his eyes as the tears streamed down his face.

Jerry continued to contort rolling onto his front and making a noise akin to a pig as he grunted for breath such was the force of his laughter, "I missed you Spank man I have not laughed like that in ages" he finally sat up rubbing his face "pass that" he reached over to Stanley taking the joint from him.

Both sat now composed looking out to the moonlit rippling river, there was a comfortable silence a pause while they both were in their own reflective worlds, "how times change mate" Stanley mused shuddering as the chill of the night air cut through his body his head now felt fuzzy he sat forward bringing his knees up to his chest "I love Ami but Anais is special" he spoke incoherently on a whim pushing his hair back looking out into the distance. Jerry who was laying prone silently still with the remainder of the long joint perched in his mouth just groaned, "what does that mean?" Stanley turned to him snatching the joint away and relighting it, "choices Stan at least we have them now" Jerry's voice meandered from high to a low husk tailing off at the end of his sentence, it was food for thought indeed and Stanley knew it looking up at the dark sky only illuminated by a crescent moon which was hidden partially by the night clouds.

The faint knocking on the door barely roused Stanley he was hanging feeling the effects of the night before he could just about lift his head which was throbbing and feeling heavy, the door was slowly pushed open and Brenda's voice disturbed Stanley's sleep further "Stanley can you hear me?" the reek of alcohol and stale smoke hit her as she stepped into the room she looked around staring and clothes strewn on the floor and Stanley's crumpled body under the bed covers, "are you going to sleep the day away then?" again his mum's heckling continued frustrating a comatose Stanley who writhed and groaned.

Brenda stepped through the minefield of clothes and shoes and pulled open the curtains letting in a bright shard of light, "mum!" Stanley growled clearly unhappy at his mums overbearing persistence to resurrect her hung over son, "it's twelve thirty I think you should get up" she continued fussing and opening the window creating as much noise as she possibly could.

Finally a grumpy and wild looking Stanley sat up his face was wrinkled eyes barely opened squinting trying to adjust to the light his hair messy, he scratched his bare chest then rubbed his face aggressively, Brenda stood in front of him none to impressed "ok wakey wakey we need to talk I'll see you downstairs" she said firmly confirming her prickly mood by stamping out of the room and walking with heavy footsteps down the stairs. Stanley groaned loudly flinging himself back down onto the bed petulantly he was in no mood to get up let alone receive a lecture first thing.

Brenda sat patiently sipping a cup of tea in the kitchen her hair was still sat in pink curlers under a black hair net she cupped her mug high in front of her face the steam rising from it past her eyes, it was quiet and she seemed pensive, every few seconds which passed she would take a slow sip from the mug slowly swallowing the hot liquid she was very still apart from one of her pink slippered feet which tapped away underneath the table the only part of her that signified any anxiousness. Again she sipped on her tea, before the sound of Stanley stamping loudly down the stairs then literally dragged his feet towards the kitchen where his mother sat still waiting. He looked tragic his hair messily tumbled down his face which was blotchy and puffy, he wore just a simple white vest and grey sweatpants he groaned plonking himself down opposite his mum coughing up his lungs and sniffing.

"Well look what the cats dragged in", Brenda sounded unimpressed her voice flat and to the point she still sat unmoved staring ahead towards a horribly hung over Stanley who now was laying his head onto the table, "so talk to me Stan where have you been?", Brenda continued she was in a straight talking mood and not ready to let Stanley have an easy morning, Stanley groaned again barely picking his head up "mum" he moaned "I was with Jerry we had a few" he managed to pick his head up enough to catch his mums eye line, "is there any tea going I'm parched" he coughed again wheezing hard as if he was dying.

"What's happened to you Stanley?" she finally put down her cup and breathed out a sigh, Stanley looked back at his mother he was tired and felt awful but he soon straightened up when he heard the discord in her voice suddenly his senses were roused, the last person he wanted to disappoint or let down was his old dear. "Mum" he began to clear his throat he knew now was the time to come clean there was no way he was going to escape her inquisition he pushed back his hair and ruffled it taking a deep breath as Brenda sat quietly and patiently waiting for the inevitable explanation to pour out of her son.

"Well I've been working" a more awake looking Stanley started to explain, "I've made some good money and went abroad too, that's why I needed my passport", he started slowly his voice still low and gruff, "I gathered that" Brenda replied digging her fingers into her hair net scratching at her scalp, "look mum I'm a male escort I escort rich women to events" he finally let it out, Brenda's expression was wild-eyed with shock "a what?" she shot back, Stanley slumped back in his chair "a male escort mum" his voice now hushed he looked down and away from his mum a tad embarrassed, "you!" again Brenda shot back in disbelief before breaking into a fit of laughter, "oh well I've heard it all now" she continued before coming to her senses "isn't that like prostitution?" she now became serious "lord give me strength" she rolled her eyes upwards towards the heavens then clasping her wrinkled thick fingers against her face.

"It's not like what you think mum it's more having fun" Stanley tried his best to explain, Brenda continued to curse under her breath then she stopped and looked straight at him "does your father know about this?" Stanley paused looking his mother dead in the eye wearily and replied with no hesitancy "no mum" he took a sharp intake of breath then got up "I need some tea", Brenda frowned and shook her head she was not convinced pushing her face up disgusted by Stanley's revelation, "well I am shocked and does your young lady know about all of this?" she continued to question a badgered and harangued Stanley as he slowly yet noisily began making his cup of tea, "yes she does now" he replied feebly turning back to face her, "look mum I make good money and I don't do anything bad it's a job a good one at that" he pleaded his case hoping that his mum would finally lay off of him he was getting moody and was certainly not up to having an early morning barney especially with his mum who he doted on.

"I'm disappointed Stan" Brenda still chipped away before pausing for thought "Oh I get it now that's why that picture was in the paper you were…" she finally twigged her eyes lighting up then actually broke into a chuckle although she tried her hardest to not be amused but in the end could not hold it back and burst into a fit of stifled laughter much to Stanley's amazement just as the kettle came to the boil and set off a large blast of steam whistling behind him.

"What are you like Stanley Spank?" her eyes went from dead and cold to sparkling and no matter how she tried to stay angry with him he always had a way of melting his mum, "so I guess you can pay me back for all that money you have loaned in the past?" she put her hand out opening her palm and became serious again staring intently waiting causing him to look back at her uncomfortably "are you serious?" he protested, "I'm saving for a holiday with Ami" he began to get into a strop his face turning redder acting as if his whole world was about to fall apart. Brenda burst into a fit of giggles "oh Stan the look on your face" she continued to crack up "I don't want your money Stanley we've done ok without it up until now, but I do want to meet this Ami", she insisted standing up from the table and walking over to help him make a cup of tea "invite her round for dinner and sit down your useless in the kitchen" she shunted him playfully out of the way.

Stanley hugged her partly out of relief but mainly because he knew his mum was the most important woman in his life, "ok I'll call her now" he kissed her on the cheek before disappearing out of the kitchen, "Stan what about your tea?" a puzzled Brenda shouted out, "I'll be back and a bit of toast wouldn't go amiss" he shot back a cheeky reply stomping up the stairs much to his mothers dismay. Brenda was able to smile she still shook her head but she knew that was Stanley and although he had now obtained this new status he would still need her, "that boy" she muttered under hear breath still chuckling.

The booming stereo thumped loudly and in amongst the din the voice of Stanley singing out the words of the Oasis song Wonderwall, the din drowned out the sound of his mobile phone which was plonked onto the quilt in the middle of his bed, Stanley leaned his head out of the window he was in good mood he felt like a weight had lifted from his shoulders he was now free from a guilty conscious no more lies even though he still had some work to do with Ami but his life was good.

The volume decreased as the song came to an end and he heard the tone of a message come through on his phone he turned around and plucked it up with zest he opened the message "Spank! Leanne is in town fancy bringing Ami for a double date?, I've booked a table at Espinolas", instantly Stanley laughed with excitement and began calling back his friend, "Dooley has the Tyford two become the Tyford four?" he cackled hard, "the awesome foursome" the exuberant sound of Jerry's response echoed down the line "Ok what time?" Stanley asked, "ok six at Espinola's eh! will be there over and out" he spoke mocking an army commander cracking up then hanging up the phone.

He had a spring in his step now he bounced around his bedroom laying out different clothes on his bed rubbing his chin trying to make a choice of what to wear he had spoken to Ami and thankfully she had mellowed from their previous meeting she was happy to go out with him and meet the famous Jerry Dooley he knew it was going to be a great night and he was looking forward to seeing Ami he just wanted to get back to what things were before and hoped she forgave him in time. Stanley emerged from his room some hours later looking like he had just stepped of a Milanese catwalk he looked fresh despite still feeling rough this morning he wore a royal blue blazer dark ripped frayed denim jeans a white shirt and black penny loafer without socks.

He knew he looked good and wanted to show Jerry and Ami this new reinvented person the Stanley Spank that his clients saw, he even afforded himself a slick side parting in his comb over hairstyle, he carried it all of very well looking every inch the poster boy, "mum the taxi's here I'm off now" he poked his head in the front room where he could hear the TV on, Brenda sat glued to the screen lost in watching her favourite soap opera until Stanley stepped in "mum did you hear me I'm going now", he commented break his mums concentration forcing her to train her eyes away from the screen to see her son standing their in all his glory.

She did a double take still sat with her hair in curlers and under a patterned headscarf "look at you bloody hell where is my real son!" she gasped standing up to look at him in detail, "well I always said you were my little James Dean" she turned him around brushing the shoulders of his blazer fussing around him "hmm and you smell nice too, better than smelling of that wacky backy" she looked at him knowingly, "ok mum the taxi is outside" Stanley started to become impatient with all her fussing, "oh quickly take a picture of me" he pulled his phone out and pressed a few buttons before handing it to his mum, "just press the red button on the screen" he hastily instructed.

Brenda stood holding the device awkwardly not really sure of what she was doing pulling it forward and backwards until she thought she had the best shot, "mum come on" Stanley pleaded, "ok I'm doing it", she pressed the button a bright flash went off while Stanley tried to quickly get in a good pose, "let's see" he grabbed the phone from his mum, "ok that's nice it will do", he kissed his mum on the cheek "see ya" he said before darting out of the door to his waiting taxi, Brenda plonked herself back down shaking her head she had a wry smile on her face she knew her lazy son was now becoming a man.

In the taxi Stanley sent a text to Ami "*on my way x*" it read while he sat back fixing himself and getting comfortable for the journey, he stared out of the window reflecting seeing the large grey clouds masking the moonlight the orange tinge of the street lights whizzed past at this moment he was so content within himself he felt assured now he had the freedom he could look forward to more work once Cassandra was recovered and out of hospital then he could start choosing his holiday destination with Ami.

They arrived at Ami's place in Underbridge "just a sec" he said to the taxi driver then got out of the car, he dialed Ami on his phone, she picked up quickly "are you here Stanley?", "yes I'm outside" he replied hearing Ami still shuffling around sounding a bit rushed and flustered "ok be down in a minute" she said hanging up the phone before Stanley could reply, "ok then" he put the phone away and looked at his reflection in the window of the taxi making sure he still looked smart and impeccable.

After what seemed like ten minutes later, Ami emerged from the building walking elegantly towards him he strained his eyes towards her watching her walked slowly in a pair of gold high heeled shoes she wore a figure hugging beige and gold off the shoulder dress which fitted her bust aptly, "wow you look stunning" he drooled as her petite but cute figure came towards him.

Stanley knew he also looked cool and went straight into escort mode stepping forward to hold her hand "good evening gorgeous" he lent forward and kissed her on the cheek, she look beautiful her eyes shimmering in the night lights, her short hair was styled with a swept fringe and her face had a dusting of make up finished with glittered pink lip gloss, "your not so bad yourself" she complimented him back giving him an air kiss on his cheek as not to spoil her beautifully made up face.

Stanley opened the door for her, "shall we" her gestured for her to get in which was a bit of a task for Ami such was the tightness of her dress but she managed to pull it off with class. Stanley carefully closed the door and walked round to let himself in on the other side, "ok Espinolas restaurant please sir" Stanley directed the driver then took Ami's hand, "you're a good looking young couple if you don't mind me saying" the old driver looked back in the mirror nodding his head, "thank you" they both responded at the same time sharing a giggle as they did so.

Espinolas was one of classiest restaurants in Tyford a trendy Spanish style venue it was mainly a haunt of the young rich types those that lived in Underbridge or worked in the upscale posh offices in the town centre so it was a surprise to see Jerry Dooley suited and booted propping up the bar with his new girlfriend Leanne they looked happy and were blissfully chatting away. Leanne was attractive very tanned fit looking with her bleach blonde hair trussed up into a bun she was donning a smart black trouser suit with a simple thin diamante studded belt around her waist, Jerry was his usual self laughing loudly as they were engaged in deep conversation not even noticing the arrival of Stanley and Ami.

"Good evening Mr. Dooley" Stanley approached keeping up his well to do English gentleman accent tapping Jerry on his shoulder, he was confident and happy with Ami on his arm, Jerry swiveled around clapping eyes onto his mate "Stan my man wow look at you!" he exclaimed loudly stepping back to admire his mates transformation, Stanley smiled a broad grin and rolled his eyes before they embraced fleetingly, Jerry ushered Leanne forward eagerly "Leanne this is Stanley and I take it you are Ami?" he did his best to introduce them all, they all greeted each other. Ami smiled sweetly at Leanne who also returned a broad smile "hello nice to meet you" they both said in unison causing them to giggle nervously as they checked each other out, "pleasure to meet you" Stanley stepped forward and planted a kiss onto Leanne's cheek he was in full escort mode in his element which was an interesting surprise to both Ami and Jerry who continued to look on at him in astonishment.

"Espinolas eh Jerry I'm impressed" Stanley stepped back and looked around admiring the classy venue, "only the best Stanley" Jerry replied back putting his arm around Leanne feeling full of himself "ok let's get a table and order some drinks" his big voice boomed enthusiastically, "we are just going to powder our noses" Leanne spoke she had a high pitched sweet sugary voice, she grabbed Ami's hand and led her away towards the female restroom watched all the way by both Stanley and Jerry. "Man we have got a couple of crackers there Stanley" Jerry bounced up and down rubbing his hands he was full of beans patting Stanley on the shoulder he was obviously buzzing and full of energy bouncing around like a cat on a hot tinned roof, "yeah you are definitely punching above your weight mate" Stanley joked laughing at Jerry causing him to stop bouncing up and down his face twisting into a serious expression, "only joking she seems lovely I'm happy for you" a cool Stanley hugged him tightly.

All four were now sat a table positioned in the far corner of the restaurant it was very sedate the dim lighting from the fairy lights which were dotted around the high beams "this is nice" Leanne spoke her high perky tone almost childlike and excitable "I've heard a lot about you Stanley the Tyford two" she giggled as she spoke her squeaky accent had a Northern twist, her face was a very orange tan she had piercing blue eyes and her teeth were a fluorescent white in stark comparison to her skin, "all the time Stanley this and Stanley that" she continued laughing looking towards Jerry who nodded taking a sip of his pint "all good stuff I hope" Stanley chipped in "of course" she giggled back. Ami remained poised one of her hands under the table perched onto Stanley's lap the other hand held her glass of white wine "I've heard lots about Jerry too" she spoke quietly her slight Swedish accent abound in her sentence "oh no what have you told her?" Jerry held his face in his hands cringing joking around hiding behind his hands, "don't worry I know you have some kind of bromance!" she laughed gripping Stanley's leg tightly and looking at him lovingly. The ice was well and truly broken as they all awaited their meals it was funny as both Stanley and Jerry were consummate diners truly on their P's and Q's entertaining their young girlfriends. Nobody would have thought they would ever be at this point in their lives, they ate drank laughed and were having a ball Ami had loosened up and was now retelling the story of how she and Stanley met, "I saw this scruffy guy in shorts and flip flops but then he came out or the dressing room in a suit a wow!" she continued clearly now full after the meal and merry from the wine "he is so handsome" she gushed rubbing her hand onto Stanley's face, "ahh so romantic" Leanne cooed "we met at a foam party drunk!" she cracked into a high pitched cackle causing the rest of them to break into a roar of laughter causing the waiting staff and other customers to look over.

Stanley felt his phone vibrating in his pocket he was still laughing hard with the others as he pulled it out he stared at the screen and could see a long foreign looking number, Ami watched him as he answered "hello Stanley speaking" he reigned in his laughter "hello Spank have you forgotten me already?" the voice was unmistakable even amongst the din of the laughter and chatter of their table sultry smoky and with a hint of irony, Stanley felt the blood rush from his face it was awkward and he knew with Ami right beside him it would be hard to disguise the conversation, "hold on just give me a second" he got up from the table a bit flustered "be back in a bit" he hurriedly walked away from the table he seemed to be alert now like a sheep dog hearing the whistle of its owner, Jerry and Leanne looked on and Ami's face was not impressed in fact she had a face like thunder watching Stanley dart outside the restaurant at speed.

"Anais how are you?" he spoke softly attempting to sound calm but knew he felt awkward, "I'm missing you Stanley how comes you didn't call me?" she asked firmly placing Stanley on the spot "I'm really sorry just been a bit busy" he replied looking over his shoulder back into the restaurant, "look can I call you tomorrow I'm out with some friends" he continued trying to rush the conversation, "ok I just wanted to let you know I'll be in London from tomorrow and I really want to see you" her husky tone once again danced into Stanley's ears "ok call me when you arrive I have to go" he again responded rushing knowing Ami would be wondering what he was up to, "ok Mr. Spank au revoir" she hung up the phone leaving Stanley feeling strangely excited but shaken. He knew this was going to be a difficult situation he turned and glanced through the window and could see Jerry Leanne and Ami still chattering away, he took a minute to compose himself before returning to the table greeted by a frosty stare from Ami which Jerry was alert to "Spank thanks for rejoining us he's such a busy man eh" he cracked a joke attempting to inject a dose of humour.

Stanley took his seat and was still getting daggers from Ami who although was clearly fuming inside but still regained her poise, she nudged Stanley under the table giving him an indication of her mood, Stanley smiled politely at everyone and turned to Ami with an ashen look on his face winking and placing his arm around her to reassure her everything was fine.

A perky young waitress arrived at the table with a small notebook, "are you guys ready for dessert?" she chirped cheerfully cutting into the strained atmosphere, "er yeah we will have two chocolate fudge cakes" Jerry spoke confidently he had now taken off his suit jacket and loosened his tie he kept his arm around Leanne and kept canoodling with her at every opportunity much to the embarrassment of the waitress "and for you sir?" she turned her attention to Stanley and Ami, "no I'm fine" Ami spoke blankly giving a courteous smile to the young waitress, Stanley picked up on her mood "no nothing for me" he followed suit much to the surprise of Jerry who again boisterously shouted his order "and a bottle of your finest champagne" he exclaimed loudly making sure half of the restaurant could hear him.

"Jerry it's ok we're fine" Stanley protested he was now sullen and not enjoying the evening he knew that Ami was not happy "no my friend we are celebrating tonight we have two crackers" he continued in his usual boorish manner looking at Leanne and Ami who's sour face just about managed to crack a smile, Stanley shuffled uncomfortably in his chair then straightened his blazer "ok champagne it is then" he conceded "but I'm paying" he continued taking out a wad of cash licking his finger and thumb before counting out some notes and laying them down on the table, "you are a gentleman and a scholar" Jerry held up his beer glass towards his mate then burst into a fit of laughter "sorry" he spluttered his face turned red as he choked back his laughter to the amusement of the young waitress, "it's fine will that be all?" she smiled sweetly, Jerry held up his hand in a mock surrender towards her "yes thanks" he continued to enjoy a hearty laugh to himself as Leanne looked on rolling her eyes "god I can't take you anywhere" she slapped him playfully on his arm giggling again her high pitched sugar coated voice sounding like a cartoon character.

Once again Stanley glanced over to Ami trying to hold her hand she pulled it away still stern faced obviously still vexed from his phone call and impromptu exit, Stanley was about to whisper something to Ami when the young vivacious waitress returned with the silver bucket of champagne and four glasses, "here we go" she placed the items down as Leanne and Ami politely cleared some space on the table, "thank you" she smiled "be right back with your desserts".

Jerry stood up he seemed to become more disheveled by the minute quickly attempting to tuck in his shirt which had become detached from his bulging waistline, he popped the cork out followed by a cheer from him and Leanne, he seemed like a different man full of joy pouring out the fizzy liquid into each glass "ok time for a toast" he continued fixing his tie then picking up his glass, they all looked towards Jerry he swayed slightly unsteady on his feet then announced his toast "to the four of us the Tyford four!" he shouted lifting his glass up high before necking down the contents of his glass, "the Tyford four" they all responded in unison Ami's tone deadpan, before she swilled down in one her glass too. "Dessert" the young waitress arrived back, "do you want me to take a picture?" she asked cheerfully sensing the epic occasion "ok cool use my phone" Stanley piped up handing her his mobile then assertively pulling Ami towards him, he could smell her fragrance as she lay back into his chest as they all posed waiting for the bright flash to go off, "that's one for the archives" Stanley said taking his phone back and looking at the picture.

It had come to the end of the night thankfully the rest of the evening had gone smoothly without any further disruption even Ami's mood had managed to thaw enough for her and Leanne to walk off giggling in deep conversation towards the female restrooms again for a final touch up.

Stanley and Jerry's eyes stayed trained on their girlfriends until they disappeared through the door, "Jesus mate what is up with Ami?" Jerry questioned an exasperated Stanley "that phone call I had to take it was from Anais" he stated sitting back and running his hands through his hair "she's still a bit narked because of the escort thing", Jerry lent forward onto the table and breathed out heavily "mate you got a lot of grovelling to do tonight" he spoke without raising his head his voice semi muffled, it was true Stanley had a long night ahead of him trying to quell Ami's wrath which he knew was going to come, "I could die for a joint right now" he gasped picking up his glass finishing the remains of his pint gulping it down and wiping his mouth, "yeah" he sighed reflectively.

Once the girls remerged Jerry and Stanley had paid the bill and were up and ready to leave, Stanley looked at Ami she looked upset as if she had been crying Leanne cleverly made a beeline for Jerry hugging him tightly much to Jerry's surprise, "you ok?" Stanley walked towards Ami reaching out to hold her hand "I'm ready to go" she whimpered attempting to crack a forced smile she held his hand limply a token gesture which sent out a clear message to Stanley.

"Ok guys we are going to walk" Jerry interjected sensing his mate needed some alone time, "ok mate was a pleasure meeting you Leanne" Stanley reached over and planted a kiss on her cheek, "lovely to meet the famous Stanley too" she quipped back still highly energised and chirpy, "bye babe" she hugged Ami rubbing her back "see you soon" Jerry stepped forward and planted a kiss on Ami's cheek, then turned to Stanley pretending to lean in for a kiss, "forget it mate your not that pretty!" Jerry joked then bounded off with Leanne "I'll call tomorrow" Stanley shouted out then turned to face Ami, "shall we?" he offered his hand to which Ami accepted.

The short walk to the taxi rank was frosty only small talk was had between them, Stanley still played the gentleman and opened the door for her she slid elegantly in her gold shoes shining in the night, "Underbridge please" Stanley shouted to the driver climbing into the back next to Ami, he squeezed up next to her and cuddled her which was initially met with resistance but eventually Ami relented and fell into his arms "that went well" Stanley mentioned rubbing Ami's arm "yes it was nice" she responded yawning wildly before she turning her face towards Stanley, he immediately interpreted that she wanted to kiss and began to pucker up his lips and lean in towards her only to be met by her hand in his face, "not so easy Mr Spank, who was on the phone?" she waited barely two minutes before getting off her chest what was bothering her.

Stanley sat back exhaling loudly "Ami can we not just have a good night and not get into any drama" he sounded exasperated maybe because he was anticipating an avalanche which made him become defensive, "can I stay with you tonight?" he fired back quickly kissing her on the forehead dismissing her question entirely continuing to smooch and kiss her around the face, Ami wriggled his kisses tickled her neck and face, she tried her hardest to resist his advances but crumbled and melted ignoring the driver turning to kiss him passionately. The taste of wine and lager mixed as they launched into a full open mouthed French kiss attracting a sneaky yet disapproving look from the driver in the rear view mirror, they continued to chew away at each others faces making loud sloppy noises until the driver cleared his throat aggressively interrupting their impromtu clinch.

"Ok five pounds please" the grumpy middle aged driver spouted clearly unimpressed by the cavorting on display, they both stepped out and Stanley handed the driver a crumpled note, "thank you sir" he nodded towards the frumpy driver before turning away. The night chill made Ami shiver on the short walk to her flat and knowing he was clearly not out of the doghouse yet Stanley took off his jacket and placed around Ami's bare shoulders "such a gent" she said toddling off in her high heels. Stanley shoved his hands into his pockets and causally strolled in behind her admiring her sexy figure draped in his over sized blazer he was still heightened by their tryst in the taxi and seemed to be full of himself now that he knew he was staying his swagger returned albeit an intoxicated one but one thing he knew is that he would have to used all of his Spank magic to charm his way back into Ami's good books as her suspicions deepened.

Once they were back home and into Ami's flat Stanley wasted no time in launching his charm offensive by shuffling up to his girlfriend from behind and removing his blazer from her shoulders she shivered feeling his cold hands touch her bare back followed by his lips pecking gently on the back of her neck "ohh Stanley" she turned around her eyes looked dreamy looking up towards him it was obvious she was also feeling a bit tipsy she giggled then pulled him towards her and engulfed herself in a deep kiss opening her mouth wide and sucking onto his lips forcefully pushing her tongue inside.

Stanley groaned cupping her head from behind then moving his hands slowly down her back onto her buttocks squeezing tightly through her silky dress material, Ami stood back and gasped taking a second to breath and gather herself Stanley was left gasping for air himself still open mouthed, "well are you going to just stand there or are you going to help me out of this dress?" Ami spoke quietly and breathy stepping out of one her shoes, her accent sounded cute and enticing as she staggered back kicking off her other shoe "whoops" she screamed then burst out laughing before Stanley thrust forward and picked her up playfully, "bed time for you" he sounded smooth maintaining the gentlemanly charm nuzzling his face into her neck and chest tripping on her shoes as they bumbled their way to the bedroom nosily in a fit of grunts and giggles.

A loud alarm bell rang annoyingly piercing into the silence it continued until the long arm of Stanley stretch out and banged the top of the clock hitting it so hard it fell onto the floor he coughed frustrated at being woken from his slumber even Ami who was curled up beside him stirred slowly barely raising her head from the comfort of the soft pillow, the air hung heavy with the smell of a bodily musk.

Stanley opened his eyes slowly his blurred vision taking its time to adjust to the light which shone through the slanted blinds he squinted his eyes rubbing them hard before he once again let out a series of coughs, "what time is it?" Ami's sweet yet husky voice questioned as she turned around and snuggled up to Stanley entwining her naked body against his, Stanley reached over and looked at his phone, "it's quarter to ten" he answered relaxing back tenderly kissing Ami on her forehead making her cuddle up to him tighter. "Last night was good" a more awake sounding Stanley reflected "hmm you are naughty taking advantage of a tipsy girl" Ami's voice croaked softly, "I meant the whole night you know with Jerry and Leanne" he continued again affording Ami a couple of kisses on her face, "yes it was nice" she agreed twisting into him to get even more comfortable.

They both lay silently for a moment Ami began to rub her hand along Stanley's waist and chest "I could lay her all day" she mulled over the thought of comfort, "I wish I could babe but I have to go to London on business" Stanley casually let slip out his intention for the day which instantly threw Ami into aggressive mode, "what do you mean?" she suddenly had an injection of energy and stopped caressing his bare chest her eyes were now opened wide "what business?" instantly her mood had changed it were as if Stanley had triggered something again. Ami sat up her face still looked tired although she was now far more alert, "oh so this was what that phone call was about" she spoke sternly looking directly at Stanley who could only concede defeat at this point he was too tired to even fight with her, "look I have to do this job it's important" he tried to be as earnest as possible but could see the fire in Ami's eyes the bone of contention had reared again "why do you have to do this Stanley?" she became upset and got up out of the bed naked picking up his shirt from off of the floor and putting it on her pale flesh exposed and only modestly covered, "I don't like this job" she stormed out upset into the bathroom slamming the door behind her forcefully causing Stanley to shudder.

He rolled his eyes to the heavens "I don't need this" he spoke under his breath before jumping out of the bed and putting on his boxer shorts before walking to the bathroom and politely knocking on the door, "Ami please open the door" he spoke softly leaning his head against the door "leave me alone Stanley" her muffled voice responded, he knew that even if he begged she would not be in the mood to listen part of him could not fault her either he knew lying to her was not what she deserved and only he had himself to blame for this dilemma he was letting her down by acting like a prized chump but also the words of his mate Jerry telling him to have fun and play the field also filled his head with the notion that seeing Anais was something he head to do, it was just the deceit towards Ami which pained him, he walked back and sat on the bed he was fraught running his hands through his hair it was all coming on top and he did not know what to do.

The sound of the bathroom door opening signalled the end of the stand off Ami emerged clearly upset her face of disappointment was hard enough for a sorrowful Stanley to look at he remained seated on the bed he knew from last night this storm had been brewing so it was time for him to face whatever came his way. Ami arms folded and red faced clearly still unhappy sidled up next to Stanley she drew her knees up to her chest sniffing trying to hold back her tears Stanley belatedly put his arm around her offering some consolation and affection "I promise after this we will go on the holiday of a lifetime", he declared hoping that this would appease Ami "we can go anywhere in the world" he enthused squeezing her tightly, "I don't want some kind of gigolo I just want you Stanley" she looked at him her eyes puffy from the crying his shirt she wore slightly ajar revealing her breast and flat porcelain stomach.

Stanley knew that when he stared into her eyes her love was deep and genuine and also he was responsible for the hurt she was feeling it was a wrench to leave her in this way but the lure of seeing Anais once more was also such a strong pull, in one way he had to know whether his Monaco experience was just superficial due to the hot sun and magnificent surroundings rather than the fact he and Anais had a special chemistry.

He was not good at this game and hated how it all made Ami feel maybe he was becoming greedy and wanted it all regardless of the feelings of others, Ami turned her body in towards his and grabbed him tightly it was as if this action summed up their relationship, Stanley indecisive and Ami attempting to hold on to something precious.

Leaving Ami in the way he did niggled away at Stanley on his high speed journey towards London he sat in deep thought not noticing anyone or anything else in the carriage even the polite assistant pushing the refreshment trolley receive nothing more than a cursory glance from him. He chewed his fingers tips gnawing away lost in thought, his packed suitcase was next to him on the vacant seat and he tapped away on the hard casing nervous and guilty at the same time a real bag of mixed emotions it made him think that with all of the arguments and pressure from Ami was it all really worth it?, it was difficult he knew having her in his life was special but he had to weigh up the fact that he loved the escapades and after this he could not go back to working a normal job at the bus company like his dad.

His thoughts were interrupted by his phone he sat up and looked at the screen it was another unknown number but he answered it anyway, "hello" he spoke softly and sounded downbeat until he heard the sultry yet distinct voice of Anais, "hello Mr Spank where are you? I'm here at the hotel waiting" her voice was bright she sounded genuinely excited which pricked up Stanley "well Ms Von Arnold my ETA is around forty minutes" he replied now sounding a bit more energetic making Anais break into a sexy laugh, "well I've texted you all the details so hurry I can't wait to see you" her velvet tones were music to Stanley's ears he could not help but get a warm feeling in his stomach whenever he heard her "ok I'll be there soon" he again switched on his charm playing up to the fact he was on an adventure, any thoughts of the guilt from leaving Ami upset melted away, he disconnected the call he took a deep breath gearing himself up for what was going to be an interesting mission.

He had arrived and stepped quickly through the busy concourse pulling his case behind him dodging the various obstacles of rushing people small children flying pigeons knocking into luggage and cases, he was casual in ripped faded jeans, converse pumps and a blue chequered shirt he was rushing to get to the taxi rank keen now to meet up with his society chick.

Stanley groaned when he arrived seeing there was a long queue of passengers ahead of him, he looked up at the big clock which hung impressively in a lofty position above the main booking hall, twenty to four the big black hands pointed to the large numbers on the clock face, "it's ok I got time" he affirmed to himself pulling out a crumpled box of cigarettes from his pocket then digging around and patting his jeans looking for his lighter "damn" he cussed under his breath with the cigarette hanging from his mouth, "excuse me sir do you need a light?" an older gentleman stood behind him distinguished in his dress sense very business like in a black pin striped suit.

He looked Mediterranean with grey hair dark at the roots similar to the actor Omar Sharif, he offered Stanley a large flame from a large gold lighter Stanley puffed away until the fag was lit, "cheers mate" he nodded to the gentleman who smiled back at him, his teeth were stained yellow with slim gold fillings on each side of his set "it's ok my friend" he replied clicking back the top of the lighter inserting into his inside blazer pocket then oddly walked off without a word disappearing into the bustling crowds,

Stanley continued to look trying to locate the strange man but he could not see him "totally random" he mumbled to himself between quick puffs.

He finally able to get into a black taxi, "where to?" the old cockney driver asked switching on the meter, Stanley pulled out his phone to check on the text from Anais, "the Hilton Mayfair please" he stuttered out his words whilst reading the text, the driver nodded and drove out of the station allowing Stanley a moment to relax and collect himself before being reunited with Anais.

Pulling into the fantastic Hilton hotel reminded Stanley of pulling up to the Grande in Monaco he was in awe at the tall skyscraper and it's surroundings he could see the well dressed doormen looking immaculate in their sharp blazers and shiny black shoes attending to other guests as a stream of luxury cars pulling up to the entrance, "thirty five pounds please" the driver cranked up the handbrake then turned around pulling the glass partition aside to enable Stanley to pass through the money.

Stanley handed over some crisp notes "keep the change" he winked at the driver full of himself before stepping out and bowling towards the entrance the way he was dressed felt out of place in contrast to the impeccable clean entrance, maybe they would think he was a pop star or something he thought as he walked past the doormen nodding politely before walking through the main lobby.

It was large clean and very classically opulent a beautiful marble tiled floor which sat a large glass table with a tall orchid centre piece the rich green leaves and ivory coloured petals complimented the surroundings perfectly. Stanley was instantly struck by its beauty casting his eyes all over until he saw the fine rich oak wood reception area, "this is why I love this job" he mentioned speaking to himself confirming his justification for making the trip, he pushed his fair fringe back and took a deep breath then strode up to the reception desk.

The look he received from the snooty nosed receptionist said it all it was demeaning to say the least she could not help looking at him with a hint of disdain, "yes how can I help" she sounded just like she looked as if she had a broomstick shoved somewhere very uncomfortable, her face was pushed up as she looked at Stanley, "I'm here to see Miss Anais Von Arnold", he made sure he spoke in his alter ego English gentleman accent, suddenly the uptight receptionist changed her stance and voice, "ah Miss Von Arnold" she confirmed her voice now perked up a notch "and who shall I say is requesting her?" she continued her tone now very accommodating and genial.

Stanley could not help himself by milking the moment "she's expecting me" he replied bluntly for once relinquishing his manners much to the shock of the receptionist her long nose clearly now out of joint "one moment please" she quietly spoke picking up the telephone her slim manicured finger pushing buttons, "good afternoon Miss Von Arnold your guest has arrived" she looked at Stanley again who smiled smugly, "ok I'll send him up" she placed down the handset "sir please make your way to the seventh floor suite1125", she smiled warmly her face now a red flush clasping her hands together looking a wee bit embarrassed "do you need any help with your luggage sir" she said hopefully, "no thanks I'm ok" Stanley shot back turning and walking towards the shiny lifts dragging his case behind him.

The loud bell rang in the plush lift signifying he had reached the desired floor he quickly looked at his reflection once more in the spotless mirror it was only after he checked himself out a few times over and the lift door slid smoothly open the butterflies really began to play in his stomach, this was the first time he was going to see Anais and in a totally different environment from her fathers super yacht and with the leers of Charles Carter. He did his best to compose himself walking along the lush patterned carpeted floor in the wide corridor which was flanked by vintage gold frame paintings the decadent surroundings were lost on Stanley he was too excited and focused on laying eyes on Anais again.

Finally he reached the room number he drew breath and paused before tapping on the door lightly for a minute he stood patiently waiting but nothing no answer so again he knocked the door but this time with a bit more vigour this time he could hear faint noises from inside the room "give me a second" a female voice cried out on the other side of the door, eventually he heard the lock being turned and the door opened, a dripping wet haired Anais stood in a fluffy white Hilton hotel labelled robe her face was wet but she was still tanned and flawlessly gorgeous.

"Spank!" she screamed delighted to see him stepping forward and flinging her arms around his neck hauling him towards her ensuring he got a full wetting as well "hi" an overwhelmed yet surprised Stanley managed to get out his voice muffled as his mouth was squashed against her fluffy toweled robe she stepped back finally letting go of Stanley's neck "wow that was a nice welcome" he exclaimed fixing his shirt and wiping his face wearing a broad smile. The feelings from Monaco came flooding back once more he was able to properly set eyes on her again, "come in don't just stand there I was having a bath" Anais demanded waltzing back into the room her husky voice calm and inviting.

Stepping into the suite was like walking into a penthouse, it was large beautifully furnished it had modern features such as the large supersized flat TV screen mounted on the wall yet the furniture was vintage and expensively upholstered a large crème sofa with plump brown and gold leafed patterned cushions. An elegant iron cast glass table adorned with an assortment of Harpers Bazaar magazines displayed on the top.

Stanley pulled his suitcase to the middle of the room then stopped to take in the spectacular views overlooking Hyde park through large clear rectangular windows, it was breath taking but not more than the view of a half dressed Anais returning to the room "you like Mr. Spank?" she asked rhetorically causing Stanley to turn around "yeah this place is amazing…" he stopped talking immediately soon as he saw her now dressed in a dainty little white vest top and matching shorts her hair was now slicked back showing off her perfect shaped face and gold bangles decorated her wrists "It's good to see you still have your looks" she quipped eyeing Stanley.

Stanley was lost for words he could only grin as she walked sexily towards him, his heart beat twice as fast and he seemed to lose all of his cool persona he began to fidget again like he always did whenever he got nervous or was around Anais, "do you want a drink?, chill out make your self at home" she continued strolling around totally comfortable in her surroundings, "yeah cool what have you got?" Stanley tried to loosen up plopping himself down into the comfortable sofa and cushions.

"So how's the Baron and your mum" a more relaxed calm Stanley began to engage looking around the room, it was weird attempting to switch to being with Anais when less than twenty four hours ago he was sharing his intimate space with Ami they were totally different types of girls he knew that but it still did not stop him having to really think hard about trying not to get their names wrong, "yeah they are fine" she yelled from the far reaches of the kitchen space which was over the other side of the room "they send their love too" she continued to shout while clinking around.

Anais came back with a large silver bucket filled with a large champagne bottle and two large slim flutes "and here's one I made earlier" she waltzed back into the lounge area of the suite, Stanley did not forget his manners and immediately jumped up to give her a hand taking charge and grabbing the silver bucket which was cold and filled with ice, "thank you" she smiled sweetly at him.

He smelt her fresh sweet aroma her fragrance wafted past his nose, "come on put it on the table then come and sit down" she spoke confidently she was clearly in charge fussing and buzzing around like a mosquito, Stanley could only watch as she elegantly sat on the sofa crossing her gorgeous long olive toned legs. "Well are you going to open it then or stand there like a butler" her wit was sharp and made Stanley laugh he loved her banter even for someone so rich and posh he loved that she had a great sense of humour.

"So Spank did you miss me?" she looked deep into his eyes while he poured her a full glass of the fizzy champagne his hand was shaking it was silly he always felt so nervous around her, she still had that mystical aura and now they were alone he felt even more vulnerable to her charm.

Stanley sat down beside her after pouring himself a drink "cheers and yes it's always a pleasure Miss Von Arnold" he spoke more confidently holding up his glass to hers, "I did not expect to see you so soon after Monaco" he continued taking a big mouthful of champagne, Anais sipped hers coolly staring seductively back she smiled whilst swallowing her drink, "well I came here for you" she replied boldly yet with a hint of shyness continuing to sip on the long flute with a little smile towards Stanley who himself was quite flattered by her statement, "really?" he quizzed unsure of whether she was up to her mischievous games again.

Stanley swept his hair back he did not know whether to quite believe her as she stayed deadpan in her expression, "I'm really surprised" he spoke quietly thinking it through as he spoke waiting for her to burst into a fit of laughter or something but she remained deadly serious fluttering her eyelids and smiling "your not joking are you?" Stanley looked at her then stretched to put his glass down on the table, "come here" he said assertively moving in towards a now timid blushing Anais she shuffled up next to him it was uncomfortable like two school kids who had a secret crush. Stanley took charge and lent forward putting his arm around her bare shoulder, he pulled her in towards him and lent forward tenderly kissing her on the lips the sound of Anais groaning with pleasure apart from their lips connecting was all that could be heard.

They both pulled away and shyly giggled "I should have done that at the door" Stanley joked, maybe it was the surroundings and champagne but Anais had an effect on him her mystique cheekiness and fragility endeared him it was like kryptonite to superman he was weak and under her spell. They laid tucked up in each others arms looking up towards the chandelier strewn ceiling Anais was very attentive stroking Stanley's thighs tenderly her smooth skin shimmering they were comfortable and for once no words were spoken in a moment of silence.

Stanley continued to sip away at his glass of champagne he was relaxed in a world of his own consumed by the lavish surroundings "hey Spank why so quiet?" Anais spoke her voice quieter than normal almost a whisper she tilted her head back to get eye contact she adjusted and looked into his eyes "I can see up your nostrils" she burst out laughing "you can be so silly" Stanley replied threatening to pour his glass over her face, she screamed covering her face and laughing hysterically then then catching her breath calming down and turning over onto her front.

"You fancy partying tonight?" Anais fixed her hair back away from her face and continued to stare up at him, Stanley looked up towards the dangling lights "yeah why not" he answered back "where's the party?" he downed the rest of his drink sitting up then burping unintentionally "oops pardon me" he apologised then cracked up laughing childishly which was followed by a slap on the thigh from an unimpressed Anais "manners please" she corrected him swiftly before contorting herself into a standing position her tall leggy frame overlooked a seated Stanley who in turn ran his eyes up and down her model figure, he was aroused just by looking at her it was weird yet mesmeric everything about her from her cute nude manicured finger tips up to her smooth skinned flawless face was beautiful.

He grabbed her hands gently and stood up he felt woozy but held firm his stance, Anais again let out a little chuckle "what's up Spank?" she spoke playfully just about getting out the question before being consumed by a big sloppy kiss from Stanley who boldly gripped her waist holding her strongly, it did literally take her breath away especially as she was in mid sentence.

Stanley pulled away making an air kiss sound "mwah", looking back at a taken aback surprised Anais "well that was nice" she said wiping her mouth slowly her brown smokey eyes wide yet admiringly looking back at Stanley who too had a reddened face flush from the alcohol "I didn't know you had that in you", again her wit masking the fact she was impressed, "neither did I" Stanley replied sweeping his hair back into place "so where's this party then?" he kept his cool running his fingers through her long thick hair and attentively touching her face smoothing his hands across her eyebrows. Anais shyly manoeuvred her head side ways making a purring noise like a cat enjoying being stroked "why did you come into my life?" she asked sounding relaxed "there I was lying on my sun lounger dreading Charles Carters visit and then bang there you were" her eyes opened wider as she relived that moment. Stanley smiled that comment injected a hit of confidence through Stanley he suddenly puffed out his chest here he was holding one of the most beautiful women he had seen in his life and getting complimented of course it swelled his ego but he knew she was being sincere, "why me?" he sounded confused, "I mean aren't you supposed to marry a prince or something?" he continued half joking, Anais face became serious she looked at him deeply before stating "I love you Spank you silly boy" lunging forward and kissing him passionately holding his face her gold bangles clinking together as she held her arms up.

They kissed for around ten minutes until finally Anais pulled away slowly they both gazed longingly breathing heavy attempting to catch their breath "did you really mean what you said?" a befuddled Stanley questioned his heart still pumping hard from their clinch, "I'm serious" she pouted irresistibly "you like me for me not for my money or my status I knew that straight away", Anais gushed still with her arms around Stanley's neck, "anyway enough of this lovey dovey stuff let's get ready to party!" she screamed then turned around and bounded off to the bedroom "I need to find something to wear!" she shouted clearly feeling euphoric.

His conscious ate away at him while he lay on the king size bed he could hear the running water from the shower coupled with Anais blissfully singing in the background, he was torn his thoughts on Ami he knew he was being intolerable by leading this double life and expecting her to still be there for him.

He also had Jerry's voice echoing in his head telling him to live life and enjoy the good times while they were there he also knew his parents would frown upon such cowardice and deceit especially his mum Brenda but then there was the happy gorgeous society girl who continued to happily test her dulcet tones in the large bathroom next door. He sat up quickly the cool cocky confident Stanley had been replaced by a confused anxious young man, he lent over and grabbed the champagne bottle which contained the last remains of the fizzy liquid, he tilted the bottle and guzzled the rest of its contents which frothed around his mouth, he then regimentally stood up and began removing his clothes unbuttoning his shirt he laughed to himself like as drunken sailor burping again as the bubbles internally fizzed up through his chest and nostrils inducing hiccups.

He continued undoing his jeans he was now in such a state of headiness in this moment nothing mattered anymore it was like he was saying to hell with it all, less than a year ago he had nothing but friendship with Jerry and a home with two loving parents now he was suffering from hiccups by drinking vintage champagne in an executive suite in the Hilton hotel in London, not forgoing the fact he had a beautiful bond girl in the shower in the shape of Anais Von Arnold.

His face wore an indulgent drunken smirk he stepped out of his trousers then peeled off his tight grey David Beckham boxer shorts stumbling momentarily as he kicked them off with his foot, he took a deep breath before striding forward totally naked towards the bathroom door which was ajar his lean pale frame stark purposely walking, he pushed the door open letting out a gust of hot perfumed scented steam as he entered "room service!" he shouted stepping into the shower greeted by a high pitched shriek followed by fits of giggles and muffled laughter which then quelled to be replaced by water splashed kisses.

It seemed like they were locked in the shower forever until they both reappeared both wet and naked Anais long legs were wrapped around Stanley as he carried her towards the large circular bed Anais continued to kiss Stanley around his face she was rampant and her breaths heavy, they both fell onto the bed in a jumbled pile Stanley not being the most graceful in lowering her onto the soft quilt "hey gently" the sultry soaked haired society girl looked up at him breaking into another fit of giggles before pulling him in towards her, Stanley was still feeling the effects from the alcohol he was giddy but the magnetism of Anais of was so strong he could not pull himself away part of him felt like he was in a dream but this was real the touch of her smooth glossed skin and the warm breaths which tickled his wet chest reminded him that this was very much reality, he paused staring into her doe eyes he ran his fingers through her wet tangled hair "you love me?" he asked profoundly with a sense of disbelief as droplets of water dripped onto Anais bronzed neck, "yes I just know.." she answered tailing off shyly sweeping his fair hair back away from his face "yes Spank don't let me tell you again" she cracked up laughing putting her hand behind his head pulling him in towards her, a wicked broad smile crept across Stanley's face his ego was soaring before he once again submerged himself in another glutton of kisses.

Stanley felt giddy not just from the effects of the champagne but the concoction of lust and Anais were a force he succumbed to his weakness apparent as he became more aroused every part of her body he touched rubbed and caressed Anais groaned with pleasure the more he ran his fingers across her smooth body, he tried to be soft and in control but he was really quite hurried and clumsy as he continued his boundless indulgence, Anais grabbed his hand just as he was groping at her nether regions, "wait" she stopped him in his tracks as Stanley continued to chomp down on her neck oblivious to Anais soft request, "wait Stanley we need to get ready for the party", Stanley groaned as he continued to make kissing movements with his lips which more resembled a goldfish sucking for air out of water before rolling over onto his back, breathing out heavily, "ok" he replied reluctantly clasping his hand over his private parts slightly aware that he was nearing the point of no return, "let's just" Anais clambered over him and began to kiss him on his body moving he head down towards his taut midriff eventually working her way slowly down to his groin area, her long wet hair snaked across his stomach, Stanley gasped sucking in air as Anais naughtily worked her magic, "oh my god" he spoke out stagnated unable to control his emotions his toes curling tightly as the sensation heightened, Anais stopped abruptly and looked up "that's enough for now" she wiped her mouth and began to laugh looking down at a defenceless Stanley who's body was contorting with his eyes closed, "what type of lady do you think I am?" she questioned playfully wringing her hair and tying it back letting the excess water drip down onto Stanley's twisted body "come on time to party Spank" she slapped his buttock then removed herself from the bed.

"Hello reception this is Anais Von Arnold ask my driver to meet me in the lobby in ten minutes" she slammed down the phone assertively now sounding fully focused, she walked across the marble floor barefooted yet dressed in a hot red pair of shorts matched with a red blouse slashed on the arms, she had a gold belt complimented by gold dangling earrings and bracelets her hair was once again slicked back into a high ponytail allowing her beautiful browned face to be the centrepiece, she was always effortless in her beauty and achieved a model look every time.

Stanley emerged from the bedroom he smelt fresh and looked very slick himself black jeans fastened with a chunky silver buckled belt with black loafer shoes and a crisp white shirt was his attire for the evening he too now looked composed his hair too all slicked back like a true brylcream boy the cuffs on his sleeves were turned up half way up to his wrists, "the car will be here is a sec I'm just going to put on my shoes" a hurried yet happy Anais waltzed in squirting puffs of sweet perfume onto her chest plate whilst still trotting around barefooted with her black shiny heels hanging from her other hand, she stopped momentarily to check out Stanley "hmm you scrub up so well I'm a lucky girl" she said excitedly planting a glossy kiss onto his cheek before plonking herself down on the sofa to strap her shoes on.

Stanley walked to one of the large glass windows and stared out pensively as he awaited he looked out to the passing traffic below the blur of the lights caught his eye it was the one thing he liked about London the buzz that something was always going on and from the relative calm of Anais swanky hotel suite he know that down below there was a hive of activity going on, he loved this part of his life it took him away from everything even Ami who he seem to have complete memory loss of in the company of Anais, he continued to stare reflective in his thoughts until the shrill of the telephone interrupted his moment, "hello…ok we'll be down in a minute" Anais's smoky voice answered "come on Stanley time to party honey" she sounded upbeat her enthusiasm distracting Stanley away from his solemn gaze, "ok let's do it" he turned and walked towards a beautiful stunning Anais who was now fully dressed up to the nines "wow!" Stanley was stopped in his tracks he stopped and applauded "classy very classy" he admired before reaching out his hand and bowing mockingly towards her, "shall we?" he asked his English gentleman persona rearing again "yes Mr Spank let's shall we?" Anais responded smiling cutely and winking at her man.

Another night and another chauffeur driven experience for Stanley this time in the back of a sweet vanilla smelling Mercedes it was clean and smooth the engine purring almost silently as they cruise along the Thames through the night traffic, "so who's party is it we are going to?" Stanley asked breaking the silence from a poised and serious looking Anais "oh just an old friend it's a small soiree but should be fun" she replied with an air of nonchalance pulling one of her signature slim white cigarettes from a small silver pocket case "fancy a Von Arnold?" she quipped shoving one of the cigarettes towards Stanley who laughed recalling the now infamous white sticks, "no I'm ok" he waved his hand much to Anais surprise "hmm staying clean I see Spank" she nodded impressed before sparking her cigarette pulling on it with her bubble gum pink lipsticked mouth and blowing out coolly pressing the automatic window down to let the smoke out, Stanley sat back admiring his beauty he felt chuffed knowing he was with one of the most beautiful girls he'd ever seen of course aside from Ami but Anais Von Arnold exuded mystique and when Stanley was around her it made him forget about everything and everyone else.

They arrived at a large house in a quiet leafy street in Kensington the car slowly drew to a halt only the soft hum of the engine could be heard from the outside it did not seem like much was going on but the distant thud of music could be heard, "let's go handsome" Anais grabbed Stanley's hand as they waited for the quiet driver to walk around the car to open the door.

They both stepped out and looked at each other giving one quick glance of assurance "hmm very handsome" Anais commented squeezing his hand tightly before leading the way towards the house, Stanley turned and winked at the driver who returned the wink knowingly before he got dragged by a sauntering eager Anais who trotted eagerly up the high concrete porch steps.

Anais pressed the doorbell which chimed loudly like the bells of a cathedral, "you ok?" she questioned staring her brown eyes adoringly at Stanley while they waited for the door to be answered "yes I'm fine" he answered back confidently leaning in to give her peck on the cheek just as the door was opened by a hyper young blonde dressed in a gold jumpsuit "hi babe!" she screamed out seeing Anais rushing out to hug her "oh my god you look amazing!" her tone squealing high as they embraced, Stanley stepped back allowing the reunion to be complete before the blonde turned to him "and who is this fine young man?" the smell of alcohol on her breath was apparent as she moved in to kiss him on the cheek, Stanley Spank this is Carmen Phipps my old friend and party queen" Anais made the introduction, "hello Carmen pleasure to meet you" again Stanley's best etiquette was on display, "well you have done well there dare I say" Carmen commented slapping Anais on her arm in approval, "come in don't just stand there" she ushered them into the house.

Upon entrance Stanley gawped at the exquisite hallway which had marble floor covered with a thin patterned carpet. The walls were adorned with expensive paintings some which would not be out of place in an art gallery along with the other ornaments and sculptured figurines lined up along the mantelpiece. They continued through the house where the sound of dance music became louder as did the murmur of chattering voices and laughter Anais once again squeezed his hand and winked at him in an act of reassurance while the excitable Carmen danced her way through some people off into the distance, "don't worry we'll only stay for a while Anais mentioned to Stanley who was still wide eyed at the size of the place.

The hallway led them through to a large marquee which was set up at the rear of the house it was filled with around forty people all well heeled some were prancing around dancing energetically under the flash of multi coloured lights "so this is how the other half gets down then?" Stanley asked sarcastically looking towards the bubbling throng, "something like that lets get a drink" Anais walked elegantly down the stairs into the marquee she had an air of confidence she stood out from the young socialite crowd her stunning body ensuring her outfit rocked against the back drop of the other young rich crowd he felt proud to walk in beside such a hot looking women knowing that all eyes were her it strangely made his attraction to her more intense if that could be possible.

The smell of weed and human musk hung thick in the air as the couple barged their way through to the bar set up at the back of the marquee "Jesus this is worst than the crown on a Saturday night" Stanley commented frustrated at having to bundle their way past flailing arms and heaving bodies to get him and Anais a drink.

Finally they made it Stanley swept back his hair composing himself "what do you fancy babe?" he tried to stay calm amongst the loud pumping beat "I'll have a martini on the rocks" she replied looking out to the hub in front of her making sure she still looked good fixing her hair, "Stanley I've just seen someone I know hold that drink for me" she excitedly commented before bolting off towards the dancing tribe, Stanley turned looking on haplessly watching Anais embrace a female friend, "martini and a pint please" he looked at the young bar man leaning against the pitched up bar, he felt a little out of his depth it seemed like everyone at the party had some association plus they were all rich types dressed smartly and chattering away but he was there for Anais and he had never really experience such a vibrant set of people.

After downing half of his pint and standing there holding Anais martini for at least twenty minutes Stanley heard a voice next to him "alright mate" the unfamiliar male tone made him spin around to see a tall smart flop haired young man stood next to him "Jackson Reece" he thrust out his hand towards Stanley who looked back at him puzzled "hi Stanley Spank" he held up his pint his hands full not allowing him to shake hands "thirsty are you?" Jackson replied with a smug smile nodding towards the martini in his other hand, Stanley looked at him before the penny dropped "oh no this is my girlfriends she's over there" he replied laughing gesturing towards Anais who was still in deep conversation with her friend.

The music still pumped at a high volume causing Jackson to lean in to talk into Stanley's ear, he was tall and wore a blue blazer with a striped tee shirt he looked red in the face which was either due to the heat or flush from the consumed alcohol, "enjoying yourself?" he questioned, Stanley looked back at him "yeah its not bad " he replied feeling obliged to answer to this stranger sipping on his pint, "look between me and you I could do with a little boost if you know what I mean" Jackson nudged him and rubbed his nose, "sorry" Stanley replied straining to hear him amongst the din, "you know mate fancy doing a Patsy Kline?" again he rubbed his nose chuckling knowing that Stanley was baffled by his suggestion.

"Patsy Kline?" Stanley questioned clearly none the wiser to his coded question, Jackson looked shifty before pulling out a little clear plastic bag full of white powder "Patsy Kline...line!" he replied to Stanley laughing clearly amused by Stanley's naivety, Stanley looked at him shocked and uncomfortable "no I'm cool thanks" he replied meekly looking over towards Anais who blew a kiss towards him, Stanley held up her drink as if to signal that he was tired of standing there holding a girly looking martini, "you sure mate this is top quality" Jackson continued his stench of sweat cruised into Stanley's nostrils, "no but thanks" Stanley politely declined before moving off into the crowd towards Anais.

Stanley could see that Anais was very popular with this crowd as she was getting greeted by different people and seemed excited to see most of them, he felt a bit isolated and like just a bit part or a trophy on Anais arm he did not have much in common with her friends it got him thinking of Ami and life in Tyford although he was making his best effort to enjoy his time with Anais, "I'm just going to find the toilet" he stated to Anais who scarcely acknowledged him whilst in mid flow conversing with another one of her friends, "ok don't be long" she partially smiled at him before getting back deep into conversation with her friend.

He entered the house and went upstairs in search of the toilet, the pint he had plus the champagne from earlier had gone right through him, he still observed the house and the different artefacts which were adorned on each shelf it showed that the owners had led a cultured and well travelled life. He had waited for around five minutes getting stared at by a couple of giggling drunk girls who seem to get fun by just staring him up and down and whispering.

He was bursting for the loo and was relieved when the door finally opened, he was about to rush in when he heard a voice behind him "hey stranger" the voice was recognisable and stopped Stanley in his tracks pausing his impending entry into the toilet, he turned around and saw the unmistakable face of Carissa Le Chad looking up towards his lean frame, "Carissa!" he shouted shocked but happy moving in to embrace her to which she responded with a warm hug, "what are you doing here?" he quizzed still looking uncomfortable as he need to relieve himself, Carissa laughed back at him and spoke calmly "do your business first I'll wait here for you" she shoved him ushering him towards the bathroom, "ok yeah thanks" Stanley responded slightly embarrassed then quickly running into the loo.

A few minutes later and Stanley emerged from the bathroom, Carissa was still there she could not wipe the smile off of her face "wow so good to see you" a reenergised and fresh Stanley returned his eyes were all over Carissa she looked stunning dressed in a beautiful little black dress with a gold head band she had natural beauty and was cute too "where's the other one?" he joked looking around for her sister Melissa, "no I'm here with a friend" she responded her brown eyes boring into his "so are you working here tonight?" she asked emphasising the work part of the question Stanley looked back at her it was as if he did not know how to answer, "well no I'm not working I'm here with someone" he spoke quietly bowing his head, "oh really?" Carissa seemed shocked "that's why you have not called me then?" she shot back she seemed hurt her beautiful face yearned when she looked at him, "no not at all" Stanley composed himself he reached out his hands in his plea, "I've just had a lot going on".

Carissa stepped forward she was now closer to Stanley's face he could feel the energy between them which took him fleetingly back to their liaison that night, her brown skin was shimmered and her red lips looked juicy and luscious the moment seem to last forever and became intense as they both stared at each other, "ah that's where you are?" the sultry smokey voice of Anais interrupted the frozen stand off between Carissa and Stanley who backed off as soon as he saw Anais coming up the stairs, "hi babe" he nervously welcomed Anais "and who is this?" Anais asked whilst grabbing Stanley's hand and looking at Carissa with an air of superiority she still looked stunning every feature still flawlessly in place.

Stanley felt a little awkward and tense in the middle of this stand off between two beauties, "this is…" he was just about to introduce when Anais took over "Anais Von Arnold" she stuck her hand out to shake, "Carissa Le Chad" Carissa replied softly putting her hand out to shake with Anais, "yeah this is er Carissa" Stanley repeated not knowing quite what to say, "and how do you guys know each other?" Anais quizzed looking at Stanley who stood almost void of a response before Carissa stepped in "let's just say we used to work together" she smiled sweetly in Stanley's direction, he could feel the blood rush to his face he pushed his fingers through his hair as he always did when he felt nervous or on the spot, Carissa sensing the slight tension took control, "anyway lovely seeing you again Stanley you look well take care" she winked at him before turning and stepping calmly away "nice to meet you Anais" again she smiled sweetly at Anais before turning and stepping slowly and elegantly down the stairs.

"I think I'm ready to go now" Anais looked up sternly at Stanley who was still trying to process all that had just happened, "ok yeah let's do it" he clutched Anais hand tightly and led her down the stairs, there were still crowds of people turning up at the front door and walking through the hallway, Stanley looked around hoping to catch a last glimpse of Carissa he saw her disappear into the marquee with Jackson Reece who had his arm around her, he felt a little bit gutted that he did not get the time to really speak with her but he knew as a gentleman he came with Anais and she was the one who always had this magnetic pull on him he was happy to step out with her and even more excited to return back to the Hilton suite with her.

The drive back was a quiet one Anais seemed to have lost her energy she was preoccupied silent and laid her head onto Stanley's shoulder he kissed her tenderly on her forehead she responded by nuzzling her head more into him, "are you ok?" he quizzed "yes I'm fine Spank" she spoke in almost a sultry whisper closing her eyes as the smooth ride cruised through city streets back towards the sumptuous hotel.

Stanley's mind drifted as the car sped along the road next to Hyde park he looked out to the trees which swayed in the night breeze only slightly lit by the street lamps his thoughts wandered from Carissa to Ami and also Anais who had fallen asleep in his arms it was awash with confusion it finally hit him that all of these girls wanted him and that he needed to choose which one he wanted to be with otherwise he would get caught up in this crazy web of emotions he was not adept at all the jumping from one to the other he knew he was the kingmaker and even with his sense of loyalty to Ami it was becoming a difficult decision especially when he could smell the sweet fragrance and feel the warm body of Anais on him.

They arrived back and Stanley woke Anais by gently rubbing her shoulder "come on sleepy head we are here", he whispered much to the humour of the driver, Stanley stepped out first and helped Anais out of the car, "good night sir" the driver nodded politely as the two slowly walked into the sparse lobby.

Whilst in the lift Anais stood close holding her arms around Stanley her eyes looked tired as she clung on tightly to her man "I love you Stanley I've never said that to anyone before" her voice a low husk the tiredness really creeping in, again this shocked Stanley he did not expect such an outpouring of emotions she seemed to want to really drive home her feelings as the time ebbed away, Stanley could not resist and pulled her towards him sneaking in a cheeky kiss just as the lift doors opened, they stepped out still with their lips locked together kissing passionately Anais cupped his face with her hands they were soft and warm against his cheeks she seemed to have found back her energy and was really going for it ravishing her fingers through his hair.

The two stood in the luxurious hallway canoodling for a while before Stanley was able to pull away, "let's go to the suite" he just about caught his breathe enough to speak, Anais giggled and ran towards the room in her high heels still looking very sexy in the red short suit Stanley was still trying to draw breath while Anais was suddenly full of mischief and euphoric "come on then" she giggled playfully unlocking the door and gesturing to him with her long bronzed perfectly manicured finger, Stanley laughed he loved her playfulness even at that time of the morning he let out a stifled laugh himself then quickly strode towards the room just as Anais kicked off her shoes and stepped into the room.

The morning after the night before and both Stanley and Anais were blissfully asleep curled up into each other, their bodies entwined their limbs splayed out like an octopus's tentacles all over the large bed, several cracks of light slashed through the gaps in the drapes filtering through the room which smelt of a mix of musty sweat and dull perfumed fragrance.

Anais stirred flinging her arms and legs around Stanley who was knocked out and did not even move, once again she moved her body clearly uncomfortable in her position this time opening her eyes blearily staring at Stanley who was out cold, she smiled yawning wildly then playfully ruffled Stanley's hair "you are gorgeous Mr Spank my own dream boy" she growled her deep morning voice barely a level above her normal husk before she kissed him on the forehead then got up out of the bed and walked naked towards the en suite bathroom her black hair draped down her back tangled yet still looking stylish, her long golden legs and perfectly arched back with her pert derriere looked majestic as she strolled into the large vintage bathroom.

The sound of the shower jetting its water splashing loudly roused a sleepy Stanley who rolled over looking for some form of contact with his sexy partner he grabbed the sheets feeling around then rubbed his eyes with vigour stretching out his long body, he just about found the energy to sit up, he coughed clearing his throat he sounded rough and hoarse breathing in heavily, he looked around him again finding it difficult to accept the reality that he was sat in a large comfortable bed in a private suite in the London Hilton hotel.

Finally he was able to haul himself up and out of the bed pulling on his tight black boxer shorts he swept his hair from his face he could hear Anais showering it seemed so surreal to be in this position and for once not working, but instead of feeling happy and content a heavy dose of guilt consumed him he no longer felt giddy with excitement or drunk from champagne the reality of his position hit him for some weird reason his first thoughts were of Ami, even surrounded in all of this opulence and luxury he had a yearning just to be home relaxing with her.

He walked over to the large windows and peered through the heavy material drapes the early morning sunshine dazzled him for a second before he adjusted his eyes to take in the beautiful view of the park opposite, he could hear Anais happily singing her voice high echoing against the back drop of the running of water, he quickly rummaged through his belongings and found his phone on the screen he saw five missed calls from Ami and a text, his heart leapt in his moment of sobriety he was quick to open the text "*where are you Stanley? call me*", he sunk onto the soft mattress of the large bed his shoulders slumped as much as the impression he made in the bed, he knew in that moment that he would have to finally make a bold choice to come clean.

He had two awesome women who adored him the problem was that he was equally enamoured with both of them too he was confused and scratched his head staring at the phone before a now refreshed and chirpy Anais walked back into the room, "he's alive!" she mocked her cheery voice happy to see a half naked Stanley sitting silently "hey good morning" she quickly walked towards him her sleek frame covered with a white Hilton branded towel her fresh face plain with no make up was still flawless she came and plonked herself in Stanley's lap her dripping wet hair lashing onto Stanley's chest "morning smelly" she laughed then kissed him passionately on his lips to which Stanley responded but only half heartedly "you should have come and joined me" her brown eyes exuded happiness she looked deeply into Stanley's eyes, "what's wrong?" she questioned sensing a lack of willingness from a lethargic Stanley "nothing just…" Stanley mumbled sweeping back away Anais wet hair from her face, "maybe you just need breakfast and a nice shower dream boy" she slapped him on his bare chest playfully then got up and went to sit at the large dressing table where all of her lotions and beauty products were located.

Stanley sat motionless he breathed in deeply the weight of guilt on his conscious was proving hard to shake off "ok I'm going to hit the shower" he spoke his voice still gruff he got up throwing his phone onto the pillow, "ok don't be long I thought we could go out for breakfast it's a lovely day" a happy Anais commented while dabbing her face with cotton wool wiping away the perfumed cream she had applied to her face.

After a long shower Stanley emerged clean and refreshed he came out with more energy his hairs slicked back in his signature style he stepped into the room with the towel wrapped around his body "so what was you thinking for breakfast?" he now sounded more himself now walking confidently into the bedroom he could smell the Anais's fragrance lingering in the air the bed was now made up and the room cleaner "hey Anais where are you?" he looked around the room with a nervous smile he walked barefooted on the soft thick carpeted floor he checked behind the door acting like it was a game of hide and seek, "hey what you doing?" he saw a dressed Anais sitting on the vintage couch she seemed sullen dressed in a tight pair of jeans and a white tee shirt her hair was still out semi dry and falling down on her shoulders, "there you are I thought you was hiding from me" Stanley quipped not sensing Anais's sudden mood change he stood there bare chested hands on hips, "what's wrong?" he asked his tone now more of an exasperated whisper realising something was up.

Anais coolly raised Stanley's phone in her hand she could bare look at him such was the hurt "when was you going to tell me about Ami?" she asked her voice croaked with emotions Stanley literally could feel the blood drain from his body he let out a sigh his shoulders sagged he could see Anais was upset but she tried to hold her composure together, "well Spank?" again she asked the question, "ok can we talk?" a dejected and defeated Stanley pleaded knowing he had to come clean and confess to his double life, "start talking or I will" she held the phone with Ami's number on the screen ready to press the call button, "ok can I sit?" he asked politely, Anais just gestured with her open palm encouraging him to sit in the vacant space on the sofa.

Anais sobbed inconsolably into Stanley's bare chest it was quite surprising the amount of emotion which poured out of her, even for such a confident young girl once she had let her guard down to expose her feelings she was just as vulnerable like a child, Stanley on the other hand just rested his head back with his eyes closed still sat with his white towel around his waist, Anais finally raised her head looking up towards Stanley she snivelled and wiped her face "Stanley" she whimpered "I can't even be angry with you" she put her soft hand onto his chest "why don't you come to Monaco mum and dad would love to have you stay?" she continued hopefully rubbing his chest slowly, Stanley opened his eyes he looked jaded and weary after his tough conversation he looked around the room surveying the beautifully designed suite his head was spinning awash with thoughts he stroked Anais hair tenderly "I have to go home" he spoke bluntly cupping her face in his hands "I'm sorry babe I can't" he manoeuvred his body away from Anais and walked back into the bedroom to get dressed leaving Anais curled up upset on the sofa.

Stanley was now dressed he had his jeans jacket over a red v necked tee shirt and skinny jeans he had packed his bag and walked back into the room to where Anais sat calmly puffing on one of her famous slim white cigarettes, she did not turn to acknowledge him instead just stared ahead she was crying silently the tears rolling down her olive skinned cheeks, Stanley knelt down in front of her it was as if he was being knighted but he was not instead it was to console Anais, he felt heavy inside but somehow he knew what he had to do was right, "listen I want to thank you, you are amazing" he began his speech, Anais could not bear to look at him but her poise was soon broken she tried to suck up the outpouring but could not be restrained he rubbed her thigh, "it's ok Stanley just go I'll be fine" again she attempted to reign her feelings in sniffing through her nose while taking long puffs of her fag, "goodbye Stanley" her voice trembled she could not bear to look at him.

Stanley got up from his crouched position he lent over a kissed her on her forehead, "goodbye Miss Anais Von Arnold" he spoke with his distinguished English accent he picked up his bag and walked away, he himself was overcome with emotion but he kept walking keeping a stiff upper lip it was the hardest thing he had ever had to do. He reached the door and did not look back stepping out and away from the luxurious suite and the beautiful Anais was a wrench he closed the door behind him and walked with a heavy heart through the corridor towards the lift, he took his phone out and dialled Ami "hi it's me I'm coming home now" he spoke softly before the golden gilded doors of the elevator slid open smoothly.

Stanley stepped in and pressed the button to take him down to the lobby the doors closed there seemed an irony in this action indicating the end of his adventure chapter. This was now the life and times of Stanley Spank.

The End

About the Author

Lyndon Haynes is a North London born writer with a colourful and eventful past.

He began his career as a child actor starring in a BAFTA-award-winning children's drama at the age of 15. He then turned his writing skills to music and featured as a rapper in the successful UK hip-hop band The Sindecut, who were signed to Virgin records in the early nineties.

After many years in the music industry, Lyndon finally followed his first love and passion for writing and began by attending a creative writing course in North London. Within three years, his first book, entitled This Functional Family, was published by Book Guild Publishing in 2011. He received rave reviews and joined an exclusive list of UK black authors.

Lyndon's momentum has continued, where he has written and directed music videos, continued to rap and feature on various musical projects, and even wrote and directed his first short movie independently in 2013. The Life and Times of Stanley Spank sees Lyndon returning to the literary world with his first novel.

Lyndon is currently studying for his MA in writing for screen and stage at Regent's University in London. Lyndon is a creative being, and words are his forte. His passion for creating a story burns fiercely.

Lightning Source UK Ltd.
Milton Keynes UK
UKOW02f0841280914

239284UK00001B/2/P